the SECRETS of JANE

Forgotten

I

First Printing Edition 2023
Copyright © 2023 by Charlotte Mallory
www.charlottemallory.com

All rights reserved.

No part of this book may be reproduced in any form or by any electronic or mechanical means, including information storage and retrieval systems, without written permission from the author, except for the use of brief quotations in a book review.

ISBN: 979-8-9862555-4-5

Editor: Heather Creeden

www.creedreads.com

Interior Cover Art by Lulybot

Cover Design and Map by Charlotte Mallory

***

WARNINGS:

Content Warning 18+: This series contains explicit scenes, depictions of war, battle violence, abduction, graphic depiction of violence, drugging, and overall a very crude world.

This is a duel POV duology and the series finishes in the next installment with a guaranteed HEA.

While this book ends on a cliffhanger, it's a very exciting one that many have loved. No cheating, no last minute deaths, etc. It's meant to wrap this book up on an exciting note.

*To all the readers who want an MMC that will
absolutely burn the world down for her,
this story is for you.*

Huntswood
Deadman's Falls
Trident's Cove
Serpent's Reach
Seafarer's Rest
Spi...
The Veil
Skull's Row
Graywatch
Raven's Basin
Restless Peaks
The Keep
The Black S...
Dryhill
Inkstone
Bala...
Talon's Perch
Ender's Bay
Coalfell

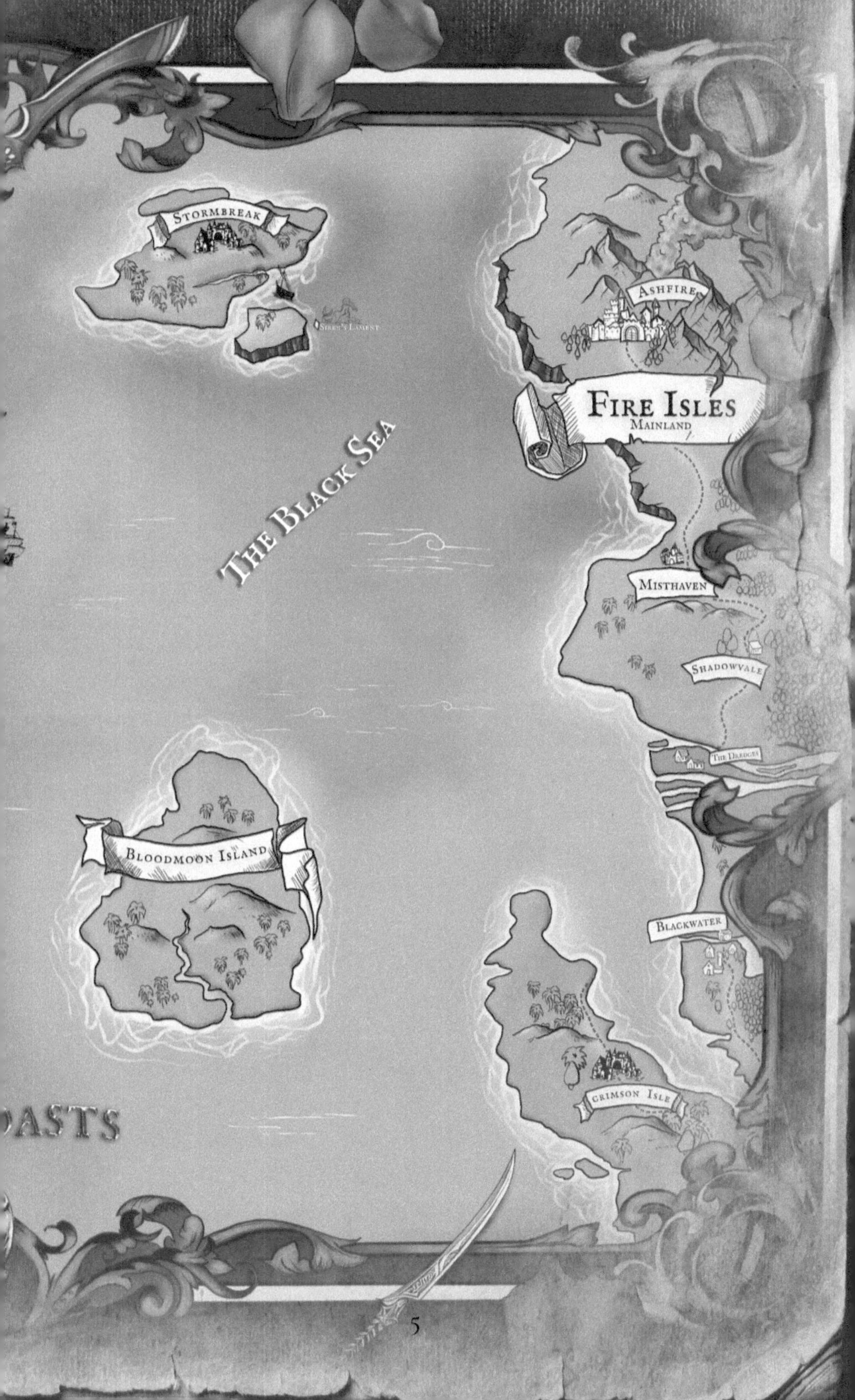

STORMBREAK
Siren's Lament
THE BLACK SEA
ASHFIRE
FIRE ISLES
MAINLAND
MISTHAVEN
SHADOWVALE
THE DREDGES
BLOODMOON ISLAND
BLACKWATER
CRIMSON ISLE
ASTS

"Bastard broke my knuckles," I grumble. My hand throbs as I exit Ern's Tavern, the ale barely soothing my pain.

"Let's go, little warlord," Kathleen calmly says, her hand on my back as the door shuts behind us—she's the only friend I'm willing to punch others for.

I laugh and groan in the same breath, placing my right hand over my left knuckles, concentrating on the well of power that flows through me. A faint blue light emits from my right palm until the pain subsides. I pull my hand away, flexing as the cracking bones fall back into place.

That man's jaw left my skin raw and red. I could heal it further to remove any discoloration, but then I'd have nothing to remember his ugly, shocked face by.

My satisfaction is even better because I can still hear the asshole groaning through an open window. He told Kathleen that she would look better on her knees between his thighs, positioning himself as if she'd actually comply.

That's when I downed my ale and struck him so hard my bones broke.

I already miss the energy of the rowdy tavern as we make our way through Talon's Perch, a large outpost near the coal miner's village where we live. Once we pass the guards sitting on haystacks that watch the border, we only have the moonlight to guide us back.

It's a trek we've made countless times in the dark, sometimes more drunk than others. I'll never forget our younger days when Kathleen stole venison jerky and ate the whole bag on our walk home—it was the first night I ever began teaching 'lessons' with my fists.

"You didn't have to go so far as to injure yourself, though," Kathleen remarks, pulling me from my nostalgia. I glance at my friend who's a few inches taller, her breasts so large someone can eat dessert right off of them—which is actually a favorite trick of hers when we visit drinking establishments.

"I think it's a perfect arrangement," I contest. "It means I really broke his nose, and I'll just heal myself afterward like I always do."

"I just hate you getting hurt, is all."

"Yeah, but what about watching *him* get hurt?"

She laughs. "Okay, I did really enjoy watching that asshole fall off his chair. Telling me to suck his ugly, fat dick!"

"See! It's absolutely worth it, being able to hit men like him. Nothing quite like it, really."

"You know, you could always try flirting with a man rather than beating him senseless—except for *that* asshole, obviously. But it's an idea, right? Might make you feel better in a whole *different* way to let yourself have a pleasurable night rather than ending it with pain." Kathleen winks as she pulls up the bottom of her white skirt while we walk through a muddy spot in the dirt road that leads us home.

I don't have to pull up my dress because I'm purposefully wearing pants. The idea of getting into a fight at a tavern while wearing flowing fabric sounds ridiculous.

Kathleen understands me, though. Probably because she's similar, in her own way, as she isn't wearing anything underneath that dress. Knickers only get in the way, according to her.

We're an odd fucking duo, and I adore it. When we go out, I'm always motivated to find a cocky asshole who runs his mouth far too much so I can leave him bruised and bloodied. Meanwhile, Kathleen bends over for a handsome wanderer when he comes into Ern's Tavern.

Even though I've always walked my own path, I also consider Kathleen's suggestion—I really do. But the thought that I'd accidentally seduce a man from Skull's Row and not realize it until morning... I *refuse* to be part of that life. Not even for a quick romp.

Is it for my ego? No, not at all. My aversion stems from knowing that the temptation to claim more would consume me, like an alcoholic being told to guard a barrel of ale.

I breathe deeply, catching the smell of smoke in the air, wondering if it's coming from a traveler's campfire nearby. Ern's Tavern is far enough behind us that it's just Kathleen and me on this dirt road. My mind drifts to the blade at my thigh in case anyone else traveling this road is less than friendly.

Kathleen continues, "You're lucky Coalfell is such a traveler's hub, or you'd run out of faces to sock." She eyes me, her face barely visible in the dark. "Okay, you don't have to do things *my* way, but perhaps trying some meditation would help."

"Why? What's wrong with my way?"

"Oh, come on. One day, it's all going to go wrong. Hit the wrong man or something. Maybe I'm getting older, but it does worry me more than before."

"It's... complicated," I reply. There's no way to properly describe how it feels to be strong when I've always been so easy to push around. "And anyway, I'm careful about it! I don't go looking for fights when a Zenith is in Talon's Perch."

"Thank the gods you don't, or I wouldn't go with you anymore. I don't need to watch what those men would do to you if they saw how you act."

"At least my death would be swift with them," I darkly joke.

Kathleen snorts. "Oh, stop it. It stresses me out as it is. I just don't enjoy imagining the day you hit the wrong man."

I glance at her again, most of her blonde hair pulled back while a few loose curls freely bounce past her ears. "Yeah, but I can heal myself. Pain is temporary. And I know how to spot a Zenith. Trust me on that one."

"Can't heal a broken skull if someone hits you too hard," Kathleen counters, pointing to her own head, "Zenith or not."

"True," I concede with an even wider grin, placing my hands on my hips, rolling my fingers to loosen the stiffened bones. "And besides, what about you? Aren't you afraid that one day you'll wake up with a swollen belly and no father to name him after?" I tease.

Her laugh carries through the trees surrounding us, mixing with the crickets. "Oh, whoever that bastard is will be *lucky* to get a say in the name. I'm naming that kid after *me*."

"Yeah, you *could*... You're aware of how it works, though.

It's the father's line that means everything." My voice is more bitter than I intended, my smile dropping. My lips thin as I press them together, the words eating at me in retrospect.

"Well, that's society's and your issue, along with whatever bugs you so much that you need to beat up random men for it. I don't care what people think. *I'm* the one that has to birth the damn baby, so they're getting *my* name."

Chuckling, the warmth in my chest returns. "Yeah... Yeah it's a good idea, isn't it?" My grin doesn't linger when my wounded soul aches like it begs to be seen. I crane my head to stare at the stars, placing a hand over my heart, mindlessly rubbing the skin there.

If only life were that simple.

"I'm all for setting new trends," I add, kicking a rock in the path as my boots squelch in the muddy patches. "But in all honesty, I don't think I can stop doing what I do. I was raised to deal with anger by getting into fights. To take it out that way. The only real rule is to always make sure the man earned it."

Kathleen crosses her arms, speaking as she slowly releases a chuckle. "Hells, Jane, that's the kind of behavior people have in Skull's Row."

My body stiffens, but I'm swift to move the conversation forward. "Yeah, like I'd survive in Skull's Row," I scoff, nervously stuffing my hands in my pockets. "I'm not *that* good of a healer. Those men would destroy me with just one look."

My somewhat humble origin is a gray area for many, and that's just how I like it. Very difficult and dangerous men would be after me if anyone ever found out who I truly am, and they'd use way more than nasty looks to bring me to the Zenith.

Skull's Row... the Zenith... all fancy names for a world that's built on the blood shed by mercenaries and warlords.

Whereas the more civilized lands of our world call their rulers kings, we call ours Zenith.

And I'm intimately aware of how dangerous they are.

My mother comes to mind, the woman I inherited my magic from. It's for her memory that I try so hard to keep myself from getting lost in the world that killed her.

I know in my bones that I'm trying to fight against a current that's never going to weaken. I was born with blood that runs hot, and I don't know what to do with it anymore. Instead of letting my shadows haunt me, I've learned to stare them down and rough them up a bit instead.

Or rough up *others*.

"Yeah, well, you can say you're not from Skull's Row all you want," Kathleen says. "The villagers might all be daft, but I've seen a lot. I know you like to keep your secrets Jane, but I can tell you weren't born to a stable master." She yawns, covering her mouth before adding, "You got another kind of fire in there. Don't know where it initially kindles from, but it's definitely not from a pacifist's village."

I sigh, glancing at the silhouettes of the trees created by the nearly full moon. I could try to deny the statement, but having someone see a *sliver* of the truth in my shadow makes me feel things I'm not sure how to interpret.

How I *wish* I could tell her.

But if Kathleen dies because of my truths...

I settle with, "You're right... I'm not from a village..." With the confession brimming in my chest, I move on before it can reach my lips. "But it's good for something, you know? The way that prick was talking to you! He deserved what he got."

"Oh darlin', it's these tits. You always get the pricks in the weeds with these girls, but they also land me my stallions." She wickedly grins while looking at her nails.

I give a belly laugh, reminded again why Kathleen and I go

together so well. She's a worldly woman, and that's something I don't come across much of anymore. If the village of Coalfell wasn't such a safe place to rest my head, I'd suggest she and I try to find ourselves new lands to settle in—

We both freeze when the smell of smoke is undeniable, a distinct glow hovering above the tree line in the far distance. Dark clouds billow into the night sky. "Are they holding a large bonfire?" I ask, although I fear I know the truth.

Kathleen hesitates before replying, "No."

We face each other, her eyes wide and lips parted, no doubt mirroring my own expression. The burning down of villages is extremely common in warring lands, but who would attack Coalfell? It's protected by Belstead, one of the largest settlements in the region. Even Skull's Row—where all the darkest bastards eat, live, and die, including the Zenith—have an unofficial understanding with Belstead, leaving their crops and villages in peace, sometimes even harvesting it themselves.

Either way, a burning village is a beacon of caution, alerting anyone outside that mercenaries have sunk their blades into it. Much like seeing a red flag on a pirate ship, knowing they will attack without mercy.

The faintest scream in the distance raises the hair on the back of my neck.

Kathleen immediately takes off, picking up her dress as she bolts for the village.

And what do I do? Honestly, I fucking hesitate, eyeing the smoke with upturned brows, knowing that if there's even a *chance* that men of Skull's Row attacked our village, then I have to stay *far* away from it.

Who else would do something like this? Even if it's not them, who isn't to say they'd find out what's inked on my chest? If I get caught...

"Kathleen!" I shout.

No, no, no.

This can't be happening.

Kathleen only runs faster. If she goes too far, I will lose her to whatever carnage waits to ensnare us.

It disappoints me how torn I am when faced with the mortality of a friend.

Outside of her, I've been a lone wolf for over a decade—since my teens. Kathleen and I have grown close whether I wanted to or not, even if I knew better.

The scent of smoke gives me tunnel vision born from deep despair.

Survival begs me to run for it, but the need to help those in danger nearly moves my feet forward. And yet, if this is a mercenary's doing... everyone who isn't already dead, will be.

If *they* catch me, they'll know. They'll know what I've been trying to hide. All this running and hiding will be for nothing.

Kathleen becomes smaller in the distance, and I swiftly imagine a future where I've left this village, *after* leaving a friend behind to die.

All for *his* secrets.

Fuck it.

I was raised to die a warrior's death, not be a coward when facing sharpened steel.

I run forward and pray to every god that this isn't a mercenary's doing, and if it *is*... well, hopefully, somehow, they won't see me.

And somehow, I'll get Kathleen out of this unscathed.

FINDING JANE

SOREN

There's nothing like the hunt, especially when the moon is bright.

I dismount my black steed, a big fucker I call Phantom. The horse never fails to startle strangers like he's a damn ghost, despite his size. It wasn't always the horse's name, but it stuck and now the stubborn ass refuses to respond to anything else.

My armor clinks together when my feet hit the dirt. The tailored hide is stained a deep red to match the shade of dried blood.

I pet the horse's nose—the only creature I show any affection for—and make my way through the outpost of Talon's Perch, running a hand through my chin-length black hair, smoothing it out of my face.

The outpost has dirt roads, wooden buildings, and gets bigger every year; soon they'll have cobbled streets. Braziers light up the main strip, windows glowing orange from the candles inside.

I ignore the myriad of reactions to my presence: most of the onlookers flee, some look at me with opportunity glinting in their gaze, and a few slender things latch their wide eyes on me, no doubt hoping I'll make their bellies swell so their sons can be attributed to a father named Soren.

As much as I enjoy fucking women outside of Skull's Row —thriving with the challenge of making even the primmest princesses buckle at her knees, willing to do the most impure acts just to please me—I have to ignore them tonight.

There's a woman to catch, a hunt that requires my *full* attention. I've been eager to meet whoever holds the Council of Zenith's interest so easily.

I don't know her name—neither do they—but I've got a description of her, and a location. I also don't know why the fuck they want her, but I *do* know that if they're going to be vague about her summons, then it's something that makes her important.

Been a while since we had a woman cause this much of a stir.

Hopefully, she'll live up to the commotion surrounding her.

I shoulder open the wooden door of a large brick building, the energy inside filling the quiet streets with sounds of laughter, yelling, and wooden cups hitting the tables. I enter the place called Ern's Tavern where there's said to be a petite little thing that gets into frequent bar fights. I don't immediately see anyone that matches the description of the woman I'm looking for.

The pungent smell of tobacco fills the air. I can feel the tension in the air as the occupants fall silent in my presence. Ern's Tavern is bright with candlelight, casting harsh shadows, and elongating the concerned faces of those who recognize me. The rest remain quiet, no doubt because it's uncommon to witness a man as large and built as I—clad in expensive armor —without assuming I'm related to *some* part of Skull's Row.

If I had my black skull mask visible, *no one* would question what part of our world I belong to.

Ern, the middle-aged bartender with a braided black beard, focuses on me when our eyes meet. Placing a wooden mug on the counter, Ern stands up straight and cautiously says, "Soren, what pleasure do we owe the likes of you?"

I may be an improper bastard of the war lording kind, but I'm not a fucking idiot. It's important to make friends with the bartenders and innkeepers. They have the best eyes and ears for gossip, which is quite necessary for tasks such as this.

I near the wooden counter, the metal pieces of my armored shoulders clinking with every step. I ignore the enveloping silence—save for a few whispers that reach my ears—all while everyone watches. "Small woman, mid-twenties. Long, auburn hair. I'm here for her."

Ern's long nose flares as his beady eyes widen. He scans the room as if wondering what in the hells this is about before asking, "It can't be because of *that* git, can it?"

He motions to a man in the corner who has a woman applying a steak to his face.

I frown, looking the man over. "No. Although it looks like I'm close, whoever she is."

She's an active little fiend.

"Please, my liege. She's a good person."

My liege. He's already calling me by whatever fucking proper titles I'm owed as a Zenith myself; an excellent cue for when someone seeks my favor. Ern already wants to protect her, and I make note of that.

I lean my head in his direction. "It's not for me. The Council wants her. Before you bother asking, I don't know why. They're being quiet about it."

Even the whispers hush, the flickering shadows more haunting than the silence. Ern lowers his head but maintains his anxious gaze on me. If I wasn't so keen on finding this mystery woman, I'd investigate the way he seems to cover a hundred expressions. "The Council... at Skull's Row?"

"Little lady has attracted quite the audience," I casually reply. The man closest to me ever so slowly creates distance between us.

Can't blame the bastard, especially if he knows who I am. It's never a good idea to be within arm's reach of a Zenith—the individual men that make up the entirety of the Council; we're a limited collection of the worst mercenaries and the most skilled at rampage and murder.

Ern hesitates before giving a single nod. "I can't imagine why you'd want Jane. Or did she finally break the ego of the wrong man?"

I narrow my eyes on hearing her name. Such a common name. I was expecting something grand or dramatic, based on who was calling for her.

Inhaling, my reply rests on my tongue when the man sitting in the corner croaks out, "Nah, fuck that whore. Gave me a black eye."

Raising my brows as I face him, a few strands of hair fall into my gaze. The man is a larger bloke with one hand resting on a gut hardened by years of ale, and the other hand holds the steak on his round face as the woman tending to him backs away. His nose is grossly swollen, and his voice is stuffy when he speaks.

"She's supposed to be petite, mate. How the fuck did she manage so much damage?" I ask.

"She's a fucking asshole! This shit will never heal straight."

I can't help but snort, although my mind is already racing and trying to piece together every detail. I glance down at my hands and then at my leather bracers while I try to uncover whoever the fuck this Jane is. That's a mighty blow she delivered, even for a normal-sized man. I face Ern, giving him a nod. "If she was here recently, then I need to act. Where does she live? Don't bother trying to protect her, Ern. She's on our list now. No one can save her, so don't get caught in her wake."

"She lives in a village called Coalfell," he regretfully says, exhaling as he presses his lips together. He cleans the glass in his hand with more rigor.

"Who is she, exactly? Why does she get into bar fights? Any family in Coalfell?"

Ern shrugs. "Don't know much about her, honestly. This is a big traveler's outpost, so she's always in here to see the fresh faces and gets a little feisty when they roll in. Don't think she's got family in Coalfell. She's got sad eyes, sometimes—"

"Sad my fucking ass," the one in the corner grunts, the tavern still dead silent.

The first time, the interruption was entertaining.

This time, it just annoys me.

I languidly look at the man, not sure what I want to do with him. I didn't come here to listen to a bastard's whining, but I also can't believe a smaller woman could give such a large man a shiner as ugly as that. A few that are near the man take even larger steps away, his one good eye opening with concern.

"Why'd she hit you?" I calmly ask.

His wet eye looks me over like he wonders if he should keep

speaking. Finally, he grumbles out, "Cause she's a jealous cunt."

The fire in the hearth *pops* with embers, but I remain as still as a large cat watching its prey. Again, the titles mean little to me, but lately, the Zenith have been keeping to their fortress in Skull's Row a little *too* often, and many of the commoners outside of our home are forgetting their proper manners.

Unlike Ern, here.

I've got nothing but impatience for people not giving me proper respect. Even if the titles feel decorative, the *use* of them indicates obedience. Without that, it's how it always falls apart; can't respect a captain that is unable to control the entire ship.

As I weigh my options, contemplating what to do, a woman's voice cuts through my thoughts from where she sits in the lap of a man across the room. I slice my gaze in her direction. She's a mousy thing, her light voice breaking up the tension as she says, "He was being rude, my liege. Jane doesn't like when men are rude to other women." She scrunches her nose. "I think she looks for the assholes, honestly."

"Why *you*—" the annoying one begins, but he silences as I raise my hand.

I can't deny I'm enjoying the reputation that this *Jane* is creating for herself. I always love roses with the thickest, most plentiful thorns. Maybe she can make life interesting for the week it'll take to return to Skull's Row.

"She'll fucking love me, then." I look back at Ern, ignoring the fat bastard for now. "A swig of your golden, and then I'll chase after her.

The man in the corner takes the meat off of his eye, sits up straight, and says, "When you find her, punch that whore—"

I shift my entire head in his direction, his eyes widening as we stare each other down. Many men of my caliber have developed their own ways of sending out subtle messages. Mine is always in my expressions.

I'm cognizant that my scowl is making him nervous for the first time tonight. Possibly the first time in a while.

A small glass filled with golden liquid slides my way, and without taking my glare off of this man, I down the burning alcohol, slapping the empty glass on the table before standing from my leaning position. The man with a viciously swollen, blackened eye straightens his back.

Slowly, I articulate, "Don't interrupt me again, or you won't have a nose to bitch about."

I head toward the door, not bothering to see the reactions. I purposefully keep my attention ahead of me as I exit, breathing in the cooler, clean air as I leave the musty old tavern.

There's no need to make a more direct threat. It's a dangerous practice to sling words around with little action to support them, and I don't have time to discipline the ugly man.

And as much as it might be fucking hilarious that a woman said to be much smaller than him delivered so much damage, it also shows she's got claws I'll need to be cautious of. I couldn't even see his actual eye from the swelling, but I bet the whites are properly bloodied. That nose will never recover, not with how crooked it already seemed to be.

Someone taught Miss Jane how to hit. How to hit *real* fucking hard. I'd be amazed if her fist wasn't damaged after a serious hit like that.

Most fathers don't teach their daughters that, not out in these villages.

A father of *Skull's Row*, however, would.

Is she from there, then? Is that why they want her? Has she pissed off the wrong man from a decade ago and they finally found her?

No… that doesn't quite feel right. Pieces are missing. If she pissed off the wrong man, she wouldn't settle in a village only a week's ride from Skull's Row. And Coalfell is a pacifist's village, one that splits up their labor between mining coal, and the other on farms. Why would a woman with a healthy dose of violence in her heart choose to reside here? She clearly misses the fight.

I stride to the border of the outpost and into the dark of night, approaching the stables. Someone is near Phantom, and I hear him mumble, "You're a big fucker. Who in the hells rode on you?"

He nearly squeaks when he spots me. With thinned patience, I backhand the man so hard he flies backward and hits the ground out cold.

Hopefully, he'll remind the people here to *also* not touch the war horses of Zeniths.

I mount Phantom, and my company of men are waiting for me just outside the outpost. It's a clear-cut team I use for swift traveling and specialized missions. Trotting off, I leave the unconscious man in the dirt. Someone will either find him, or they won't.

He's not my fucking problem right now.

No, *Miss Jane* is my problem.

Being out here is also how I know Jane has baggage that not even a mule could carry. A Zenith doing this work is only reserved for serious infractions, and I'll even don the black skull mask if needed. Aside from the message it sends, the powers it grants me might prove necessary.

I'll find out, either way.

I give one curt nod to the thirty riders who wait in the shadows of night as we head toward Coalfell. I could always go in alone, in case Jane's the fleeing type. But if she's shrewd, even a whisper of someone looking like me entering her village will tell her she's been found.

Might as well have thirty men with me when that happens.

I'm not sure how much time has passed since I left the tavern, but I grip the reins tighter when I notice the billowing of smoke in the distance that looks entirely too much like a village on fire.

Holding a hand up, I pull Phantom to a halt, my heart racing for the first time that night.

The stampeding of horse hooves of my flanking men silence as they stop next to me, neighing and huffing.

As a mercenary—and a warlord—I'm used to the site of burning homes. I clench my jaw when a tower of spinning fire spirals high into the night.

Fires don't do that on their own.

Riding up next to me is my right hand, Bones. He's a dangerous bastard with a proclivity for slicing flesh. He wears a necklace made of his enemy's finger bones like they're damn seashells. His tanned skin darkens easily in the sun, making his one blue eye stand out, especially with the other being brown.

And whereas I don leather stained in red, Bones wears the darkest colors known to man because he likes how the necklace stands out against an ebony backdrop.

Bones' gruff, raspy voice grates next to me. "That's more than a village fire. That's a fucking barbecue."

On my other side, Anya approaches, a woman so pale she's easy to see in the dark. Her short, black hair is greased back, that long nose of hers smelling the air, no doubt breathing in the smoke. "That's a poor decision. Isn't Coalfell a part of Belstead's supply chain? One that supports *us*?"

I nod. "Which means if someone's burning it down, they don't fear what comes after them. Could be a local issue gone too dark, or a mercenary from over the oceans who doesn't know Coalfell and that burning it down is going to piss off the wrong people."

That's also the damn village that Miss Jane is supposedly in...

Won't do us any good to collect her charred bones.

I narrow my eyes. Could this all be related to her? But who in the hells would she have pissed off so much that not only the Council of Zenith is after her, but now people are burning down her village just to get to her?

And how the fuck have I never heard of this broad? No one has bitched about an auburn-haired woman by the name of Jane, nor about *anyone* in this region.

I concentrate on my surroundings, seeking any information I can gather before I say, "Find Jane. She's the priority. Leave whoever did this to me if we find them. But *we* find Jane first."

THE BLACK SKULL MASK

JANE

The whole damn place is on fire, thick black smoke engulfing the clean air. People run and scream, and many have flames burning their clothes. The heat only adds to the panic, and from what I can gather, it's not a fire caused by a knocked-over candle.

It's a rumbling inferno, as if the homes were deliberately set ablaze by magic. Could that be true? No, it has to be my paranoia to assume this is a fire mage's doing.

Or would the Council truly send a fire mage after me?

"Kathleen!" I cry out, scanning the terrified faces for the one I care about-most.

I've lost her among the chaos. I had been hot on her heels, but as soon as someone spotted me, they begged me to heal a face with leaking blisters. Of course, I took care of them. How could I know when I've known everyone here for a decade?

I remained vigilant about any dangers that could appear while doing so, feeling rushed and also like I was not doing enough.

If only I followed Kathleen right as she took off... where did she go? To her grandmother's, maybe? I can't lose her. I can't lose another person in my life.

Fuck.

"What happened?" I ask a middle-aged woman named Maryanne when I come upon her as she sits against a tree with singed leaves. Swollen, red skin lines her body. I immediately hover my hands over her shin that's gashed *and* burned. My heart's pounding so hard it nearly fractures my rib cage, my voice trembling from a whirlwind of emotions and memories that these flames mercilessly stir. It's hard to steady myself.

"Ransacked!" she cries, wincing when blue light emits from my palm to heal her, contrasting the golden glow of death around us. "We need to get everyone out," she pants. "I sent the kids with Todd and came back to try and get the family gold... I-I needed a bit of a rest." Her chest rises and falls with labored breathing. "Oh Jane, what if it's mercenaries? Who else would do this?"

"Let's not stick around to find out," I manage to say. She has no idea how haunting that idea is to me.

Burns are a tricky thing to heal, and scarring will most definitely occur. Sending minimal regenerative energy into her skin is the most I can provide, or else I'll exhaust myself. "I need to keep going, but you get out of this smoke, okay? Can you walk?"

She gives an unconvincing nod. "Yes. I got the gold

already," she replies, patting at a deep pocket in her dress. "Just tripped and hurt myself."

"Don't stop until someone else is with you," I order, helping her to her feet.

Once Maryanne is on her way—even if stumbling—I wipe my sweaty palms on my leather pants, raggedly breathing in the smoke. I resort to squinting with how bright the fire burns. Every so often I check my skin to ensure it isn't bubbling. My only ailment seems to be stinging eyes. I'm not sure how I'm not burned, but I won't question it now.

All the while, the fires rumble like a thousand horse hooves circling the city.

Every time I try to peel away and seek out Kathleen, someone else needs me. My gut screams to take care of myself, but now that I'm here among them, how can I ignore wounds that would easily lead to infection unless I intervened? They're probably suffering *because* of me, and they don't even know it.

I have a limit, however, and before long I'm only good for placing damp towels on burned skin, my vision tunneling after each use of my magic.

A few hard sleepers straggle out of their homes—some clinging to their pets—while others utilize coal carts to ferry their household goods out of the burning center. The rest have fled.

What the hells is happening? There's so much damage, and yet I haven't seen a single perpetrator.

Does the attacker plan to kill everyone and make me watch? Hoping I'll talk in order to spare the remaining villagers?

Fear twists into anger—I don't fucking know what to do.

Focus on finding Kathleen.

I make my way to Main Street, where Kathleen's grandmother runs her apothecary. The village is moderately sized, with only four dirt streets running off of this central one.

Stumbling through the flaming carnage, I place my hands over my eyes when a roof caves in from a nearby building. Embers spit out like splashing water as someone screams nearby.

I stumble away, glancing back when I spot Kathleen by the apothecary. Scorch marks mar her dress. The acrid smell of smoke and swirling ash fills the air as she supports her grandmother while they slowly move down the street. Her dress is tinged and she's helping her grandmother through the street.

Quickening my pace, my lungs screaming for better air—I pause, panting with my hair in my eyes. Someone on a horse strides around the postal building, riding right onto Main Street.

I'm at the end of Main and Kathleen is on the opposite side. I stand there, my eyes watering as the smoke and ash burns them dry. The horseman rides by one of our neighbors, slicing the man's head clean off, the body slowly slumping to the ground as the head rolls.

"Oh, fuck," I mutter through a hard cough.

Kathleen is right in his path, shielding her grandmother.

On the off chance they're here for me... I scream as loud as I can, "HERE!"

The horseman looks in my direction, yanking his reins to charge right at me, striding past Kathleen.

"Fuck, fuck, fuck."

I'm exhausted, sick from the smoke, overheated, and surely suffering from some kind of burns I haven't discovered yet. Despite all that's slowing me down, I run for it, searching for a building to dash into. As I round the village's community structure, I stumble over a charred, dead man, adrenaline and survival urging me forward.

To my horror, one of the blazing buildings shoots its fire high into the dark sky, swirling above the village in completely unnatural ways—a fire mage's magic; there's no doubt anymore. Then again, fire mages don't attack villages, unless at the hands of someone with a lot of money or power.

In our world, it ranks by cutthroats, mercenaries, pirates, warlords, and then the Zenith that triumph over them all.

This isn't the work of a cutthroat, that much is clear. Just how high up did this order come?

I survey the area for a black skull mask—just in case—as only the Zenith bear those masks, and they are notorious for being the only ones with enough influence to hire fire mages.

Unless this person is from overseas... from the Order of Ash?

Finally risking it, I glance over my shoulder to see the horseman is gaining on me, his ugly face plain as day. Which means no mask to cover it. So not a Zenith? Or is the Zenith nearby, and this is a lackey?

More importantly, what direction should I run?

I don't know how to outrun a horse, especially with my magic draining so rapidly. The end of this road means running right into the woods, and I'm better at running through elaborate city streets than a forest.

I choose not to chance what I cannot see or maneuver, especially if more are hiding in there.

Nearly tripping when I stop, I clumsily pivot on my tired feet to face him, ready to roll right toward his horse—out of the man's sword range—and bolt toward the other end of the village. Maybe even slice at the leg of the poor animal if I can manage it so it crashes.

If I have to run, let it at least be toward somewhere I know.

It's a risky fucking move, but as long as I have some kind of a hand after this, I can heal whatever carnage I may suffer—

Behind the horse rider is a site that numbs me so juxtaposed to the incinerated village. A giant man rides on an ebony steed, wearing a black skull mask with unique, golden designs.

And the way he smoothly throws his dagger absolutely matches the skill of a Zenith, striking the rider in front of me square in his back. The man slumps off his horse and hits the dirt with a hard thud; the beast running past me.

If I hadn't been so shocked that it was a bona fide Zenith, I may have tried to grab the horse as it ran by me.

But I don't move.

It's been too long since I truly had to think on my feet like this. A Zenith should never be out here. Then again, neither should I... which means if he's here, he *has* to be after me. I wince when his horse stomps on the fallen rider, blood spattering onto fur and dirt roads.

Dead tired, I force myself to run for it again. This time, even risking the woods. I can't consider my earlier stunt on this one. A part of me knows it's futile to even try and escape, but it feels important to make the effort.

The stomping of heavy horse hooves resonates in the ground underneath me. I glance over my shoulder to see he's right on me, towering over like a shadow of death, his vivid, pale eyes visible through the holes of his black, expressionless mask. I cry out as the masked man grabs me while he's still on his damn horse, hoisting me up by the underside of my arm.

Panic drowns out any drive for retaliation as I cling onto anything stable when the horse trots faster, my head on this man's thigh. His leather is a deep red, something about the color unnerving me.

Only rich men have armor like this.

Holy shit. They really sent a Zenith after me.

Once I realize I'm not dead or injured, I'm about to fight back in any way that I can to make him drop me, only for him to release me on his own once we're outside of the major carnage.

"Rope her!" the Zenith shouts with a deep, raspy voice that's slightly muffled through the mask.

For a minute, I think he says rape and I'm about to unleash every ounce of fury I have, death or not. But then someone is already on me and pinning me to the ground while a woman with rope approaches like I'm a wild hog they caught.

"Get the fuck off of me!" I yell, kicking the man who holds me down square in the face like I have countless times before, aiming to break it.

"Son of a fucking bitch!" He looks like he might punch me, but I refuse to flinch; I'm ready for it.

Blood gushes down his lips. He doesn't reach for his face, however, and continues to restrain me as crimson drips onto my clothes. He handles pain well, it seems. I stare at him long enough to see he's got one blue eye, the other brown, and both brimming with immense hatred. Deep scars on his face remind me of the caliber of these attackers.

The one on the black horse rides by, jumping down while his steed slows its trot. Seeing the mask deeply haunts my soul, subduing me more than any rope could.

"Knock her out," the Zenith commands.

"Like hell—"

I can't tell who strikes me, but in mere moments, pain lances through my skull, my vision fading as I'm out like a wet candle wick.

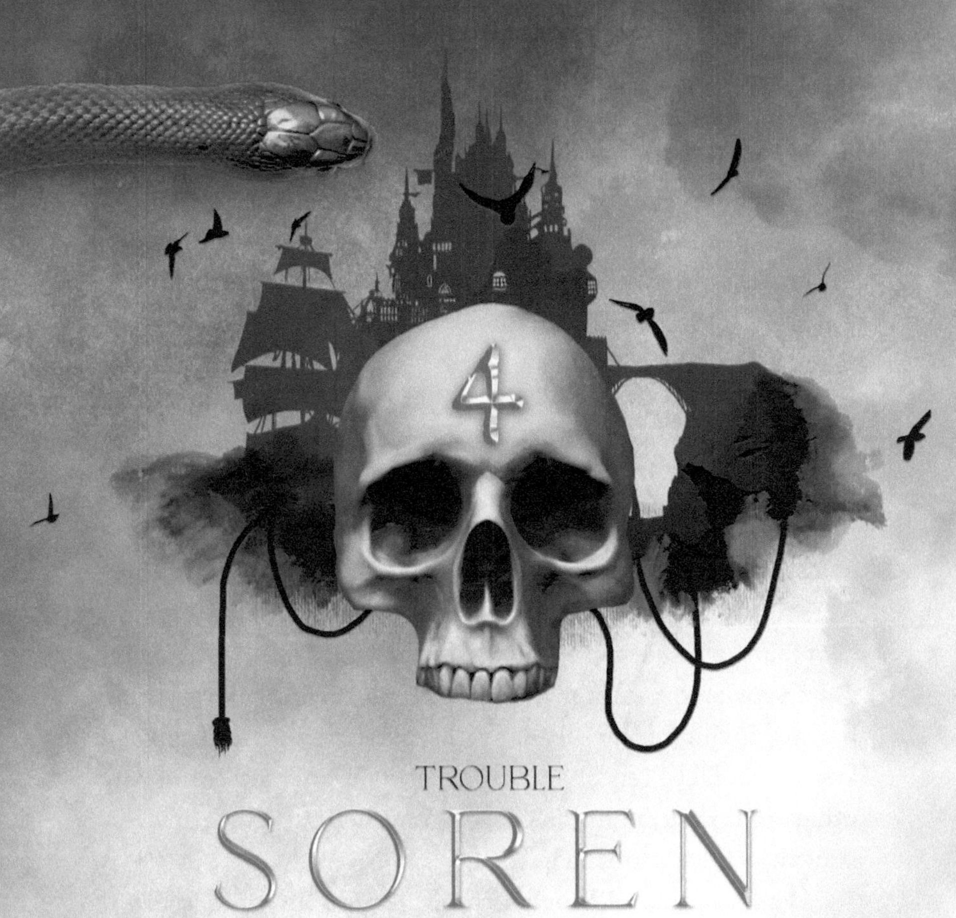

SOREN

Th is burned-down village is starting to reflect more of what I expected when I first pursued a woman requiring someone of my rank.

But this thing lying in the grass? I take her in: Jane's curvy but small, her face quite proportional, all with plump lips to top it off. And that deep auburn hair of hers...

Why the fuck is she worth all this? She looks more like a lord's daughter than some vagabond causing issues for the Council.

My blood runs hot from the heat and violence, and now from seeing the first pretty creature since leaving Skull's Row.

In a world where beauties are so scarce and hard to come by, it's impossible not to make the mental note that in any other setting, she'd be quite *distracting*.

"We need to get her out of the area—Anya, give her *whispering words* so we don't have to deal with her fighting us. Then, we'll place her on Phantom with me. We ride back to the Talon's Perch and begin our way to Skull's Row on the morrow, " I instruct, eyeing the others that arrive on foot, some sheathing their blades. Bones finally puts pressure on his mess of a nose, wincing and groaning, examining his bloodied hand to assess the damage. Anya continues to wrap the rope around a rag-dolled Jane.

I survey the group, fire glinting off the metal of their armor. "Someone also needs to grab the fucker that I killed. Strip him, search for any markings or tattoos, and then take everything he has, including his head. We'll spike it and see if anyone knows his face. Ten of you are to remain and search for any other signs that might indicate who burned this place down— stay away if it's a fire mage.

"Those of this village that can walk are allowed to follow if they aren't remaining. We'll send any of the survivors who follow us to Belstead." I observe the two dozen before me— noting that I'm missing a few—and wonder if the others have found anything. "Whoever I killed wasn't the fire mage, and this is clearly a mage's doing. We need to ask every survivor if they've seen who it was and where they went."

Anya stands, staring at Jane who's listless on the ground. "Who the fuck do you think sent a fire mage here?" she asks, wiping her hands on her pants. She then digs into a leather bag at her waist and pulls out a very sharp, small knife and a vial of clear liquid. Coating the metal, she pricks Jane right on her dainty, pale neck.

"I don't know," I say through the mask, searching the area

once more, staring at the tree lines. "But whoever sent them isn't here anymore, if they even came at all."

"You're sure?"

I remove my mask, which contracts from its leathery texture to form a hard, distinct ridge like it's made out of clay. Its magic allows the edges to merge with the wearer it was created for, unable to feel it even when it's on.

"You know I am," I reply, feeling no other energy in the air.

If it wasn't Anya asking—the brains I rely on—then I'd be snarkier about the comment. But she too sees the magnitude of this village being burned.

Coalfell supplies minerals to Belstead while we take their crops. It's like burning down the king's food, except from a kingdom known for its vicious monarchs. Someone will pay, and it will be a grisly affair. "We need the identity of the one I killed, though," I say, clicking my tongue so Phantom comes to me.

The giant beast stands still as I affix the skull mask to the outside of my bag, so others can witness who I am. It's a unique creation, able to sense its location no matter where I last had it.

And these masks have a way of reappearing, even if one loses it.

I mount the horse, positioning myself so Jane's body can fit in front of me. I nod to Jane, and Anya motions for someone other than Bones—who's still tending to his face—as they grab Jane with ease. A little too carelessly.

"Hand her to me. Don't be rough. The Council wants her in the best condition possible."

Although, unfortunately for her, it's not to make sure she's happy. It's so she has elongated endurance for torture. As to whatever the fuck she's hiding, the Council is willing to do whatever is needed to procure it.

The limp woman is lifted upright toward my saddle. I grip Phantom with my thighs as I grab her by the ropes that bind her, swinging her thin yet firm leg over so she sits more naturally. Jane's head slumps forward, her wavy, silken hair smelling of smoke and her skin smeared with ash.

Securing her against my body with one arm, I grip the reins with my other hand.

"My face fucking hurts," Bones complains through the blood as he stands. "The fucking bitch."

"You'll live," I reply.

My eyes narrow when I feel a distinct aura of magic emitting right between my thighs. Pulling her closer, the sensation flows all through my chest. What the hells is this? I release the reins and use my free hand to grab her wrist. Sure enough, even in the dark, there's a fucking mark in blue ink—a healer's insignia, a design created without equal for each one that bears it.

I snort.

"She's a fucking healer," I rasp, eyeing Bones, who's silhouetted by the burning village. "You're in luck. We'll make her take care of that when she comes to."

As I grab the reins and turn my steed to leave, a woman comes running up—or bouncing up—depending on where someone is looking. Bones glares at her through his blood covered hand. He's going to be quite enamored with her.

"What are you doing?" the woman asks, breathless. Her blonde hair is in disarray and barely restrained by her two clips at the side, like it might have once been well put together. Soot covers her face, her clothes singed and completely grayed over.

"This one is wanted by the Zenith." I nod to the small woman secured between my legs. "Go back to your people."

The blonde looks me over, spotting the black mask attached to the outside of Phantom. "Oh, shit. I know that color leather," she mutters, speaking as if declaring the fact will help her come to terms. "You're Soren."

With heavy sarcasm, I retort, "And you must be the village's scout."

A few of my men snort, looking at her like she might be a fresh picking. I glare their way; some of my kind rape and ravage when pirating or ransacking villages, but I only tolerate the ravaging bit.

Rape is for weak men, and the world is already full of enough bastards with broken mothers.

Bones moves ahead, dropping his hand to reveal the wreckage of his nose. "Please tell me you have plans to stay at the outpost tonight?"

"Shut the fuck up, asshole," she grinds out, scowling at him.

My smirk rolls into a laugh. "The fuck is wrong with this village." I pull at the reins, planning to trot off. "You all act like you're born in a damn tavern."

"Wait!" the woman shouts. Her gaze flicks to Jane as she ignores Bones, a possessive gleam staining his eyes like she's a precious thing. Great. Her ignoring him will only make him want her more. "We need help! We are protected by Belstead, and we feed Skull's Row. Please. We still have laborers left. We have value, and a lot of us need protection or help to get away from here."

In a world of killing, good labor is priceless for crafting armor and weapons, while the others tend the fields that keep us strong. Good on her for being willing to approach me, just to take care of the survivors.

"You're a brave lass," Bones croons. The man is a good foot taller than her as he towers behind her like a shadow creature born out of the flames.

She burns her gaze into me, treating Bones like he's smoke.

I admit I'm impressed—she must be aware of the risk in surrounding herself with mercenaries as defenseless and vulnerable as she is.

"Ten of my men will trail you. Whoever makes it can come with us to Skull's Row, where we will get you on a ship to cross the Black Sea, or a caravan to Belstead." I acknowledge Anya. "Stay here and lead the reconnaissance. Ensure the survivors are left untouched."

The villager's worry stands out, even in the dark, Bones watching her with mesmerized calculation. "What are you going to do with Jane?" she asks like she doesn't want to admit this is happening.

I eye the auburn hair in front of me, contemplating. Rather than tell the blonde that she's probably never going to see her friend again, I choose to be unusually nice and simply say nothing.

I turn Phantom around to face the darkness that will lead me to Talon's Perch. "Send the fastest horse to ready the Black House."

Phantom breaks into a full trot at my command.

The woman in my lap begins to stir, but it'll be a while before she's coherent again. Speaking in her ear, breathing in her smokey scent, I say, "You're in a world of fucking trouble, little one."

JANE

I fade in and out of coherence, only aware of my body rocking back and forth. The throbbing in my head prevents me from concentrating until, at some point, it clicks that this undulating of my hips means I'm on a horse.

I'm taken back to my childhood, where I've just woken up from napping on a horse as Mother and I travel to a village. It's for a routine trip where her services are offered to assist in birth and heal any trauma that might arise.

As my eyes fully open, I register the inky horse that I ride, a stranger's. My mother's horse, Honey, had a coat the color of fresh cream.

The last memory I carry of my mother is of her being stabbed in the heart, a place that I couldn't heal, no matter how I poured my life's energy into her, tears and all.

My throat constricts. *No, she's long gone. So is Honey.*

As I wake, I register that my back aches. A jarring reminder that I'm in my mid-twenties, and not a child.

What happened to me?

I blink—but may have fallen back into unconsciousness—as the next time I open my eyes, the surroundings bear a striking resemblance to Talon's Perch, its silhouette etched against the brilliant, star-filled night sky.

I stare for a while, the heaviness of my breaths exhausting me.

The pressure around my body forces me to groggily look down. Not only am I bound, but there's a very large, thick arm wrapped around my waist. A firm body presses up against my back in an all-encompassing sensation, like I'm cocooned into them. "What…"

"I got no problem dropping you if that's the kind of lesson you need," a gritty voice warns. "It'd be a shame to waste such a pretty face since I bet you are perfectly firm underneath these men's clothes."

I grew up with criminals just as bad as him, so his words mean nothing to me. The vestigial smell of burning air sullies my nostrils, and my stomach aches as I recall the frightened faces from the village. "You attacked my village?" I slur, trying to concentrate my vision on my surroundings.

"No, it wasn't me. I was only there for you."

My brain understands what has happened, and yet I can't quite form a proper reaction. I remember the Zenith skull, but surely that's just a figment of my broken mind.

Why's it so hard to focus?

I breathe out, "What kind of killer are you?"

He snickers, his deep and raspy voice like that of a giant, very scarred wolf. "Let's wait until you're on solid ground for that, Miss Jane."

Time passes easily as we near the outpost, its weathered walls greeting me for the second time that day. My dazed mind perceives we're suddenly dismounting, but I can't quite figure out what I'm doing. *When did we reach the stable?* As he slides off the horse, I take a tumble in a desperate attempt to create *any* distance between us—even if bound—only for me to crash into his chest as his massive arms catch me.

They're anything but comforting.

My head throbs, and my knees are weak as he puts me on my feet. Everything is out of focus. "You gave me a damn concussion. And... and, something else. I'm too out of it for this to be... from someone... hitting me."

"Not my problem," he grunts, pushing me forward. "Made my ride easier."

Why are we here? In Talon's Perch? Did Kathleen make it out alive?

The delirium thins enough that I realize if this man has a black skull mask, then I know *exactly* where we're going.

In all outposts within a certain mileage of Skull's Row is a blacked-out dwelling, usually tucked away in its own area where only the Zenith reside. Staff are always ready to cater to a Zenith that *might* stop in town for the night. Those killers travel around like how an alpha wolf might patrol his terrain.

The horror stories some of the workers tell at Ern's Tavern... I always make sure I'm nowhere near Talon's Perch when one is visiting.

I try to glance over my shoulder, only gathering that he towers over me like his horse did before he turns my face forward, pushing me with his other hand. There's so much strength in that simple command.

"Keep walking," he rasps.

The sound of clinking metal trails me; haunts me.

We pass by Ern's Tavern, a few familiar faces exiting the building and quickly darting back inside, only for more to pile out.

They all know me.

And now I'm being herded by a fucking Zenith.

I glance over at the tavern and glare at the fat ass that told Kathleen her place is on her knees and between his thighs. He leans against the building as he laughs. His swollen eye looks like a donkey kicked him, and I hate the way he clearly thinks he won by the smirk written all over his stupid face.

A moment of clarity returns like I wiped at a foggy mirror and can finally see myself. I'm almost certain now that I was drugged to some degree. My heart races, my body is *exhausted*.

Worrying about the village, wondering who died... The pain can't help me now. I can mourn them later once I'm safe or alone, but right now every detail needs to be observed. If I want *any* chance of escaping, I can't rest my mind for a single breath. Which includes ignoring those at Ern's, who will continue about their lives while any mention of me will be reduced down to rumors spread as drunken tales.

All the while, I'll be living an unfathomable nightmare.

No, I'll escape. One way or another, I'll figure it out.

We traverse in silence—save for the sound of leather soles on dirt and clinking armor—and veer off onto a darkened lane. Just outside the main strip is a settlement consisting of one large building that's painted all black, along with a few smaller buildings adjacent to it. The roof, the framing of the windows, the chimney... all of them are the color of night.

Stationed men wait outside, opening the front double doors as we approach. Braziers light up the siding of the Black House, the stars bright above us.

My body is screaming at me to wake up as adrenaline courses through my veins. "Who are you..." I mumble.

He doesn't answer.

I nearly stumble with my bound arms, but he grabs the rope to steady me, guiding me forward.

We enter the dark structure that has housed blends of agonizing screams, moans of pleasure, and just about every-thing in between. My breathing is ragged, and I'm torn between panic and also wanting to go out like a warrior. But there's one thing for certain—I'm absolutely fucked.

No one goes in these without the permission—or by the force of—a Zenith.

The doors shut behind us, candles barely lighting the entryway, red velvet and gold decorations accenting the black-ness of it all. Two servants jump up from a table, looking as if we interrupted a very deep and private conversation. They're quick to give the Zenith his privacy, leaving the two of us in the foyer.

My captor leans in behind me, my body stiffening like a demon has just decided to make contact.

I shudder when he says, "The name's Soren. You've found yourself on the wrong list, Miss Jane."

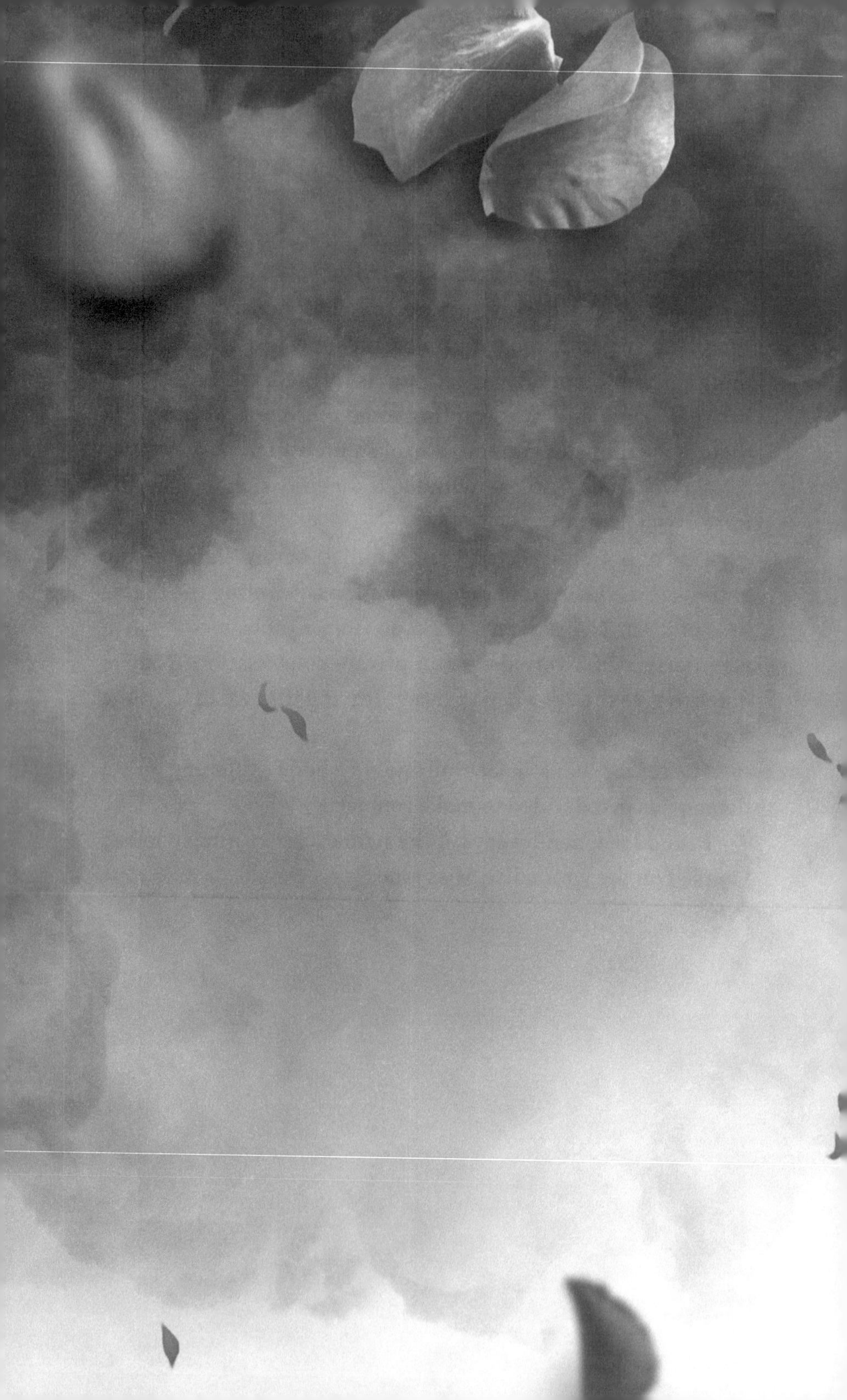

FACING FATE
JANE

My entire life chaotically swirls together while staring at Soren when he faces me. I take a few steps back, my eyes drifting to his lower half. My father always told me to judge a man not by his words, but by his boots: they're worn, thick, expensive, and purely militant.

Well... he's the real deal. He's dressed like a mercenary, from his thick leather pants that are stained red, to his leather vest and braziers, all bearing the marks of countless clashes with enemies. Let alone all the knives, daggers, and shiny objects lining his body, especially the metal armor on his outer thighs and shoulders.

And what a *terrifying* body—everyone calls themselves large when they hit a certain height, but this man is... massive. Broad and thickly muscled, like all he does is kill people for a living. His weathered, dirty hand reaches for the hilt of his sword. His unnervingly clear-cut eyes stare right through me.

"What are you doing here?" I demand, jerking my head to get some of my hair out of my eyes. "Why were you in Coalfell? Why were you after me?"

Soren's face is interesting, I'll give him that. It's hard, very hard, like the skin of his cheeks have been thickened by war. Probably mid-thirties. Yet, he's handsome, but not in a conventional way—just unnaturally attractive for a killer. Everything is in proportion, those eyes the palest, clearest blue, his jaw strong and masculine. There's a deep scar along the side of his face, along with three healed gashes over his left eyebrow, but it completely fits the rough, dirty demeanor.

One would think being attractive has very little to do with survival, but lessons from Kathleen whisper in my mind.

Would Soren be easy to distract? In *that* way?

I quickly decide he's attractive enough for me to play whatever part I must, as long as it means I'll have a shot to run for it.

"You just going to stare at me, love?" he asks, dark curiosity laced in his captivatingly rough voice, ignoring my question.

I drop my gaze, not sure what to do or say. I'm in Soren's grip and I'm not dead, yet. As mercenaries are, they're only allies to whoever is paying. Then again, he's a Zenith, so *he'd* be the one paying... just how much cruelty is he willing to use on me?

"You going to hurt me?" I ask, my lighter voice contrasting against his. I clear my throat, like it'll somehow make the tone deeper.

He takes me in like he's examining bound cattle. The rough

fibers of the rope burn into my skin, tightening with my wriggling.

"If that's your thing, I suppose I can. Whatever it takes to get you to tell me who the fuck you are."

His manners certainly match his demeanor.

With my arms tied, I'm pretty sure all I can do is headbutt his armored chest, but hells, it's better than standing here. If he's going to resort to hurting me, then I'll put up whatever fight I have to.

He removes his hand from the sword at his side, as if deciding I won't be requiring such measures. Rolling his fingers, I catch the detail of the mismatched rings he wears—a sign that he loots and steals what he likes.

"Who wants me?"

"The Council." He tuts, strutting over to a side table lined with many, empty crystal glasses. He may have given his back to me, but I know his guard is anything but down.

Soren pours himself a glass of golden liquid and examines it, setting the decanter down with a dull thud. "Sounds ridiculous, saying the name out loud. They can come up with Skull's Row, the Zenith... and then the *Council*. Was there really no better option?" He faces me, those icy eyes penetrating as smoothly as his steel blades. "It's my equals that want you, though. And for some reason, they want you badly."

My lips part, empty air escaping. I can only imagine they're after one thing in particular, but I also don't know how that's possible.

No—I have to evade this, one way or another. Whether I have to fight or fuck my way out of this remains unclear, but I *will* change plans at a moment's notice to accommodate survival.

He nears me, his footsteps heavy on the wood, sipping on his drink, not even blinking. His gaze trails my face, licking his annoyingly enticing lips when he lowers the glass. "You look like someone that might bite a cock off rather than suck it like those pretty lips could," he says, reaching out to run a thumb over my mouth.

Oh, no he doesn't. I take a bite at his thumb, and he snickers while jerking his hand back, like he's pleased by that. "Your hair is quite nice... But I don't think they want you for that, either—" his gaze slices to meet mine "—so if they're not after you to fuck you, then who in the hells are you?"

"Funny, that. I'd *also* like to know." So... he's curious about me? "And why don't you know, if you're one of them—"

A sensation of vertigo almost unsteadies me, my knees weakening. I swallow thickly and crane my head to look into the face that's so cold I doubt it's ever felt warmth. "I need to heal myself," I mumble.

He cocks his head, raising a dark brow. "You also need to heal my man's nose."

I huff. "No. He held me down while I got hit in the head."

Soren shrugs, his leather crinkling with the motion. "I gave the order."

"Then you're lucky I'm tied up," I mock back.

If Kathleen were here, she'd be pushing me away, apologizing profusely for my ill temper. She's done it more than once at taverns. *She better be alive and all right...*

He laughs, the expression almost inviting. "Little one, I could control you with my *foot*."

"A real tough man you are then, needing me bound," I quip, raising an eyebrow in challenge.

He takes another slow sip of his liquor. I don't like that he's so hard to read. Is he violent for no reason? The harassing kind? Or is he going to just hold me close to the flames all night, only ever singeing my hair?

"You really threatening me?"

I suppose I am. I'm in the home of a Zenith, wanted by the Council. This isn't going to end well for me, no matter what I do, so I might as well go out with some control over the situation. It'll either kill me, or I'll miraculously escape.

What's there to lose?

I sigh and look down at my binding, my head aching, my bladder reminding me it's been a while since I voided it. "What are you going to do when I have to piss?"

"You're not staying that way, so don't start bitching about it." He places his drink down so he can unsheathe a blade, and my heart freezes. I'd rather choke in the flames than be cut to pieces. He holds it to my neck with such fluidity that I'm certain he knows how to stab me ten times and miss every artery. His face is in mine, his breath smelling of smooth alcohol, those pale eyes captivatingly haunting. "You run from me, and I'll break both your fucking ankles and bind your healing hands so you can't fix them. Do you understand?"

"I won't run," I quietly say.

"I don't believe you," he states, as if the idea is interesting, lowering his blade to snip the rope. "But I could use the entertainment."

It falls to the ground, and I immediately scan the floor for any bit of help. Any weapon.

The search is pointless because a second later, he throws me over his shoulder. I start flailing, but he's a big fucker, and I'm, well, not very big at all. Darkness threatens the edge of my vision, my pulse beating at my temples. My head hurts so bad that all I manage is a groan. I stare at the back of his legs, holding onto his hips for stability to minimize my brain from jostling as he walks.

Staring at my hands braced against his hips, I consider fumbling for a blade.

No. Observe your surroundings.

His voice echoes in my mind, piercing through the chaos to chastise my erratic behavior. I let it linger so it can help me focus... what will pissing off Soren get me? Nothing more than an escalation of pain, and I need clarity to make it out of this, not torment.

We descend into what appears to be a dungeon, the rough surface of the dark stone bearing the weight of hidden secrets, the air damp and smelling like candle wax. We make a turn, and I can see more boots before entering what seems to be a room, guards standing outside the door.

Soren sets me down.

"What is this place?" I whimper, my agonized skull pounding so badly I want to vomit. Survival pieces ugly ideas together when I stare at the plain bed inches away from where we stand.

"Some Zenith like their toys afraid. Or bound and desperate. Or locked away for months so they'll do anything when they see them," he explains, amusement laced in his rugged voice.

I face the armored behemoth as he runs a hand over his black hair to smooth it back. He blocks the doorway. My eyes flutter as I slur through the agony, "You say that like you've done it."

"Course I have," he calmly quips. "But for now, it's your little dungeon—" He takes a step back, placing a hand on the door, those frigid eyes smiling at me, even if his lips remain poised. "Good luck trying to escape."

"This is cruel!" I get out through heavy breaths, the sparse environment inducing claustrophobia. I take advantage of it to attempt any pity that he may harbor. "Just deliver whatever the hells you're going to give me."

He hovers in the doorway, the mercenary too trained to reveal what he's really thinking. "I don't make the orders, love.

But I'm one of the Zenith, and if they all want you, then I owe them loyalty before you, obviously. We start our journey toward Skull's Row on the morrow."

He backs away, shutting the door while maintaining eye contact before all I see is wood. The subsequent slamming of a bar feels almost deliberate, as if to make it a point that I'm stuck in here.

I don't know how long I stand there, shocked, and horrified. My village is burned down—thoughts of Kathleen sear my heart—and there was most certainly a fire mage present. Still waters now have ripples in them; wars always start like this.

And now Soren, of all the damn Zenith, is assigned to take me somewhere inhospitable. It's like having a council of kings and sending one of their own to get the job done, and this particular Zenith is ascribed by legends of carnage, paired with an ability to snatch anyone, no matter if they're as thin as smoke.

How the fuck do I escape this?

I place a hand over my heart, between my breasts, where my tattoo is. All they have to do is look for it, and they'll know.

They'll know everything.

So why hasn't Soren searched for it, yet? Wouldn't that have been the best way to confirm my identity? It would be all too easy to strip me of my clothes.

Then again... what if that wasn't why I was taken?

I huff. That *also* means I can't seduce him, not unless I want to try and explain how I got an impossible tattoo on me.

Then again, does any of this even matter? I doubt they're doing all of this to merely ask me a few questions. They'll strip me, sooner or later. My story has a bloody end—that's all I know for certain. I won't make it easy, then. They'll need to take me kicking and screaming.

I scan the spartan room, holding a hand to my head, healing it: dark walls and floors, a simple bed, nightstand, and an empty chamber pot. I walk near the mirror on the wall—hand still placed on the center of my forehead as blue light emits—looking at my image.

Tears blur my vision, as I look fucking terrible.

Kathleen once told me that I'm pretty enough to offer myself as a concubine to a warlord—even a Zenith—if I was lucky. Now, I look like I crawled out of the ass crack of a cavern that had been engulfed in flames.

My face is utterly covered in soot, my hair a feral mess. There's no way I'm tempting Soren, or anyone, into giving me freedom when I look like this, even *if* I could somehow explain the tattoo over my heart.

My lips drop into a frown, eyeing the auburn hair of my mother, and the honey-brown eyes that neither of my parents possess. I roll in my plump lips, thinking of Soren's rough thumb touching them. My admittedly pretty, gentle face contorts to reveal a rage that I've buried deep.

No... I'm still Jane. And they can't have me.

There's a water basin on the table next to me, along with a single towel. I wet it and clean my face like I'm a warrior putting on face paint, my eyes wide and listless. I even wipe my hair clean to reveal the Jane I want the world to see me as, something about the act feeling important.

Then, I cover my fist with the towel and punch the glass with an expression so incensed they'll never have to guess where I'm from. The glass shatters, broken shards reflecting the dull candlelight of the room as they clink to the floor. I grab a large shard, turn around to stare at the bed and stab a pillow like it's the heart of the Council themselves.

I won't be taken like a sheep.

Even if it means destroying a perfectly fine dungeon. My

blood is born of too much chaos to not make a grand statement in my departure from this world.

I'm a daughter of Skull's Row, and if they're forcing me to return, then this is how I will confirm that for them, since I know that's what they're trying to understand.

Blood, sweat, and tears mix on the fabric of the room as I destroy it.

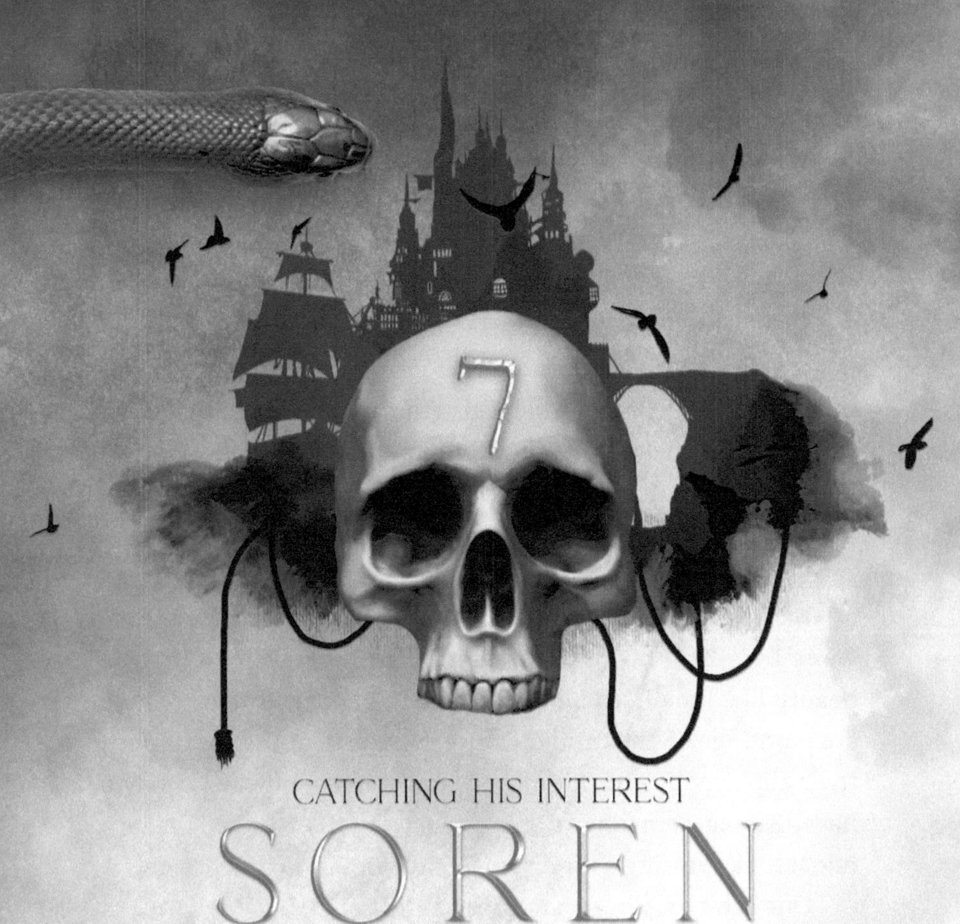

CATCHING HIS INTEREST

SOREN

I sit in the foyer, watching the golden liquid shimmer in the light as I gently swirl the glass. There's a strong, charred scent from whatever barrel it sat in. My rather deranged m ind thinks back to the village and how I bet there's a few good, charred pieces of wood to be utilized by whoever distills this.

Staring at nothing, I try to understand what crazy bastard may have attacked Coalfell...

Could this pyro be from outside our world, if not connected to Jane? From across the ocean? I'd be fucking shocked if it came from the kingdoms in the opposite direction of Skull's

Row—they only have their lofty, soft worlds because they're too far from the cliff-lined coasts that men like me call home. They'd also know that we'd burn down their cities if they ever waged such an attack, no matter the distance or the mountains that separate us.

Does Jane know who attacked her village?

It's almost disappointing how easy capturing her was. In our world, magic is a subtle trait granted only to a select few, tipping the scales of power until our society birthed what we have—mercenaries and warlords ruling over many of the lands, and pirating legends dominating the seas.

She's only a healer, though.

And what a fucking pretty thing she is... is that why they want her? Zenith are all well-traveled, but even so, a true beauty like Jane is something scarcely happened upon. There are paintings of beautiful creatures—mostly of the sirens with their abnormally enchanting, oceanic allure—but that's all we have. Seeing someone in the flesh is another ordeal—like a man at sea spotting a forgotten island with buried riches.

One can't help but want to ensnare it.

I've had many pretty pussies, but there's something fun about one sprouting up out of nothingness—with all this drama surrounding her—that makes me so damn curious. Granting her freedom within that dungeon will reveal who she is.

Will she try to injure me? Be forced to expose another magic of hers that she's hiding? Assault another? Escape?

She'll *never* escape, that I'm sure of. Standing at chest height, she doesn't present much of a threat, and can only deliver damage when someone's guard is down. Didn't even go for my daggers when she was over my shoulder. I snort into the glass as it hovers near my lips—rippling the golden liquid —when I remember she tried to bite my thumb.

Jane's just a snapping turtle.

I sip more of my drink, staring at a painting of an ocean framed in ornate bronze.

Perhaps one of the Zenith are wanting to travel overseas, where the lands are rumored to be in utter turmoil: perfect pillaging environment. A pretty healer would be quite the accessory.

The Council of Zenith only send one of their own for the most extreme circumstances. It's annoying they haven't told me why they want her, but I assume it's because they know I'll find out why. I *always* do.

Speaking into the glass as I take another sip, I mumble, "Miss Jane is hiding a large secret, I bet..."

I down the rest, slam it on a table, and stand to open the heavy front door, alcohol loosening my muscles. A few houses are scattered right outside for those traveling with their Zenith. I say to one of my men on guard, "Get Bones."

I wait patiently as the message is delivered.

Emerging from a smaller establishment—suffused with a warm, golden glow from the inside—comes my most trusted man, his eyes swollen, and his nose definitely shattered. Despite the evident pain plaguing Bones, a mirthful laughter escapes my lips at the sight of his disheveled state. "Gotta admit, she disappointed me in how easy she was to catch, but she kicks like a damn mule."

"Little bitch," Bones grumbles, bitterness lacing his voice, cracking his knuckles. "Maybe I can break her feet as a sign of *gratitude*."

"The Council wants her intact, unless necessary measures are required," I reply, my gaze sweeping the darkness, sensing out any disturbances. "But sure, if she becomes a pain, you can do the honor."

"Good, because I don't care what they want. I want my

nose intact." His voice is stuffy, dried blood caking his nostrils. He'll need the healing if he doesn't want his breathing fucked up for the rest of his life.

"We'll make her heal it. That's why I called you over."

He nods. "I also learned a few things about her. Villagers were *very* cooperative, although a few were loyal. She apparently appeared in Coalfell around the age of thirteen, out of the blue, orphaned. Refuses to talk about her life. Has even gotten a few proposals but turned them all down—*they* were willing to reveal truths about her the most. Kathleen, the *blonde*," he says, using his hands to accentuate his chest area, "is her only true friend. Won't say a fucking word about her."

"I still say that's an odd choice. They usually tell you *everything*."

"Aye. Something's important about her, and I want to find out what it is before we reach Skull's Row."

I re-enter the confines of our sanctuary as Bones closely follows, descending the worn stone stairs, and immediately I sense a great deal of anguish in the air—one of my more hidden skills. That anguish runs deep, staining the air with rancor. Sounds of muffled mania makes me move faster.

"What's happening?" I demand, eyeing Jane's door as the discordant sound of an enraged woman makes it seem like a damn torture chamber.

"She's destroying the room," one of the craggy guards dismissively responds, like she's a pest.

I shove him to the side, swing the wooden bar upward, and open the bedroom door. The sight before me is utter chaos: the room is torn apart, blood staining the fabrics of the bed. She's stabbing a pillow with a broken piece of glass in her bloodied hand, panting and snarling like a rabid animal.

She doesn't look up from the bed, fixated on her brutal assault of the damn pillow.

I slice a scathing glare at the guard. "You didn't hear this?"

"You said to let her suffer. Sounds like she's doing a right job at that," he says, placing a lazy hand on his hilt, peering in.

Idiot. Should have used my own men down here rather than the locals, but it's too fucking late now.

Bones laughs as he peeks in, widening his eyes to get a better look. "Bitch is fucking nuts."

My gaze narrows on Jane like she's a wild cougar, especially as she pulls the broken shard through the last, good pillow, fabric tearing and goose feathers flying everywhere.

"How you doing, love?" I ask, holding my hands out like I won't hurt her. She's gone bat-shit crazy, and yet still took the time and effort to clean her hair and face.

This is more of what I was expecting.

"Really great," she retorts, glaring at the pillow, still on her knees. A few white feathers are stuck in her frenzied hair.

I hold very still, devouring everything I can of her. "Whatever you fucking say," I gesture with my head to the door, "You still need to heal Bones' nose, Jane."

She snorts, flicking those warm eyes up at me that are coated with a wild edge. "Nope. You need me alive, I've gathered. So, I know I don't have to do shit, because you can't kill me." She points the shard at me. "And break my fucking ankles. Go for it. I'll just heal them. Even with broken hands. I'll find a way."

Bones enters the room. "The fuck is wrong with this one? She's like a personification of Skull's Row."

I watch how Jane stabs the pillow, *right* as Bones speaks. Well... that might be an idea. There're thousands of people in Skull's Row. Wouldn't be hard to believe she was born there and left without anyone noticing.

But why is she so interesting to the Council? I take a step

closer, hands still raised. "What do you want in exchange for healing Bones?"

"Go find another healer," she grunts, tossing the pillow, eyeing the room like it's useless to her now, seeing as there's nothing else to rip apart.

"I'm kind of curious what it'll take to get you to heal him."

She throws her gaze at me, a flicker of her defense removed before it's back up. Did she really have to clean her face and hair? She looks even more like a lord's daughter, one that all the knights would fight for. Except I'm gathering that she's the type to stab them in their sleep if they stole the covers in the night.

"Set me free," she demands.

I snort. "No."

"Then, find someone else." Jane raises a judging brow at Bones, like she's disappointed he's not more damaged.

"You going to hurt yourself with that?" I nod to the shard in her hands.

She scoffs and rolls her head to face me. "What does that matter?"

"I have strict orders to bring you in alive, so it's a little relevant," I explain, taking one step closer.

Jane straightens her back, contemplating my words. The tear in her tunic—right at the collar—reveals her shoulder and collarbone. It's almost like an invitation to let my gaze wander and take in her feminine shape, considering *many* things.

I still can't believe this woman is wanted like she's a warlord herself.

"Well, when you're done staring at me," she finally says, unabashed. "You need to understand one thing—I *will* go out on my terms. Don't care why the Council wants me. It's my life, which means *my* death."

Why the fuck am I getting hard? She gives me commands

like she's got a secret army hidden away somewhere. Taming her savagery would be quite fun... ferocious beauties like Jane are immensely rare, even in Skull's Row.

That's only frequently found among the sirens.

"You're just a sharp little fucking rose," I muse, completely entertained; it's been a boring fucking two weeks searching for her. Each step I take heightens her vigilance like she's ready to pounce if I get too close. "Why have you been hiding this whole time in a boring village?"

"Going to write a book about me?"

I push down any thoughts about laughing. "How about this—" I begin, eager to see her reaction. How can I not? I have to stoke this flame. She's no doubt the type to respond to provocation rather than torture. "They offer to kill you, I'll take you as my concubine."

The singular laugh from Jane carries a tone of disgust, but she doesn't fail to look me over like it's a thought that doesn't offend her. That just makes me all the more fucking intrigued.

I'll unwind her, one way or another.

"Lucky me," she grinds out. "You're the worst of them."

I place a hand on my chest, feigning an expression of sincerity. "I've *never* claimed to be a knight in shining armor."

The corner of her lips quiver like she might find me funny. "You're deranged."

I glance briefly at Bones and then back at her, finally laughing. "Says the woman who tore a whole room apart." I motion to the shredded pillow and bloodied feathers in her lap. "With her blood smeared all over the damn place."

With sanity no longer guiding her, she lunges right at me, feathers flying.

I grin wildly, expecting this.

She might be much quicker than most women, and can take most grown men by surprise, but I'm a fucking legend for a reason. Right as she swings her arm toward me, I grab her wrist as the shard hits my vambrace, disarming the bloody shard. Not once do I remove my gaze from hers, fixing both my legs on either side of her, pinning down her arms against the bed. She squirms under my pressure.

Now, my cock is hard for every reason that makes sense, especially as her rapid movements rub the crotch of my leather pants.

Her eyes are wide, and finally, the fear is unfiltered: deep, all-consuming dread. A sliver of my humanity recognizes the wild, primal distress. She's cornered, and this is her mind processing it. How many men have I killed that looked at me like this before I ripped their hearts out? Or gouged out their eyes before carrying on about my day like none of this violence matters?

This is different, and I know it. *None* of them were wanted alive by the Council, which means, I'm not allowed to think about killing her because that's not the deal. With death removed, her humanity speaks to me more than it otherwise would have.

"Enjoying yourself?" I ask as she continues to writhe underneath my weight. I have both of her wrists pinned above her head now, my weight restraining her. I almost want to warn her to stop moving so much, especially when her hips rock in just the right way in an attempt for freedom. My unhelpful cock is already twitching for me to grab a fistful of that pretty hair and hold her still.

She stops, as if realizing the futility. I stare into honey eyes that long lashes whisp over. With a quiver in her voice, one that I feel disappoints her more than she wants to let on, she nervously asks, "What're they going to do to me?"

Ah, *fuck.* My cock is slightly less hard now. It's only fun when she's feisty.

"I don't know." I lower my face slightly, half expecting her to headbutt me or bite my face. "But like I said, I'd happily take your crazy ass with me. Peace is quite nice, but it does get a little boring."

"What the fuck is wrong with you?"

"Do you really want to get into that now, love?" I ask, an unhinged gleam in my eyes. "Or should we first talk about whatever the fuck is wrong with *you*?"

I'll learn every shadow of her history before delivering her to the other Zenith. No matter what it takes. I'm not turning Jane in until I know who exactly I've got in my hands. If I have to fuck it out of her, then it'll simply be one of the more enjoyable interrogations I've led.

The more I get from her, the more I'm understanding that perhaps the Council hoped I would deliver her without question. Which means whatever she hides might be tempting enough for me to break a few rules.

We *all* have a tendency to be selfish, so they'd be well aware of this trait within me.

Either way, it's all a mystery and I *love* solving these riddles.

She averts her gaze, which was the wrong move. Now, she's exposed her pale, soft neck to me, and I quickly lean in. Her resurfaced struggle is quite useless underneath me, especially as I lean the weight of my chest into hers, quickly whispering into her ear, ensuring my voice is hot on her skin. "You tell me why they want you—every truth—and I'll help keep them away from you. I think your response here shows you know they won't let you go alive... but I can keep death at bay."

She subdues, her heart pounding so hard I can feel its frantic rhythm against my chest, her soft breasts pressed right against my leather armor. "Why should I trust you?" she breathes out, but I hear the interest.

I hear the bargain.

"I'm a man of opportunity, and I want to know what the Council isn't sharing." I run my nose against her hairline, smelling her. It's pure ash and smoke. I catch the way, for an unguarded moment, her body betrays her as it relaxes. I grin, although she can't see that. *That's it. That's my way through to her.* "Think about it, little one."

In an instant, I release my grip and slide off of her, not giving her enough time to try anything she'll regret. Once I'm at the foot of the bed, the woman is still splayed out, staring hopelessly at the ceiling.

"Hope you like sleeping in broken glass."

"You were supposed to kill me for this," she confesses, breathing heavily, lowering her gaze as she tries to stare right through me.

I pause, considering that. "What?"

"I don't want to die at their hands." Her eyes aimlessly move all over, staring at nothing in particular, lying among her carnage like it's nothing bothersome, blood still leaking from the lacerations of her palms. "They can't have me."

I need more of this from her.

Time to play a very careful game of chess. "Heal Bones for me, and I will have them clean this up," I offer, using a gentler tone.

Her gaze finally latches to something in the room, unblinking.

Jane deliberates for a long while before giving a single, curt nod.

CHOKED OUT

JANE

I only agreed to take care of Bones because it's better than engaging in combative behavior with either of them. Weaknesses reveal themselves when one thinks they have control, so I'll grant them that illusion.

Besides, I can't quite focus, anyway. Not when I'm wondering what in the *hells* is going on with my reaction to Soren's touch?

He's darkness personified, and here my body is betraying me: the weight of his armored body, mixing with the vibrations of his gruff voice in my ear... it *enrages* me.

The simple men of Coalfell were never interesting, a loathsome reminder that altering the core of my identity is, well, impossible.

Soren confirms *everything* for me. The bastard has captured me, bound me, had me assaulted, and I'm fucking turned on by him—especially when I was immobile underneath him.

I observe Bones, his face reminding me of a toad with the way his nose and eyes have swollen. So far, violence hasn't helped me at all. Perhaps healing Soren's man can get me into his good graces, even by an inch. *Anything* to keep me away from the hands of the Council.

I doubt he'll truly keep the Council off of me... but damn, it tempts me.

Bones saunters over with a confident gait, his slightly curly black hair tucked behind his ears, barely reaching his shoulders. Scooting closer to the edge of the bed, carefully avoiding the broken shards of the mirror, I notice a deep scar on his outer neck, another slicing through his cheek from chin to ear.

Bones leans down on one knee in front of me, his intense glare warning that if I so much as *sneeze*, he's going to cut me. "Try anything on me other than to heal me, and I'll carve my name in your skin."

Soren watches in the background like a sentry, and I note that he doesn't seem to mind the threat in the slightest. All he does is stare at my face like my thoughts are scrawled on my skin for him to read.

Rolling my eyes, I hold my breath so I can steady my anger. *Play nice. Do this so you can understand Soren better.* Through tight lips, I say, "Well, if you're done being dramatic, then let's begin. This will hurt for a moment. You'll feel things shift around, and then the swelling will start to subside."

He doesn't move; not even to blink.

I hold my hand out, glimpsing the blue tattoo on my wrist that's scrawled in a language I can't read, shaped into a circle. I hover my magic over his nose, the inky lines glowing blue as a faint light emits from my palm. The way it feels to heal another is akin to waves of vibrations, and I can interpret the way they feel when they return back to me, gauging the damage so I can properly direct the powers gifted to me.

Every healer is born with an innate ability to mend, the tattoo connecting the gifted ones to the ancient roots that made us.

His battered skin moves to accommodate the healing cartilage, wincing and grunting when the most painful part begins.

I stare at his mismatched eyes, concentrating hard to remove the swelling. For a moment, my head grows so light I worry I'll pass out; I nearly forgot how exhausted I am.

The effort is enough to get the job done, though, Bones breathing deeply through his unclogged nose when it finally straightens; I pant from draining what little reserves I had regained.

It's almost annoying to note that Bones would be rather handsome if he wasn't so brutish. I can now see he's got a square face with another scar on his lip, that one blue eye fascinating against the darkness of him. He even wears a necklace consisting of many knuckles hanging around his neck, the only thing standing out besides his eye.

He rises to leave, reaching up with weathered hands to stroke his newly healed nose. "Don't fucking break it again," he grunts.

"Then don't hold me down again." I sweetly smile, a little *too* cordial. I can't help myself; he's fun to annoy.

Before Bones can properly retort, Soren motions for him to leave with a minor flick of his fingers—it's all that's required to leash Bones and keep him off of me.

Soren's attention is mine once more, which is an unnerving

experience. "You can either sit out in the hall, or in here, while they clean."

I don't trust a single hair on his head—not even his eyelashes—but I know sitting in this room is the last thing that will help me. "I won't try anything," I say while standing.

My heart races like a caged animal who's centered her attention on the open gate.

"Sure, you won't," he says with absolutely no conviction in those words.

I think about his previous offer of becoming his concubine, even if it *was* offered in jest, taking in his formidable body when his back is to me as he exits the room. What would he be like as a lover, even if it was just an exchange to keep me alive? Is he rough? Will I know what every inch of him tastes like by the time he's done with me? Will he force me on my knees to worship his cock like I've seen so many of his kind do?

There's no way the Council isn't planning on killing me, which means any option for survival *has* to be considered. Fuck Soren for a few months, get his guard down, then cross the Black Seas into wilder lands where no one will know of me...

It *is* a solid plan.

But I'm not ready to concede. Not yet.

I follow him out of the room, the dim candlelight only adding to the misery of this dungeon.

He sits down in a seat that's brought for him, the Zenith almost too big for the damn thing. I sit in another when a guard places it down, the wooden chair cold against my skin. Soren watches me like he's not truly looking *at* me, but something else.

What that is? I'm not sure. And I'm so tired that I don't know if I have the energy to process it. *Just relax, be patient. Show you can work with him. Then get some rest and try again.*

Bones strides up the stairs at Soren's command, breathing extra loudly as if to make a point that he got his way.

We awkwardly sit in silence, my fists clenching as I observe his men cleaning my mess. I harbor no remorse for making them do such a thing, and why should I, anyway? I'm a dead woman walking, and they'll all rest their heads on soft pillows long after I'm gone. It felt good to get that pent up aggression out, and it clearly bought Soren's attention.

Completely worth it... even if his intense gaze never releases its hold on me.

"Why are you after me?" I mutter, not averting where I stare, but watching him in my peripheral. I'm wasting precious time in this silence. "Why did they send *you*?"

He finally relinquishes that unnerving stare and looks ahead like he contemplates whether or not he wants to answer. It's *then* that I steal my own glance. Unwavering calculation fills his eyes, a sinking pit forming in my gut—outsmarting this monster might prove entirely useless.

Soren sighs through his nose, the muscles in his jaw flexing. "When the Council needs to get a job done, they send one of their own." His head rolls to look at me, my pulse quickening, "And I haven't failed *once* in collecting a bounty, no matter *what* I have to do."

Fidgeting with my injured hands, eyeing the drying blood smeared on my skin, I listen to the guards complain as they clean up the feathers. *Keep going, Jane. Prod more.* I practice the words in my mind before I attempt a gentler approach, "I didn't do anything, you know, to make them come for me. I really didn't."

He snorts. "Sure, you didn't, love."

I roll my eyes, something about that word grating on me. It's demeaning, like I'm his entertainment. "I'm not your *love*."

He snickers, adjusting in his seat as he languidly trails his gaze to the hands in my lap. "I call all pretty women that."

A blush lies just underneath my cheeks—this fucker thinks he's smooth. *Keep it together, Jane.* "I didn't do anything. Truly. This isn't fair to punish me, and you're wasting your time. *Both* of our time." I drop my gaze to the stone floor when staring at him is simply too much, like he teeters on which side of patience to choose. "And who burned the village down? Did you catch them? It didn't look like an accident."

"That's all still a mystery, just like you," Soren slowly replies, turning it right back on me. "You're clearly hiding something, *Jane*. Healers don't end up in random villages... Not with a story like yours, anyway: orphaned young, lives alone, appearing with no backstory and refuses marriage proposal after marriage proposal."

I clench my teeth, steadying my breathing. How in the hells— the *villagers*. The drive to march out of here and yell at every one of those betrayers is almost enough to bring me to my feet. *Stop. Keep calm. Don't get mad at them for talking. They're fucking terrified. He's using that to make it seem like he knows more than he actually does.*

"Well, good to see you did your research," I reply, trying to act as calm and in control as possible. "How is everyone, then? Since you seemed to have spoken to them all?" I think of Kathleen, my tongue nearly tying at the thought of receiving bad news. "Was there a woman, a blonde one? My age?"

Humor etches in his tone. "Yes... we saw who I imagine you're referencing. She was worried about you. Bones is quite infatuated, in fact. Doubt she's going to get rid of him anytime soon."

I glare at him, my blood running so hot it nearly damages my skin. "*That* man? He's unhinged."

"You don't say?" he sarcastically replies.

Glowering at him, I snap my attention back to watching the men clean, my lips nearly forming a snarl. Suddenly, the seat is entirely uncomfortable, the air stuffy down here.

Focus! I want to say more, to ask for protection for Kathleen, but I also want to avoid placing too much attention on her in case that backfires. What if they use her as a means to get me to talk?

No. Keep her out of this. I shouldn't have even asked.

Honing in on my surroundings, I'm reminded of the peculiarities about openly chatting with a Zenith as his men clean a room I demolished; I'm not sitting out here because Soren is feeling *nice.* "Why are you talking to me right now?"

He sucks his bottom lip to his teeth, watching as they carry out the sheets. "Well, I'm not wandering far from you since you're my captive, which means I can go sit by myself while you sit restrained... *or* I can try and pick apart whatever the fuck you are."

All right, a reasonable answer. What do I do with that, though? Play the victim? Maintain my attitude? My nerves speak for me, "Well then, this will be a rather dull conversation. Like I said, I don't know why they want me."

Circles. We're going round and round with no progress, and I don't know if he's patient or not. It's been so long since I had to talk my way out of something, that my skills have completely rusted over.

His attention returns to me, that gaze of his making my heart race in ways I don't bother to interpret. He speaks like he's entertaining me, but not for my sake. "I'm sure you have a *guess.*"

I swallow thickly, nervously running a hand through my hair, regretting that decision as it irritates the injured flesh of my fingers. I choose to lie, "No, I don't."

"You're going to be a stubborn bitch, aren't you?" he asks, although his tone isn't as cutting as his words.

"You're just charming the pants *right* off of me," I grind out, throwing him an insolent look. "Really makes me want to open up."

He returns it with a knowing grin, revealing a rather nice smile.

This stupid man makes me want to blush even more. In an effort to distract myself, I use whatever energy I have left to heal my lacerations, holding up my hand to examine it, thinking I might see glass in there—

Soren lunges at me, his blade pressed against my throat as he forcefully grips one of my wrists and pins me to my seat. I inhale through clenched teeth, my eyes wide, remaining absolutely still with that cool steel against my flesh; I'm too exhausted to fight back, worrying I don't have enough energy to heal something as deep as a neck injury.

"What the fuck?" I quietly mutter.

The guards pause with concern, but quickly return to cleaning when Soren is clearly unthreatened—perhaps he often behaves like this with others.

He's fixated on my wrist that's in his hand, dark brows furrowed. With his blade steady at my neck and my head craned back, I'm unable to see what has him so bothered.

Soren suddenly releases my wrist, blood pooling back into my hand. The steel never wavers in its spot, the mercenary looking *right* at me—every gear has shifted to reveal the ruthless man he is, not an ounce of remorse or humanity in those pale eyes.

His voice vibrates against my lips as he leans in. "There's a scar on your arm. It's got a translucent, purple hue to it."

My expression deadpans.

Of-fucking-course. I had forgotten all about that. No one in the village knew what it was, and it's so close to my healer tattoos that it blends right in.

No point in hiding it. I know enough to understand that will only anger him; *truly* anger him.

"So, I do," I admit with a stark tone, returning that unnerving glare right back at him. So much for not having at least a *guess* on my end.

There's no humor reflected from the mercenary this time. "That only appears when naprese gold touches your skin—" the blade presses deeper, my jaw shaking as I crane my neck further back... I *hate* being cut by others "—that shit is as rare as a Zenith, and only found in the heart of Skull's Row when they make our masks... which means you've been in *our* world. The Zenith's world." A wicked glimmer flares in his gaze. "Who the *fuck* are you?"

My heart pounds all the way into my ears. This isn't fair. I left that world, didn't I? Why does it have to haunt me now? I lick my dry lips from all the panting.

But fine—if they want to kill me for this, then so be it. With as much stiffness in my tone as I can muster, I reply, "I'm obviously not saying anything to you, so do what you need."

His eyes terrify me with the hundred promises of violence hidden within... I know that's the look he gives to the souls right before ending their life. "Maybe we bring that one named Kathleen down here? Since you asked about her..."

No. No, no, no.

My hidden truth is what this man craves, which means it's my buffer to keep others safe. Is it worth trying to negotiate? Or is it simply my time? Do I allow him to kill me now, in an effort to save Kathleen?

I grew up among dangerous, difficult men. I've been ready to die for a very long time, as one can never be in that world without seeing violent endings as the inevitable: Either Soren will kill me, or the Council will.

The thought of meeting the Council burns my heart just as much as the smoke burned my lungs. And returning to them would mean I break my oath about never setting foot inside of Skull's Row again.

I choose to die in Soren's hands.

Nearly smiling, I move quick enough to headbutt the Zenith, while also slicing my neck in the process. It's not deep enough to bleed out, but the blood quickly warms my skin all the same.

If I thought I had already glimpsed an idea of his brutality, I was wrong.

Everything about him changes.

In a blurry motion, I'm off my chair and Soren's knife drops to the ground, the man instantly at my back in a fluid motion. My head's locked in his arm as he chokes me, my feet barely scraping the floor.

Even though I just agreed to meet death, I can't kill the instinct to claw at his armored forearm. "Just. Kill. Me," I manage out through a constricted airway, hoping I won't wake up after this. I know he said he can't kill me... but maybe he will. They're *all* bloodthirsty, in the end.

The world fades to black while locked within Soren's grip until my body is limp in his arms.

JANE

Everything hurts.

My head, my hands, my neck... all of it.

My crusted eyes beg to open, but I sew them shut as it all rushes back to me. That familiar sensation of rope binding my arms momentarily weakens my resolve; I feel like a sailor anchoring my ship near an island surrounded by steep cliffs. Will shore come to me? Or am I destined to succumb to the stormy waters until they drown me?

I make a wish to whatever gods exist that Kathleen manages to escape and get far away from this place. Surely, Kathleen and her gran will find refuge *somewhere*.

"You're obviously awake," Soren's voice penetrates my somber reprieve. He has an odd effect on me when he speaks; if I weren't bound and afraid for my life, I'd find the roughness of it rather enticing.

"Are you watching me like a vulture?" I ask, eyes still closed. Even now, I simply can't let go of my snarky side.

It's all one really has left when facing the void, alone.

"Yes, actually, I am." I hear something heavy being set on a nearby table. "Do you feel better after that outburst?"

There's an edge of impatience in his tone, like he pities himself for having to be stuck with me.

"Oh, clearly," I counter, coughing, my dry voice cracking. "Barely feel a damn thing."

With an exasperated sigh, I finally open my eyes and squint; my head pounds like nails are piercing through my skull.

"You're a mad woman."

I groggily look around, the need to drink consuming me. "I'm thirsty."

I stare out one of the windows, eyeing the moon-lit clouds. Tonight was supposed to be simple, consisting of tending to the injured coal miners leaving their day shift... maybe even enjoy a hot meal of lamb stew.

Taking shallow breaths, I loathe the way the smell of charred wood clings to me. Screams echo in my memory, the heat terrifying to recall, guilt choking me—No. I need to lock that away. It won't help me now.

Soren strides over with heavy steps. I'm disoriented on my side, only his thighs visible in my view. His virile, veined hand grabs the rope that binds me and sits me up straight. I groan from the pain in my throat, the scratchy twine pinching and digging into my skin.

I'm a fucking mess.

I can see the room better now, however; we're in a much nicer bedroom with a massive four-poster bed, draped in crimson velvet curtains. The bedposts are carved with intricate designs of anchors, an adjacent large hearth emitting a warm glow. A bay window is partially curtained, reminding me of a captain's quarters on a ship.

Ships.

Everything in here reminds me of a life that's a ghost to me now—I really *am* being forced to return.

My lip quivers as every wound reopens in my soul. *Bury it. Numb it all. It's the best way. Those feelings belong in the grave of my childhood.*

Breathing deeply, I observe Soren—most of his exterior armor is removed, revealing a simpler layer beneath his battle-worn exterior. He pours a pitcher of water into a wooden cup before bringing it to me, placing it at my lips. I gorge on the offering, water dribbling down my face. Soren sets the empty cup on a weathered end table and walks away, not saying a damn word.

This man confuses me. Why did he choke me out instead of killing me? Does the Council need me *that* badly? And why can I not look at him without losing my damn mind?

You know why, Jane.

When I was a younger girl, I used to dream of marrying a man that could slay all of my enemies. My father ensured I knew his standards—any man not willing, or capable, of slicing his way through an army to save me, was beneath me.

It's a rather fucked up requirement, but anyone would understand if they knew who my father was.

That command feels so empty now, as he failed to save Mother...

I had to stab her killer in the neck, his blood having bathed me in warm spurts as she died behind me.

Grinding my teeth, I'm infuriated at the swift deterioration of my resolve. I was doing so well at keeping all these emotions at bay, and now they move rampantly within my heart. And all the while, this asshole mercenary removes the rest of his armor while the dwindling flames in the hearth gently crackles. It's almost peaceful, like my crumbling life is just another day for him.

Those dexterous fingers move with finesse, untying his connecting pieces. His black hair hangs in his unnecessarily handsome face.

What an annoying bastard. He gets to exist as my captor, living a lofty life, while I smell like charred bones.

When Soren removes his vest, there's nothing left but a tunic and his leather pants. Even his shoes and socks are removed.

And then he *pulls the tunic off.*

"What are you doing?" I ask, my voice unrecognizably scratchy.

He ignores me as I confusingly devour his body from a distance. Soren has thick valleys of rippling muscles, deep scars laid out in mismatched patterns. One of his arms is a collage of ink that reaches his hand, rings still adorning his fingers. Once his back is straight, I see the black tattoo down his spine like someone took three quills and held them steady, pulling down until they reached just above his sacrum. His rough voice fills the room as he drops the tunic on the table, "I'm going to sleep, and not with my armor on."

"And I'm sitting right here," I counter. "You're just stripping in front of me."

He flashes that pale gaze right at me, something unsettling in how deeply it penetrates. "Watching is your own choice."

I harden my glare. "What about *me*?" I ask, wriggling as if to show I obviously can't sleep while being bound. "I can barely move, and my shoulder is aching. Let alone whatever you did to my neck. And what if I need to piss?"

He thankfully keeps those pants on and nears the bed, bare feet on wood. "You pissed yourself when you passed out, so I doubt you need to void your bladder any time soon. I watered you. You're good until morning," he says, sitting on one side of the bed, stretching his body in gentle movements.

I can't stop staring at the way that scarred man moves, how I can see all the rippling cords of strength whenever he twists or turns. And that black and gold skull tattoo right on his chest, denoting he's a Zenith...

The stupid fucking Zenith.

"So, is this the state I'll be in until we get to the Council?" I croak, still fighting for my dignity, not surprised I pissed myself based on the disgusting moisture below. "Can I at least look presentable when taken to my death? And *not* be covered in piss?"

"I gave you a nice, cushioned room in that cellar, one that had a water basin so you might clean the ash off of you, but you destroyed it," he replies, narrowing his eyes. "And I lost my patience when I spotted that scar on your wrist. Especially when you headbutted me. I really didn't think you'd follow through. First person in a while to land a surprise hit."

Sure enough, there's a small mark on his forehead where the skin has split at the eyebrow. I didn't even remember making contact with him, not with how much the blade hurt when it sliced me.

The scar on my wrist... that wretched mark has ruined everything.

"It was an accident," I mumble. "The scar that you saw was just a dumb accident I got as a kid sneaking around where I shouldn't be..."

The pleading nearly hurts, especially when I so badly want

to tell him he *deserves* the head injury, but I refrain when a coldness returns to his eyes; he doesn't believe a word I said.

I admit, the scar doesn't look good. Access to the naprese forge can't be reached even by the stealthiest of us.

Someone let me in. I don't honestly remember who it was, the tea I drank beforehand disorienting my memory. But I never could have just wandered or snuck in.

We both know that.

A childish desire to cry gets lodged in my throat when all I want is to free my hands. Being bound makes everything feel... it's a dishonorable way to leave this world. "I can heal your eyebrow," I offer, hoping he takes the bait.

"Would require freeing your hands, love, and I'm not doing that." He leans over, licking his fingers so he can pinch out the candle on his nightstand, the dwindling fire our only source of light. "Unless you tell me the truth about how you got that scar."

"I just told you it was an accident," I plead once more with my lie.

He lifts the comforter and slides in like he's a normal fucking person and not a renowned killer. "Because that's not vague at all."

I grunt, trying to concoct a story that I can easily sell to him, but I can't muster anything. My mind is worn down, and so is my body. "Can I at least get a blanket?" I quietly ask.

He groans, those massive arms outside the covers and resting on the bed as he stares at the ceiling. "You're a stubborn mule."

"I'm not a fucking mule."

"That's exactly what a mule would say."

I nearly scream until the mere thought makes my throat ache. "Why am I even in this room with you?" I grind out, annoyed by every breath he takes. I'm not even sure what's holding my sanity together.

Pure spite and survival, probably.

"You have a naprese scar on your wrist. Even if you told me the truth, you're not leaving my sight. Not until I know *everything*."

Groaning, I concede to that argument. He then has the audacity to lick his lips, close his eyes, and lay there like I'm not even here. My listless gaze drops to the floor, then to the ropes that bind me.

I wiggle my body, grating the rough twine against my arms as I try to pull free. I'm bound so tight my skin will have imprints for days, possibly bruised. Looking through my lashes, I consider biting him in his sleep... right at the jugular.

I know that's an idiotic decision, even as I consider it. Killing a Zenith will put an entirely different bounty on my head, and I can only afford that if I'm close enough to the ocean to ride a ship far fucking away from this place—

He speaks, and I hold my breath, hoping to hear an ounce of pity in his voice. But instead, it's merely a threat. "If you move anywhere other than to that couch, I'll chain you real nice and tight to it after gagging and blindfolding you."

My thoughts drip with murder... but I'm beat. Physically, emotionally, and mentally.

Refusing to answer him, I manage to lie down with what little movement I can make, nearly falling off the couch as I do since I can't brace with my arms, ensuring I'm facing the room, not willing to give him my back.

It's so gentle and quiet as I lay in silence with Soren, the fire casting long shadows on the bed that the monster sleeps in. I can't see him from this angle, other than that he's a giant mound moving underneath the covers when he turns over.

Whether or not he sleeps remains a mystery; will he actually let me lie here as he slumbers away?

I should be worried that I'm only feet away from one of the most established killers of the Balar Coasts, but this silence offers a surprising reprieve—I get to properly consider my next steps. It seems like Soren will be my ultimate obstacle until I get to the Council, and I can either affix myself to him or find a way to evade him.

The way every ounce of him went cold makes me nervous, a reminder that if permitted, he'll kill me without thought.

Wouldn't that be for the best, though? I either convince Soren to somehow let me go—which, realistically, will be impossible—or I die before setting foot inside the city of murderers to preserve the oath I made.

Prophetic warnings from a siren are like words etched in stone...

Once, after fleeing Skull's Row, a siren named Melona spoke to me with foretelling... '*Be careful, young human. If the Council ever learns, they will want your blood all over their walls... never let them have you, or return to Skull's Row without paying your debt, or hundreds, if not thousands, will die. Don't ask why... just know your untimely presence will ruin everything.*'

The debt I owe her was never clarified, either. I just assumed, as a kid, someone would eventually find me and explain what my debt was. Until years passed, and my isolation solidified. Her existence became lost to time in my head, seeming as if the whole memory was something my young mind conjured up. How can I possibly manage to heed what she told me? At this rate, I'm going back, one way or another.

So, what if I tell Soren the *smallest* detail? What if he lets me become his concubine, or hells, *anything*? I'm ready to die, while simultaneously not *wanting* to die if I can avoid it.

My heart races as reality sinks in.

The images of Coalfell villagers dying are real—my throat constricts as I suddenly want to cry. *Not right now, Jane. You owe Melona. You have to heed her warning.*

Soren... yes, the fucking annoying man sleeping only a few feet away from me. *He's* the one in the way of my freedom. I admit that I'm worried my heart is too broken to filter through the complexities of my past. What if he can pick me apart better than I'm prepared for?

Does that even matter?

The minute Soren learns my father was a Zenith, one that fell from grace and disappeared...

This is going to be a rough few days.

⸎

I awaken when the sun brightens the room, squinting and wishing for the darkness to return. Daybreak means we will be on the road today, beginning our journey to Skull's Row.

I haven't been there in over ten years.

My eyes widen when I recall there's supposed to be a mercenary somewhere in this room. Soren sleeps soundly as if my impending doom doesn't bother him in the slightest.

I stare at him. How odd is it to see a Zenith so non-threatening? One that had cut my throat, choked me out, and bound me with no blanket while I'm covered in dry piss?

A gnawing instinct warns me that I've only witnessed the spear's tip of this man's anger and power.

The ache in my throat becomes too much and I cough—

His eyes shoot open, staring right at me like a dog that heard movement outside the home.

"Sorry," I grumble. I'm not *really* sorry, but that primal look when he thinks he has to go into action is enough to make me apologize without thinking.

He rolls his eyes and deeply inhales on the soft, lovely bed. At least, I imagine it's such a thing, especially with this rock-hard couch underneath me. He stretches, those flexing muscles begging for a neglected part of my body to stare longer...

He sits up, running a hand through his hair, a light stubble on his face. Without all his armor on, he's undeniably tantalizing; at least to a messed-up woman like me who apparently prefers savage killers to simple farmers.

I look away, not out of embarrassment, but because I know I look terrible in this state. Then I frown, my shame confusing me even more.

He paces the room, silence binding us once more, save for his footsteps and the sound of him pouring water into a cup. He nears me, sitting me up like before, his movements rough. I wince, everything aching so greatly that my eyes water. When he presses the cup to my lips, I greedily drink, eyeing the raised scars of his muscled stomach.

So many women from my childhood sought after these Zenith, desperate to fill their wombs with these men's children, and even more acclaimed—to own their hearts.

Aside from their title, there was *nothing* attractive about some of those men.

This one, though... I'm not blind, and it pisses me off, my body releasing itself into the reckless seas of imagination, eager to know what it's like to touch a person like Soren, and to have someone like him *let* me touch them. To see those cold, calculated eyes grant temporary reprieve, and then for those rough hands to take what he's owed... what *I'm* owed, being the daughter of his kind.

Gods, I'm fucked up.

I'm just as bad as those women always trailing father's shadow, none of them aware he was married... they all just thought I was a kid seeking glory as I followed him.

When I'm "watered", as Soren puts it, he goes over to a table with a bowl and mirror, sitting down on a stool.

"I have to piss," I mutter. "And I'm starving."

"I'll have Anya take you in a moment. She will feed you," he replies, lathering his face in white shaving cream. Apparently, the asshole has to shave before I'm allowed any relief.

"Can I please not be bound? For a *moment*?" I ask in futility.

Soren raises a brow, still looking at himself in the mirror. "Do I have to explain why that's not happening?"

No, no he doesn't. I'd take that blade as soon as his guard was down and stab him in the eyes, or maybe his heart. Yes, his heart would be best. It would feel good to watch the life leave his gaze as he realizes he lost.

Feeling absolutely useless with only my imagination as my weapon, I stare out the window, knowing that Skull's Row is only a week's ride from here.

There's not much time.

"If I give you a hint, what does that get me? Surely, there's something I can say that can at least grant me a few moments to scratch my face."

He looks at me in the mirror, pausing with the blade at his chin. "Depends on how big that hint is."

SOREN

Jane hasn't answered me, and instead, peers back out the window. She's covered in blood, dirt, and grime, her determination frequently overpowering exhaustion, those honeyed eyes burning with an intensity lit from the same wick as when I found her in the dungeon room.

I continue to shave my face, wondering what the fuck to do with her.

I've not survived all these years by believing the words of strangers—her story of that scar being an *accident* means very little to me. No one can enter our citadel without proper clearance. All of our soldiers know every face and name, and we have *sensors*.

The higher towers of the Council are notoriously difficult for thieves, let alone the disastrous fate of whoever *attempts* to steal from us. The forge for naprese gold is deep within the cliffs, and only the family or wives of a Zenith can go near the blacksmith that smelts our gold, the ore requiring very delicate magic to get it just right. The metal turns translucent when fire is held up to it, so no one can mimic its purity.

She knows someone important. Important enough to get everyone to look away.

Someone at *my* level.

Jane continues to stew in her mind, and I don't have all fucking day. I *do* want to know who and what she is before we get there. I may owe some loyalty to the Council, but it's a selfish one.

I wouldn't mind robbing the Council of spiking her head if it means she makes a good pet on any upcoming pillages, sitting pretty at my side, able to heal my wounds. I may even be open to fucking her until she's begging to come on my cock.

Keeping her alive has to be worth my time, though, which means I need to know *everything*. Anything less is a liability. It will take an immense amount of convincing the Council to keep her if that's what I want to do, but I know I can do it.

I'm their manipulator for a reason.

I sigh and say, "Ask me for a favor, and I'll tell you what I need in order to grant that favor."

"I want to heal myself," she says without missing a beat.

"Give me the hint, then," I reply, rinsing the blade. "A *real* one. Something to indicate how you got *that*," I nod to her useless wrists, "close to the Zenith."

"I wasn't born in that village. In Coalfell," she quickly explain.

I don't even bother looking at her. "No shit. Try again."

I swear I hear a *chuckle* and latch my gaze on her through the mirror, catching a flicker of a smile on her pretty face.

What the fuck is going on with me? I don't usually feel bad for captives. Especially not ones taken for the Council—usually they're just as corrupt as me. But there's something sad about the way she's covered in blood, tears, piss, and fresh wounds, while bound and smiling at my comment, that makes her seem pitiful. Not in a way where she's pathetic, but just... unfortunate. Like perhaps this isn't the worst moment she's been through.

What a waste of such beauty and wit. She's got scars from deep in the heart of Skull's Row, which confirms to me that the Council will no doubt kill her for whatever treason she committed to be that close without permission. She's going to have to make it worth my time if I'm going to stick my neck out for her.

Jane rolls through the options in her mind, her lips wordlessly moving until she says, "I... I may have been born in Skull's Row. In the Silver District."

I nearly cut my neck. "You fucking what now?"

I had suspected her origins as being from Skull's Row, but not the *Silver District*. That's where extended family of the Zenith live—I turn to face her, eyeing the bound rope, right at her heart. "What's between your tits?"

"The fuck?" she asks, frowning, her tone tightening in agitation.

"On. Your. Chest." I articulate very slowly.

She blanches.

My blood runs hot. I wipe the cream off my face and stand, facing her. "Show me," I demand.

"No," she mutters, barely audible.

"Or what? You'll fight me?" I have to confirm the truth.

There's no way she'd have *that* because that would mean... well, who the *fuck* is she? Just who do I have in my hands?

She looks frustrated enough to ignite into flames. "I just... I tried to live away from it all. I lived in that village for thirteen years. I stayed away. I left them *alone*. Why is this haunting me now? They didn't seem to care for the last decade."

A cornered animal.

I bet her heart is pounding against that rope, her anxiety nearly leaking out of her eyes that flit between frayed emotions. I can play gentle if I need to, especially to get *this* answer. "You let me look, and you can get a warm bath, heal yourself, and eat a hot meal."

She scoffs, looking at me like *I'm* the crazy one. "You're fucking with me."

Jane's warm eyes are frenzied, her shoulders leaning forward as if she might charge me. Nearing the red couch, I slowly crouch down, eye level with her as her honeyed gaze tracks every movement of mine. "You'll know when I'm fucking with you, Jane."

Her cheeks redden; I refrain from smiling. Her pretty, grimy little head went straight down the drain like rainwater.

I can't make heads or tails of this woman. She's vicious enough to attack a room and smear it with her own blood and challenge a Zenith, but blushes when I make a comment like that?

"I want a hot bath. Not a warm one. And I want to *soak* in it," she blurts out.

The corner of my lips betray me as they almost quiver into an actual smile, the surprising emotion frustrating me. "Deal."

Her nostrils flare, her frantic eyes moving all over me. Then, she gives another, single nod. "Take off this rope, then, and I'll show you."

Leaning in, I untie it, watching her closely. She breathes

slowly, staring right at the ground. When the binding is loose, she hotly sighs, her gaze boring into me— "I'm *not* removing my shirt, either. Just lifting it."

Many replies nearly slip off my tongue, but she's like a rare, feral animal—cautious steps are required in order to approach. I sit across from her in the other chair, staring intensely at her. "I'll sit here while you show me."

With determination and no shame, she scratches everything that must have itched but couldn't reach. When she's done with that, she breathes heavily, staring at the hearth that smolders from a dead fire. She turns her head like she's stuck in an internal monologue.

Then, the bold cunt stares *right* at me as she lifts her tunic to the center of her chest. My cock twitches at her daring personality, made worse as I stare at the bare, smooth skin of her stomach.

My morning wood rises to press against my leather pants, wondering if I should fuck her for a quick release, as sort of an interview as my traveling-healer-concubine. I don't control the pleasant surprise in my eyes, my brows arching tall, the underside of her round breasts revealing themselves—my blood stills.

I stare at a black and gold tattoo of a Zenith skull, right over her heart.

I'm on my feet before I realize it, reaching out to touch the tattoo. Jane braces herself, stiffening her back; she understands I have to feel it to believe it.

I'll have to fuck a whore after this. A feisty, auburn-haired whore. Squatting down, I run my finger over her warm, soft skin. The black ink feels normal, as expected, but the gold throughout is rough like sandpaper. Swiftly moving to the hearth, I grab a small burning piece of wood, returning to Jane who hasn't moved; she watches me like she's plotting out the most difficult escape plan.

Holding the flame close enough to make her nostrils flare from the heat, her eyes flash with fear in a way that reminds me of men reliving days they'd rather never see again.

Her village...

It doesn't matter. I see what I need, which is a translucency manifesting in the golden design, her skin appearing as if clear ink carved itself out of her skin once the heat is close enough.

I toss the wood back into the fire, embers spewing out as it crashes into the others, the solid gold design returning once her skin is room temperature.

Once I'm standing back in front of her, I nearly reach out to grab her neck and hold her still, to stare into those eyes until the truth reveals itself... but I hesitate when I glance down and see the blends of deep red and purple bruises from being choked out, an even uglier, festering line on the side where my blade cut.

The unusual hesitation to not hurt her unnerves me. So, I back away before the thought can linger, Jane lowering her shirt. "So... the mystery of your identity begins. You're too easy to knock out to be a Zenith yourself—" her jaw drops in offense, like she might rise to hit me "—so either the widow of one, or the child."

It still makes no sense, even as I say that. None of it does. Daughters are *never* branded. Wives have their own marking, different from the one Jane carries, laced with the color red to denote the blood that will be spilled if any harm comes her way. Only one woman has ever become a Zenith, but that's because she's the storm incarnate.

So where does Jane fit?

"It's personal," Jane mutters, raising her hands to heal her neck. Blue light emits as she closes her eyes, no doubt relieved to feel the pain leave her.

I pace the room, needing to connect these dots. Every detail in this space that's crafted for luxury feels foreign now—extravagant wood carvings, gilded knobs, lush red velvet... the style belongs to a collection of killers that owe each other the bare minimum. The Zenith are a means to an end for me, not my life's dedication.

What do I owe them now? Do I deliver Jane without question? Clearly, some of them knew she had this or they wouldn't have sent me, and yet they didn't tell me. *Peel her layers back and decide what to do after.* Flashing my gaze at her, I ask, "How did you get that scar on your wrist?"

She sighs with futility, head slightly craned back, hands wrapped around her slender neck. "I got the sear when I got the tattoo. It was rushed. I don't remember much, because I wasn't coherent when it happened."

Good enough for now. "How old are you?"

"In my mid-twenties," she says, huffing as she peeks through her lashes and catches me glaring right at her. "Fine, I'm twenty-five summers."

I think on that, trying to piece together a timeline. She's almost a decade younger than me. "Are you a child bride?" I question, hating that aspect of our world but *everything* has to be considered. Even then, the tattoo is still wrong, as it's not a bride's tattoo; but this entire picture is *also* wrong.

Do our rules even apply when trying to unravel the secrets of Jane?

"No. I'm not married. Never was." She doesn't look at me, but everything about her seems to tell the truth.

"So, if you're not married then it's a father that branded you, or as good as..." I pace more, never taking my eyes off of her. "Whoever your daddy is no longer belongs to the Council,

I wager. Or else they wouldn't want you in this manner. He'd have threatened to kill me if I so much as ruffled your hair... so a dead parent? There's only a handful of Zenith that have died or disappeared in the last two decades. And why would the Council want you for *that*?" I nod to her wrist, thinking of the blue ink etched onto her skin. "And whose wife was a healer?"

The healing line is a maternal magic passed onto daughters. Jane is no bastard with the black and gold skull mark between those perfect breasts... so her mother was someone that was married to a Zenith, and a healer at that.

"Should I start calling you inquisitor?"

I smirk. "At least it's clear why you have so many thorns..."

I can only think of two Zenith that were significant enough to warrant such a drastic response that requires sending me to collect her, but both would be impossible. One of them was forced to be a eunuch right at puberty—so incapable and too young to breed—and the other never married. No records of children or a wife; not even a concubine. Some thought he just preferred men.

But even then, his child would *never* receive the mark without a record of it, and I can't recall anything.

So, who is her father? Who broke all these damn rules and got away with it? What was the purpose?

I consider gauging her reactions.

"Charles Ritter," I say, wanting to see if the names spur any reaction if said without warning. Jane's only movement is to clench her fists, staring right at me. "Marcus Harrow."

"Is that how you sneeze, or something?" she asks, raising her brows.

My scowl quivers as I nearly laugh—she blushes and then looks infinitely angry at such a response. My blood runs hot in so many ways that it interferes with my concentration.

"No... those are two Zenith that disappeared within the last two decades." I stop my pacing and stand to squarely face her. "When did you get the tattoo?"

Her eyes vibrate back and forth as she looks into mine, a thousand emotions tying her tongue. I can't deny, the thought of surrendering her to the Council seems so boring now. Almost wrong.

"That's as far as this goes," Jane says, standing. "Now I want breakfast. And a *hot* bath. Don't forget that part."

"You are bossy."

"What I am is hungry, and disgusting. In *so* many ways..." she shakes her head in bafflement.

My gaze trails over her, very slowly, observing every detail as if she's new. So many things run through her head... it's almost difficult to discern the emotions that ensnare her the most.

Jane's not the only secret holder. I can feel things others can't and read their emotions in ways against nature. A magic of my own perhaps, one that the Council utilizes when seeking out the truth. There's very few out there like me.

In Jane's heart, on top of every piece of anxiety, rage, and fear sits a desire she can't shake–she wants me, and she hates herself for it.

It honestly amuses the fuck out of me that out of all the things to enrage her, it's her begrudging attraction to her captor that has her mind spinning like it's caught in a cyclone.

Because I'm a mad fucker that can't stop himself, I near this woman until I'm close enough to lean into her ear, wanting to watch her squirm. She admittedly doesn't smell great. She has endured *way* more than most women—or men —can handle.

For a moment, I register how it's not intelligent for me to feel anything other than indifference for Jane. I respect very few in this world, but the way she's handling herself now is impressive.

Right now, a thoughtless temptation draws me to her, ready for her to hit me in this proximity as I speak into her ear, my lips grazing on her skin, "I can feel you desperately fighting what you want—" I grin, eager to see her fire flare, looking at the wall behind the couch she stands in front of "—There's no shame in wanting my cock, Jane."

"You *mother*—" she aggressively places her small hands on my chest, pushing with as much force as she can, even pounding hard enough to take my breath away; I deflect her, all the while pushing her down onto the couch. I lodge a thigh between her legs, one of my hands resting on the top of the couch and the other free, as if threatening that I can use it to knock her out if I so need to.

I ease my weight down, just slightly. Her hair is spread all over the cushion beneath her, warm eyes seething.

"Don't get mad at *me* for that. I'm not wrong," I say.

An internal heat rolls off of her like steam from a dragon. Something about me pisses her off in ways she can't understand.

Maybe pushing her will help break the shell that hides who she really is. I always see—and feel—the most of her when she's like this.

Her silence makes sense when she throws a kick that barely misses contact, eliciting a sinister laugh from me while moving to the door of the room, knocking on it five times. "Come fetch her."

"You're a cunt," she grinds out. I can tell that words much more venomous than those nearly pour out of her, but she knows better than to run her mouth before she gets her bath.

Aside from her deep hatred of me, all I feel is her longing to *bathe*. I stride back to my seat to finish shaving. Jane bolts to her unbalanced feet, eyeing my neatly laid armor and weaponry on a table.

I say, "Go ahead. Take whatever you want, love. Although I don't recommend using my sword to stab me. Doubt you can lift it for more than a few seconds." I lather shaving cream back on my face, staring into the mirror. "A fair warning—I'll know before you grab anything, to which I'll use this razor blade to chop off whatever touches my shit."

Sensing others means I can *always* feel when someone is about to attack, *and* how. Jane only successfully headbutted me because I just didn't think she'd actually do it.

I snicker to myself; how wrong I was there. No, she's not dull enough to be that predictable.

She doesn't have long to think about what she wants to do before Anya enters the room, the heavy door groaning as it opens. I eye them both through the mirror. "Tie the rope around Jane's neck as you take her outside. Don't let her linger. Bring her back to me immediately. She talks to—and touches —no one."

With one last menacing look from Jane, Anya pulls her from the room. I lower my chin to observe my blade when I hear them on the stairs, the steel catching light from a nearby window. Will Jane be more fun if she doesn't fear her death so much? Life rarely sends such mysteries my way, all wrapped up in such a delicate, thorny bow. One thing's for certain—riling her up has been the best method of communication.

Perhaps I can enjoy playing with my captive before returning her.

"Little Jane," I say to myself, tying my hair back into a low mess of a bun. "What else do you have hidden for me to uncover?"

LICKING STOMACHS

JANE

Soren echoes in my mind for every minute that passes, his words slicing open deep vulnerabilities that are best kept hidden. He's such a dipshit for saying what he said to me, and my crotch is also a right idiot for getting *wet*.

How does he know I want him so badly? Is he that cocky? Does he see me as someone to easily take advantage of? Anger fumes inside, hating that he has *some* semblance of control over me.

Revealing my tattoo bought me his curiosity, and I can't waste it, even if he makes me mad. I simply need to ignore what he does to me and realize there's always opportunity in chaos, as long as one knows where to look. Opening up to him —on *my* terms—might be the best way to manipulate him.

I refuse to lose. Father would disown me if I didn't at least *try*.

There's *one* good option for escape, and I'll have to use it soon before resorting to stabbing him.

Staring at a half-eaten loaf of bread, I chew the giant piece in my mouth. I already pissed outside and sipped on some hot soup. I sigh, listlessly staring at the worn wooden table.

The woman named Anya stares at me as I eat, the two of us sitting at a dining table with a white cloth on top, pewter plates, and mugs set out for the both of us. Even *that* angers me. The scene is too nice for a captive.

Fucking my way to freedom was easier before this turned into some kind of power play.

Maybe I *don't* have that in me.

Relax, Jane. Don't let him get to your head. Focus on breaking his resolve.

Finally, Anya speaks. Her gentle voice seems to rest on the edge of brutality. "You had a rough night."

"Aye," I dully reply.

"Do you have any idea why they want you?"

"That's supposed to be *your* job."

"I never claimed—"

Heavy footsteps echo on the stairs, my body shivering when I hear Soren's voice. "Ready the horses to leave in an hour."

I spin around to glare at him, the mercenary all dressed in his armor, clean-shaven. "My bath?" I will fight like hells to get one, especially after what I revealed to him.

"It's being drawn, *princess*," he chides. "You get until that sundial hits the sixth line, then we leave."

I scarf down the rest of my food as Anya watches the two of

us like she's indexing this entire encounter. I glance at her before leaving the table, the mercenary woman dressed not much differently from Soren, except wearing less armor.

"Where do I go?" I ask, nearing the devil I'm ready to make a deal with.

He raises a brow, standing at the bottom step. "Are baths really your thing? You're *that* easy?"

"I hate bathing in cold rivers."

Mother always had someone draw hot baths for me. It's a treat that strikes deeply at my childhood... and it will comfort me.

Plus, I need this smell of smoke off of me.

His shrewd eyes graze over me in judgment, then he looks at Anya. "Get the men ready. I'll take her upstairs."

He nods back up, stepping to the side—oh, absolutely not. Why does *he* have to be the one to escort me? I was enjoying how quiet—even if a bit *too* observational—Anya was. She'd be easier to escape from too, I bet.

I fidget with a protest in my throat, but I'm also wasting time. Trudging past him, my feet echo softly compared to his, the sound of his armor a haunting reminder of who controls my destiny.

"In the room to your right," he instructs.

I open the door on its squeaky hinges, briefly remembering the depths of Soren's barbarism, expecting something awful to happen, but inside is just a small bathing room with a large, wooden tub in the middle, stagnant water steaming. Soren moves to occupy an empty chair in the corner, pulling out a blade and whetstone.

"Yeah, I'm not bathing with you in the room," I say, motioning for the door.

He doesn't look at me. "If you want a bath, you will." He

points to it with his knife. "You're too *interesting* to let anyone else guard you. I don't trust you. Get in."

Fuck. He has a point. And I'm wasting time. Attacking him seems to get me nowhere, as if he can predict all my actions. Perhaps I *will* have to use alternative tactics... but not yet. I'm proving a point that I'll enjoy my bath, even if this asshole watches.

"Look away, then."

He huffs in annoyance but does an action that makes me feel uninterpretable things—he actually turns around in the small chair, looking away. *He's a Zenith, Jane. One they send to capture people. He's a manipulator, and that's all he's doing right now. It doesn't matter if his angry stare makes you melt... You can sort through that mess later.*

I strip while locking my eyes on him before sliding my body into the water, shivering from the heat before melting into it, soaking down underneath it all.

I slowly resurface for air, running a hand over my head to smooth out my hair. Soren now watches with a curiosity that he's getting worse at covering, his eyes haunting my peripheral.

Fine, if he's going to watch, then he can. I begin washing my hair, keeping my chest submerged. My eyes roll behind closed lids as I scrub my scalp, using extra scented oils to remove the stain of smoke. I clean the rest of me, relaxing with what little heat is left when I feel done.

All the while, I hear the sound of metal sharpening.

Cracking my eyes open, I immediately note that he's watching me. Unwarranted chills of pleasure coil down my spine, and I nearly laugh at how ridiculous that is. *Talk to him. Don't waste having his full attention.*

After a few steadying breaths, I'm re-centered.

"Can I stay with you if the Council wants to boil me alive?"

I question, circling my finger on the bath's edge. "I *am* worth something as a healer, you know."

He snorts and shakes his head, another *swipe*. "I don't know if whatever you hide in your shadows is worth my trouble, no matter how tempting you look."

I avert my gaze when heat creeps into my cheeks, the foreign sensation as annoying as Soren. Men never make me blush this easily. It fuels my desire to want to make *him* speechless. Show him he doesn't hold all the cards, even if he's convinced he does.

The organ in my chest pounds harder, and my eyes struggle to focus. Melona warned me to stay away from the Council, at *all* costs. Gears turn inside my skull, one by one, click by click, moving with intention as I consider *every* option.

Opening up to Soren can only help me escape. Being physically close is required, and I doubt I'll be able to go near the mercenary unless he thinks he's got the upper hand.

My lips part, the words like heavy lead on my tongue; I can't seem to get my mouth to cooperate. Quietly, and with great apprehension, I say, "My father was a Zenith."

The sharpening stops.

My heart pounds so hard I'm shocked there aren't ripples in the water, knowing I'm risking *everything* right now. But Soren's given me a bath and deems me important enough to keep me within arm's length. There's opportunity in his caution with me.

"What happened to him?" He quietly asks. A calming voice. *He wants this information, and he wants it terribly.*

It's so hard to imagine what Dad would do right now, given I only knew him from a child's perspective. *It's all right. You know what to do. Lower Soren's walls, even if by an inch, then strike with the one move you have.* "He's not around anymore."

Silence. Contemplation.

The Zenith's rough, deep voice remains steady as if treating me like an ocean storm that might strike down a ship without warning. "How do you have the tattoo, but no records of you?"

I dare a glance at the killer. "How do you know if there are records of me or not?"

"We are always aware of who is out there, related to a Zenith, former or alive." His eyes are completely devoid of any emotion. "Of all the Zenith missing, none of them has a daughter. The tattoos are also always listed."

I honestly don't know how my father managed to escape that. I barely remember the night I got the tattoo. "I don't know," I mumble, chewing on my lip. Do I give him more? Yes. He'll either tie me up and gag me, or he'll want to pick me apart—I'd wager the latter if I make it worth his time. "But I didn't grow up around the Zenith. I lived with my mother, who was a healer. Dad would visit when he could."

Soren places the whetstone down, his scrutinous gaze scanning the room as he stands. I remain still as he nears me with heavy footsteps and clinking armor, the man kneeling down next to the tub. I stare out the window, gripping the edges of the tub with white knuckles. He points that freshly sharpened knife right at me, my nostrils flaring, but I remain immobile. "I'll admit, I'm intrigued." He leans in, my breathing quickening, but I control my expression to the best of my ability. "But you're unpredictable. I know you want freedom, and I may even be inclined to help. Not unless I know the *whole* story, though."

My heart races to an unhealthy degree. I doubt he means that he'll actually *help*, but I don't need a knight in shining armor right now—all that matters is he thinks my walls are down, so I can manipulate him when he least expects it...

"I'm willing to talk *if* you agree to help," I concede.

"You must know some damning secrets if you're this desperate to strike a bargain with me," he muses.

"You know what, I *am* desperate," I reply, trying to look his way without meeting his gaze. I throw out a line to gauge the depths of his negotiations. "It's unfair, honestly. This whole situation. I'd do a *lot* to live. Even be your little healer pet, if needed."

Without warning, he runs his hand through the wet hair on the backside of my head, pulling so he cranes my face toward the dark ceiling. I gasp as he looks right down at me, hovering in my line of sight. He studies me, and I try not to meet those piercing eyes.

"No. I won't take another Zenith's daughter as a pet. That's not your place." He tightens his grip, and I instinctively arch my back to lessen the pain, my warm, exposed skin pebbling from the cooler air. "You seem to not like that you're aroused by me, anyway," he cheekily adds.

A sardonic chuckle rolls out of me, stuck in this uncomfortable position. "I tried to reject your kind," I say, finally meeting his pale gaze. I lick my lips, my chest rising and falling before I softly confess, "I can't do it. I'm born with blood as bad as yours, and it makes me *angry*."

Let's see what that makes him do.

He doesn't change his calculated expression, as if every word I utter sends his mind down a labyrinth of choices. "Is that why you get into fights? You got aggression like a small dog that needs ran?"

His words defile my veins with a familiar anger and I try to hit him, but he grabs my wet wrist as if I told him I was about to do it. I glare at him. "Will you stop predicting my moves? Just let me hit you. *Once*."

His laugh reveals an unnaturally alluring smile for a killer.

Staring up at him while he holds me like this, my body exposed... oh, I will *burn* these thoughts one day.

"Tell me his name, and I'll keep the Council away from you, little Jane."

Scoffing, I reply, "I'd be thrilled to believe you, but you can understand why I *don't.*"

"Perhaps, but I also see value in preserving you. I doubt the Council want to do more than kill you for the sake of posterity, which means they won't fight me if I make it difficult for them."

The hand gripping my wrist releases, sliding his fingers between my breasts, hovering his touch on the tattoo while still holding onto my hair. I hate the way his touch feels on my skin, my nipples hardening from the cold.

It *better* be from the cold.

He muses, "My guess is the Council has seen you're alive somehow and are not happy you have this mark. You broke a rule, and they love to kill their rule breakers."

"You don't have to touch it a second time, I know which mark you mean."

He grins, moving only his eyes to look at me. "You just offered to be my pet. That will require me touching you."

"Desperation does weird things to people."

He slides that hand up to my neck, my body flinching as muscle memory wants to fight being gripped there again. Instead, my hands clasp the side of the tub, showing him some form of submission that will no doubt speak to the brute; I'm torn between acting as the Jane who gets into fights and being the Jane that can successfully manipulate.

My body remains tense, even if his grip isn't the same as yesterday. No, it's to steady me as he lowers his lips to my ear, completely securing my head. His hot breath does everything for me, which simultaneously destroys me.

Soren laughs as if he can read my mind and releases me, standing. "That's not desperation, love. It's called arousal."

"Oh, fuck *off*," I grind out.

"When you want to tell me who daddy is," he says, sitting back down across from me. "I'll agree to keep the hounds off of you. But you can only take my offer *before* we meet them."

Well, if I thought he was confusing before, I'm not sure what he is now. He's so clearly trying to goad me into talking without any *real* reassurances. "Sure, I'll just believe you like I'm an idiot. At least strike a real deal with me."

He leans back in his seat like it's a throne. "Listen, my life's purpose is *my* priority, long before I owe anything to the world as a Zenith. We're a collection of liars, killers, and thieves. Honor only matters to those that share our blood or oaths. Everyone else is expendable, including the Council." He rests his arms on each edge of the seat, spreading his legs. "Makes sense why they didn't say anything to me in the first place. Your daddy being a Zenith could prove useful to me, in one way or another. But I can't tell *how* useful you are until his name is given."

I stare at the bath water, soaking in how I'm naked and bargaining for my life with a dangerous man. I frown. "Yes, but *what*? Do *what* with me? You're just going to spare me then let me go on my way?"

"Don't know yet. But how about this—I won't kill you," he offers.

His voice seems sincere, I'll give him that. I incline my head in his direction, raising my brows and nearly shaking my head. "You can promise me whatever you want, even a pretty pearl crown, but it's only as good as empty air to me. Meanwhile, I give you *all* of my secrets? That's a little convenient."

He leans forward, the leather crinkling. "What other options do you have? I kept my word on your bath and food."

Sinking my fists into the water, staring at my protruding knees, I think about that. There's not an inch of him that I trust, but surely this offer *has* to be worth something? Even if it only buys me an extra day free of the Council's grasp, or an extra layer of his patience... "And what would we *possibly* make the deal on?"

"Your desperate hope that I keep my word."

My lips betray me as they quiver upward before I press them together in a hard line, refusing to laugh.

I weigh my options: maintain silence on dad's identity, or participate in a negotiation. If I know Soren's kind at all, he'll gag me until I speak. So, logic would reason that remaining mute is a waste of my time.

Lifting my head to stare at the blue sky through the window, I can't lose a single day to being stingy. The further from Skull's Row that I am when I try to escape, the better. "All right. I'll tell you. My last name is Ritter. You got it right when you said Charles Ritter."

Soren's anchored silence has my teeth nearly clattering from adrenaline. "The *Scorpion* was your daddy?"

"Yes," I mutter.

"He never had children," he says as if still trying to understand.

"That you know of," I counter, glancing at him through my peripheral.

"Yeah, they definitely will want to kill you," he replies, watching me with eyes I'm not sure how to read. Soren adds, "We record *everything*. Every bastard. And even if you escaped Skull's Row, Ritter still marked you. They're going to pick you apart like starving beasts eating a fresh kill, wanting to know who betrayed them to allow you permission to receive our mark."

Okay... now what? How do I take advantage of this?

"You're also hiding something," Soren adds, rubbing his chin. "Best to speak up on it."

"Quit pretending you can read minds," I quip, glaring at him.

His gaze burns into mine. "You're not the only one in the room with magic in their veins."

"What?"

"I'm an empath, of sorts. A very astute one that sometimes can read more than emotions. I can feel people. It's why I'm good at killing. I can move through pure darkness and always find my target and feel their moves. I can feel *your* motives. They're foggy because of how lost you are, but I can tell when you're being honest. You've never felt so pure and true until you confessed your daddy is one of us."

Fucking great. Of *course*. I'm almost not even angry, as nothing seems impossible right now.

I roll my eyes and ask, "What if my true purpose is that I am just here to seduce you, hmm?"

"Then hurry the fuck up because you're slow at it."

My laugh spills out before I have the ability to reign it back in. I don't like the genuine banter. I can't be *chummy* with him, especially when something curious crosses his gaze. "Why do they want me?" I ask quietly, trying to pretend that never happened. "Have they really not told you?"

"No. They know not to trust me to that degree... and I'm guessing they learned who you are. Or at least that your mark exists."

"How did they learn, though?" I ask, uncertain as to why he's speaking so openly, but it's also not like I'll waste this.

"All it takes is one bath in the river, and someone seeing you."

"I always bathed with my chest covered."

"You're also a little thing getting into frequent bar fights.

That's a Skull's Row move, love. So of course, we send men out to investigate."

Perhaps.

Either way, they clearly found out, one way or another. "What are you going to do with me now? Seriously. Just be honest, if you can be such a thing."

He seems to consider many things while his thumb rubs over his bottom lip. His eyes are slightly gentle as he says, "I won't kill you. That's all I can promise."

The lukewarm water is starting to feel cold, and I'm losing interest in it, but I keep pushing for any crumbs. "By keeping me, you'd be keeping a rather illicit secret."

"Love, I was a warlord before a Zenith. There are no illicit manners, just handshakes that we all know have a limit to our promises."

Okay... so I'm definitely dying in Skull's Row. Even if he keeps me alive to fuck me for a week, he just admitted that his selfish desires will triumph over *any* agreement. Escaping is more paramount than ever—I shut that off, in case he can feel it. To distract myself even further, I place my hand over my neck, sending healing energy into it to soothe the deep ache. "So, you can hear what others are thinking? Or just feel it?"

He indulges quickly, and I'm still not sure why. "I can wade through the bullshit more than others." He stands, grabbing a towel and standing above the bath, holding it out. "It's how I know you want me, but don't like it," he says with a slow grin and places the towel on the edge. "Get out. We're leaving. I can also tell you're mad it's no longer warm."

"Turn around," I say with a defeated sigh. How in the fuck did I end up with an *empath*? This will get old fast.

He actually turns his back to me again. The first time felt like he wanted me stripped and bare to reveal any vulnerability, but to do it *again*... is it an offering of peace? To show he means his words? I eye that man, breathing heavily. One quick, unsuspecting strike—

He laughs. "That fast? You're already thinking about killing me?"

Why in the fucking hells does that turn me on even more? "It's a habit. Get used to it."

What a complicated situation; he's right. I'm massively attracted to him, and that makes me a bad person, especially being his captive that he wants to use for his own gain. Fucking him as a pet could have been easy—it's a transaction. He gives me safety, and I pleasure and heal him.

But apparently, I can't get over the thought of *enjoying* the process. Is it only men from Skull's Row that make me happy? The murderous villains that they are?

I get out, water dripping down my body and onto the floor as I quickly wrap myself in the dry towel.

"You know, you send the most hypocritical signals, Jane," he says, his grating voice doing *things* to me.

I use the towel around me to dab at my hair, frantically holding it to my body when he turns around.

"I told you to keep your eyes to yourself," I bite, glaring at him, nearly tripping on the tub as I back up.

"Where's the flirtation?" he asks like I'm his entertainment.

"Close your eyes and I'll show you," I mock.

Avidity glints within the ice of his gaze. "Go on, then."

What the hells is happening? He raises a brow as if challenging me. *He's fucking with you, Jane. Another tactic.* My heart pounds in my neck, and I'm so far at the edge of chaos that I'm willing to give *anything* a shot. *Embrace being attracted to him. Use it.* Cautiously, and not believing he'll actually do it, I say, "You have to close your eyes, like I said."

He actually complies.

An impending death has a funny way of making people behave against their nature. Or is *this* my true nature, and I just want to believe I'm better than this?

Like a wolf that refuses to shed her sheep's clothing, I'm still called to the primal howls of the kill in the distance.

I near him, my wet feet on the cool floor. I can look at him now and observe all the details. His hair has the faintest wave, although currently pulled back in a loose bundle. Perhaps it's not even black, but the darkest shade of mahogany. I can see the minute twitches in his face, no doubt feeling me out. I'm within arm's reach, inside the lion's den, but I don't care.

Everything I knew about my life, about who I *wanted* to be, no longer matters. Skull's Row calls me back, and I can't remember the last time I wanted to jump a man's bones this badly.

That's why I always resorted to punching people to get this frustration out of my system.

There, that's familiar—I start to think about assaulting him. Knocking him out and running for it, leaving him with a misshapen nose to remember me by, even if it *would* be a shame to ruin his face. I raise my hand in thought, just to look at it, but it's enough for him. Pale eyes flash open, his armored arm swiftly striking out to grab my wrist, glaring at me.

My towel drops to the floor.

His eyes fall to my damp body. I breathe heavier, lost in that same headspace that I occupy when at the taverns. Reckless thoughts burn away good decisions, just wanting to understand my heart. Everything shifts in his rapacious expression as he looks me over.

"Oh, that was a poor decision, love."

Warm and jittery sensations flood my navel, contrasting the air that chills my skin. He can probably ravish me, and no doubt knows a woman's body like a wet dream. He slides his gaze up at me. I'm pulled in every direction, stuck in the stagnant middle. His other hand touches my outer thigh, an electric need filling my body.

He looks me over and then stares right at my pussy. "You have a fucking *lovely* body. And I mean that."

Not a single word forms in my brain. I want him so badly that I can only swallow the lump in my throat. I want the world I'm owed, to taste the adoration of men that would have *killed* to be with the Scorpion's daughter.

The hand on my thigh slides around to my hip and ass, my knees weakening. Who cares if Soren's my captor? It's not like I plan to stay. Don't I deserve to enjoy something like this? Use him like he's using me?

Then he leans in and hovers his warm breath right over my navel. Soren has the gall to give it a slow, languid, hungry lick. I'm immediately slick for him, and I internally panic. "Why the *fuck* did you do that..." I moan, wanting his tongue *everywhere* now.

Some remaining sense of my dignity tries to back up, but his grip is iron, and that confusingly turns me on more. He smiles against my skin, then slowly rises to stand, all the while grazing his nose against my flesh—over my tattoo—his hand swiftly grabbing the nape of my neck, partially fisting my hair. The other cups my chin as his thumb pulls my bottom lip down.

He looks at me like it's taking every ounce of his control to not mount me.

"I'm going to have to fuck a whore now," he rasps, looking into my eyes. "But that sweet pussy of yours will be on my mind for a while, Jane. Curves like these don't appear every day."

My head spins in desire. "Fuck you," I mumble, his thumb still on my lip. I want to kick him, but I don't. Because I *also* want to see where this goes, inspired by the part of me that stares at danger and simply walks head first; the part of me that belongs in Skull's Row.

"I know you want to," he says with a wicked grin and pulls away.

I groan in displeasure. I want him back here, touching me. Licking me. *What the fuck?*

He snorts. "Get dressed. We're leaving."

"I don't want to go to Skull's Row," I say, turning to face him in my nudity, speaking to the authority I know he carries. Maybe my *curves* can tempt him to come back, so I can try to slap him again. Maybe the trick is to not think about it and just do it.

That's how I will use my one good escape plan when the time comes to it. I will slide it in with ease...

His eyes are all over my body, a desire in his gaze that almost scares me. "You have to go—that's non-negotiable—but after seeing your lithe frame, I'm certainly not letting them kill you any time soon."

MAKE HER SQUIRM

SOREN

I stand outside the bathing room, crossing my hand over my wrist, holding it to my chest as I mindlessly rub the fastenings of my glove. Jane dresses inside with the door shut behind me. My attention is locked onto her emotions, seeking out any thoughts that indicate a *hint* at her hidden truths.

That heart of hers is a complete fucking mess, and for a moment, her entire body had begged for me to touch her. Maybe the thorned rose needs me to show her how much she wants me, because she just can't ask for it. I don't need to have a unique sensitivity to know that, either.

Feeling others, I imagine, is a lot like how animals communicate with the smallest nuances in body language. I can sense what goes through another, can perceive someone's presence even if I've never smelled or seen them before. I'd be dead by now without that ability, as I'm a tenacious fucker and didn't get my reputation by playing it safe; my heightened intuition has saved me from death's embrace more than once.

I snicker at the thought of sensing Jane as she had raised her hand. I could tell she didn't mean to attack, but I had to teach her that she'd never be able to surprise me, not as long as she was close enough to feel her. My ability to dissect a person only increases the longer I'm near them, too.

And oh how close she had been...

My cock twinges at the thought of tasting Jane's flesh. How could I not steal a lick of her warm skin while she smelled so sweet? Especially as a daughter of my kind? I *did* release her when she revealed a deeper hesitation... but before her heart revealed that layer, she *craved* me. And I wanted to see what she'd do if I dismantled any of those fortified barriers of her heart.

Her reaction did not disappoint.

Maybe the demanding bitch with large tits will know a whore around the area with auburn-colored hair; she seems to know *everyone*. I won't be able to focus like this, not with Jane's gasp in the echoes of my mind.

Let alone all the other shit I just learned about her.

That fucking tattoo...

I've never fucked a Zenith's daughter before. Claiming her heart and cunt would be a different kind of sweet, like finding a rose blooming in the desert. And as I imagine plucking that rose, careful to avoid the many thorns that Jane wears—I halt the idea. Wouldn't making the effort to steal such a flower make it more special than the rest? Why bother elevating her importance when there are roses all over if one knows where to look?

Something in my subconscious answers that—Jane feels like a treasure chest found deep within the sea, sucking someone in like a siren stealing the hearts of men, drowning them in the pitiless ocean.

It's probably a good thing she lived so far away from Skull's Row. The men there would do desperate things to claim they'd fucked a woman with a last name one can only inherit, not steal.

Jane *Ritter* is rare.

"All right, I guess I'm ready," she says, her feminine voice muffled through the door.

Nerves. All I feel are nerves as she opens it. It's something I can quiet if I want, but I'm fucking keyed in on her; the smallest variations in her thoughts are as clear as crystal to me.

I pivot to look at her—she wears a rather plain outfit of an emerald tunic and some leather pants, and I'm annoyed at whoever handed these clothes for Jane to wear. Would have been nice to see her in a dress, one that hugs her perfectly and leaves her neck and cleavage open for my viewing. Even then, she's still tempting with her cleaned-up face, her damp hair leaving little darkened spots on her shirt, her plump lips and high cheeks slightly rosy from the heat of the bath—

That predictable reaction suddenly happens whenever I look at her. Jane's face hardens as her heart mixes dangerously with her thoughts.

I take a step to the side. "Ladies first."

"What?" she asks, raising a brow, like I might be an imposter.

With a snicker, I lean in and cock my head. "I'm not giving you my back while we walk down the stairs."

Her pretty face scrunches as she huffs, rolling her eyes.

Careful love, that eye roll does things to me.

She focuses ahead of herself, her chest swiftly rising and falling as she passes me. I start to wonder how wet her pussy is, if she'll moan with her lips around my cock... those thoughts make me grin, and when she's close enough—when I can feel someone the deepest—I want to say she's almost mad that I didn't pull her out of that tub to fill her cunt with every fucking inch that I can give her.

Well, little Jane, if that's what you want...

I follow her down the stairs, my common sense telling me that she doesn't matter; she's dangerous. She's a flavor of honey I've been eager to find, and that's how all men fall.

But haven't I survived long enough to say, 'fuck it'? Shouldn't I pluck the damn desert rose, just to see what fucking happens? I've got the gold, the men, the title, the lands, and the scars to tell the stories of my triumphant warfare, and yet, something about Jane intrigues me. Pestering her is a kind of fun I don't often get to indulge in.

I can be patient, and let her warm up to me... but I won't be subtle.

No. I want to watch Miss Jane squirm.

⸺⸻◈⸻⸺

Bones stands guard in the foyer, his armor covered in more metal pieces than mine. He claims everything on him can be used as a weapon, and who am I to stifle a murderer's capability? Bones eyes Jane as she descends the stairs. She strides right past him like he doesn't even bother her, and my gaze is locked onto the back of her damp head. In Skull's Row, I could have her fully pampered; all the oils and soaps to make her smell like the softest temptation, just so I can ruin her.

And how fucking glorious it would be to watch that heart of hers betray her pride—then I can proclaim that not even a Zenith princess can deny me.

I nod to Anya, who stands near the door. Her brown leather armor looks freshly polished, the scar on her cheek more visible than usual with her cleaned face, the interlocking design of a snake's body carved out in the front of her chest— my sigil.

I'm the snake one never sees coming, one bite being all it takes to destroy a man. Only those high enough in my ranks wear the same sigil, except for Bones. His loyalty has never been given to anyone but his own fucking self, and everyone still believes that.

The delusion benefits us, nearly everyone convinced that he's not my man through and through.

"Get Jane on her own horse, then tie that horse to mine," I instruct.

Anya nods, opening the door of the home to call out to the stable master, the light outside silhouetting Jane who spins to glare at me. "Don't tie me to your horse. I'm not stupid enough to try and outride your entire *group* of men."

I rest my hand on the hilt of my sword. "And I promise never to fuck a whore again."

Bones snorts.

Jane's plump lips crook upward into a smile, the humor making her whirl around so quickly she nearly stumbles, only wanting to ever give me her cold shoulder.

Jane crosses her arms and remains silent, moving only when Anya approaches and grabs her by the arm. The little woman initially fights Anya, and something odd in me stirs at seeing her struggle in another's grip, but I ignore it as

Anya gives Jane a rather dangerous glare, subduing the little fire.

With a slow step near the open door, I survey the area that has at least two dozen of my men waiting for my command. The citizens of Coalfell slept in barns with haystacks. It's not up to me what they do with their lives, but as is custom for this part of the world, survivors can follow for protection as long as they don't get in the way. I speak to Bones, "Has any more information been uncovered since we last spoke?"

"No. We've got the head of the one you killed, sending it with Bryon so he can deliver it to the other Zenith while it's still fresh. The villagers didn't know who the attacker was. They claim the men with fire just wore black capes and black masks, tossing torches into homes as they were devoured in flames unusually fast. Unusually simple, some said. Same with their weapons." Bones takes a pause, and I watch as Jane is led to a horse. "My kitten reckons they're not from here. They didn't seem to know their way around."

I pause and frown, looking down at the grass. "Your what now?"

Bones speaks in an unnaturally gentle manner. "Kathleen. She said her name was Kat at first, so now I call her kitten."

Oh, fucking hells. "I'm sure she loves that," I say, stepping out into the bright sun, keeping my watch on Jane, wondering if Kathleen will be stuffed away somewhere for Bones to play with. One of the most ruthless and stone-cold killers I've ever met sounds utterly smitten by that damn villager.

Bones' ragged voice follows me. "She blushes when I call her that, seems to piss her off, too, but I've caught her staring at me, those pretty cheeks turning pink... unlike that stupid bitch who just tears apart perfectly nice rooms." He nods toward where Jane stands.

My body stiffens. I'm not sure what to do about the foreign

reaction to Jane, other than knowing that treating her like cattle is the wrong decision. "Don't call her a stupid bitch."

Bones' demeanor completely changes, stepping closer as if to hear me better. "Why not? She sucks cock that good?"

"It doesn't feel right to do so." I'm unsure what all I can share with Bones. "I learned some things, and my gut doesn't like treating her poorly. I believe we just found ourselves caught in a riptide with her, but I don't know the extent of it yet."

"Wait, what?" He scans the area to ensure we're alone before staring at my face, like it might not be me. "Does it matter? The Council will kill her just to make a point, at the bare minimum."

I don't meet his mismatched gaze.

Something eats away at my instincts: Charles Ritter was never confirmed dead. Allowing Jane to be slaughtered brings a sense of foreboding I've learned to listen to a long time ago.

Bones looks off like he's contemplating a very deep philosophical question. "She can't be *that* important."

"I'll tell you soon, but she's no ordinary person," I conclude, stepping forward to Phantom.

Jane sits on a brown horse underneath the shade of a large tree, the reins of hers tied to mine by a long rope. She looks down at the creature, petting its neck. I'm not quite sure how I would act if I couldn't decipher her truths from lies. She speaks about Charles Ritter like she believes it's veracity... and yet, I still can't fathom that being a reality.

Either way, if she's going to feed me what her heart believes to be the truth, I will let her have free hands as she rides on her horse as a reward.

I mount Phantom, the horse so black he seems to absorb light rather than reflect it. Settling into my saddle—the black skull mask affixed to a bag on the back—I say, "If you pull any shit on our ride, I'll tie you up and drag you behind for good measure." I glance at her, and she's only partially looking my way as if she's trying to ignore me. "But maybe you like it rough. Which, of course, I can always oblige."

"Oh, shut the fuck up," she grunts.

I grin.

Any other woman and I would reprimand her for that... but instead, I just kick the horse to get us to move, everyone swiftly mounting their steeds to follow me.

It's time to pick her apart.

I'M NOT YOUR TAROT CARD READER

JANE

There's not much to say as we ride.

It feels important to consider my life and the options before me. The weight of knowing that I'll be entering Skull's Row in less than a week's time—a place that already burns my throat with the bitter memories of how my family fell apart. It leaves me feeling very small.

And I *hate* feeling small.

Behave Jane, so you can ask to speak with Kathleen.

I had seen Kathleen in the distance with Bones, utterly relieved to see she's alive. I know I have to find a way to talk to her, even if Soren keeps me utterly separated from the rest.

All I want is to tell Kathleen *everything,* like a deathbed confession. But instead I'm stuck riding next to this behemoth that's mounted on an even bigger beast.

I can't trust him for shit, and I hate to think he might be able to feel my affection for Kathleen, making her an unintentional target.

The best decision feels so murky, like I'm staring through salt water while trying to read.

What would my father's advice be? For most of my life, he always managed to be at the right place at the right time, scaring men away even if they didn't know I was a Zenith's daughter; it's why he branded me so young. If something happened when he couldn't be around, maybe the tattoo would make them reconsider.

As I yearn for him, I also battle with my anger for what happened to me. Why would he brand me if he didn't think we were in danger? Why didn't he tell me to be extra careful?

I once loved the life I lived, the way my parents emboldened me to be as rough as leather, Mother reminding me to *also* be gentle with my healing gifts. Then it all disintegrated. Mother was murdered. My father disappeared. Then, I was alone, and not a soul to care for me.

Maybe my father ran off, abandoning me.

Soren is as selfish as the rest. One way or another, he's going to reveal his mercenary motives and I have to remind myself his offers to save me will *always* have a limit.

"You're a thinker," Soren says at some point while we're riding to wherever the hells he's taking us.

I've been aimlessly eyeing the world around me, his voice drawing me to look directly at him before back at our surroundings. We're on a dirt road that carriage wheels have dug small grooves into. Tall trees tower over us, but I know in a few days they'll reveal open terrain and green pastures. It's just the two of us, with half of his small caravan quite a ways ahead, and the rest far behind.

"You've been quiet yourself," I counter.

"I do well not to die by staying focused on the task at hand." His voice grates against the soothing terrain of a late summer's day.

"Same," is all I say, my mind in too many places to concentrate. Even as I stare off at a woodpecker drilling into some bark, I swear I can feel Soren's gaze penetrate. "What am I feeling right now, since I know you're reading me?" I challenge, my tone clipped. I wish he wouldn't use that gift of his, even if just for half of a day.

He scoffs, straightening his back as he faces ahead. "I'm not your fucking tarot card reader."

Now I just want to know for the sake of it. "Answer the question."

He's quiet before settling on, "Something with dread, and something bittersweet. I've learned that usually means people are thinking about their past, or about something significant that breaks their heart."

The conversation after hours of silence scratches at my boredom, which also eases some of the anxiety. "When did you know you could feel people?" I ask, needing the abstraction.

"That's a very personal question."

"You licked my stomach."

He wickedly grins, rubbing his chin as he breathes out, "We'll see how the Council goes before I tell you details about my life."

I huff in disappointment, his response ruining my hope of a proper distraction. Why do I have to be tied to *this* man when every breath brings me closer to the Council, who will no doubt rip my heart out while it still beats?

"You're just like all the others, then," I utter in frustration, shifting in my seat when my ass starts to hurt. "Always hiding behind a mystery, but in reality, you're nowhere near as complex as you portray."

"That's a lazy perception," he chides.

"I've only ever been burned by those from Skull's Row. It's a pretty well-established observation."

"It's still an over-simplified observation from you, even if I never claimed to surround myself with men of high morals."

I make a funny sound as I force a cough, my lips twitching in a threatened grin. "If I wasn't tied to your damn horse, I might actually be able to relax and consider your propositions."

His laugh is loud enough to make someone ahead look back. "Even if you *could* escape, I'd catch you. So, I'm eliminating the failed attempt preemptively. I don't have time to mind you like a child. No, actually, I *do* have the time. I just don't want to."

What a prick.

Fine, if he's not going to talk to me, then it's back to my imagination. Scenarios of escaping flood my mind. Crossing the Black Sea is one's *true* escape, sailing it to reach outside the Balar Coasts and onto lands that are more wild than here. I hear that if one goes even deeper, where it's colder... peace settles like snowflakes on a cold morning.

It's a hard life in the bitter winds, but people out there are left alone.

Is *that* where I can go?

My heart tells me no. I need the warmth and the ocean. Perhaps escaping to Belstead will prove useful, the largest city of the Free People, just beyond the Restless Peaks. The tang of blood stains my tongue from biting the inside of my lip too hard, worried that I can't go there with the mark of Skull's Row on my chest. If anyone ever saw that, they'd hogtie me and deliver my sorry ass straight to the Zenith.

I only ended up in a pacifist's village because Father said he'd meet me there...

"You're deeply afraid, over there," Soren hums, ever entrenched without invitation into my heart.

I swallow away all the passive-aggressive remarks clawing in my throat. He's not wrong, I *am* afraid, and I need to talk to *someone,* even if it's Soren. "I fear the unknown of it all."

"Do you think you'll die?" he asks, his grating voice bearing no comfort.

"Maybe. Probably." I decide to turn it back on him. "How often do you chat with those you are carrying to death, anyway?"

"I can count on a single hand the times I've felt some version of sympathy, or curiosity, for those I've killed or captured." He takes a swig from his canteen after popping the cork out. "You're probably the third."

For some reason, that surprises me. "Do you not regret the other two?"

"Everyone has a code. Every Zenith has their role and a task we perform when it's necessary. We have a few Zenith that kill indiscriminately, even if it's a newborn babe. I don't go after those that haven't properly pissed me off or earned it through a heavy bounty, so no, I don't regret it."

"And have *I* earned it?" I ask, lightly tugging on the rope that connects our horses.

He doesn't answer.

Fucking great. That just makes it worse. I have to look truly pathetic for someone like Soren to feel sorry for me.

He offers me the canteen with a lazy gesture, and rather than give him my suspicion, I greedily take it, put it to my lips, and drink until it's drained.

"Well, that was fucking rude," he says.

I wipe at the dribbles of water with my shoulder before tossing him the empty thing, Soren catching it with one hand. "Was really parched," I say, my belly full of water now.

"If you wanted to get wet again, there was no need to down my entire fucking canteen," he smoothly says. "Unless you just like to be fucked hard and without mercy."

"You should find a whore to fuck," I boldly state, controlling the squeak in my voice. "I'll take care of myself."

Oddly enough, he only gives a small snort as he ties his canteen at his waist again. I don't understand him or why he flirts with me. Maybe he's trying to undo me through methods *other* than torture so my feelings on my father bleed through with ease.

Perhaps I'm also in over my head and have no way to gauge what's best for me.

Silence sits between us for the rest of the ride, Soren never more than a few feet from me. By nightfall, we arrive at the next city—a bustling trade post that grows richer every year, known as Dryhill. It used to be infamous for banning all liquor, in the era before the Zenith were even invented. Now it's as wet as I am for Soren...

I've been here before with Kathleen as it's always nice to have a little change of scenery, but I try to avoid frequenting too often since Skull's Row bleeds heavily into it.

Soren's men wait for him at the walls—it's a giant fortress that's all packed together inside, winding alleyways connecting to the main roads. A black flag with a golden skull hangs above, gently waving in the wind. I immediately lower my head, wanting to scoot my horse closer to Soren in some last-ditch effort at survival.

Anyone bearing the flag of a Zenith owes their loyalty to Skull's Row and carries out their traditions and laws.

Soren's words will be as strong as iron here.

It didn't used to bother me when I was just staying for a night with Kathleen, always feeling like that threat was far away. Now, though? It's those very laws that will have me swinging from the gallows, or get my head spiked.

We wait for his other men to arrive, the first group lost in jovial snickering and telling stories of their greatest kills. Soren remains silent as he stares into the blackness of night that surrounds the settlement, his maroon leather standing out against his steed.

My expression hardens when Soren speaks quietly, so only *I* hear him. "You'll be sticking with me in Dryhill. Don't say anything about why you're wanted, or I'll gag you—" There's no sexual innuendo in his tone "—If, on the other hand, you behave, I'll let you sleep without rope binding you."

I sigh. "Will it be at the foot of your bed this time?"

He leans closer, speaking lowly. "If that's what Miss Jane likes, then I can indulge."

I grip the reins, trying to embrace those wild thoughts so they may suppress the excitement I have for being alone with him. There may be little I can do about the Zenith, but I didn't grow up as a baker's daughter. My "daddy", as Soren likes to put it, was a damn Zenith.

My silence from earlier stemmed not only from my fear, but I've also been trying to consider a plan for escape while convoluting it with other thoughts so Soren doesn't register it.

If I'm to make a bold attempt to escape, *this* is where it will be. I've got one single shot, and I'm going to make it count. And I'm going to need Soren alone, his guard completely down.

Gods help me.

TAVERN THINGS

JANE

The gate to Dryhill is a very tall, wooden door with thick steel chains that hang down, creating a dull *clink, clink, clink* when it lowers. My horse lurches forward when Soren's begins to move, riding only about a foot away from me as we enter together. Flickering braziers guide our way, the moon hidden behind clouds.

Determination eats away at the anxiety, something about being here allowing me to accept this *is* my reality.

You're fine. You know your captor now, you have an idea of why the Council wants you, and Kathleen is alive. Plan the next steps.

Inside, a few people are still traversing the streets despite the late hour. Homes are tightly built next to—and some on top of—each other, candles lit inside in a warm glow against the bleak buildings. This is a world where people make money by selling goods and services, existing as a safer place than Skull's Row for trade.

If my mother had desired to be associated as a Zenith's wife, I would have walked these streets like royalty next to my father, known as a *Ritter*.

Now, I'm just Jane.

I ditched my mother's maiden name of Foley for protection, which I used as a child. If anyone ever did bother to seek my last name, I always told them Wood. There's no grand reasoning for it; it's just the first thing that came to mind when someone asked me all those years ago when I was young and alone.

Torch fires lick against stone in the rather quiet streets, save for the taverns. We turn down one cobblestone street that has a rather notable butcher living here, recalling the days when Dad used to buy us food if he ever snuck me here. I only eye the wooden sign of *Ramsay's Meats* for a fraction of a moment before latching my gaze to a tall building directly ahead–it's constructed out of richly colored wood, the second story boasting a lavish balcony with many spindles. Over the main doors is a siren carved out of the same dark wood, wielding a metal spear—Moor's Inn.

We approach the stable master, the man nearly falling over when he spots Soren's mask. A cascading of horse hooves begins to halt as his men crowd around us, which is partially drowned out by the energy inside of the building ahead. The Zenith dismounts, and I slide off of mine. Just as my feet hit the stoney street, Soren is right on me, red rope in his hands. It's completely black outside but the various flames create haunting, moving shadows, his pale eyes warning me not to challenge him in public.

He nods to my hands, which are resting on the saddle of my horse. I chew on my lip before arguing, "I behaved the whole ride."

"Do you see how busy this place is?" he asks, grabbing my hands with his indomitable strength. I give a *small* struggle, but let him have his way. I need to be on his good side tonight. He speaks as he binds me, "No one here knows why you're with me. Someone with bound wrists, in a trading post like this, usually means a bounty has been caught." He finishes the last knot, making eye contact with me. "And this red rope is one that I use. They'll know you belong to *me*."

Whatever fleeting sensations of being enamored by him completely fades, the pinching sensation of rope ruining everything. "You're branding me."

"You're welcome."

He puts a hand on the back of my neck, the touch commanding. It doesn't feel like it did back in the bathing room—Soren's just a mercenary to me in this moment, laying a claim to his capture. He guides me through the drunken and slurring crowd, men throwing knives at a wooden wall and crying out when they hit their mark.

The smell of fish assaults my nose, and yet it reminds me of home—Skull's Row is salty, rocky, and coastal.

We're getting closer.

Many move away from Soren and eye me like I'm a bound beast. I imagine getting a personal escort by the Zenith makes me look quite dangerous—which only fuels my ego, throwing a few death glares at lingering eyes, challenging them to attack the person requiring Soren to subdue her.

They don't need to know I just have a flare for drama. It

simply feels good to be feared, the only control I've ever really had in life.

It's better than looking submissive, anyway. Being bound in an area like this is dangerous as all hells, having seen many people be stolen right from their seat like they're a small, valuable puppy for the taking. *'Steal the treasure and ask questions later'*... a motto of these men.

But the red rope, admittedly, should keep most at bay.

Laughter erupts in one corner, and I watch as a few women wearing corsets saunter around, carrying ale and food. A rugged, middle-aged man donning an eyepatch sits by the fire with a woman on his lap, telling some kind of tale to those who will listen. His black hair is tightly braided, just like his beard. He wears the single, golden earring drop in his right ear —a man of the sea.

Soren guides us to the bar where three men run the operation and leans me against it like I'm a wooden board he's temporarily putting down. The noise of this tavern uneasily mixes with the dread blurring my heart. Many have taken note of Soren's arrival, although they don't loiter or stare. The Zenith are known to enjoy their meanderings in establishments, like a captain of a ship who drinks with his men. Some still flee out the back, as they always do.

No one is *truly* safe near a Zenith.

Their grandeur is only elevated by that mask of theirs, granting them power when they wear it. Nothing overwhelming, but they *are* stronger, faster, their senses heightened; sometimes even their wounds are magically healed. The Zenith are dangerous for that alone, not even counting the skills they have as a basal man.

At least the others should stay off of me.

Soren leans into my ear so I can hear him better. I *wish* I could trust him; I yearn for him to be familiar. But he's foreign, and I'm reminded how alone I am in this world. "When Bones comes in, I'm going upstairs and having a fucking drink."

The first thing that comes to mind slips out of me. "Oh, yes, it's *so* stressful being someone's captor."

He snickers before pulling away, looking at me with a calculated expression like he's compelled by something I can't interpret.

Then I hear, *"Oh, you're really all right! He wasn't lying."*

"I'd never lie to you kitten... not directly!"

I spin around, my jaw dropping when I spot Kathleen—she wears a new gray dress with a thick belt cinched at her waist, her curly hair free. I move toward her without even looking at Soren. Reaching out my arms in a hug, I pause and hold up my bound hands in defeat. Kathleen wraps me in her arms anyway.

"Oh, Kathleen," I breathe out.

She quickly pulls back and looks over my head like she's about to apologize; Soren, no doubt, gave her a scolding glare.

Bones is behind her, watching like he's caught a glimpse of a siren. "So, you *do* give hugs, kitten."

I raise my brows, jutting my head out as my gaze darts between the two of them. "What is *that*?"

Kathleen sighs and waves a hand, still not looking at the man behind her. "I can't get rid of him. He's like a lost dog that won't fucking go away."

Bones looks at her curly hair, his one blue eye blazing with interest while the charcoal one emits avarice. "I'll take being compared to a dog. They *are* loyal beasts. Which, you should know, is something I don't give out often."

Kathleen rolls her eyes, but I know that look, the one with the *slightest* smile on her lips. She's intrigued.

Soren speaks behind me. "Watch over Jane, Bones."

"Aye," he replies, dipping his head in a low bow.

There are so many unspoken words that race through my mind. I lick my dry lips, and the first thing I manage out is, "What happened to everyone? How's your family? Are they all right?"

Vengeance sears my heart at the thought of her suffering. There's no doubt those who attacked were there for me. Why else would they be there? *Unless it's related to Soren, and this is all a grand scheme to gain my trust... maybe they know dad is alive somewhere and hope I can point them to him?*

Kathleen leans on the bar, tucking her hair behind her ear. "It's a miracle the family is fine. I think they're still in shock, really."

I'm unable to get my hands in a comfortable spot and give up, leaning in the same manner as her. Kathleen flexes her left hand as the other mindlessly moves a steel ring on her middle finger—something she acquired before we met and refuses to tell the story of. I've only seen the inside of it once before, a few rubies hidden within the steel.

"That's about it. Lots are wanting to go to Belstead," she solemnly says, her green eyes eclipsed with exhaustion. "It was horrible," she sighs and stares at her ring. "I got my gran out, but she's staying at Talon's Perch. Knows the local baker. The rest of my family are leaving for Belstead, getting the fuck away from Skull's Row."

I wish we could plan something together, like some means of escape, but my death looms far too close behind me to dream of anything happy. I know I'm going to attempt an escape tonight and there are so many things that could go wrong. *Very* wrong.

That siren, long ago, was so dead-set on the Council not having me. And those creatures of the ocean are notorious for beauty, mystical powers, *and* their sight.

Receiving a vision from one should *never* be taken lightly.

Melona's warning is eerily accurate with what plagues me now, and in that, her words are the only stability I have in this; I'm compelled to do everything I can to heed them in order to save others. I don't even know who these people are in Melona's warning, or how they'd die, but I can't risk it.

I simply can't.

Do what you can to help Kathleen. Then get out of here and ensure others don't die for you.

My heart is eager to offer her perfect words of comfort, but I've never been good at finding them. Mother was always better at that than me. I manage out, "What about you? How are *you?*"

Kathleen surveys the crowd. A few more of Soren's men are sitting at various tables. I notice how tired her eyes are up close, like the surprise of seeing me temporarily erased her worries. Bones listens intently as she leans in to meet my gaze. "Me? Well, I left Talon's Perch because I didn't want to leave you alone," Kathleen explains, lifting her head backward to reference the towering man behind her. "And this one is basically kidnapping me."

Bones raises an offended, dark brow, a strand of his wavy black hair in his eyes. "I said we can come back to your Perch, once we get *her*—" he nods to me "—situated."

"Oh, thank you, kind kidnapper," Kathleen exhales through a defeated sigh.

I watch Kathleen *very* carefully, in case I catch a hint of her truly being upset or threatened. "Why is he so obsessed, by the way?"

Bones slices his gaze at me like I just said something extremely belligerent. "Have you not seen her?"

Kathleen tilts her head down to look at me through her brownish blonde lashes. "He's a tits man."

"And more than that," he adds, looking up and down from

behind. "You've got a nice, sharp tongue. And you're brave… and quite hardy in spirit for looking so soft."

I'm utterly bewildered by him. "Are you sure you're good, Kathleen?"

Kathleen barely nods so Bones might not pick it up. He glares at the back of her head, trying to decipher any answer from her—

Her attention shifts from me to something else, and I pivot to see a man approaching us. The first thing I note is his greasy, blonde hair. He raises his head up like he's looking down on us from over his large nose. His emerald-colored clothes are a little *too* tailored to be an average citizen. "You a bound wench? You're in the wrong establishment for that. We keep that business for the building across the way—only established escorts are permitted here."

Bones cringes. "Ah, yeah, that's not smart, mate."

The man ignores Bones and Kathleen straightens her back. I'm the shortest among them all, doubling my vulnerability with my bound wrists. He looks down at a golden pocket watch that he swiftly pulls out, then tucks it back away, staring at me with wet, black eyes. "The name is Hector. Hector Bolin."

Bones frowns. "No one gives a shit. Leave us alone if you know what's good for you."

Hector sneers. "I'm the mayor's cousin. His righthand, in fact."

"I still don't give a shit," Bones chides.

"Well, you *should*. We are a Free City now, you know. As a part of our eastern alliance for the Silken Pearls trade?"

Bones grunts. I forgot all about that—Dryhill recently engaged in trade from much further east where they spin fine silk in exchange for pearls. The Western kingdoms only agreed to work with Dryhill if Skull's Row granted them the title of Free People as an extra measure of safety for their merchants.

I was surprised that the Council agreed, but then remembered how much they love their silks.

Hector looks back at me, side-glancing at Bones like he's considering arresting him, just for the attitude. "As I was saying. You're all bound," he nods to my wrists before his eyes flash up at me with a disgusting edge of selfishness. "A slave wench? Belonging to Soren's company? There's a room for women like you, but again, it's *not* at the bar."

I'm simmering to hit someone and contemplate kicking *Hector* right in the balls. Would that make Soren mad? I hate that I even have to consider this, but I do need his guard down for my escape plan to work. Will he tie me to a couch if I retaliate?

Kathleen snorts, "You're a real dumbass."

Bones leans over and says, "I love the way you talk."

"She talks just as bad!" Kathleen motions to me. I can see where she'd like Bones—she always liked the rougher ones, even if he makes me nervous.

"Nah, she's a bitch that broke my nose," he casually replies, leaning in ever so slightly, speaking as if he considers his words romantic. "But I'd let *you* break my nose. Maybe smack me with those beautiful assets of yours."

A laugh nearly pours out of me, and I'm shocked to see Kathleen *blush*, but not before she mentions *not* to call me a bitch—

The man named Hector places his hand along the bar, closing the space between us as I press every inch I can into the counter. "Yeah, whores all right. The blonde can stay while we figure out what to do with *you*."

Bones' demeanor changes like nothing but frost coats his heart; he scowls at Hector and adjusts his posture like he's readying himself to reach for a blade, his mouth opening with a threat—

"I'm not a fucking whore, and you're a fucking idiot," I say before Bones can speak, moving to face this man fully. "But come closer. Let me show you why I'm really tied up."

Give me a good reason to bite your nose, you bastard.

"Who roped you?" he asks, completely oblivious to the danger he's in. "Isn't that Soren's color? I heard he was in here. Are one of his men planning to fuck you all night? Might need him to provide me with a special tax if you stay in here... I also wouldn't mind collecting it *now*, in order to keep you here."

I nearly gag, the little food I ate churning in my stomach when his gaze drops down to lewdly stare at my body. I roll my eyes to look at Bones, wondering why he's not stopping this man. If I'm left to defend myself, I could do something that pisses Soren off, which is the opposite of what I'm supposed to be doing. It's honestly one of the first times in my life that I hope for someone *else* to do my job.

His wild eyes slice to Hector. "Say anything else about the blonde, and I'll turn *you* into a proper fucking whore."

Hector blanches, then gives an uncomfortable nod before placing his attention back on me. He even touches my thigh with his free hand, my skin crawling as I try to lean away. "Now, come along."

I'm stuck between my dignity and debating what's best for my escape, but when his hand slides up just a little too far, I decide I'm not going to let him touch me this easily. He's lucky my hands are bound or I'd punch him right in the cock, maybe grab what I can and twist so hard he'll become a eunuch. I ready myself for the unbearable crunch of cartilage as I figure biting his nose is the best way to send the message. I'll greatly enjoy spitting whatever chunk I get onto his unscuffed boots...

Kathleen steps forward to try to help but Bones snakes an arm around her waist, pulling her closer to him. I don't understand why he isn't helping unless Soren's words really mean nothing and I bought a lie.

Just as Bones says— "Nah, leave it, my kitten. He's already got a death glare on the man, and Soren's been itching to gut someone—" someone suddenly stabs that hand of Hector's resting on the bar, a crescendoing scream leaving his thin lips.

I jump, turning around to see Soren on the other side of the bar, appearing seemingly out of nowhere, a door just around the shelves of liquor swinging closed.

"The fuck do you think you're doing?" Soren asks with wide, ruthless eyes, leaning over the counter, the man's blood pooling from his hand. "That's my rope's color. Yet, you decided to touch her anyway?"

Hector's jaw drops to pronounce an aged double chin. "You stabbed me, you cunt!" he squeaks, bellowing loudly as he shudders when he tries to move his hand. "My cousin is the damn mayor! This is a Free City! And you stabbed me! You can't do this!"

Soren growls, those crystal eyes voiding all emotion as the killer takes over. It makes me scoot closer to Kathleen, who is still locked in one of Bones' arms. Soren removes the blade and walks around the counter—many are now watching—a premeditated, hollow gaze staring Hector down. The injured man holds his hand up and shudders as blood drips all over the floor, gushing down his arm to discolor his rich clothes.

Then, Soren moves so swiftly that Hector can barely defend himself—Soren stabs the man right in the neck to elicit a wet, choking sound, crimson liquid pooling in Hector's mouth. Soren leans in.

I watch, unblinking.

"No, *now* I've stabbed you," Soren warns. "And you owe allegiance to Skull's Row, Free City or not. All we agreed to do was give you more freedom in your management of trade, not to give *us* orders or reprimand. Let's hope this lesson sticks."

The blade is removed with a sickening suction of blood. Hector holds his hands to his gushing neck, knocking a barstool over, his beady eyes wide and consumed with fear. Soren looks at the room and watches with apprehension. "This one here? Auburn hair—" Soren points to me with the bloodied blade, a few drops landing on the floor "—any of you touch her, and you'll be castrated right on this bar counter, your balls spiked just outside this establishment's door. You can stare at them as you starve while tied to a post right next to it."

The Zenith throws his gaze right back at me, then at Bones, his expression still wrung tight with murder while the dying man clings to the counter. The woman sitting on the pirate's lap rushes over after she seems to think the threat is over, her long brown hair jostling as she runs, gripping Hector's neck. Blue light emits from her healer's insignia, blood pulsating through her fingers every time Hector looks like he swallows.

All these prominent establishments have healers in these parts for reasons such as this.

Bones calmly says, "Knew you were coming. Thought he was worth the stabbing with the way he talked like he owned this place. Didn't seem to hurt to let himself dig his grave further."

Soren cleans his blade on Hector's shoulder blades, the man squealing with gurgling fear when he's touched by the Zenith's blade. One of the bartenders lazily drops a few rags to clean up the blood as if this is a nightly occasion.

Hector stumbles away once the woman heals the deepest wounds, trying to make space between him and Soren.

When the Zenith sheaths his blade at his hip, he looks at

me as if the severely injured man doesn't even exist. "We're upstairs," he grinds out, the words still laced with violence.

Soren glances to a nearby table, holding eye contact with a dark-skinned man who nods back, then stands, and mans the door's entrance.

And do I panic about the idea of sleeping next such a homicidal person? Absolutely not. If anything, my heart leaps with the hope that this all might truly work as intended, the Zenith still keeping me close. I just need him alone.

For a fraction of time, I swear Soren reads every crevice of what I consider. *Push those thoughts away, Jane!*

Breathing heavily, I focus on the healer tending to Hector who now is leaning against a chair, choosing to narrate the scene in my head as a distraction: it's been a while since I saw another woman like me—we're uncommon, something only those with prestige or money can obtain; a sign that Dryhill is doing well for itself. *Yes. Healers. Other healers I knew... Mother. Yes, use that. Make him feel pity.*

My diversion sinks quickly into nostalgia, and rather than ignore what I feel, I let the bittersweet memories remove any aberrations.

My lips press together in a frown as I wonder what my mom would think of me now?

Soren's mirthless gaze relinquishes. He turns around, and I trail him up the stairs to the second floor of the tavern. When Bones nods for me to follow, I see Anya waiting in a corner booth next to a bay window.

The Zenith speaks to her and she gives an obedient nod before he faces me. "Anya will take you and your friend to my room, where you will stay for the night. You can have *one* drink in there." He glares at me when I look like I don't believe him. "I need to speak with Bones, and reestablish who the fuck runs things here."

"Don't have to tell me twice," I say with a polite bow of my head. I'd even kneel to him if it gets me something taller than a pint.

Bones watches as Kathleen and I are guided to an exterior door, walking across a covered bridge that connects the tavern to an inn. But we don't go to an ordinary room—we visit *another* section reserved only for the Zenith. It's tucked away with its own balcony in the front, a double door ornately carved with giant skulls and ocean waves.

These details make me nervous, a steep reminder of where we're close to.

Of what I must escape.

JANE

Anya uses a key on a brass ring to open the barrier that confines me to Soren's chambers for the night, golden candle and firelight washing over us. It's already teaming with warmth as if they immediately began preparing it upon Soren's arrival. I know places like these have more than one room for our mercenary kings, especially being so close to the Zenith's world.

Anya follows Kathleen and me inside and actually unties the rope binding my wrists. "Uh, thanks," I say, not trusting this at all, rubbing the skin where it dug in the most.

Anya places the crimson rope on a table near the door,

taking two large pints from a grizzled soldier just outside the doorway. She speaks as she hands one to each of us, her voice smooth and feminine, contrasting her appearance. "You should know that Soren is offering quite the luxury right now. Don't fuck it up."

"Cheers," I say, holding the pint in Anya's direction.

She raises a scarred brow like she's about to say something more, but just presses her uneven lips together and shuts the door. There's something about her that makes her almost pretty, and yet she looks as rough as Soren.

Now, Kathleen and I stand in this room with ale in our hands... well, shit. Are we alone right now? This easily?

I smell the hoppy liquid from the wooden mug, rolling my eyes with pleasure. If I didn't need mental clarity tonight, I'd have requested an entire barrel.

"Holy shit we're actually alone," Kathleen says, listening at the door. "Sounds like she walked off. I mean, could be messing with us, but I still can't believe we're in *here*, sharing ale!"

I take a drink of the warm, pale fluff, its strength hitting me instantly. "No, we're never alone with someone like *Soren*." I go to one of the windows that overlooks the street behind us, moving a heavy maroon curtain aside to peer around. "I bet ten men are watching, even if we can't see them." I let go of the curtain, nearing Kathleen, speaking just above a whisper. "Did you know he's an empath? Soren?"

She nearly chokes on her drink, holding the mug with two hands. "*What?*"

I nod feverishly. "He can feel things... and he's quite fucking accurate at readings emotions, almost like he can partially read minds. He'll even know if I leave this room, I bet."

Kathleen whistles, looking around the elaborate room

that's nearly the same as the Black House in Talon's Perch. "What the fuck is going on, Jane?" she quietly asks, taking another long drink, focusing on a giant painting of the ocean, framed in gold as it hangs on a black wall. "Do you even know what's happening?"

I move closer once I realize what the painting is, thinking very carefully about that reply. The painting isn't just of the water—it's a wide view of Skull's Row from the ocean. It depicts a huge cliff that powerful waves lap against, and many inlets where giant stone islands are connecting via wooden bridges. The cliffs are carved out at just above sea level with many ports tied to the rock. Enormous wooden buildings with elaborate support structures are affixed to the sides so ships can be pulled and hung out of the water to clean the barnacles. Only ships made in Skull's Row can land there, using materials from the nearby forests that possess magic, preventing the bottoms from breaking against the rocks.

Throughout the cliffs are carved-out windows and balconies until it reaches the very top where a monumental stone structure—a jagged, black stone castle—unevenly spirals upward with many connecting towers, surrounded by pine forests on the lower level. I stare at the little strip of paint that's meant to illustrate the spirals. That's one of the places where they hold their prisoners, the storms freezing men to death that far up as they rage and batter the stone with cold rains.

The thought of dying in there makes everything seem so pointless.

I almost tell Kathleen all of my secrets, to answer her question about what's happening. What if she doesn't like what she hears, though? The last thing I need, on my deathbed, is a look of disapproval from the only person I genuinely care about.

The truth of it all never reaches my lips. "The Council really does want me. It's not a mistake. It's related to my childhood, but I can't speak more on it."

She gives a pause, like she knows that I need silence. Quietly, and with a small smile, Kathleen says, "Okay, so then let's talk about what Soren is doing with you in *his* room."

I snicker, rolling my head to look up at her. "He claims he has to keep me close. And what about you? What is Bones doing with *you*?"

"I landed a nutter with him," she says, taking a long drink as if to hide the smile that twinkles in her eyes. The wild ones captivate her in the same way that Soren's brutality does to me.

Oh, how I want to sit and talk about where our lives ended up and dream of where they'll go. But I already know where it's leading for me. I then consider that if I flee in the night, it means leaving her with Bones.

I take a step near her, speaking just above a whisper. "Kathleen... if I leave... are you okay?"

"What?"

I speak as low as possible, nearly mouthing the words. "I don't want to draw attention, but if I... *disappeared*... are you going to be okay?"

I know I need to flee, but I'd feel terrible leaving her with these pirates and mercenaries. She puts a hand on my shoulder, my body stiffening as I dread her disappointment. "Love, don't worry about me. I grew up in a whore house, one that was similar to this city. I'll find my way."

"But you came for me."

"It didn't feel right to stay in Talon's Perch, not when some of the others were following Soren. Lots of the miners are hoping to take their family north where there's more coal, so it's easy following you. Also, you're my *friend*, and I wanted to make sure you're okay."

"Oh, great friend I am, then. Just leaving you behind with Bones."

"Are you kidding? Flee the fucking continent if you can. What's the alternative? Walk to your own death? What good will you be to me then? That's not worth sticking around for an extra day or two. And don't say I should come with you. I can't, with gran—" she sighs, pressing her plump lips together, then tilts her head to the side in a sad way "—Look out for yourself right now, Jane. If I'm desperate, I'll just fuck Bones. Pretty sure he'll consider us married, then."

I laugh into my drink, then swallow a long gulp. My heart aches at the thought that I will never see her again. "I wish we would have left years ago, like we always planned. Go somewhere that not even Skull's Row can touch."

"We always make better decisions in hindsight..." Her hand slides off as she scrunches her face. "Do you *really* think you'll die?"

I groan, downing another gulp, the beer burning my throat from drinking too much. Through a cough, I say, "Yeah, it's a real possibility. They have reasons to kill me."

"What did you do?" Kathleen's eyes vibrate in her skull like she has a guess but doesn't want to force me to say it.

"It's what was *done* to me. It's who I *am*."

"You can trust me. In the whorehouse, our code is to look out for pussies before cocks, because those wankers have a tendency to wander in loyalty."

Gods, I love this woman. I grin like it's been years since I've truly smiled. "I—" I begin, my smile faltering as I stare at the crackling flames. The truth nearly slips out, snagged by a thread that's unable to risk losing her in this final hour. "How about this, if I somehow survive, I'll tell you."

Her bright green eyes turn sad; if I survive, we both know

I'll never be near Skull's Row again. Which means we might never cross paths.

"Let's tell stories," I suggest, motioning to the fire and pull a chair closer to its warmth. It's what Father and I used to do back home whenever I'd start to worry about his next "adventure". "That'll make us feel better."

I stoke the fire with a skinny piece of wood, returning to sit in the cushioned chair. "But really, before we begin... *are* you good? With Bones? I really don't want to just leave you with him. Not after everything we just went through. I'll stay and figure it out if I have to."

She crosses her legs, laughing as she looks at her fingernails. "I've never met a man like Bones, and I can't deny I kind of like how he basically worships me already." She clears her throat like remembering something imprudent.

I smile. "Coalfell was too boring for the pair of us."

"Oh, *most* definitely." She scoffs. "But I could never just run away with someone like Bones. My family would kill me. My gran, more specifically."

"Yeah, I understand. Have any of your family been threatened at all?" I'll tell Soren a hundred secrets if he promises to keep Kathleen and her family safe.

"No, thankfully. I told Bones that I wouldn't push him away as long as he *promised* that we were going back to Talon's Perch to check on my gran. That's all I care about right now. I'll find the rest of my family once this is all said and done."

In true Kathleen fashion, she's only worried about her gran. It took a while in our younger years for me to really pay attention to how much she deflects when asked about her history and other relatives.

Maybe it's why we get along so well—we never pry about the secrets that the other keeps. At the same time, this might really be the last time I see her. I dare the question, "I know we don't talk a lot about our childhood… but… how'd you end up in Coalfell? I know you said your mother was a petal, but what made you come *here*?"

Calling someone a petal is a more polite term for describing an esteemed—and expensive—lady or gentleman of the night, as floral perfumes are prominent near pleasure houses.

Kathleen's eyes never focus on anything, in particular, her hands fidgeting. I almost retract the question before she says, "My mother was a fine petal, as you know." She mindlessly rubs the wooden mug. "My father used to travel with his uncle when he was a child and came back to his favorite haunts as an adult. Met my dear mother, they had a few encounters, and then she had me… she died when I was around thirteen. I found my father and he didn't want me, but my gran did. He warmed up to the idea, eventually."

I always knew her mother had died, and Kathleen always openly spoke with pride about who her mother was, and that her dad was a piece of shit that often gave her bloody, busted lips. I didn't know how they met and made Kathleen, though.

"I'm glad your gran was there for you," I say, not bothering to ask where she grew up. "I'm also sorry your dad is an ass."

"Maybe I'll fuck Bones just so he can deal with my father for me, give him a few new scars for breaking Mom's heart and treating me like a disease. Bet Bones would do that if I make it worth his time," she cynically muses, the hairs on my arms raising at seeing this side of her. She blinks rapidly and drinks more ale. "Sorry. That was a bit morbid."

I sigh, offering her the only thing I can, "It's nothing I haven't heard before. Hells, we just heard what Soren will do to someone's balls just for touching his bounty. It doesn't bother me at all, really…" Drawing out a long sigh, I know it's time to tell her *this*. "I, well… I grew up in Skull's Row."

Our gazes meet, a layer peeled back that makes me feel like maybe she *wouldn't* judge me. I have a feeling Kathleen's secrets run much deeper than they appear, just like mine.

Because Kathleen is an amazing fucking person, she doesn't pry. "You better live, Jane. So you can tell me all about your life."

"I'm going to give it my best shot," I say with a lame attempt at a smile, raising my wooden mug.

We fall into reminiscing about our adventures together, unaware of how much time passes—only that the fire needs more logs—when we hear talking outside the door, followed by Soren's deep rasp.

Everything in my heart changes, and the ale going to my head doesn't help. I greatly enjoyed this small reprieve, and seeing that giant man's hardened face enter the room sent a thrilling mixture of dread and desire through my veins. *Fucker can probably feel that.*

Kathleen stands right away, bows her head, and says, "Thank you, sir. I'll be going."

I almost forget who he is when it's just the two of us, but her behavior is more of how I should be treating him—I nearly snort at the fat chance of that. I push away all thoughts about what I'm planning to do to him—about the siren's song and subduing Soren with a lesser-known part of my magic.

To avoid my thoughts slipping through, I concentrate on the chemistry from earlier; the desires I have for my captor. I'm going to need them if I'm to be successful.

When I *do* stand, it's to hug Kathleen. "This isn't the end for us," I whisper. "Be safe."

"No, not at all. And you be smart, Jane," she says, kissing the side of my head before parting ways. "Don't be too hot-headed, you hear?"

Soren watches Kathleen leave. A deeper part of my heart

mourns the idea of never seeing her again. It's enough to nearly make me bawl my eyes out, to reach back out and spend my remaining days with the primary person I care for rather than cling to this measly chance of survival.

If it wasn't for that damn promise I made...

The door shuts behind Kathleen and it's only then that I notice some of Soren's armor is missing, the remainder of it in his arms before he places them on a wooden table. His hair is out of the low bun he wore, tousled and tucked behind his ears. He's bleeding pretty good from a wound that his black tunic covers at the shoulder, but acts like nothing is wrong.

Waste not a second.

Like a tired parent, I ask him, "What did you do to your shoulder?"

"Generic tavern things," he rasps, locking the door and begins to take off the rest of his armor, but not before boldly looking me up and down, as if his eyes can scan every word spoken to Kathleen.

I shiver, wondering what my life would have been like if things didn't go the way they did. Would I be married to someone like Soren? Would this scene instead be one of me traveling with my imaginary, mercenary husband?

Probably.

I lean into that fantasy, hoping it makes everything easier for me.

Soren begins to peel off his clothes and I watch as I sit by the fire, accepting that he's the only kind of man that I can truly desire in this world.

Why wouldn't he be, though? I'm a daughter of Skull's Row. Soon, he'll be reminded of that.

He glances over his bleeding shoulder as he removes the last chest piece before he wears nothing but a bloody tunic. "Enjoying yourself as you stare?"

"There's nothing else to look at," I quip, downing the last bit of ale.

He snickers and shakes his head, and then wipes his injured shoulder with a towel. It still bleeds. "If only I had a fucking healer with me, that would help *so* much."

I hate the way I like his humor. "What do I gain for healing you?"

He walks over to the large mirror where his shaving equipment rests, his footsteps heavy, and looks at me through his reflection. "I gave you a night alone with your friend. You see how friendly I am. That was a nice gesture."

"Fine," I say, committed to doing anything that gets him to think he's won. I stand, the burning alcohol rushing into my legs. At least the drink should help loosen me up. "But no touching. I don't need any more stomach licks."

A part of me—a side that can't be blamed on survival— regrets telling him that. I'd very much like for him to lick much more of me, but I can't dive straight into fucking him too quickly or it might look suspicious.

He laughs, his cold eyes contrasting his smile. "If the Zenith princess says so."

Our gazes connect in the mirror. With a racing heart, I near the mercenary legend, fully planning to heal him. I'll know when the time to strike is.

Until then... those damn, penetrating eyes of his will be the death of me.

THE GREAT ESCAPE

JANE

Soren removes his tunic, that body nearly criminal in how all the muscles move like a silent promise of his power. I watch from behind, staring at the tattoo on his spine. I finally remember why those three long streaks look familiar. It's an insignia from a gang of mercenaries—a dangerous band of men called Death's Wing.

So, he probably belonged to them before becoming a Zenith, and here I am, casually tending to him.

A gaping wound oozes blood on his shoulder, the skin red and angry. The cut isn't *too* large—glass, maybe? For a sliver of a second, my heart races with genuine panic as all I can picture is being covered in marks like these when I get to Skull's Row. Will the Council stab me? Slice my flesh? Ensure I can't heal myself as they inflict whatever cruel punishment they have planned for me? Will Soren be involved as the one to 'read' me while I beg for mercy, locked high in the Spiraling Stone as I plead for the cold to end my misery?

Or will they throw me deep within their dungeons to rot away while the world forgets I ever existed?

It's one thing to slice my own hand with a broken mirror, but another to be at someone's mercy. At least in the bar, I can fight back.

"You are convinced you're dying when we visit Skull's Row, Jane."

"Aren't you the captain of observations," I reply, breaking out of his spell.

He snorts. "I've told you I can keep them at bay. All you need to do is reveal to me your secrets. It's that simple."

I glare at him; his back is only an inch from my stomach as he sits there. "And I've told you I don't trust you as far as I can throw you, so basically not at all."

Placing my hand on his shoulder, I focus my energy right on the tattoo on my wrist. The blue light of my palms reflects against the blood that continues to leak from him.

I can feel right away that some muscle has been cut, which will take a good moment to heal. I find my gaze moving to his hair, which is surprisingly healthy, even soft looking. He seems to value grooming, which I find interesting. Quietly, I ask, "Why don't you have a healer with you?"

"We did. She died on a mission."

"What?" I meet his gaze in the mirror and find he's still watching me.

"It's a long story," he says, wincing when I can feel some of the muscle tying back together. "She's hard to replace. She worked well with the core team." He cocks his head to the side, narrowing those ice-colored eyes on me. "Could *you* work for mercenaries?"

The corner of my lip twitches as I angrily try to subdue a smile. "Is this an interview?"

He grins like he's won something. "You did apply to be my pet, and responded so well when I licked your stomach. Healing, on top of that, would nearly guarantee you the job."

My racing heart makes me blush *again*, pushing more of my energy into his shoulder so it heals faster. "Stop that."

Then, he does that thing where he gentles his voice, just enough to sound like he might actually be attempting sincerity. "Life is too short, little one, to turn away from what you want."

Focus, Jane. He probably gets off on you being a Zenith's daughter. Use it.

"What I *want* is for Skull's Row to go well." I can feel his skin starting to vibrate; it will suture shut soon.

"If it goes well, it means you come right back to me," he silkily replies. "The Council will only let you free if they think you become my pet."

Forbidden attraction rouses inside of me like a wave of heat, the idea absolutely tempting. I'd get to live while treating my body to what it needs and *also* see Kathleen. For the first time, I consider what he says as truth. I wouldn't be surprised if he found value in my father's name... It's been a *very* long time since I've felt the leverage of my lineage; I nearly forgot it was there. "Then what?" I quietly ask, eyeing a strand of his hair that's loose.

"Don't know," he concludes.

I lift my hand to take a look and it's healed, the faintest line appearing where a scar will form. That answer isn't what I wanted to hear, and yet it also feels more true than anything else he could have said.

Soren dips a towel into the water bowl reserved for his shaving and hands it to me, water droplets unevenly falling. I wipe my hands with it, smearing the fabric with red, before cleaning away at the blood on his skin.

I don't move away from him once I place the towel down. It's as if my heart is lying to me, telling me that if I stay near him long enough, he'll finally offer a good reason for why I should trust him; somehow conjure an offer that I can't refute.

"If you could heal my left clavicle, that would also help your chances for the Council," he adds.

His words pull me away from that hope, indecision grounded by reality. In truth, there's nothing he can offer me that I would trust.

Returning is simply out of the question, even if I wanted to.

I sigh with a nod, taking a step back. "Turn around."

He does so, moving quietly on the stool to face me. A neglected part of me registers how smoothly he does this, and how massive he is in comparison. He won't take his eyes off of me, staring right at my face—I don't risk losing my sanity by making eye contact this close, so I examine his shoulder, noticing a swelling where it might be fractured rather than broken. The injury explains why they already took some of the armor off. "Why are you injured in the first place?" I ask, focusing my powers once more as I take a step nearer.

Even when standing between his thighs, Soren doesn't touch me, resting his veinous hands on either knee.

"I stabbed the mayor's cousin," he says in a derisive tone, still watching me. "Some of his men came to inquire, and a rather big fucker said the wrong things that pissed me off."

"I bet you were *completely* innocent, you poor bastard," I offer with sarcasm.

That intense glower of his changes in ways that make my heart flutter, his eyes softening as humor replaces his intensity.

"How did you know?" he plays along.

Oh no—that makes me smile. A *real* smile. We can't be having chummy conversations. "Is your armor useless?" I ask, trying to move on.

"He had a rather large war hammer."

My eyes widen with concern as I imagine someone having to fight against a *war hammer* before returning to an empty stare. "Then this should have been shattered."

"Well, I dodged most of the impact, obviously, as one should," he says. "Had four of his men on me, though. Can only move around so much."

"How did I not hear that?" I ask, trying to recall if we heard anyone yelling.

"It was over very fast," he says as if asserting his prowess, then his tone turns to tease. "But thank you for being concerned, love."

I look him right in the eye, close enough to see a deep scar on his bottom lip. The minimized space between us is nearly nonexistent. "I can make this hurt, you know."

"Going to ruin the mood?"

"Yes, the mood of where I'm going to Skull's Row to probably die?"

He rolls his eyes and sighs, looking away. "Can't help if you won't listen to me. I've already told you they're not going to kill you on my watch. You're Ritter's daughter, so on that principle alone I'm not letting them kill you. Your daddy was a brutal man. I'm not handing his branded daughter to her killers."

"You're a Zenith, Soren," I counter. It's the first time I've said his name and his eyes seem to narrow as he catches that, slightly inclining his head as if he likes what he heard. "Why should I *possibly* trust you? Truly? I highly doubt you actually want to help my father. I don't even know if he's still alive."

Jane, stop. Fuck. What am I doing? At this rate, I'm going to slip and reveal crucial details.

He looks around the room, his clavicle nearly healed. "You're free, in my room. Is that not enough of a good gesture?"

His shoulder jolts when it completely heals, his lip twitching from the pain. My hands drop to my side, but I don't move.

I'm genuinely confused. That's actually not a bad point he just made. Why am I in his room, unbound? I can't possibly be *that* interesting to him, just because of who my family is.

He answers what only my heart can whisper, looking right at me. "Oh, but you are."

I suddenly realize why he's been staring at me like that. He's reading me like a damn book.

My heart pounds so hard that I'm nearly lightheaded. "I don't even know your last name," I irrationally spit out, as if that matters.

I still don't move away from him, though.

"It's not very interesting."

"Tell me," I urge with a partial smile. "It can't be that bad. Unless it's Cockburn or something, which I *have* heard before."

His stifled chuckle nearly turns into a full laugh, his lips twitching, his nostrils flaring. It almost makes him look like a real person, and he clearly doesn't like that, fighting the humor in the same way that I do.

As if to move himself on from such an emotion, he admits, "It's Latham."

I stand up straighter, looking him over, my eyes landing on the skull tattoo over his heart before eyeing the elaborate ink down his left arm that's made of waves, daggers, and even a siren. "Soren Latham, then."

His eyes soften like he finds that confusingly curious, making my reckless heart behave in extremely unreliable ways. What if I kiss him? Why shouldn't I greet death after a good romp? If my escape doesn't kill me, then at least I got to fuck a violent man from Skull's Row before leaving it for forever.

That invasive thought snowballs until all I can think about is him touching me. I'm just staring at his brutally handsome face, his hair down and tousled. I want him, badly. But I don't want myself to want him, because I know this could all backfire in catastrophic ways.

"You look awfully confused and lustful for someone who claims she doesn't want me at all." His voice is like honeyed sandpaper, and I feel like an idiot for thinking that. I don't move, just staring into his eyes as I thickly swallow. He raises a scarred brow. "Well, too bad. I'm not touching you. I made you a deal."

This fucker... is that why he's just sitting there? I open my mouth, but nothing comes out. In turn, his handsome, scarred lips curl into a wayward grin.

Screw it. I allow my desires to drown out the doubt. I deserve to have what I want as long as it's not hurting anybody. Right?

His guard will be *completely* down after this...

Releasing reservation, my barriers are removed as I stare at him with yearning. He picks up on the change, his calculated gaze focusing on me with eyes so intense it might scare the average woman. I lean in, but he doesn't move. I feel some sense of safety in wanting him as long as I take it very, very slow like I'm confirming that I *do*, indeed, want this man. I even hover my lips in front of his, not looking him in the eyes. I can smell the scent of ale on him, along with tobacco from the tavern. He doesn't move a muscle, but I can feel that he breathes faster.

I continue to look down at his cheeks, my throbbing pussy already five steps ahead of me, wondering how and when my pants will be removed.

Distract him.

Breathing steadily, I brush my lips on his, Soren's soft lips moving with experience, the warm air from our lungs mixing.

My groan parts us from the kiss as I open my eyes, his untamed icy gaze devouring me, watching me, judging me... reading my soul. My breathless words leave me without hesitation. "Fine... you can touch me."

He does, immediately.

The sensation of Soren's arms surrounding me weakens my knees, his roaming hands large and powerful. His whole body moves when he deepens the kiss, like a man eager to prove his control. Exploring this desire makes me feel so alive when I fear death so greatly.

His touch sliding up my back elicits a moan from me. Soren growls into my mouth, his warm, wet tongue parting my lips to command the space. He's so smooth in his actions, so confident. It's such an odd thing to realize I'm touching the shoulders and chest of my captor in this manner while I'm reveling in it.

He's removing my shirt before I realize it, taking a short moment to admire my exposed breasts—Soren's rapacious gaze devours what he sees. His dominating grip pulls me closer, his teeth grazing my nipple.

I gasp.

He moves quickly.

Soren grabs the back of my thighs, hoisting me up as he stands. His shoulders are my only stability before I'm placed on the bed.

The beast of a man towers over me as I lie on my back, Soren already untying my pants. My blood is a wretched thing; it turns me on to no end that this Zenith is captivated by me.

The cool air pebbles my skin as he drops my pants onto the floor. Soren stands there, muscled, scarred, and tattooed, just taking me in like he doesn't know where he wants to start. He touches my hips, slowly gliding over my stomach, his head moving with the motion. "You are gorgeous, love."

I whimper, breathing deeply. I want him to be rough. To force it all out of me. He leans down, licking my stomach while lifting his chin to look at me like he fucking wins; my body nearly shakes at having his attention.

Something in me greatly weakens as my desires belong to Soren at this moment, his victorious glower preceding a sharp pull on my hips to dangle my legs off of the stiff bed, spreading me wide. Extreme vulnerability makes me want to close them, my pussy completely exposed to this brutal human.

He runs his coarse, virile hands down the inside of my thighs to keep them split, moans betraying me as they escape. He doesn't play with me for long before he slides his touch right over everything sensitive—my sounds nearly echo off the walls. I need this man to fuck me.

Icy eyes hook into mine as he slides a finger inside, the muscles in his forearm flexing. My sounds morph into breathy groans, amazed at how small any voice of opposition is.

Turns out I *did* need a good fucking, but only from someone like *Soren*.

He slowly growls, the grumble so unrefined compared to what vibrates in my throat; I have the mercenary's complete and undivided attention. "You're so damn wet..." he pulls the finger out, languidly licking my slick off of himself while boring his gaze into mine. "How do you taste so fucking good?" he rasps. My rapt attention is on him when he fucks me with his finger again, hoping he leads every inch of this so I don't have to. His gaze falls to between my breasts where my tattoo is, running his other hand up the outline of his hardened cock that's still in his pants.

Warm flutters fill my navel, my breathing shallow as he not only moves his finger in and out but crooks it upward as my body is overcome with carnal pleasure.

I don't need to read his mind to know something about me messes with him. No doubt it's the mixture of my tattoo, and that I'd brutalize someone just as fast as he would. I perch onto my elbows, deciding to prod the beast. "Want to fuck a Zenith's daughter, is that it?"

He smiles, shoving two fingers in without warning, our eyes connected the entire time, that stroke of his cock now more forceful than languid; I stiffen, trying to withhold showing the pleasure that laps at my mind. "And what of you? Just want to fuck a Zenith yourself? Squeeze my cock while you drip for me?"

I almost rise as if I'm about to tell him off while he's finger fucking me, but he's fast and that free hand ceases stroking himself to place a knee on the bed and lean over, gripping my neck as he shoves me back down, pushing his fingers in past the knuckle.

Like an idiot, I moan like it's the first time I've ever been touched.

"You're not going *anywhere*, love." Something in me turns to liquid mush as he's holding me down, those thick fingers penetrating me like he has to open me up for what's to come. He tilts his head to the side, speaking while leaning over me. "What's going to happen is you're going to come for me, then I'm going to properly fuck you. And then you will come *again*... maybe even a third time, if you're not loud enough for the first two."

My eyes roll, my pussy squeezing him as the only means of

my permission. He seems pleased and releases my neck as he pulls back, spreading my legs again with more force; he's barely making an effort, and yet he's overpowering me with ease.

Soren kneels and doesn't hesitate before he's licking my clit with greed, asserting himself. I whimper, gripping the covers, back arching. His fingers move faster. I'm annoyed at how good he is, how much my body just completely unwinds for his touch. He snickers, holding me down with a hand on my hip, locking me to him. Into my flesh, he says, "You think *you're* annoyed? Imagine how I feel when I'm actually considering telling the Council they can fuck right off just so I can enjoy whatever the fuck you are."

"Whatever I am?" I moan. I meant to sound combative, but my voice is soft... curious... *needy*.

The deepest look he's given so far—a possessive edge wrapped with confusion—leaks out of those hungry eyes. "A distraction."

I grin, my head lulling when his fingers move at just the right pace. "Oh, are you frustrated?"

"*Very*." He gives a sharp lick, his feral groans making me grab his hand that pins me down. I don't know what kind of sex we're having but I fucking like it.

"*Fuck*, Soren..."

A third finger stretches me without warning, and I gasp at the invasion. The hand on my hip is removed as he uses it to lift my left leg, pushing it back and holding it from behind my knee. Rapacious pleasure spreads those perfect lips of his into a ravenous smile. "You'll need to stretch more than that for me, love. If not, you'll be in a lot of pain for your horse tomorrow."

I swear he's enjoying his expert command over my body as much as I am—we're like two pieces of chaos colliding, our instant attraction pushing us to the point of doing what we're doing now... my orgasm swiftly threatens to consume me.

"*Soren*..." I whimper.

That does it for him. His shoulders tense, returning to suck on my clit, those fingers working *oh* so perfectly. He growls right into my cunt. "*Louder.*"

I'm helpless to my desires. "Fuck, Soren!"

He continues fucking me with one hand, looking at me like there's an underlying beast that needs to be fed. "What was that?"

"Oh, don't fucking stop!" I retort, perching on my elbows, failing to move the leg he grasps.

He grins, his forearm still flexing as he keeps working me. But it's not enough. I try to close my legs in anger, but he holds them open with an almost bruising force. "Say it. You want me to make you come. Admit it, love."

Fuck this bastard—I refuse to leave this bed until he delivers the ecstasy that I need. "I want to fucking come!"

"Say *who* you're coming for."

"*You*, you bastard."

He tilts his head like I'm here for a lesson, and he's more than obliged to be patient as he teaches me. "Close."

I roll my hips and loudly shout, "Fuck you! Finish the job!"

He looks like he might pull away, but the way he moves makes me think he's about to pull his cock out to fuck me like this is the next part of the lesson. My pussy clenches with glee at the thought, and I nearly want to smack her for the betrayal.

No, I want to come on his stupidly handsome face, because, well, my damn ego demands this. "Fine. Please, make me come, Soren!"

His lip twitches. "That's a good girl."

"Oh, fuck *you*." His lips nearly suction my soul out of me

when he returns to finish the job, my head thrown back. I break a barrier and touch his hair in my need. Something fleeting crosses his eyes, like he might yell at me for doing that, but he seems determined to imprint in my brain that he's the one to bring me rapture, working his tongue in a deliberate rhythm. I watch that man's face between my thighs as my legs are completely spread.

And then it builds.

I'm going to come for this man.

My gasps turn to whimpers. Waves of pleasure lap at my body, that wonderful feeling escalating to a point of no return. He growls with so much pleasure that ecstasy nearly drowns me.

"Oh... oh, *fuck*," I mutter.

Muscles tighten as I hold my breath, *needing* this, my body shuddering when my clit is over-sensitized as all the build-up crashes from its precipice, Soren releasing a smooth, deep groan as if to tell me *'good girl'* while I come with his fingers still inside. His tongue milks every last drop of what he took from me.

I pant, a fraction of a thought dedicated toward knowing this is *the* moment. I need to act, and *before* he fucks me. I'm not returning to sanity if this man unwinds and fills every inch of me, pressed against his body...

I tug on his hair that's still in my hand. "Come here," I whisper.

Releasing my grip, that hand pulls away as I lay my arms at my side. He grabs my hips and moves me further up on the bed, and goddamn I don't need to know what it's like to have him hold me *and* fuck me at the same time. He spreads my thighs with his knees, the ridge in his pants stealing my atten- tion. His lips crash into mine with so much control; so much lust. He's going to fuck me raw, and I bet more than once. And because I'm hopeless, I let my mind wander with thoughts of him making me choke on his cock, too.

He growls into my mouth, smiling. My smell is all over his face, tasting myself on his tongue. "Oh, you dirty fucking girl. You want me to fuck your throat."

"Shut up," I say, grabbing his face, kissing him back.

I melt. Fuck him, but I melt. The way that tongue had just massaged my body to a rippling climax, and now it battles with my own, his hips dipping down to grind right between my legs; I can tell I won't ever forget this night, like it's an acceptance of who I am.

I push on his chest, showing him I want on top. "Let me," I insist.

He gives way so I can straddle him, his rough hands sliding up my thighs and cupping my ass as his restrained cock is right underneath me. For a moment, I actually regret everything. I really, genuinely do. My smitten, confused ass frets on wondering if I'm making the right call.

He pauses, sensing that.

And the bastard is fast to switch gears, that massive body tensing, those eyes removing every bit of undoing that I did to him.

I commit.

I switch every ounce of my powers to sedating him, my tattoos glowing when I place them on his chest. His icy eyes widen, the unnaturally pale color completely devoid of humanity. He attempts to move every limb in protest, his stomach flexing, but I lean down and begin to sing in the foreign tongue of the sirens, the one that they use to lull sailors and pirates into their waters, the men falling asleep before they are pulled under.

It was taught to me by the siren that found me abandoned all those years ago, the one named Melona, whose vision warned me against the Council or returning to Skull's Row.

She was the last creature to take care of me before I had to take care of myself, the last person—aside from Kathleen—to interact with me simply because they wanted to.

Soren's nostrils flare, his jaw clenching, his chest heaving. Those damning muscles go limp, his eyes the only unsubdued part of him, that massive body barely writhing between my thighs. I sing quietly, just for him, while also sedating him with my healing powers, slowing his heart so he might sleep. His lips part as he pants, mumbling incoherently. He struggles to stay awake, let alone speak. But his eyes say it all—he'll personally chop my head off for this.

He's a strong bastard because when the song is over, he's still conscious. Just barely. I stop pouring my energy into him in case I might need more for myself. His eyes still track my movement, his breathing growing deeper. I lean in to speak to him, and I can still smell myself on his face. I only just learned his last name, but this mercenary does something dangerous to my brain.

Maybe it's because I can't deny the ruthless existence of my ancestors anymore, as if Soren found the lost key to unlock a chest that contains my *real* identity.

My reawakening.

There's a moment, where my chest is pressed against his, that makes me want to stay. I was having great fun with him, even if I didn't want to admit it. I speak gently now that I have the upper hand, almost as if to rub it in that I'm not worried. I press my cheek against his clean-shaven one, his breathing increasing, but that's all he can do; I've momentarily immobilized him. "It's nothing personal, Soren. But I don't want to die, and I know better than to trust a Zenith I just met." And just to fuck with him, because a part of my ego wants this man's attention, I smile as I stare at the pillow that he rests on. "But it *is* a shame I didn't get to know you more. I did want that if I'm to be honest."

I back away, his eyes watching me, his blinking languid. There's a wave of complete remorse in my heart; what if he *would* protect me? Let me in? Maybe this could turn into something bigger than just fucking him, and I wouldn't have to go on the run for the rest of my life... and that *is* tempting. My brain bargains with the thought that maybe I can somehow stay and tell him '*My sincerest apologies for the random attack. Please don't be mad. Won't happen again.*'

But the feeling passes as his eyes mostly close, hovering in a sleep. No, I have to leave. Staying was never an option, even if I believed it would work. It's now or never, and survival tells me to look out for myself.

Just as Melona warned me.

Very few humans can use the *siren's sunder*, as a siren has to teach it to someone for the magic to be effective, or else it's mostly singing empty air.

My father did *something* right, it seems. I was only granted the privilege of singing it because of a deal he made with Melona at the very end.

I dress while Soren lies there, twitching from time to time like his subconscious begs for a fight. I'm impressed. I've never seen someone do more than deeply breathe when in this trance. Pulling on my pants feels wrong, my core still slick from desire and his mouth. But I keep moving. I spot a bag of his coin by his armor, picking up the leather pouch to examine it; it's heavy.

Tying the money bag through a loop on my pants, I quickly work to add some boots and a shirt. I throw on a cloak, just for good measure, then near the door with a pounding heart.

I slowly open it, the air cool compared to the warmth of

Soren's room. Anya is out there, nearly snapping her neck to glare at me. I expected another guard rather than her—she seems shrewd. Too shrewd. I mumble, "I need to use the outhouse. The ale got to me, and I don't feel like shitting in the chamber pot."

She peeks inside the room, completely ignoring me; fuck. She frowns. "He never sleeps that hard."

"You can check him, if you want," I say, letting my mind run free with every theory on what I might have to do. Her boss isn't awake to weed through the things I think or feel.

She nods forward. "Inside."

I do just that, thinking the plan over and over and over. I could sing the song to her, but Melona warned me that the effect only works the longer I wait to sing it again. It's best used once every few months, at least for a human. So that's not an option.

The door quietly shuts behind us. "What's wrong with him? He didn't drink but one pint of ale. He *always* wakes if someone enters a room."

I lunge at her, considering punching her in the throat. There's no time to pretend.

But this woman is clearly from Skull's Row, and unlike me, she never left. Her blade is immediately drawn. All right, I can do this. I'm ready for it—she stabs me right in the gut as I try to hit her in the throat.

The searing pain and discomfort convolutes my concentration, my hands only gripping her throat as I channel all of my healer's power on subduing her, a blue glow radiating off her armor. Her dark eyes widen, looking at me like I've committed a deep betrayal. I can't use all of my reserve or else I won't be able to heal my stomach.

Do I kill her? Or just knock her out?

Her death seems like it would deliver a certain death from

Soren himself, and maybe he'll remember that I left them all alive when I could have slit their throats. There's a chance he still finds me, and I know better than to prematurely burn that bridge.

Blood leaks from my wound, blooming into the fabric of my shirt. I *hate* that feeling of something sharp digging deep into my organs. When she stumbles from my sedation, I punch her hard in the side of the head to knock her out, shaking my hand as the familiar pain floods me. Anya falls to the floor in a slow collapse, Soren sleeping in the background. I hold my breath, grip the hilt of the dagger with my good hand, and slide it out. I shudder, placing the blade on the ground so it doesn't make a sound, warm blood completely staining my clothes. I heal what I can, mumbling curses under my breath. These take too long to fix. I lean on the wall, watching Soren as I feel the bleeding slow, my intestines healing.

Fuck. I messed this all up. How long will he be out for? A few more seconds? Minutes? He's still twitching, his eyelids opening like he's waking up, but then drooping back down.

Stupid, big fucker. The song is supposed to wipe people out for *hours*.

Once the bleeding is manageable, I figure I can heal the rest once I'm on a horse. I double-check that I have the bag with Soren's money, clean off Anya's blade, and stick it in my boot, opening the door for a second take. This will either work, or it won't.

But I have to try.

Slipping out is easier this time, my hood up; the private deck is empty. I quickly pace in the opposite direction of the tavern. No one follows. I find a side set of stairs and descend them, keeping to the shadows of the night. I freeze when I hear Bones— "Hold it. Where's Anya?"

I glance over at a room that's on the bottom level and see

that Kathleen is standing in an open doorway. Bones is looking up where Soren and Anya are—it makes me realize they didn't have many guards outside the room, although I see his men patrolling all over.

Did they think so little of my capabilities? *Idiots.*

Kathleen spots me and quickly grabs Bones by the wrist. "Fine, you can come into my room."

She tugs on his wrist.

"I can what now?" he asks, completely distracted as he drops his head to look down at her.

She kisses him, running her hand up his arm and the madman melts at her touch. I know it's my cue to leave.

My one, major regret is not telling her that the reason I cannot stay is because of Melona. Otherwise I'd strike a bargain with Soren and pray to all the gods he keeps his word.

It destroys a part of me to think that Kathleen believes I'm leaving to save my life, when all I want to do is save *others.*

But it must be this way, whether I like it or not.

I manage to sneak out into the streets, heading across the city to the other stable master so the one here can't recognize me. The entire walk is the most nerve-wracking I've felt in a long time, everything in my peripheral feeling like it's moving. I try not to fidget with my cloak too much, wanting to appear as indiscreet as possible. I can't help but wonder how long Anya will be out, how long Soren will rest, and if Bones will realize Kathleen kissed him as a rather obvious decoy.

But I reach the other horses, handing their charge a small bit of coin that I stole from Soren.

I'm absolutely dead if he ever catches me.

The stable master looks at me funny, but I ignore him and almost fail to get on a horse when my injured stomach spasms. *You can feel sorry for yourself later. Get out of here!*

Once I'm on the horse, panting as if I ran for an hour

straight rather than just walk a few hundred feet, he says, "Ride 'er only to our sister cities. She's branded to Skull's Row."

"I know the drill," I grunt. If this horse gets found outside their boundaries, someone will notice I've stolen a horse from the men of Skull's Row, stirring the pot I'm desperate to keep untouched.

I plan to ride straight east and get on a fucking ship across the Black Sea.

It amazes me that the northern gates to Dryhill actually open as I trot right on out. I'm even more shocked that no guards are rushing to find me.

It worked.

I choose one of the trails that's less traveled, knowing it will lead to a road with heavy commerce and footprints. They'll think they have me, but the end of this dirt path is a grand intersection. All it takes is them choosing the wrong path and I'll gain ample time on them.

Anything I can do to lose them, even if for an hour.

Once Dryhill becomes small enough that I can barely see the flickering of their braziers behind me, I let out a deep belly laugh, only to double over and groan in agony.

Slowly, I begin healing myself once more.

When I feel truly free, like my shadows are clear of any threat, a nagging disappointment creeps into my heart.

Kathleen shouldn't have helped me, not with Soren's powers to read her. Fuck. What if this backfires?

Melona didn't just warn me, she made a deal with father and gave me an official prophecy, glowing eyes and all... I owe her a debt, but she never clarified what that was. Without that detail, it's not like I can pay it off, which means all I can do is avoid Skull's Row at all costs.

"You better not hurt Kathleen, Soren..." I mumble to the void of night.

I yearn for comfort, for one of my parents. To ask all of these questions to someone who has no motive other than to help me. I grip the reins tighter with one hand as the other begins to wipe away the tears.

Once the salty water trickles down my cheeks, I sob in ways that I haven't cried in over a decade.

CYPRESS

JANE

I actually found her.

Coming here was a spur-of-the-moment decision I made once I felt that Dryhill was far enough behind me.

Once I reached the crossroads, I decided that I *did* need to speak to someone, and there's only one person in all of the Balar Coasts that I trust with information that plagues me.

By a stroke of fate, *she* was on the way to the coastline.

An ancient aura exudes from the hut before me, constructed out of worn riverstone that stretches up into an uneven cedar roof. Deep green ivy covers the structure, and lozenge windows reflect the surrounding forest.

Whisps of smoke lazily curl out of the chimney. Melted, unlit candles line the property; a rather figureless effigy made of obsidian perches in an alcove by the door—the dark god that the witch inside worships. Its name is Solerin, if I remember correctly, a being that controls the manipulation of shadows and use of blood magic.

Its eyeless face haunts my peripheral, the surrounding air vibrating with power as if every leaf is an eye that stares at me.

Perhaps they do.

Cypress, a woman with no true age known, is a witch whose legend speaks of her ability to exist in more than one place at once, like a mirrored reflection that has no ends. It would be akin to leaving a double of myself with Soren while this version sought refuge.

Cypress also *sees* things... and she is greedy in her tolls for those truths.

The red door to her home slowly creaks open, my blood frigid at the eerie movement among the stillness. Dad always said Cypress is from beyond the Black Sea, bringing with her a magic that many on this continent couldn't *dream* of over-powering.

And she's the only person I can think of that might help me.

Long fingers wrap around the edge of the door before a pale woman with inky hair peers out of the threshold. Heavy-lidded eyes connect with mine, their color as black as obsidian.

"Jane," she croons, her velvety and ethereal voice caressing my name. "Jane, Jane, *Jane.*"

Every bone within me can sense how dangerous this is, but desperation drives me forward. As steady as I can say, I mutter, "Hello, Cypress."

She opens the door further, appraising me slowly as if every inch tells a different story, the poor condition of my clothes not helping my presentation. Or maybe it will, and she'll take pity on me. I suppose it depends on whether her and Father had a good last encounter.

Cypress adds, "Last I saw you, you sat on your father's horse as nothing more than a child."

The words are ones that *could* be spoken by an old friend, but her placid tone contrasts any possible hospitality. Her neck reveals signs of aging while the skin on her cheeks and forehead are smooth and unmarred.

"Yes, it's been a while," I say, moving forward when she calmly raises an arm to greet me inside. I hastily take in the rather simple black robes she wears, thinking this decision over one last time before committing. Passing by her, intrusive thoughts burn into my mind of her grabbing my neck and choking me, claiming my soul as an offering to her faceless god.

The vision is so strong I half wonder if it's a bewitched warning rather than my subconscious telling me how damning this is.

My reckless side, as always, wins over and pushes me forward until I'm standing inside the hut that smells of wood, herbs, and something musky. A large fire roars to lick the black, overhanging kettle. Rubies of all sizes, encased in various fixings, adorn the space, their crimson hues shimmering all around me. "You still trade rubies, I see," I say, attempting small talk.

My gaze remains still when I spot a collection of necklaces and earrings, recalling my mother. Dad would often visit to buy her jewelry from here, as it was her favorite gemstone.

Charles Ritter trusted Cypress.

It's the only thing I have right now.

Cypress circles me, her long robe dragging on the floor. Glossy eyes peer into my skin just like Soren does, the witch not answering me.

I can't believe I actually wish Soren was here right now, knowing that he could help navigate this if he weren't the one I'm actively running from.

He's out there, hunting me. He has to have awakened by now.

If I thought the silence incited anxiety, my heart pounds into my ears when I spot a pile of raw meat on a table, the amount *far* too great for a single witch. For some reason it feels entirely unnatural, even if it could be as innocent as her having skinned an elk.

Maybe I'm just on edge.

Cypress doesn't turn around to confirm what I see before saying, "Those are for my hounds. I called them off to allow you to approach."

Okay, take that. She wants to talk. "So, you saw me?" I ask, my composure as thin as paper while she leads me to a wooden seat at a table.

"I see it all, Miss Ritter."

My breath hitches as I sit, ignoring how it feels to be referred to as a *Ritter*. I'm honestly not sure what to do with Cypress, or how to ask for aid. Am I supposed to offer anything? Staring at the table with many gashes, as if it's been stabbed repeatedly, I say, "Then you're aware I need help."

"Oh, yes, you most certainly do." Her grim voice holds an air of inevitability, the witch scooting a chair on the wooden floor to sit across from me, dirt filling in the underside of her nails.

"I don't know what to do, or what to offer you." I lift my gaze to meet hers, her heavy lids raised to reveal eyes so removed of emotion she may as well be a corpse. I nearly stutter as I say, "But I want your help... please."

She arches a brow, still not blinking. "You will offer me nothing, and I will give you nothing. Other than a pair of ruby earrings for a discount."

My lips twitch in a threatened laugh, although all humor fades when I look into her stony face. No matter how much I replay those words, I can't make sense of them. "Wait, what?"

"Your father used to come here to buy them for your mother," she plainly states.

A lump forms in my throat, my hands tightly lacing together. "Why would I take nothing but a pair of earrings at a time like this? I'm fleeing for my life. I assaulted a *Zenith*. What will *earrings* do for me?"

Her head slightly tilts, obsidian eyes locked in her skull much like an owl's. "Don't you want something of Eleanor's?"

I look down so abruptly that my hair falls into my face. Why is she doing this, and not helping me? I haven't heard Mom's name in over ten years, especially her full name over the nickname of Nora. I wipe my nose, rapidly blinking. "Obviously I would," I say through a trembling voice, collecting myself. "But I need *help*," I plead. "I have a very dangerous man after me, and I need off this continent as soon as possible. But I need to know if I'm making the best decision."

She slowly smiles, revealing aged teeth. "And you're wondering what to do with Melona's warning?"

"*Yes*," I quickly confess, eager to make progress here. "I—I don't want to leave. I don't *want* to flee."

"Then don't."

My lips part, a tiny sound escaping my throat that hints at a poorly controlled grunt. "*Okay*," I say, overpronunciating that word as my temper gets the best of me. "But if I don't leave, then I'll go to Skull's Row. Melona gave me a siren's prophecy. Not only do I have to heed her words, but If I go back on my promise, I can *never* enter the oceans again or the sirens will take me. You *know* this. So why tell me not to leave?"

No one quite knows where the sirens take mankind when they sink their claws into flesh and pull them under. Legends say the souls are morphed into something inhuman, affixing to the sea floor in a monstrous memory of their life, forever stuck that way as sirens use their scales for their magic.

Breaking the prophecy not only means that people die, but if I get near the ocean, I'll be subjected to a horrendous fate.

I couldn't even consider that when near Soren, or else he'd wonder why I was worried about sirens. The man is too sharp to have risked that.

Cypress has a stillness to her, even when she speaks, that makes my skin crawl. "You have already paid your debt to Melona."

Leaning back in my seat, a chill runs down my spine as those are the *exact* words I wanted to hear, even if I didn't realize it.

She's toying with me; *has* to be.

"My dad trusted you," I state. "Is that not honored at all?"

Two fingers raise as her only acknowledgment. "And *you* should trust me as well."

My anger helps combat the fear I have for her, staring boldly into eyes that reveal the whites above and below her black irises. "This advice makes absolutely no sense. I'm supposed to buy some earrings from you, trust that my debt to Melona is magically paid, and then what? Just go about like nothing ever happened?"

"You have to return to the land of your blood, Jane."

I huff, flattening my palm on the table. "Well, seeing as how you *refuse* to tell me how I've paid my debts, I think it's safe to say this is a waste of my time. I need to be on the move, not talking to someone who speaks in circles or lies to me."

She shrugs. "Then don't listen to me. I can't force you."

I knew she was cryptic, and that she drove many mad with her vague words, but I came here because her precision in the *sight* drives everyone to try and understand her riddles.

This just has me confused.

I'm about to pardon myself and get back on the trail when Cypress stands.

"Let's get you a pair of ruby earrings that your mother once bought. They're the sister set, ones I saved for a moment just as this," Cypress suggests. The oddest thing occurs as humanity returns to those black eyes like I've been speaking to another version of her this entire time.

Have I been?

"Well, no, wait. What do I owe you for something like that?" I half expect her to ask for a blood oath. "I'm not giving you anything."

"You are as ardent in personality as Charles." She nears a collection of shelves, not looking at me as she adds, "Five of the gold coins you stole from Soren will do."

She pulls out something wrapped in animal skin that's stained black. When she places it on the table and unwraps it with nimble fingers, she says, "I sold the sister pair to your father, as I said. Keep these wrapped in this goatskin for extra protection until you choose to wear them."

I can hardly do anything more than stare at the two pendants encased in gold, a golden ball sitting between the two to connect them, *just* as Mom had. The weight of my mother's presence is heavy in my heart as if I forgot what it's like to remember her.

"This is so entirely useless..." I mumble, even if tears silently stream down my face.

"You have paid the debt of Melona's prophecy whether you see it or not, just as it was intended when she received it. It's not by happenstance that you never knew the debt, as you staying put in Coalfell was necessary for fate to align. The sirens will not take you into their depths, nor will innocents die in droves. So do as you wish now, Jane. I trust the fates will guide you."

Without thought, I reach out for the earrings like they're a gift directly from Mom, staring at them.

Well, even if Cypress said what I wanted to hear, I'm slightly shocked that it means so little to me, my mind only seeing her as a merchant speaking whatever they have to in order to sell their goods.

"I'll take these," I say, sliding over Soren's coin, having no idea where this will get me. Perhaps hearing comforting words —and *not* being assuaged by them—was the answer I sought.

Greed glints in her eyes as she wraps her fingers around the coins, sliding them off to place them inside an ornate, crimson box.

"Is that all?" I ask, gripping the earrings. They feel silly to have, but I guess it's better than leaving empty-handed. *Watch all this be just a way to make some coin off of my fear.*

"Yes. Be careful, Jane Ritter," she hums, her back to me as she nears her fire. "It will all make sense, in the end. You may see yourself out, now."

Standing, I survey the hut one more time before nearing her door, opening it slowly as I look over my shoulder.

My breath stills when she's already looking at me, the *entirety* of her eyes completely red as if ink stains them.

That's enough to send me fast on my feet, leaving her behind as I lightly jog up the dirt trail that first led me to her home.

A day had already passed since leaving Dryhill, night nearly upon me once more as I realize I don't even have a lantern, nearing the settlement of Inkstone where my horse is. The last thing I need is to be in her woods when the sun is down.

Panting—those creepy ass eyes burned in my brain—I'm

up on the stable with many checked-in horses, placing a hand over my aching stomach that needs another round of healing. I spot the one I rode in on, hastily caressing its fur.

A thought crosses my mind, considering stealing *another* horse, since this is the last post that I can take my branded steed to before heading to the coasts.

Wouldn't hurt to add *one* more layer of subterfuge.

Yes, I definitely need a fresh horse, no matter the direction I choose to go in.

I stare into the horse's black, glossy eyes as I think over possibly the most important decision of my life—do I flee? Or do I stay in these lands and try to hide once more?

Only a few hours after Jane fled...

When I come to, everything is wrong.

Anya is in my room, her head bleeding. Bones peers over me like I might be dead, and I can't feel that confused heart of Jane *anywhere*.

I slowly push up into a sitting position, staring with wide eyes across the room before looking down at my body. I'm still wearing nothing but pants, my shirt on the floor near the mirror where she healed me...

That fucking bitch.

She knows the *siren's sunder*. Who the fuck taught her? And how did she hide that from me?

"Good," Bones says with a dramatic sigh. "We were just about to round everyone up to find her—"

"How long was I out for?" I stand, feeling as if I merely took a pleasant nap, surveying every available detail for context. It looks as if it's early morning outside, the hearth dwindling but not dead.

"Quite a few hours," Bones replies.

Anya adds, "The men are all rallying outside, ready to ride. Like Bones said, we were just about to go after her and leave you here—"

"No. No, I go alone to find Jane."

Anya watches me with a determined calculation. I know she's reading me the way I read hearts—except she's got no magic for that. She's just shrewd.

I examine my armor, thinking over a plan as I near the table, stopping to stand over a vast pool of blood. "Who bled?"

Anya replies, "I stabbed her."

I glare at her over my shoulder. My blood runs hot at the image of Jane being stabbed right in front of me while I was sleeping like nothing fucking happened. "You *what?*"

"Sir, she attacked you. Then *me*," she explains, shock widening her dark eyes, looking at me like maybe I've forgotten who I am.

I lower my head to stare at the stain that's already dried. Anya didn't behave wrongly, not with Jane's ability to heal herself. "Where did you stab her?"

"In the lower stomach. I know we still need her alive. Figured she could heal that enough." Anya carefully adds, "What happened, sir?"

Bones watches with a curious glower. I ignore the lipstick

smeared on his face, honestly amazed that he pried himself away from his 'kitten' to check on me.

"She knows the *siren's sunder* and can use her magic to subdue others. Much like a sedation," I explain, rubbing my neck. "Didn't know healers could do that."

Anya groans. "I *knew* it was the sunder. I *told* you that's what it was," she says, pointing at Bones. "Although, I also didn't know about the healer part. That's definitely new."

"What did you two do while I was out?" I ask, touching the leather of my vest, considering everything. "What all has happened?"

Bones dramatically nods to Anya, who says, "Well, we searched all of Dryhill. Found that the northern stable master gave a small woman a horse for some coin, so we sent out three scouts. You were breathing fine, so I figured some kind of magic knocked you out."

Bones adds, "We were giving it until the sun was fully up before sending out the rest of the men."

"You're sure you want to go *alone*," Anya confirms, her tone flat. "Let us trail you, at the very least."

"I may be back tomorrow, in a week, in a month. But I go alone for this," I reply resolutely, squatting down to stare at the red pool... the lack of bloody footprints leads me to think she healed it before leaving. "She says it's business, but it's personal now."

I turn around to check for my coin, in case... "The bitch stole my fucking coin." My voice actually cracks, incredulously holding my hands out to the side.

Holy shit. Do I even admit that I'm impressed at the brass balls she has? Stealing from a Zenith is a death sentence. It's even codified.

Anya winces when she prods her head at a delicate spot. "Didn't peg her for that type of woman. That bugs the shit out of me that I read her wrong. Guess it makes sense though, if the Council wants her."

Bones nears a window and peers out behind the curtains. "Should've seen her when she attacked her room. She's like a spawn of Skull's Row."

I don't know what I feel. Or perhaps I don't know how to *interpret* what I feel. I'm enraged, obviously, and have a natural desire to find her, kill her right on the spot, and tell the Council everything I know of her after placing her pretty head on a spike.

Then, there's the strangest emotion—the one that contrasts the familiarity of my indifference: sympathy. The way her regret mixed with victory as she subdued me confuses me the most.

She meant those words she said to me.

Some part of her genuinely wanted to trust me, only terrified of what would happen to her, choosing to look after her own skin. She could have killed me if she fucking wanted, or left me wounded.

Instead, I feel completely well-rested.

"Someone ready Phantom for me," I say, not caring which one does it. "Put my armor in a bag and attach it to the horse." Grabbing my skull mask, I remind myself that Jane's father once bore his own, too.

My time of doubting her capabilities is done.

The hunt begins.

⸺⸱⸺◈⸺⸱⸺

Heavy clouds dim the moonlight, and the northern stables are rather quiet. I ride Phantom up to a man who sleeps a little too carelessly in a bed of hay, my steed stomping his foot to wake the stablemaster. He nearly trips when he stands, strands of dry grass stuck to his clothes and hair.

"My liege," he manages out, his words slurred with ale.

"Did a woman take a horse?" I ask, burning my gaze into him. I'm wearing the skull mask to enhance the powers I possess—I can feel traces of Jane like a bloodhound catching a dying scent.

"Aye," he says, nodding to the first stall, the space empty.

"Where was she going?"

"D-didn't say, my liege."

"How fucking useful," I growl.

Kicking Phantom, I ride to the gate and shout for them to open it, the door still in the process of lowering as I charge forward, Phantom's weight smacking the wooden door down. Outside of Dryhill, horse hooves litter the dirt road canopied by trees, but I can feel her. If I were to turn south, I'd lose all sense of Jane.

The little thorn in my side, the one with her name carved into it, shines brightest in the east.

Present time, quite a few hours after Jane left Inkstone...

The first rays of dawn pierce through thick clouds, casting a pale light over this smaller outpost known for its trading of inks and rubies—Inkstone. Skull's Row traders often roll through here, only being a week away from our kingdom and near the coast. It used to be called a burrow, trees nestling deep into the soil as vines wrap around the buildings.

Now it's a proper fucking city, one that a particularly notorious witch infests.

I dismount Phantom and leave him at the entrance, unbound. The horse has been branded to my magic, and if I need him, he'll appear for me and know not to wander far.

It's so early that even the wild dogs sleep, the only sound being the padding of my boots as I follow the traces of Jane to a tavern, my hand on the hilt of my sword. A few horses are tied to posts—there's one with a burn into its fur that's of a skull.

Could be Jane, or could be someone else visiting.

As I stare at the building in front of me, my attention peaks as I hear someone open their front door to send their child on morning errands.

Even though I *know* she was in the tavern based on the traces of her aura—perhaps stopping for food—I can't fight the gnawing sensation that the tavern is a waste of my time.

If anything, I'm drawn to the right.

My heart races with annoyance when I wonder if this is leading me to *her*.

I fucking hate witches.

Following the traces of Jane through the main street, all of the homes made of half-timber and brick, I pass underneath a footbridge that connects two of the largest buildings.

Winding down and traversing a few flights of stairs, Jane's aura grows bright in my mind's eye as I pace along a dirty path until I reach a ramshackle hut sitting on the edge of a clearing, smoke lazily curling from the chimney. The prickling of witch's magic taints the air, giant beasts—the size of Phantom—

sleeping outside of a nearby building; hell hounds. They're the size of a grizzly, their hide so thick that not even a sword could penetrate it, all wrapped in silver fur that contrasts the bright red of their eyes. The black paws of one stretches out, claws as sharp as talons.

Hellhounds are nasty fuckers that even give *me* a run for my money, and witches *love* taming them. Especially to guard their dwellings.

Jane's aura is laced so heavily in there, I almost wonder if she's still present...

A witch's house is where the Zenith princess hides, then?

The witch inside is one I know very well, and I hate that bitch. She reads me like I read others, and the thought that she has information about what truly lies inside of my heart makes me want to kill her every time we, unfortunately, have an encounter.

No one should have that kind of knowledge over me.

I near it nonetheless, the hellhound's eyes widening as a deathly grumble emanates from their throats.

The others awaken.

Creatures born from magic always feel different to me. Their motives are clear, but I can't seem to anticipate their attack—only knowing how they feel. Eyeing the beast that licks its lips, I say, "I want to see your mistress."

Red eyes sharpen, the growling intensifying as their muscles stiffen. It doesn't like the skull mask. Grunting, I remove the face covering, the material hardening in my hands. I hold an arm out as if to show the beast I'll play by its rules, even if it annoys me. I don't have any time to waste—

The bright red door to the hut creaks open, and an older woman with inky hair stands in the gloomy threshold. "I knew I sensed you."

The eyes of a witch always unnerve me; completely

unreadable, especially as they hide any true thoughts or intentions with their own magic. They can see things beyond my own capabilities, the annoying vulnerability a reminder to keep this encounter short. Her hounds watch carefully, waiting for their master to display distress.

"I want to talk, Cypress."

"I bet you do. Last time it was about Serena—are you here about her, again?" she muses, opening the door further into her obscure dwelling. The hell hounds crane their monstrous heads as if questioning her life's decisions. "No, no I think not... come in for some morning tea, Soren. There's much to discuss."

She watches me carefully, her eyes half open as if she's waking from a sleep, and yet they're completely alert. The cunt is leaving a trance, then. Probably watching me as I approached.

If that's true, then she already knows I'm here for Jane, which means mentioning Serena is an unnecessary stab at my pride. At the part of me that not even Bones or Anya gets to see.

Each step toward the hut feels like a betrayal to myself, entering a den of magic that's wholly dangerous. But Jane's presence pulls me closer. Her emotions saturate the inside of this space like a permanent imprint.

What the fuck was she doing here?

I duck to enter, the door groaning behind me as it shuts. The morning sun reveals the dust floating in the air, my gaze scanning the room for any sign of a hiding fugitive. *No, she's not here anymore.* The air is thick with the smell of herbs, the floorboard creaking underneath my boots.

Ruby jewelry hangs all over, the crimson glow intensifying the mystic atmosphere from the candles lit all around. I've been hearing that Cypress has taken to hell hound breeding, and with how careless she leaves the jewelry about in this place, it makes sense now; she doesn't have to worry about any thieves here.

Nearing a table where I can almost see Jane's ghost, I sense right where her ass was perched as she sat, trying to imagine where in the hells she's fucked off to.

Either way, I'm getting closer.

With measured steps, I approach the stool, my hand instinctively running over the table. "This isn't about Serena, and I already told you that I'm not speaking to you about her further." Anger twists inside of my veins like barbed wire. "I want the woman with auburn hair that was in here," I demand.

"Miss Jane has you quite ensnared..." she replies.

"Why was she here?" I assert, locking my gaze with the witch's obsidian one.

Her laugh fills the quiet hut, the aged woman nearing a corner where a stove heats a pot of whatever the hells witches drink in the morning. "Don't waste your threatening glares on me, Soren. You hurt a single hair on my head and those hounds will rip you apart. Would be such a waste to have you die for no reason at all."

A waste? This whole damn conversation is a *waste.* "Why did Jane come in here?" I press.

More importantly, why is the damage to Jane's heart so profound that it's almost as if she's still here? *Witch's magic, maybe? She could still be here, but hidden.*

Cypress removes the steaming, black pot and pours a dark, watery liquid into two cups. "Poor dear. She's quite terrified. She came here because she's desperate."

"I bet she is," I chide.

"Taking her to the Council will get you nowhere, Soren. At least, it will not help you achieve what you truly seek. It's also a waste of time, as she's innocent," Cypress defends, bringing the tea to the table at which I stand. "Sit."

I sit in the chair, considering every possible layer of Cypress's words. "Her innocence is not mine to decide, nor do I give a shit."

"Since when do you bow to the Council? I've never known you as a follower of other men's codes. Even if the Zenith have marked your chest, we both know it was a sacrifice to help you acquire your *true* objective."

She sits across from me, pushing what smells like a cup of tea closer. I don't move, except to stare at what she offers. It smells like soil, the steam spiraling upward.

The last time I drank one of these from her, my ability to control myself and my emotions were non-existent. It's the only time I've managed to slice my blade into Cypress, who gladly took the wound as the action of me drinking her tea gave her access to *all* of me.

And for fucking what? I still don't know.

"We're at an impasse, Soren. I won't tell you why Jane was here or where she went, and you won't kill me."

My path before me is so unclear that there's no point in considering what direction to move in. I could leave and follow the path that Jane lays, but the nagging sensation in my gut tells me to *not* move from this seat. That's usually a foreboding warning from the gift that guides my intuition, demanding I heed it. "Fine. But I'm not drinking this, for *obvious* reasons. Let's also skip useless conversations. You knew Charles Ritter?"

"Of course, I did. His wife bore a fondness for rubies."

My eyebrows twitch as shock distorts my concentration. "*Wife?*"

She sips on the steaming tea, smiling at me. "Ask Jane herself if you want to know more."

"That woman knocked me out and stole my coin. The last thing she's sharing with me is her life story."

"Of course, she stole from you. She wants to live, doesn't she?" Cypress stares me down, her black eyes unnerving as they begin to widen with concentration.

Staring across the room as I consider any other approach, I see an old window resting against the wall, many pegs glued on so ruby necklaces can hang off each one.

Everyone has a vice, and Cypress adores her coins. Everywhere she exists, she indulges in some kind of sales of luxury items. Was Ritter's vice the fact that he wanted a family but no one could know of it?

Could Jane be setting me up from the beginning? If I couldn't read souls like ink on skin, I'd perhaps believe it.

But that soul of hers is so tormented it's completely raw in places.

He was never found dead... "What do you know?" I ask, facing her again. "You want me here, so tell me what you planned to tell me once you knew I was coming."

Her cup lowers, those eyes so intense it's as if she's awoken from a slumber. Leaning back into her seat, she seems almost proud to say, "It's a warning. If you're even remotely associated with Jane's death, Charles Ritter *will* find you, and the plans he has for those that hurt his wife and daughter would make even *you* squirm. Seeing as how the wife is dead, that means Jane is *everything* to him."

"So, he's not dead?"

"They never found a body," she replies, lazily shrugging her shoulders. "And before you ask, Jane doesn't know he's alive."

Adrenaline heats my blood; my jaw clenches as my nostrils flare. Breathing heavily, I don't know how to process the details. "Why tell me? Why let *me* know and not her, if this is even true?"

She points her finger at me. "Because you'd do best to put your energy into preserving the life of Ritter's daughter rather than appeasing the council of killers. She'll find out in time when it feels right for you to inform her. Not before then."

"So, you want me to gamble on a woman I don't know, all the while I'm supposed to hope it goes in my direction, all because you and I had this conversation? *After* what happened in our last encounter where you nearly raped my soul?"

Her grin is slow and shaky, as if she nearly forgot. "Tell me —what action do you think will return Serena to you?"

The audacity of this witch, to use *her*. I lean over, staring Cypress down, not caring that the hounds outside growl with a warning. "*Don't.*"

Her cackle raises the hairs on my arms. "You can't *stand* that you can't read me, can you? To face someone that uses similar powers as your own? There's no shame in wanting your sister returned, Soren—" my hands shake with a need to strangle her until her eyes pop "—but if you need proof, then it's proof I shall give you."

Heaving a dramatic sigh, Cypress stands, pulling out a scroll from inside her black robes to unroll and reveal blank parchment. She then nears a cluttered wall where her attention falls on a knife that seems as if a giant ruby was cut to be the blade. The witch moves to a nearby window, unlocking the latches as wood strains against itself when she opens it. One of the hellhounds peers in, sniffing in my direction. She speaks to it in a foreign language as the beast opens its mouth, saliva stringing between the teeth as it allows her to slice its tongue. Red liquid pools from the wound, Cypress carefully moves to our table and she cuts her palm, lowering her hand to smear the shared blood on the blank page.

Lines form like roots, spreading outward in a unique design until they glow, her black irises turning crimson, the color stretching as if staining the whites. She enters a trance as she sits, one hand on each side of the scroll, her sacrificial palm bleeding onto the table in a messy expanse.

Her hypnotic, terrifying eyes stare off into the distance as if she stares at an invisible painting with moving parts. "Miss Jane felt compelled to come east, allowing *us* cross paths, Soren," she says, her voice low and gravelly. "The energy of our world is changing... right now, ancient powers and dynamics are being threatened by man." She squints and tilts her head. "It's not the end of the society, however, but the gods are *not* pleased. Poor Jane is wrapped up in this in ways she doesn't understand."

Cypress looks me in the eyes and I hold my breath. "In particular, the Sirens are angry. Jane's father made a deal with them when his wife was struck down and Jane's life was threatened. The Scorpion has waited over a decade to strike perfectly rather than embark on a mindless rampage—as his moniker denotes. Keep Jane alive, Soren, and you will live another day to see your sister, as she is still very much alive. Let Jane die, and the Scorpion will torture you in ways that only a Zenith who has lost his family would."

Deep emotions, ones I *never* let out, resurface at her mentioning Serena in such a way. It pisses me off so much that a hound snaps at the open window when I move my hand— even by an *inch*—toward a blade at my thigh. "I didn't ask to be Jane's charge. I'm not agreeing to this, all because a witch put on a nice show."

Cypress's eyes return to normal, disappointment clear in her expression, like she wanted to remain in the vision for longer. The blood on the parchment rescinds before disappearing as if wiped away, her hand healing, the table clean once more.

"Yes, well, I didn't ask for the ringing in my ears as I've

aged, and yet here we are," she snaps in an uncharacteristic display of normalcy. "It's a part of life. I'm only here to deliver the message, Soren."

"All creatures in this world are selfish and will do what they need to survive. You're clearly working with Jane, *and* her father. And now you're using my sister as a means of manipulation to keep them safe. I *loathe* being used."

She rolls the scroll back inside her cloak. "It's not my fault you've never learned to trust the motives of someone if you can't read them." She presses her lips together as she stares at me. "Do what you want with that information. Just understand that Jane must remain ignorant about her father's whereabouts. The gods work with man as their first resort before relying on the ruthless powers of the mother goddess to ravish the lands until the humans bow down once more. We are currently in possession of controlling our own fates before our world is ravished by the wrath of our creators.

"I'm merely a branch in the tree of life, just like you, and my role is to inform you that helping the Scorpion will get you closer to saving Serena more than the Council ever will, which means to help, and protect, Jane."

An incredulous laugh escapes me. "And how the fuck did I get tied into this?"

"Because *you're* the one the Council sent." She huffs, her patience thinning. "Sometimes our ties to fate are profound and deeply woven, and other times, we're just caught in the web."

ANTICIPATION

JANE

"So, you're traveling through?" the barman inquires.

"Aye." I gulp ale from a black, horned mug at the lively tavern in Ender's Bay. The salty smell of the ocean fills the air as I sit alone among a crowd of seafarers.

I decided to book passage across the ocean, even if just for a few months while collecting myself. If Cypress wanted me to stay, then it's not my fault she didn't offer me a more genuine reason to listen to her. Saying the *exact* words I wanted to hear almost makes it worse. How much of an idiot would I be if I just believed her?

No, this is the best choice. Get away and think things through without Soren haunting me.

"Where you from?" the man asks with a high voice that contrasts his rough visage. He has dry, wiry gray hair all over his head and face, like he's been worn down from the salt of the ocean.

"Skull's Row," I say with pride.

It feels good to say that out loud after all these years of living as a healer among pacifists. Screw it. I'm a spawn of one of the most feared men around, and I finally have to accept it.

He frowns, his rag partially sticking out from inside of the mug as he pauses. "And what are *you* doing, living there?"

"I'm a baker," I say, belching. Worrying about manners seems rather pointless, now. "I make the best muffins, and I got a secret recipe that only *I* know, so no one kills me in return."

I can't mention that the secret recipe is pure, organic bullshit, as I spin that story from nothing but the memory of baking lemon muffins with my mother.

Then again, there's *some* truth in it. I once knew a baker who made the *best* sourdough, and a Zenith put a golden skull on his store, denoting that he's not to be hurt in any way, shape, or form. They call those skulls *'The Zenith's Promise'*. It's made of Naprese gold, just like the ornate designs of their masks.

No one can reproduce the way the gold becomes translucent when right next to a flame, like a unique stamp of authenticity. An invisible shield in many ways, torches usually burning right underneath.

The barman seems to buy that, or at least, he doesn't pry and moves to chat with a more grizzled lot. I eye them as I eat my stew. People change the closer they get to the coast, their outfits are worn and made of wool, and nearly all the men have facial hair, often times braided.

I'm so close to being free.

It seems risky to sit at a pub and drink when Soren *must* be hunting for me, but I've hit the end of my road, now waiting for passage across the ocean. I chose to come to Ender's Bay since I know it doesn't have near as many pirates in these ports. The least amount of drama I get involved with, the better.

Going north into the wooded lands above us *did* cross my mind, but again, I don't know forests. I only know mercenaries, pirates, and the ocean.

The next ship leaves at dawn, which means just a few more hours of waiting. Surely, I've made it far enough. If anyone comes looking for the horse I stole, I'll just give them all of Soren's gold to keep them quiet.

I pause, realizing I should have just left some coin in place of the horse to preemptively take care of that. *No, because then his men would see that and know you took it.*

It's not as if any of that matters, it's too late to change plans. I just have to trust in the small lead I have. Taking another drink, I hope it can help subdue my nerves. I'm far from relaxed; every little sound or moving shadow scares me, waiting for *him* to find me. Soren has a few dozen men that he's probably already sent out as hounds.

Tapping my foot, I stare out a window as I desperately wait for the sun to rise.

HAUNTING HER
SOREN

A few minutes prior....

The tavern in Ender's Bay is oddly packed, but it only helps blend me into the background.

I stare at the auburn-haired woman sitting at the bar, spinning tales about being a *baker*.

What the hells is Jane doing?

She scans the tavern like it's a bad habit that she has, and every time she does, I can feel how she's searching for me.

My lips curl upward.

I don't know how she got here while leaving her horse in Inkstone, unless she stole someone else's. I have half a mind to walk out from behind this door with a one-way mirror that I watch her from—just to see her pretty face as she realizes how deeply she fucked up.

I can hear her as plain as day with the cracks between the door and the wall as she speaks to the man serving her ale.

No, I'll let her think she's free of me, for now.

She will learn.

Once she's minding her own business and sipping on her stew, I scan the crowd as they begin to sing, thumping their feet on the floor. From behind Jane, in a corner, I spot a man who doesn't keep his eyes off of her, nor does he partake in anything else. And he's not watching her in a *curious* way. If I had my coin, I would bet the entire bag that he'll follow her after she leaves.

Jane *better* have my fucking gold somewhere on her. That wasn't a small amount she stole.

The bartender moves to the doors near me, which squeak on their hinges as they open and close. The aged man looks at me and quietly whispers, "Did you get what you need?"

"For now," I reply, moving my gaze back to Jane.

"Well, is she dangerous?"

I snort. "She bites harder than she looks. But she's not dangerous for *you*."

He grunts, grabbing a bottle on a nearby shelf and takes it back out, her pretty eyes observing every move the bartender makes. Her heart bleeds with pride, and I get the sense she thinks she's outsmarted me.

She's going to *hate* learning that she was so wrong to ever assume she could.

My eyes widen when Jane pulls out *my* bag of coins and

pays for her food and drink, getting a fair bit of change back. Good girl for not losing that. I leave through the back when she makes for the entrance. I'll follow her aura, keeping a distance in the guise of night. I've left my armor off so as not to make a sound. As I stand in the shadows, the air crisp in my lungs, I watch as she traverses the dirt roads, kicking a rock. She begins walking along a path that leads closer to the piers, and I hesitate to move when the tavern doors open. The man that was watching leaves too, searching around as the warm light from inside diminishes when the door shuts behind him. When he spots her, he swiftly follows and moves like he wants to avoid being seen.

Well, this is *not* his lucky day.

As Jane walks without being a bit wiser about the situation, I follow the man. When he picks up his pace and unsheathes a blade, like he might run in and pounce on her, it's time for me to act as I come in from behind, unsheathing my own as I grip the hard steel hilt. In a swift movement, I press my dagger at his throat while my other hand grabs his wrist that drops his weapon, pinning it behind his back. "Speak a word and I'll paint the streets with your blood."

He doesn't move.

I release his wrist and rummage in his pockets, pulling out a very unique coin that has a flying crow on one side, and a skull on the other. *The Crows.*

"Well, this is shit luck for you... you're from a nasty group of privateers. Why are you alone?" I mutter.

"What do you want?" He rasps, his breathing ragged. His emotions are the easiest to read yet—there's no real fear inside of him, just annoyance that this is happening at all. I can sense that he *really* wants to reach for a blade at his hip.

"Answer the question."

"I'm *visiting*."

Lies. He's hunting. Moving his wrist so I can look at it, I spot a black crow right in the middle. "You snag women and take them to be used and sold."

"The fuck do you care?"

Oh, he's *so* unlucky tonight. I think of Serena, not knowing who took her, only aware that she was taken in a very similar manner.

Which means this man has done this before. I allow him a few seconds of life to really examine his heart, and when all I can feel is the undisciplined lust for power that rapists all share, I don't fucking bother dealing with threats tonight.

"I'm sure the world won't miss you," I say, slicing his jugular so deep I cut through bone. Blood sprays out against the wall we stand adjacent to and all over the dirt. Slowly dropping his body, to minimize any loud sounds, I clean my blade on his clothes, ripping the back of his shirt off to wipe at my hands and face.

A door opens somewhere behind me, and I turn to see the bartender has left through the back door. He partially yells and partially whispers, "What the fuck are you doing?"

"Killing Crows," I explain, nudging the body at my feet with my boot. "What are *you* doing?"

"Didn't like how he eyed that woman. Don't tolerate that behavior in these piers."

Rather than reply, I simply start to walk away so I don't lose Jane's trail. In the background I can hear the bartender grumbling, probably wondering what to do with the dead body now.

Returning to the road, I realize rather than going down to the docks, Jane has left to traverse on a pathless journey, her energy leading me right up the cliffs that overlook the ocean. I stay back and wait until she's far enough away that I can follow without her seeing me.

Where is she going?

I'll give her until morning to have solace with herself, right before her escape ship leaves. So she knows that even when she has her grip firm on hope, I will *always* find her.

PLOTTING FREEDOM

JANE

The salt-laden breeze gently moves through my hair, my gaze fixed on the horizon as I watch the sunrise. The blackened sky is eaten away by a pale blue. The sun will make its appearance any moment now, and then I will be on my way across the Black Sea.

No matter what, I also just can't see how I've already paid my debts, and the idea of cursing myself from ever touching the ocean again sounds like a terrible mistake.

I *need* these waters if I ever want to leave, and I also refuse to become a siren's curse. I'd honestly rather let the Council have me and grant me *some* kind of death, rather than live for hundreds of years below the waters.

I'm sitting above the shipyard where the cliffs are just beginning to form; if one travels a few days north on horse-back, the cliffs will rise to create the giant, sharp edges of Skull's Row. For now, I rest on a cold rock surface, loose pebbles beneath my feet.

Realizing I will never see Skull's Row again grips my heart in ways I was *not* prepared for. Memories surge through like a turbulent tide, my isolation finally hitting me.

Tears stream down my face as I take in the scent of my childhood—salty air and wet stone. Palming an eye, I look back down at the shipyard that's so small I can barely see the men. The captain said an hour past dawn and he would leave. *I guess this is really happening.* I hoped Cypress might've helped me uncover a creative solution out of all of this, or given me a good reason to believe her words rather than just say them, but I guess I at least have an 'heirloom' of sorts.

It's better than nothing.

The breeze picks up, the ropes of my escape ship flapping in the air, the crew arriving to begin lowering the sails.

I'm leaving soon. All of it. My home, memories, Kathleen...

My face morphs into a genuine cry at the guilt I feel for leaving her. But if my debt to Melona *isn't* paid, then it means my presence in Skull's Row *has* to be avoided or apparently it will wreak havoc on more than one soul. Let alone my own that might get tormented for who knows how long.

Why do I also feel like I'm mourning an entire life? As if I'm dead and I'm the only one to attend my wake?

I don't know. I think I always imagined Dad would somehow appear when I needed him most, and taking this option means he's truly gone.

The loss of my life and identity rips at my soul, twisting relentlessly.

Throwing my hand down, I hit the rock beneath me with a closed fist, rage begging me to hunt down anyone who might be asking for a fight. *No, you can't hit people until you're off that ship. It's not safe until then.*

Between hiccups and deep breathing, I swear I hear something behind me. At some point, I glance over my shoulder, my nose stuffy–

I scramble to my feet in a flurry of panic, my lips wordlessly moving before I shout, "Get the fuck away from me!"

Quite a few feet above me, the faintest glow of dawn reveals Soren crouching down at the edge of the rocky wall. He's wearing dark pants, boots, a black tunic, and a long leather jacket, his mask right at his hip.

The man towers over me like a vulture circling a dying animal.

"Did you enjoy the delay?" He languidly asks, his pale eyes barely visible. "What a useless waste of time this was."

My mouth is dry, my jaw shaking. "You know, it was going pretty well until you ruined it," I grunt, searching for an escape route. Truthfully, it's only up; right where *he* is.

Unless...

Don't think about it. Just do it.

I dash to my left and slide down a section of the cliff that's not so steep to cause a free fall, but it sure fucking hurts to descend, grunting when jagged rocks cut my legs through my pants. Moving like a thief, I brace myself every time I land something solid before swiftly adjusting to keep sliding. When the ground rounds outward to more stable land, I run without a second thought. The waters below are always a reminder of what will consume me if I fall.

Panting, I taste the salt in the air. Daring a glance, I pause when I realize he's not behind me. Did I lose him? Or can I just not spot him among the dark stone?

Not waiting to find out, I stare at a thin ledge; on the other side is flatter ground. Pressing my back against the rock, balancing myself against the jagged surface of this formidable barrier, I concentrate only on reaching my destination. Pieces of rock crumble and drop what must be five stories down into waves that slam into the wall below me.

Well, at least dying won't hurt if I fall.

Once I'm finally on a flatter surface, I begin climbing up. Ocean winds twist my hair into my face, the sound of heavy waves both terrifying and invigorating. My fingers ache as I climb, some of them bloodied, but once I touch the grass at the top, I grip it like its rope.

Pulling myself over with a victorious smile, I scream before I'm firmly on my feet.

Soren is *right* there—*fuck!* He just followed my intentions, didn't he? Knew which direction I was running in? "Get out of my head, you bastard!" I shout, attempting to run for it.

The truth is my body is tired. The wound in my stomach still needs proper rest, and I'm low on sleep. My endurance is utter shit.

I don't get far before his indomitable grip ensnares me like a cage, my legs kicking in futility as my back is against him, my arms subdued. Soren's grip tightens, my resistance utterly useless within his strength. I search my surroundings, desperately seeking any path to freedom.

How do I escape someone who can sense every crevice of me? More importantly—how did he not sense the *siren's sunder*? If I could tap into that...

He rasps into my ear, "I sensed you thinking of sirens, but I admit—didn't imagine you knew the fucking song."

"You seem to be able to read more than my *emotion*," I

grind out, still thrashing. "Bet you couldn't even find your foot without that skill of yours. Admit it—I outsmarted you. You cheating *bastard*."

The rugged coastline stretches out behind us, a mockery of how close I had been. In a burst of adrenaline-fueled instinct, I reach for the blade at my hip—my hands still free even if my arms are limited in movement—unsheathing it in a smooth motion. Just as I stab backward with no care as to wear my steel lands, Soren moves the both of us so my blade completely misses, striking empty air. "*Fuck* you," I grind out.

Through a myriad of struggling and a sudden, piercing pain in my thigh, the pressure around me releases. I don't question how—I bolt.

Running on the grass and trying to make my way to town where I can find a horse, it's not until I'm utterly out of breath that I realize something isn't right. Why did he let go? Eyeing the shipyard again, anger pierces my heart like a thousand stab wounds; my victory is right on my tongue, but I won't be afforded anything more than the slightest taste. Even if I barrel down to the docks, I can't get on the boat or they'll side with Soren and round me up for him. Running into the small town of Ender's Bay feels wrong, too, knowing his horse will be far superior compared to anything I could steal.

Looking up, I stare at the grassy top where the ocean and land meet.

In a panicked decision, I run upward and away from humanity, my aching legs pumping until I'm at the edge, my breathless state confusing me. Am I just this exhausted? Steadying my breathing, I close my eyes as the salty winds brush over exposed skin, my head spinning.

I can't return to Skull's Row. That's the priority. Fuck the others, even Cypress. I owe loyalty to the only one who helped me. I told her I wouldn't go back. That I'd fight.

Opening my eyes to take in the moving, gray waters ahead of me, I release a steady breath. Turning around, I wait as Soren slowly nears me, his dark clothes contrasting the morning light. He's a confident pillar against my chaos, moving as if I'm nothing more than a hindrance.

I barely challenge him, and it's *now* that I understand why they sent him—he can hunt me with that power of his, the one I don't completely understand. I can't imagine how else he would have known I was on the cliffs, let alone here.

I'm not escaping him.

"You were going to stab me?" he asks, his eyes empty of humanity. "I felt that. You didn't care where you landed."

"Am I supposed to care about the *Zenith* pursuing me? You must have hit your head along the way if you believe that."

He stops walking, heaving a great sigh. "If you just cooperated, you wouldn't have to panic like I'm a fucking spider you're outrunning."

My arms flail, looking in every direction. "Oh, right, go with you and hate my life until I'm executed. Sounds *so* tempting."

"Based on our last encounter, I'd say you'd enjoy yourself quite a bit."

My racing mind halts, finding something *interesting* about him openly mentioning what we did. Mindlessly, a laugh rolls out of me, so utterly lost. I have no escape plans anymore. Nothing.

Except to tumble over into the waters and hope I somehow live.

If not... then death it is.

"You know what? I *did* enjoy myself," I say, unable to fight the current. If I'm drowning, I'll do so with my identity intact. "And, *actually*..." I pull out his bag of coins, moving hair out of my face, and open it to grab a pair of ruby earrings. "I also *loved* buying these with your coin."

He squares his shoulders. "You *what?*"

I don't bother explaining that it's still an odd trade, one that makes me feel like Cypress simply made some coin off of my circumstances, but I *do* love seeing his face so engrained in shock.

Imitating him from earlier, I innocently place a hand over my chest. "I've *never* claimed to be a princess. Although these rubies might make me feel like one."

I've tried many approaches, but now, *nothing* matters. I've even tried to escape. There's no point in being cordial.

The mercenary tilts his head to the side, his indomitable eyes barely blinking as he motions with two fingers, grinding out, "Come. *Now.*"

"I already did that."

Whatever has gotten ahold of my tongue is relentless, freedom blossoming in knowing that I don't have to 'behave'.

I'll die before he takes me.

His chest steadily rises and falls, almost *too* methodically. "And what alternative do you have? You jump and it'll take too damn long to heal whatever injuries you suffer, *if* you even live."

I shrug, my voice shaking with more desperation than I prefer. "Don't care. I'll die with beautiful earrings and money still left to spare. Better death than most. Could use some wine or rum, but that's life, isn't it?"

He continues to stare at me. A nagging voice related to survival makes me wonder if there's a reason he's just standing there. He's *too* calm. Too collected.

I initially wrote off my body's weakness as just natural exhaustion, but it seems to be taking over with more force. Frowning, my heart also seems to pound uncontrollably. I stumble, looking down at my legs, my pants ripped from the tumble I took, and another spot looks deliberately cut, a bit of green mixing with the blood on my skin.

Did he...

"Asshole..." I manage out. Soren's poisonous assault explains his patience.

I mean to fall back so gravity may carry me over the cliff-side, but my legs give out as my body slams into the cold earth, my head spinning, hair in my eyes... my arm hangs off the edge, and I pull myself to peer over, the lapping waves hitting the rocks below. Maybe Melona is down there. Sirens have a similar *sight* to Cypress, so perhaps she knows I'll be plummeting soon—

The ground is removed from beneath me, Soren scooping me up effortlessly.

I'm limp in his grip as the drug consumes my consciousness. Panic is the last thing I remember as I accept that my grand escape has slipped through my fingers.

DECISIONS
SOREN

Jane's listless as I carry her, her dirty hair partially in her face as an arm dangles and sways. I eye the cliff edge; that had been far too close for my comfort. She demonstrated a clear modicum of a soldier's honor, harboring that sense of loyalty required to survive in Skull's Row and on the oceans we sail.

She's willing to die for her little siren friend more than trust the witch she sought. For whatever reason, all I felt when she spoke of Cypress was distrust.

It's not the reaction I expected, which means I need to tread carefully.

I move Jane to a flatter region where Phantom can reach us, laying her down on the grass so I'm not carrying her the entire way. There's no point in exhausting any ounce of energy if I don't have to, not when the air feels wrong. It's like the change in the sky before a storm approaches, although this is something only *I* can pick up on. I search Jane's body until I find my bag of coin tied around an empty belt loop, pausing to examine the laceration on her thigh.

Taking the bag off of her, I open it, looking at how much she spent. My brows raise as I see something wrapped in goat skin—the very thing she had pulled out—and unwrap it to confirm there are, indeed, ruby earrings from Cypress in there.

Great. So that bitch knows where we're at.

Cypress can see people easier through the fog of her visions if they wear her jewels. This leads me to wonder why the Scorpion would give these very jewels to his wife...

Unless Cypress was lying about the entire story.

Jane will have a lot to answer for when she wakes. As tempting as it is to chuck these earrings into the ocean, breaking or destroying her precious things will only make my life more miserable.

I can't have that while I'm still contemplating what Cypress told me.

Tying the coin back at *my* hip, I grunt at the idea of trying to coax the truth out of Jane. She's willing to die for her secrets. It's a pain, really. It's so much easier when someone responds to torture.

Sitting down next to her as she lightly breathes, I don't know what to do. In truth, she wasn't wrong at all—without my skillset, she *would* have gotten away. If she *had* gotten on that ship, it would have created enough of a gap that might have delayed me by an entire month.

Stopping to see Cypress might have cost her everything.

The decisions before me are vast and complex, like a butterfly wing about to flap and unravel fate. What if her father is the key to all of this? Do I go looking for him now? And when do I share that her father is alive? I'm assuming I'll know in the way I know everything else—it will eat away at my instincts until I act upon it.

She'll probably try to skin me if she finds out I know of her father and didn't tell her.

I smirk at the idea.

Looking ahead, one thing is for certain—*everything* has changed. Charles Ritter is a variable in this chaos I never anticipated. At the same time, Jane has to prove that if I loosen her chain, she won't run again.

She won't like it, but I *will* be keeping her *very* close. Bound, even. I may hate Cypress, but that's for personal reasons.

My gut screams at me to listen to the witch's words, which means Jane has to live.

I glance back down at her. There's something peaceful about her pretty face when she doesn't have the weight of the world wearing down her expression. "You're like trying to tame a fucking ship's cat," I mumble, running a hand over my head. "And I'm the idiot that keeps trying to feed it to hear it purr."

It doesn't take long for Phantom's black frame to appear in the distance as he makes his way to us.

I don't give a shit what the Council thinks anymore, not if the Scorpion is the way to my sister. I only joined their ranks because of their vast network and influence. Serena is the first person I've ever completely lost, following her trail across the Black Seas and into lands that I swore I felt her in... but *lost* her.

If Cypress hadn't stripped me bare the one time she fed me *dreamer's root*, I wouldn't believe her powers were as effective as they truly are. She had dug so deep that she saw my Serena, over those oceans, alive... and my intuition had never screamed louder that she was telling the truth, as if whatever magic flows through us connected in a maelstrom of insight.

Either way, I still have to take Jane to Skull's Row. Disappearing feels entirely wrong, something drawing me back to that dangerous whirlpool of villains.

For whatever reason, she has to go back.

And *then* we can leave.

Once Phantom is close enough, his thick black mane blowing in the salty breeze, I pick Jane up and place her on the horse before sitting behind her, getting her settled between my legs. I scan the scene, wondering if Charles Ritter is watching from somewhere.

Nothing would shock me anymore.

I kick Phantom forward, Jane securely in my grip. If I'm going to help her, we will need to establish some *very* concrete rules of engagement.

And since she responds so well to my touch, I might just have to fuck her into submission, so I can reap whatever fate has sewn.

BOUND

JANE

When my cognizance returns, I'm more alert this time. *Very* alert. I consider playing it off like I'm still asleep, listening to my surroundings to understand my predicament.

Nothing. *Silence.*

Summoning the courage to face the unknown, I cautiously open my eyes, surprised to realize I'm lying on a bed.

A *bed?*

Did I misremember my last encounter? Soren had taken me, right? My eyebrows knit with confusion, my elbows shooting outward in expectation for them to be met with the resistance of rope. I'm shocked when they move with freedom. Even my legs seem completely unrestrained.

I instinctively check for a window to understand the time —black curtains are tightly drawn, streaks of white light visible at the edges. It's well beyond morning.

For a few, long seconds I try to somehow reason that perhaps the ship is still anchored in the harbor. But I know it's not, and that skinny, bright streak of sun burns through me as if I'm staring into a mirror that only reflects my ruins; I can't believe this is my life.

I actually failed.

Survival demands that I accept the ship has sailed, as the longer I rely on hope as my savior, the more I waste precious time to try and escape the clutches of this man *again*.

Slowly moving my head, I languidly look around the place. Urgency is no longer scratching at my heart as if I know escaping won't matter. Besides, I don't even know where I'm at. The chambers have a simplicity that I wouldn't expect from Soren, only a few candles casting long shadows across unadorned walls.

As much as I'm eager to get to my feet, I lie there. I'm so tired of this. Not just with the shit related to Soren, but for hiding over the last decade—

The door to the room opens with a dramatic creaking of the hinges, my head craning to see Soren standing in the doorframe. I move to my feet, only slightly unsteady from the lingering effects of whatever he gave me. I pad at my bloodied, aching legs, searching for any of my things, but all I feel are layers of ripped clothes.

The bag of coins is also missing. While I *did* steal it from Soren, my origins in Skull's Row tell me I have every right to consider it mine now. The rubies mostly definitely are. "*Where are my earrings?*"

"That should have had you out for longer."

A bitter laugh escapes me as I lower my gaze to find where he sliced my skin, my futile resistance blurring the lines of indifference. "Feels exactly like urchin's kiss. Dad used to give it to me to lessen the effects, since it's so common," I say, leaning over to heal and numb the pain. "Now, where are my earrings?"

He stands there, dressed only in a black tunic and leather pants, all of his effects missing. Icy eyes are impossible to read. "All of that effort to free yourself and subdue me, and all you care about are your *earrings* from Cypress? Ones bought with *my* money?"

"How did you know where I went?" I ask, wondering if I had ever escaped him at all.

He moves purposely into the room, the heavy door closing behind him with an ominous *thud*. Dimly lit, his penetrating eyes pierce through, ensnaring me like a web I've worked so hard to escape but is impossible to untangle. "My ability to sense my environment manifests differently, much like how you can knock a man out with your magic rather than just heal. I'm more adept than others like me, which is why *I* have the Zenith tattoo. I will *always* know where you go, Jane.

"Now, we need to chat, because we aren't leaving this room until we have *both* come to an understanding, because I won't be so kind the next time I have to hunt you down."

My heart races so fast I nearly choke on my own spit when I swallow, still trying to heal what I can, in case I need to run.

Stop. Talk to him, first. You're not bound, so maybe he doesn't plan on beating you senseless. I attempt an appeal at any humanity he may possess while moving my hand to heal my knee. "I want the earrings because I don't have anything of my mother's, all right? I wanted the rubies she liked to buy, and

Dad got them from Cypress herself, and she was on the way. Please tell me they're still here."

Soren remains silent, his inscrutable indifference as annoying as Cypress's. "Why did you go to her? It's not just about the earrings, Jane. I can tell."

Don't lie. You're not hiding anything when this exhausted and he can feel it. "My dad visited her often. I thought she could help."

When I stand, I watch as a depth flashes across his face as if those words mean something. "He trusted her?"

"Does that even matter?"

He looks me over. "You're not the only one deciphering this situation, Zenith princess."

I scoff. "What does *that* mean?"

"It means I'm trying to understand what to do with you... You hit one of my men—Anya—and stole my money. Let alone knocking me out. Tell me... what do *you* think I should do with you?" His tone is clipped *just* enough to hint at potentially sinister things as if this room is about to become my torture chamber.

"*You* tell *me* why you aren't bashing my skull in," I reply, my body stiffening when my back hits a wall.

"Your little witch said some interesting things. It has me rather curious." He sucks his bottom lip to his teeth, his nostrils flaring. His gaze devours my face in a familiar tactic to decipher every crevice of my soul.

My mind halts in confusion when I replay his words. More gently than I meant to, I ask, "What did she say?"

Another step closer, the space between us thinning. "Ah, ah. I don't think you're the one to be asking questions, Jane."

"You could have met her years ago, then realized I liked her just now, and decided to tell me a bunch of lies."

The surrounding darkness adds an eerie depth to his grin

as he takes *another* step, slowly placing a hand on the wall to entrap me even more as if every inch of space between us matters. "I worried the same thing, that perhaps she was telling me half-truths or outright lies. But *if* her words have *any* weight... I've been thinking them over since I left her. Which means we have to have a conversation about your proclivity to flee."

My heart and mind are pulled in a dozen directions, torn between accepting the reality of my re-capture and the surprising change of his tone. My gaze inadvertently lowers, fixating on his low-cut black tunic that reveals the top design of the skull tattoo visible on his chest. There's a faint scar, pale against his skin, just above the gold ink that flickers as if made of liquid metal.

The connection of our fates is murky at best, my obligations no longer clear to me. Melona warned me with a vision I *couldn't* ignore, and yet Cypress seemed strangely unconcerned when I begged for help. Soren might be silent while I filter through everything that overwhelms me, but I know he's absorbing everything I consider. What's the point in fighting it anymore? He's able to hunt me in ways that make any effort useless. He's my survival line, whether I like it or not because he's also my anchor. I confess, "The siren that taught me the sunder told me the Council can never have me."

When I look up through my lashes, his eyes burn with insight. "*That's* why you're so panicked?"

"Well, other than the *obvious*. I'm fond of living at the moment, so that's a big factor," I sarcastically reply. "Plus, you know how it goes. A siren gives you a prophecy and you have to heed their words, or else get sucked under if you go near the coasts again. Returning to Skull's Row means I break her prophecy, so I'm currently trying to avoid that fate."

"What else did she say?" He gentles his words again. "Tell me the truth. I can't help with half-truths."

I'm at the point where I have to gamble now. Silence isn't going to yield any respite from death. The nagging suspicion that this is all an elaborate ruse to get me to speak pecks harder at my brain, but I also can't give up and do *nothing*. "Fine. She told me that the prophecy would relinquish when a debt is paid, but didn't tell me what that debt was. So all I had to go by, for years, was that I can't go back to Skull's Row. If I do, it'll start a catalyst of death for many innocents. Let alone the horrible fate for *myself* if I break it in general," I begin, trailing off as I stare at the ink on his chest once more.

He articulates very slowly, his rough voice leaving no room for dissent. "Keep. Talking."

I draw in a shaky breath as I add, "There's honestly not much more to say. I promised her I wouldn't go back, and in turn, she taught me the sunder, mentioning that once the debt is paid, my life will be free. But again, she didn't *tell* me what that debt was, saying something about how I couldn't know or else I'd seek it prematurely—" I pause, but before deciding to keep going. "We bound it in a blood oath, and then she drowned me so she could revive me, my soul branded with this promise."

By the craggy gods that must exist, does it feel good to finally confess this to someone. Even the part about being drowned, something I haven't told *anyone*.

I'll never forget my lungs filling with frigid salt water... even if I wish I could. Turns out, I do *not* like drowning.

A low grumble emanates from his chest as if he's considering those words like they mean something. "And your witch? What did she say when you visited her?"

I huff, moving my head with my words as I dramatically

reply, "She just said what I wanted to hear and then offered me those earrings."

"There's more, Jane."

"*Fine*. She told me that I already paid my debt to my siren... but I simply don't believe her. That's ridiculous."

"That's because you don't believe *anyone*."

My fists clench, ready to hit him right in that tattoo. "It doesn't matter—going back sounds like a rather terrible idea overall, so, I regret nothing."

"You do understand I *am* taking you to Skull's Row? Not only does it feel like something I must do, but hiding you wouldn't do any good. They'll eventually send more than just me."

This simply won't do. I need reassurance that they won't get to do with me as they please. I look into his eyes. "Okay, let's say I *did* pay my debt and I can just suddenly go about my day like the prophecy never existed. If the Council tries to stick me in the spiraling tower to freeze, or place me deep in their dungeons to be lost forever, you have to promise to stab me first."

"No," he declares.

I tuck my chin into my neck, almost offended. "So, a painful death is my fate, then?" My voice cracks. "You want me to just accept that?"

"You're not useful to them, so they do not need to imprison you. To which *I* will keep them at bay. Stop being stubborn."

The *words* are what I want to hear, but the *offer* irritates the part of my heart desperate to trust; so very aware of how easy it would be for Soren to manipulate me. The man remains as still as stone, only his chest rising and falling in front of me. I hardly blink as I ask, "You changed your mind this much because of something Cypress said?"

A few moments pass before he replies, "I became a Zenith

because the mask is feared, and I agreed to the rules of the Council because they have a collective network that I need. Your little witch gave me *another* opportunity, and it involves keeping you alive. So, I'm keeping my options open."

I crane my whole head to look into his face. He's a scary fucker with little scars becoming more apparent the longer I stare, the man an embodiment of the very world that makes me a hopeless creature to men like him. "And I'm simply supposed to trust you? Trust Cypress? No one is giving me *anything*. Only Melona gave me something concrete, but it's not like I can ask her for insight. I don't even know where I'd find her."

His tone is gentler as he replies, "We both know there's nothing I can offer you that would gain your trust, other than to free you. Same goes for Cypress. I suggest you find a way to accept that things have changed, even if you have blatant trust issues."

Taking in the stubble lining his cheeks, my heart is fascinated with the intimate side of him.

His kinder voice is like sustenance to a starving man, filling the void that's eating away at itself. Knowing that he can even attempt to be a man worth bargaining with is somehow more painful, like I managed to get just *that much closer* to the surface.

The fight inside my chest is eaten away by exhaustion. Melona's warning once guided me like a northern star, and now I can't spot it in the sky anymore. "Give me my rubies and I'll cooperate."

His lips twitch into a stifled laugh, those battle-hardened eyes softening.

I add, "I'm serious. I haven't touched a piece of home in *years.*"

An energy changes about the Zenith, reminding me of

someone who caves when they know they shouldn't. Much like I do when he touches me. He sounds almost amused as he says, "Would go nice with your hair..."

My eyes widen as I grind out, "I don't like you."

Unphased, he says, "We both know that's a lie."

"It's only because I've lived among simple men for too long. Don't get an ego over it. You're not special," I defend, not sure what to do with my hands. The drive to assault him doesn't exist like it did before, not when I recall how he held me down...

"I wonder if you'd say those words when I'm balls deep inside of you," he boldly states.

My body's betrayal is a familiar friend when it comes to Soren, my mind numb to any obligations I may I owe.

His thumb rises to touch my bottom lip. "You came so easily, love."

Soren's words melt away at what resistance I had left. Which is a terrifying idea. Maybe I should stamp hard on his foot, and just run for the coast and hope the sirens will help me—

His grip around my throat tightens, nearly hurting me. "Don't even try it."

I wish I could read him the way he can read others. He gets in my face, Soren's walls fading as a deep craving clouds his gaze; it's the only warning I have before his lips crash onto mine in an unforgiving kiss. His forceful tongue fills my mouth, and because I'm no better, I kiss him back with a heart that has no idea what to feel.

A carnal passion engages in a battle of tongues, lips, and teeth. There's a raw intensity that's different from the other night, as if the enraged behemoth channels his frustration in this aggressive exchange.

His calloused hands run underneath my tunic and across

my skin, yanking my shirt off while hair shrouds my vision. My nipples harden as my skin pebbles from the air.

"What are you doing?" I manage to utter, my lips swollen from our fervent exchange. I hope he understands I mean the question in the broader spectrum of our actions.

"This whole situation has completely fucked everything up," he complains, throwing my shirt onto the floor before tearing off his own. "So, I'm going to angrily fuck you and hope it helps."

"Don't make me swoon all at once," I halfheartedly joke before I take a step near to place my hands on his face and bring him to my level.

And that tongue of his when we kiss again, the way it claims my mouth before he bites my lower lip while his hands untie my leather pants, has me blind to the world. "Take them off," he huskily commands.

I remove them as quick as I can—because I *also* want to angrily fuck Soren. Once both legs are out, I realize I failed to notice that he pulls out a piece of red rope from near his cloak on a dresser; *his* color.

I fixate on what he holds, but the man is quick like he's done this more than once. Just as I'm about to move away, the killer is on me with my back to his stomach while his powerful arms hold me in place. He loops my hands through a pre-made knot, pulling it to immobilize my wrists. He ensures it's taught —despite my squirming and stomping on his boots—then releases me.

Naked and exposed, I turn to glare at him as I try to move my wrists through my constraints. The reckless side to my heart revs with hunger, while my remaining sanity tells me to be prepared for *anything*.

Whatever mercy he has will be my salvation.

Soren's domineering gaze haunts me as he unhooks his

belt, the two ends dangling as he closes in the space between us. I jerk my hands away because I still don't know who he truly is and what his intentions are, but he grabs one of my arms to hold me still, sliding his belt from his pants to loop through my bindings. Yanking gets me nowhere, his smile the only tangible response from him.

Soren pulls me toward the bed, the understanding of truly being at his utter mercy slowly sinking in. My mouth hangs open with words I'm eager to speak, and yet I remain completely mute.

I simply didn't picture this when I imagined him coming for me.

The Zenith pushes me on the bed and I fall with no grace. He grabs my bound wrists and lifts them above my head never allowing me a moment to adjust. My restless legs are useless at this angle, my flailing body and grunts only an embarrassment as he runs his belt around one of the metal frames to the bed, buckling me to it. All I can really do is watch the muscles of his stomach move, craning my neck to see his concentrated face.

I give the strongest jerk I have once he drops his hands, but there's no give at all. My heart races and my jaw trembles, never having been so restrained before, while confusingly *liking* it.

He dares to lean down over me, gripping my jaw while I'm immobile, some strands of his bound hair in his eyes. I try to jerk my head away, but he holds me still and says, "Being bound is what you get for your last stunt." He releases my face and I jerk it to the side as if to convince myself I'm not completely subjected to his whim. I give him a look similar to how he was looking at me back when he realized I was singing the *sunder*—I'm angry and horny as hell. He runs his hand over the pink scar on my stomach from where Anya stabbed me.

"Stop behaving like a scrappy fighter, and you won't get

more of these," he says, those eyes locking away his true thoughts, and I don't have any option but to watch how he touches me. "Especially if you knock me unconscious again."

I'm silent, turned on, and *so* confused. Soren steps away from the bed to untie his pants, his forearms rippling with the motion as I bareface watch him; his hips become visible. *Fuck, what's wrong with me? I should be thrashing, kicking, or biting the air. Shouting for help. Anything.*

Instead, I simply exhale with a heady need at the way his veined, hard cock is revealed, the damned thing large enough to concern me. Primal cravings hypnotize my rationale, realizing he's going to have his way with me, and I'm *very* confident I will relish in it.

Where did the Jane go that would fight to the death when entangled like this? Who is this silent woman I find myself inhabiting? And why does this work so perfectly? I still feel an obliged confliction in my desires for Soren, and this sets me free of that.

His body is perfection, thick with muscle and healed wounds slashing through his thighs. Neither of us speaks as he mounts the bed, the furniture taking the weight of him as I grip his belt to hold me steady to prevent my arms from stretching too far.

All right, I indulge. I'm enjoying this, even if I worry that he's going to betray me... even if I'm afraid that being intimate with him sabotages any ability for me to have a normal relationship after this.

Closing my legs seems like an interesting option—I'm caught in the wake of whatever power exchange is happening, and I want him to pry them open. He gives a dark glower when my knees tightly sew together, his lips curling into a smile as he can no doubt feel that I *want* this.

He slides his hands in between my thighs and parts me

open, all the while devouring my face to translate the storm inside of me. He lines himself between my legs so the back of my thighs rest on top of his, his cock resting right on my cunt as I shiver from anticipation.

I'm so close to moaning, that dignity seems unable to exist inside my treacherous heart.

"When we get to Skull's Row, are you going to run?" he asks, maintaining this posture of dominance.

"I don't know," I confess.

"I'm a disciplined man, Jane. I can stay here as long as you need before the lesson sinks in that you don't run from me while you're in my charge. The time spent to track you down was a *waste*."

I'm so slick at this point, distracted by thoughts of what he's going to say when he finds out how wet he makes me. He slowly rocks his hips, watching me with unblinking eyes as he grazes my clit. I actually moan as my eyelids lower.

When I can't find any words, Soren deftly adjusts his alignment as I feel the tip of his cock find its place before sliding inside of me with a singular motion, his gaze glued to mine like he's enjoying the thrill of me losing myself to him.

"*Ah*!" I gasp, which rolls into a loud moan.

My pussy burns from the sudden stretching, but the way he deeply penetrates has my legs going limp.

His laugh fills the quiet room. "You're so *fucking* wet."

I moan so loud I'm ashamed of myself. Soren leans over, every bit of his powerful stomach and shoulders moving as he pushes further into my slick heat, and I'm so full of this mercenary that I swear I can't fit any more of him.

The dying fight inside of me manages to speak through my debauched haze, "For all I know, this is a part of the plan. They sent a Zenith that's—well, that looks like you, to lure me in..."

He smiles, slowly moving, and never pulling out far. It's

like he wants to bury himself into me over and over, and the sensation of being *filled* by this mercenary legend takes me to another level. "You're going to have to complete that thought."

"No, I don't," I grind out, but the shake of my arms reminds the both of us that I'm in no position to negotiate.

"You're the one bound, love, and you can't touch me with your magic, either. If you sing your little song, I'll just shove my cock between those pretty lips."

My eyes roll while I look away, groaning, especially when his thighs are flush with the back of mine. My legs willingly spread more, helping him.

I've neglected this side of me for far too long, and Soren is playing me like a rusted instrument, cleaning me for his use.

"Say it," he commands, one hand gripping the back of my thigh as the other touches all over my ribs, breasts, and tattoo. "I'm a Zenith that's... finish the thought."

"You're fucking attractive, okay?" I grind out, not looking at him.

He moves a hand to grab my face, and it's not like I can stop him. His piercing eyes are raw with captivation. Soren thrusts in as my body shudders, leaning over to crush my lips with his. Just as annoyed, he says into my mouth, "And you're such a pretty thing that I can't focus."

I *hate* this man.

His laughter taunts me. "You are so fond of lying to yourself."

Soren changes tempo, moving in and out so when I look down, I can see his slick shaft disappearing into me, over and over. His pants turn into groans when I squeeze his cock, sounds of pleasure flowing out of me unconstrained; I even rise to kiss him, and he happily leans down to greet my lips, sliding the hand that's on my jaw underneath my head to fist my hair, his tongue smoothly gliding against mine. The bed moves with his rhythm, the wooden floor creaking, my hands still firmly bound.

The hand behind my thigh slides down further, his stomach now touching mine. Our matching inscriptions of ink nearly graze at times.

Soren parts from the kiss, watching my face as he growls when my eyes nearly roll. I stare at the handsome, scarred face, those lips perfectly plump but still masculine. "Why don't you just hurt me?"

He pushes harder into me, pleasure spreading across his face when I gasp. "We're in the same boat, love. Annoyingly attracted to the other." He shoves in hard once more, the bed creaking. "But don't fucking take off again," he gets rougher, more unforgiving, and I just pant with an unholy bliss. "Or I'll fuck your needy cunt right in front of my men."

"*Gods*, I loathe you," I moan out. My eyes beseech me as I glance down to watch his hips move as he fucks me, whimpering when I feel an orgasm rising.

"Come for me again, Zenith princess." Soren's voice is raw and needy, fucking me purely for his own gratification.

His name escapes my lips, his groan sharpening with possession. I chase that feeling, knowing my release is close. Screw it, I need this. He angles just right, a sexual whine crooning in my throat.

I close my eyes when my clit rubs against him, trying to imagine he's someone else—

His body stiffens as he rasps, "No, you look at me and come on my cock knowing *exactly* who's fucking you."

I hold my breath, staring into those pale eyes... Soren Latham. The Zenith sent to capture me is who I'm coming for. Euphoria rushes over me and there's a moment of clarity where I realize I'm actually going to come for him and there's nothing I can do. I can't stop his perfect rhythm or shift my body, and the way ecstasy consumes me as I scream out—the mercenary swiftly fucks to his own rhythm before pushing deep into me one last time, his stolid face contorting with a lack of control when he reaches his climax nearly at the same time as me.

We both pant, our bodies so thoroughly interlocked I can feel him pulsating as he continues to spill into me. My body is blissfully spent, the weight of Soren leaning into me, making me feel oddly calm. He leans down so our lips graze, staring right into my eyes as he says, "I'll *always* find you, Jane. Never forget that."

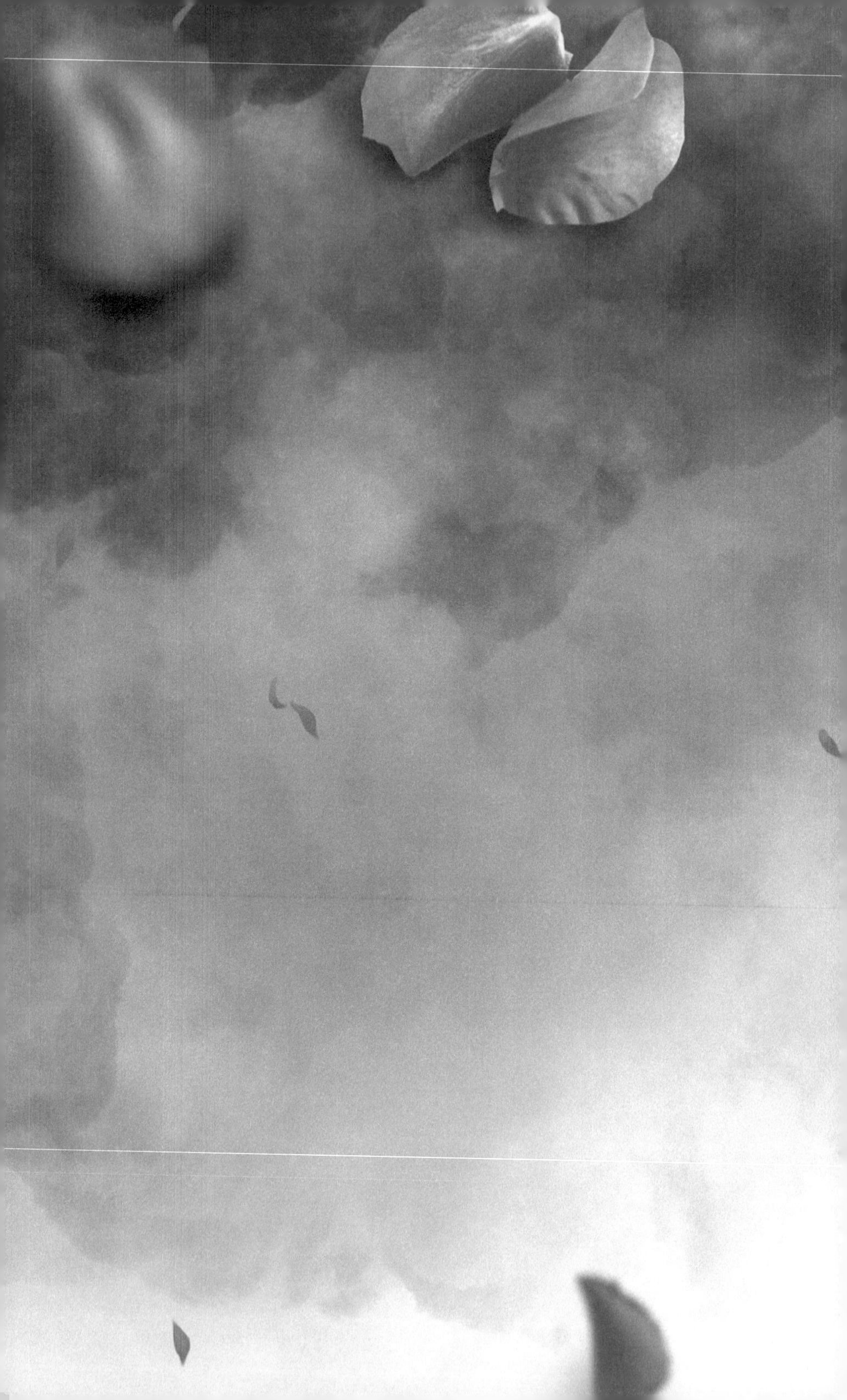

ACCEPTING FATE
JANE

I've *never* been taken in such a way, nor have I ever felt so satiated. Unbinding my hands removes the visage that I didn't want or need him in such a way, the man reaching up to unbuckle me before lifting himself off to stand.

Once I sit up, he unties the rope before it unravels into my lap. Without another word, he nears the mess of clothes on the floor until he finds his pants.

Observing him dress makes him look, well, like a *man* rather than an otherworldly creation of Skull's Row. Soren surely has his own wants, desires, hates, and *some* kind of fear.

I have to tap into that, somehow...

The mood of the room is bound by a curious silence, as if he hadn't fucked me so hard that I'm worried about an uncomfortable horse ride. Nearing my pile of dirty, shredded clothes, he hands a cloth towel at me, and I clean myself. I start redressing, unable to hold onto a single thought.

Is this really my life? Did I enjoy that more than I should have? After catching him searing his unique perception into my skin more than once, I finally say, "I know you're reading me when you stare at me like that."

He chuckles as he laces his boots. "Get used to it. I can't turn it off. Since you're as hard to pry information from as a greedy thief, I have to resort to reading you."

He stands, grabbing the rope on the table, nodding toward my hands. "Now stick out your hands. Since I still don't trust you not to run, you're going to be tethered to me, and your wrists *will* remain bound. But once we're inside Skull's Row, if I tell you to jump three times and give me a twirl, you better do it."

"You don't want me twirling."

"That's not for you to decide." He motions to my wrists.

I can't honestly say why I am going along with this as I stick my hands out. Did me fighting him get the two of us entangled in something Melona left out in her prophecy? Or does Cypress's apathy to Melona's vision give me the permission I need to pursue Soren?

Perhaps I don't actually know how to make these decisions anymore. There's so much uncertainty and unknown; I dread making the wrong choice.

"What is the fear for?" he asks, his tone patient and also tired.

"I don't know what I'm supposed to do anymore," I mumble as I watch him.

"Neither do I." When the last bit is taught, he steps away,

taking his bag of coin and attaching it to his belt loop with a snap of his wrists, as if to assert *that's* where it belongs.

"Where are my earrings?"

His shoulders rise with a sigh before he opens up the leather pouch to show me they're in there, wrapped in goat skin. My muscles stiffen as I want to snatch them, but he's already closing the pouch before I can. "You'll get these *after* the Council."

I huff, although I still don't fight him. What's the point when I'm basically being forced to trust him? If Cypress isn't lying, then I *can* return.

Trusting someone is very hard for me to do, the act of doing so dredging up horrible sensations of abandonment.

He nears the door to open it, glancing back down at me. The setting is intimate in its own way, the animosity removed in a false sense of security. My heart flips, making me blurt out, "I like the stubble."

"Want to know what it feels like between your thighs, love?"

My lips purse as I hold a smile down, walking through the open door. "Stop that."

"Yes, wouldn't want us to do or say anything inappropriate to each other."

I'm too tired to hold back my laugh, the juxtaposition confusing me the most. If it weren't for the rope around my wrists, we might look as if we had known each other for a very long time. Glancing over my shoulder, I glimpse an erasure of murder in his eyes, the mercenary stiffening once my gaze is on him. Spinning around, I refuse to even acknowledge how that struck at something deep and needy within me, as if it's a vision into what it might be like to have him as an ally.

I shiver from the cold morning when we leave the drab inn, assuming we're still in Bensen's Bay. A woman shouting for her sale of oysters makes it almost seem casual, until everyone spots Soren—no doubt eyeing the mask at his hip—and focuses their attention on us.

My body trembles from the cooler air, having lost my warmer clothes in a bag while I was trying to escape. Soren seems to have predicted this, reaching into a bag bound on his horse's saddle and pulls out a dark wool cloak that he wraps around me. I ignore the gratitude I have, the two of us not speaking a word.

Discipline, Jane. Control yourself.

Soren and I stand next to Phantom who is so tall I can't mount it by myself. For a moment, the mercenary and I just stare at each other, the horse swatting flies with its tail and stomping a foot. Soren nods to the saddle, but I don't move.

It's not in me to go *this* easily, not when I don't think I'm ready to face the Council. I've been so busy trying to run away that I didn't prepare myself for actually *going* there.

"Jane..."

"Soren..."

"Put your hands on the horn, and I'll lift you."

He raises a brow before sighing, understanding I'm being a stubborn mule again. He grabs my waist and hoists me up without warning; I grab the horn of the saddle for stability, throwing my leg over it, not wanting to fall off this damn thing. He mounts Phantom from behind me, his large body acting like a wall to lean against. There doesn't seem to be much point in preventing my ass from rubbing against his crotch—might as well be comfortable.

He lets me adjust however I need, both his arms on either side of me with his hands on the reins.

I don't bother to say anything about riding together as we trot off, my hands still bound as we pass by those living in this port town. Meanwhile, he rides as if none of this bothers him. I begin to wonder if I'm the first person to distract him this much, or if he's just this good—

He leans in, rasping into my ear, "Yes, you are."

I sigh, looking up at the heavy clouds as we leave civilization behind us. "I just *love* having a conversation while not talking."

Our bodies move to the rhythm of his horse. "You're going to realize how much time was wasted worrying that I'm going to feed you to the sharks. I wasn't going to, even *before* Cypress."

"You don't even know why the Council wants me. How can you predict if you can keep me alive or not?"

"Because I am among them. I bet it's their damn pride that they're angry over."

"And if that's not the case?"

"We'll figure it out, then."

I eye the red rope on my wrists. "Also, why am I bound when it's just us? What am I going to do, jump off and run into the woods?" I ask, scanning the surrounding forests now that the bay is behind us.

"Given our most recent encounter, it's for your own good."

"Or yours, so I can't subdue you."

His laugh is laced with incredulity.

I smile, but only for a moment, as I try to imagine sitting like this for over a day as we ride back. "Why did you come alone?"

"You said it was business, but it's personal."

"How?"

He's unabashed as he says, "The last thing I remember before the fucking lights went out, was you feeling regret. You're lost right now, and those words you whispered snagged my curiosity. So, it's personal."

My spine shivers with a new kind of revelry. I'm all

wrapped up in his darkness and I just want to burrow further into it.

"Why did your mother prefer rubies?" He asks.

I can't tell if he's curious, or simply wants to gain more intel. It's only when I actually consider the question that a profound sadness returns to me. "I never asked her, actually."

He's quiet for a long moment before asking, "How did she die?"

"Someone came to murder her. It caught us by surprise, especially when he stabbed her in the heart." I hardly blink as my expression deadpans with recalling the details. "I'll never forget his ugly face and that gap between his teeth. I grabbed a dagger and jumped on his back, stabbing him in the neck." My voice quiets. "When we fell, I took it out and stabbed him in the heart, over and over until Mom said my name. I went to her —" my voice hitches "—and I tried to heal her. But some wounds are tricky. Impossible, even. I bet... I bet if I was older, though, I could have figured it out."

"Perhaps. Perhaps not. Being stabbed in the heart has never been something many heal from, if at all," he says, his voice the gentlest yet. "I'm sorry to hear you lost her to such brutality."

Fuck this asshole. He thinks he's so smooth... but gods help me, because for a very long, profound moment, I find myself eagerly desiring nothing more than for this to turn into something completely unexpected. Especially as I wipe my eyes, the strength of his body behind me almost comforting.

And the fact that I know he can feel that, and doesn't say a word, tempts me all the more.

The ride is long and full of silence ever since that conversation, and yet when we arrive back at Dryhill in the very early morning, it feels like no time has passed. I even found myself slipping into slumber somewhere along the journey, waking up at one point with Soren's arm around my waist to prevent me from falling.

I didn't thank him for that.

That's not within my capabilities. Not yet. Not right now. I don't fully trust the man… not until I witness his behavior with the Council. He will only receive my gratitude once he's proven he can keep his promises.

His men are waiting by the northern stables, probably seeing us arrive from a turret's watch. The front gates are open, welcoming back their leader whose chest I've been using as my resting board. It's that perfect time of morning when everything feels calm.

I have to admit I'm impressed to see how effortlessly everyone falls into line for Soren, a reminder that at least it wasn't a random fisherman that managed to track me down— I was up against the impossible.

He snickers and leans into my ear again, breaking the long silence. "Impressed by me, princess?"

"You and your nicknames," I chide, covering a yawn, my back starting to ache.

"They're called pet names, love," he corrects, humor laced in his stupidly alluring voice.

I'm about to retort, but my body stiffens when I see Kathleen on a horse at the open gate, Bones standing right by her. "Kathleen is coming?" I ask, my heart racing with worry.

"No idea. I've been a little busy chasing *you* down." His subsequent sigh is laced with a weighted annoyance. "Do you think your friend can even handle Skull's Row?"

"Kathleen can take care of herself. The bigger question is will toad-face take care of her, or use her?"

He laughs, nearly all of his mercenaries giving their full attention when they hear humor come from their commander. "Toad face?"

"He looked like a toad before I healed him," I say, glaring at Bones from a distance.

"I suppose that's warranted. And I can't promise anything, as I don't know her, or her intentions with Bones," he replies, and I purse my lips when that's a fair point.

"I don't want Kathleen to get hurt," I insist. I figure there's no point in hiding our friendship from him—he's probably already deeply aware of the affection I have for her.

"I'm not about to have strangers travel among my company beyond what we owe the villagers. My men don't keep long-term pets that we take with us." He dismisses my worries as he follows his statement with, "So what nickname would you give *me*, then?"

It's hard to flirt with him when I'm worried for my friend, although I see opportunity in letting my desires get the best of me—any bit of negotiation room I can manage is crucial. Kathleen is relying on me.

A wicked smile comes to my face when I try to imagine something to slash at his ego... but the smile fades when I can't think of a clever one; the only things coming to mind revolve around praising him: *handsome tempter, annoyingly sexy...* or there's the more offensive *captor, asshole, tyrant...*

But something tells me he'll only laugh at those.

Maybe... what if... *yes*. Maybe I should say something that will make his head spin in ways he doesn't anticipate. See if I really *do* have his attention.

"I'd simply call you *handsome*," I say, straightening my back.

He moves in the saddle as if to get a better look at the back of my head, gripping the reins tighter, his voice the most playful yet. "Are you openly flirting with me, Jane?"

It takes everything I have not to grin like an idiot, aware of how *everyone* is watching us from a distance. "And that's all you get, Soren."

It's so tempting to look over my shoulder to see his face— to witness the sway I *may* have over him—but instead, I worry my lip to the point that it almost bleeds, trying to stifle a grin that threatens to form. Especially when instead of replying, he lets out this low grumble, like he takes it as a challenge he's very eager to accept.

I need to jump into the cold ocean after this—hopefully that'll shock Soren right out of my system.

Or punch someone.

Oh, how I miss hitting people. It was so simple, back then...

He dismounts Phantom once we're at the gates, helping me down as all eyes are glued to me in anticipation. One of his men approaches as if to lead me away like a prisoner, while Anya fishes out pieces of Soren's armor from a pouch on Phantom.

Soren eyes the man nearing me and sharply reprimands, "Only I handle Jane. No one else."

The admonishing eyes of the mercenary leader make *everyone* step away from me, even if they were already a few feet away.

Soren looks back down at his bracers and works the buckles as Anya dutifully brings over his chest piece, the woman not once looking at me while she removes his leather jacket. Bones gets the rest of his men in line, Kathleen eagerly watching on. When we make eye contact, I give her a reaffirming nod, then raise my brows, inclining toward her as if to ask if she's okay.

A firm, stiff bend of her neck gives me affirmation, then she smiles before looking away. Well, at least she's all right.

I also catch Kathleen's cue—we shouldn't look at each other right now, or else it might highlight our friendship in front of the others. *Of course.* I need to get my head on straight.

I uselessly stand next to Phantom, watching as Soren gives commands of where we're going, completely avoiding delivering any remarks about the events of my recapture, despite the eagerness in everyone's eyes. So, that's how it will be, then? He and I will share our little secret with each other that rather than coming to hurt me, he chose to fuck me?

My heart tangles within itself, unable to make heads or tails of my predicament.

Once he gets his blades affixed, he nears a riderless brown horse and brings it over to me, tying it to Phantom.

He lowers his head to look down at me, and I realize I've been staring hopefully at this man the whole time, like I'm eager for any sign of him *really* helping me. Him not saying a word about my capture is a good start.

As he runs a hand on the soft fur of the horse, he quietly says, "It's your choice now, Jane, on how you act. If you want your freedom, then your fate is yours to write. Either listen to me when we arrive or don't. Your decision."

Clenching my jaw, I brace myself as he reaches for my hips, hoisting me onto the horse and leaving no room for reply. Once I find my balance and have my feet in the stirrups, Soren mounts Phantom, completely leaving it all to me.

Well, I didn't quite expect that.

Is that his tactic? Do things I don't expect so as to get my guard down? I yawn again, looking down at the reins in my dirty, bound hands, kicking my horse when Phantom leads us back through the gates as my ass already aches.

The Zenith's company rides straight northeast toward Skull's Row.

Well, with Melona's prophecy apparently null and void, and after meeting with Cypress, I suppose I have to grit and bear what comes next; hope that I truly *am* free.

Whether I like it or not, I'm finally going home.

SOREN

No one has asked me about Jane; Bones's glare is the closest to questioning what in the hells happened, but that's it. I know everyone is wondering why someone I've been sent to capture—who subsequently escaped—merely looks tired and unharmed.

And it's none of their fucking business.

The clouds give us a reprieve from the blaring sun on the fifth day of our journey—despite it being rather brisk outside —and I sense how tired Jane is on her horse.

Her body is aching, even if she doesn't tell me.

I'm still processing how if it weren't *me* that was assigned to her, Jane would have managed her escape. What the fuck do I do with knowing I'm not even mad at what Jane did to me? She's acting as a daughter of a Zenith should. It would have been comedic to see the rest of the Council's faces if they heard she *escaped.*

Unless they know who she is... but I never got that sense from any of them. All I ever heard was that a few scouts spotted a suspicious woman, Blackwell demanding she be brought in and that his reasoning would be made clear once she was among us.

Jane yawns, the energy exhausting me as a wave of her fatigue washes my way.

"I'm going to fall off my horse at this rate," she quietly says.

"It will help if you look a *little* miserable. And we're getting closer."

She looks my way and I slowly meet her gaze; those round, yet lively, honey-colored eyes capture my attention. My cock hardens as I remember how full of lust they were only a few day ago, how she couldn't admit that she enjoyed when I bound her.

"Staring at me for more information?" she asks, yawning again. "Don't you have enough?"

I smile, glad that we ride so others can't hear us, the rhythm of Phantom's movement mindless to me at this point. "You've been guarding them since you learned of my powers. Means I have to exert extra effort."

She snorts. "Only an idiot would let you read them like an open book."

Scanning the lands that pine tree forests line, I lift my head to see where the sun sits in the sky. *Perhaps a break isn't unwarranted. Then again, we're almost there.* I can see Jane's not lying about being tired. Her breathing is slower, like a deep sleep is about to consume her. It *would* be nice to have her sleep against my chest on this horse, to further add to her confusion about why she wants me. I greatly enjoy being the one that binds her tongue, tempted even more by the fleeting thoughts that perhaps hinted at something deeper brewing in her chest.

She *wants* to trust me. To use me as comfort.

Facing forward, I give a call that's strictly for Bones, the sound like that of a bird.

The black horse he rides slows down, waiting for Jane and me to be nearby. At least this conversation should keep her awake, Jane's weariness already staving off at the sudden break in monotony.

Bones rides next to me, eyeing Jane carefully. I haven't spoken about her since I returned with her on Phantom, and I know someone like Bones sees the undertones. We've been on these dirt roads for five days already, Jane kept at a distance and sitting alone when we rest for the night.

I nod ahead to the blonde he so carefully watches over, the woman surrounded by others. "None of the other villagers have followed this far. Yet *she* has. It's time we talk about her, Bones. We can't take random people with us. She has to go her own way in Skull's Row, or you house her there."

Bone's gaze flicks at Jane—I know he's aware she's not just a prisoner anymore. I don't know what the fuck she is, but I'll steal the woman straight from Skull's Row if *they* make it complicated. Let alone all the words that Cypress spoke about the Scorpion being alive, and having to protect his daughter.

I have yet to confide that with Bones or Anya. I'm not quite sure if I should keep it all to myself or not.

Bones says, "I'm taking my Kathleen to Skull's Row and getting her situated there. She won't travel with us once I get her settled."

Settled... so he plans to keep her? I start with, "Does she *want* to?"

"What of *your* treasure? Does she like being bound like that?" he asks, looking at Jane with annoyance, flaring his nostrils.

I wickedly grin, knowing that she does. "She's currently a captive for the Council. The sooner we get that over with, the better. She stays bound. It helps that she likes it."

If I were to look at her, I bet I'd see Jane glaring at me like she's going to stab me. I try my best not to laugh at how quickly her fire burns.

Bones's voice grates against the air like it's made of sandpaper, "Kathleen didn't grow up in that village. My kitten is a worldly woman," he says with pride. There's a threat in there as well; he won't give her up so easily. "She will survive Skull's Row. There's no reason not to take her there."

Discomfort bleeds from a silenced Jane. These two are like testy fucking dogs fighting over territory. "Then she can handle a conversation with me," I say, a fraction of concern flashing through Bones. "You stay here with Jane. I'm riding ahead to Kathleen."

I've watched her from afar for the last few days. Not much exudes from her other than an undeniable interest in Bones. Sometimes fear.

She hardly seems to feel any *real* emotions, though. Either she knows about me, or she harbors a vacant heart.

And I'm about to find out.

I don't bother to wait for a reaction from either one of them as I untie Jane's rope and hand it to Bones. All I say is, "Ignore Jane if she gets an attitude. That's for *me* to deal with."

It doesn't matter if this bothers Jane or Bones. There's something about Kathleen that doesn't fit the usual frame. Riding ahead, I stare at the back of her head until she looks over her shoulder, her eyes widening when she realizes it's me, not Bones. "Kathleen," I command. "Ride back with me."

The others with her watch like vultures, no doubt bored. It's been a while since we had a good fight, and I know my men need to be bled soon. Perhaps a good pillage after all of this is said and done.

Kathleen slows her horse's trot, not looking at me once. I even let the silence sit for a while, the woman doing the best she can to breathe slowly.

"So... you seem to be coming with us," I begin.

Her lips part, but nothing comes out. Her heart frantically tries to cover itself, which tells me she's deliberately trying to keep me out of there.

"I know you're aware I can read you. Don't know how you know, but it's clear you do," I warn. "Jane guards you in her heart, which means you two are close. Risking Skull's Row for her is quite an act of loyalty."

"Why are you asking me this now?" She inhales deeply and dares a glance at me. "You had this whole time. Did something happen to Jane?"

"Initially, I was preoccupied with little Miss Jane. You never let off anything out of the ordinary—just normal feelings of dread and fear... but you didn't remain in Dryhill with the others. And you're starting to relax around us."

"I can't leave her to go through this alone," she defends, facing back ahead. "She's my friend. I know you're aware of that by now."

Fine. Time to pry. "You distracted Bones when Jane was trying to escape."

Fear freezes the moving parts of her mind. She barely controls the wavering in her voice. "Or Bones distracted *me.*"

I stare at her while her aura seeps into the air around us. Little truths are fleeting around her, echoes of Jane attached to many of them. Kathleen's trying to hide it, to think of other things, and she's failing; I can read her so much better now without Jane nearby. "What are you hiding?" I ask, still trying to be gentle. I'll only be rough when the time calls for it.

She doesn't reply, her thin fingers gripping the reigns tighter, staring down at the mane of her horse.

I softly threaten, "If you don't tell me, I am leaving you behind."

There it is. Something crosses in her mind and heart that she's desperate to cover as if accidentally letting something slip and reclaiming it as fast as possible. She might sit there like a proud woman who can control the fear on her face, but underneath is a deep sea of anxiety. And *he* is in there.

My eyes widen. "Seems like you have secrets of your own, *kitten*," I hiss.

"I'm not going to talk to you."

I laugh. "*Yes*, you are." I slowly lick my lips. "Why the fuck are you hiding things related to the *Scorpion*?"

It's the first time she's glanced up to truly look *at* me. Her lips press together like she's forcing certain words back down her throat until she can't contain herself. "You're a bastard for having that skill, you know."

I raise my brow. "Little bit mouthy, aren't we?"

"You can handle it. Jane is unable to *not* be mouthy, and she's not dead."

"No, but she's also not *you*. I don't trust *you*."

"I don't owe my loyalty to you."

"You do if you're sticking around. Do you also understand that Bones is not a normal man? The violence that lives inside of him will tear down those around you. Betray him, and he might only give you an hour's start before he hunts you down himself."

Familiarity. For some reason, that only brings up memories for her that make his actions seem normal.

"No matter what, Jane is my friend. Bones attaching himself to me isn't my issue."

"No, you're right. Your *issue* is that you avoided telling me why underneath all those layers in there, I can sense Jane's father." I stare intently, those words, so far, being the only thing to truly shake her foundation. "There hasn't been much chance for any of us to demonstrate *why* we're of the Zenith's world, but don't mistake Bones's fascination as being our hospitality. One of the reasons they send me is that I can feel whatever haunts you. What kind of pain *terrifies* you." I ride Phantom closer, looking down at her. "And with a world full of healers, torture can be uniquely lengthened to a disturbing degree... I wonder how long your grandmother would last before her heart gives out."

Pleading eyes connect with mine as she snaps her attention back on me. "*Please*, don't."

"Might want to try another tactic."

She fidgets in her saddle, reminding me of a thief who's been caught but still is certain they can weasel their way out of it. She's battling something in there, wondering who she owes the most, until she blurts out, "I swore an oath."

I roll my hand through the air as if leading to the next words. "To whom?"

"Charles Ritter."

✦

When I kick Phantom to turn around after getting everything I need from Kathleen, I trot my horse back to Bones and Jane. The two are as tight-lipped as captives sworn to die rather than to speak. Rounding them until Phantom is facing forward once more, I take the rope from a concerned Bones, his aura exuding that he wants to ask about Kathleen without actually doing it.

"Ride ahead, Bones. She's not a threat."

I don't know *what* this all makes Kathleen. The information I pulled from her confuses me, making this entire mess like a drunk trying to draw a map. Oddly, it makes me feel like I'm betraying Jane, knowing more about those around her than she does.

Including her father, now.

Bones doesn't wait for more orders before entering a light gallop to reunite with the group ahead. I eye the woman next to me, who doesn't say a word. "You're oddly quiet."

"I'm exerting self-discipline." Jane looks down at her hands, her pretty lips thinned and her jaw clenched. My mind races with thoughts of wondering what those hands would have done if they weren't bound a few days ago... does she dig her nails into flesh when she's on the verge of climax? Would she slide her fingers through my hair? Or how would they feel as they grab my legs for support when she's on her knees and choking on my cock?

I withhold those thoughts from reaching my expression. I'm not sure how dangerous it is to let them fester, my interest in her growing beyond the initial fucking. Instead, I ask, "What do *you* know of Kathleen?"

She sighs. "Just read me instead."

"I want to hear you speak the words, and then have it align with what I feel."

Running a hand through her dirty, reddish hair, she then covers a yawn before saying, "Her and I both appeared in Coalfell around the same time and have been friends ever since." She heaves a great sigh, the Zenith's daughter finally moving with the riptides of her predicament rather than fighting it. "Let me speak to her, before we get there, in case something goes wrong with the Council."

"No. Not before. There's decorum that needs to be upheld."

She raises her brows like she's so shocked, her anger hasn't quite reached her heart. "*Decorum*?"

"I'm sure your father taught you this," I reply, my tone resolute.

She silences, shaking her head. She knows that men of Skull's Row, especially mercenaries or any of those belonging to warlords, are very cautious in giving their attention to lovers, even if they're mere pets. Our world sniffs out weaknesses like blood in the air.

Jane must remain my prisoner until the Council has met her, or else they will talk; prisoners simply don't have conversations with their friends. And while I trust my men, I also trust how easy it is for words to slip.

I add, "We're going to arrive and go straight to the Council. Get this shit over with. Then you can sleep."

That heart of hers spins and twists like it doesn't know how to operate outside of survival mode. Should I say anything else to her? Let her know of any plans that I have? Of what Cypress told me? Of what Kathleen's been hiding from Jane this entire time?

The sun breaks through the clouds, furrowing my brows to partially block it out as she holds a hand over her eyes. I decided to give her *something*. "Spin whatever lie works best on your tongue, and I'll tell the Council it's the truth."

She doesn't speak for a while. "You're serious?"

"Yes." I don't like answering that question, as it's already against my nature to help someone to such a degree that's not my immediate family or those within my circle. Reaching for some water in my canteen, I pop the cork and drink the warm water that tastes like leather. "What were your plans after the ship, by the way?"

"I'm not saying. I may need them," she replies with absolute conviction.

My head tilts to the side, knowing she needs her deluded plans of escape to survive. I grab the rope connecting our horses and pull us closer, handing her the canteen. She takes it, her balance off with her bound hands, and she downs it in an almost dramatic fashion as if to display I won't have a drop left.

"That's the *second* time you've done that."

She coughs as she laughs, then hands it back to me, wiping those plump lips. A victorious pride spreads through me knowing that she still can't hide that she finds me funny. "Whatever. If you want water, anyone here will give it to you. Who knows when I'm getting my next drink."

Such a good little Skull's Row fighter.

I have this urge to fist the back of her soft hair and kiss her until she's moaning as if to prove I can. Prove that this creation of a world that I revere belongs to me.

Instead, I release the ropes so there's slack, our horses getting to a comfortable distance next to each other.

We ride over a hill as a salty breeze brushes through the tall grass, the pine trees smaller as we reach the forest's edge. On the other side, we pass by our first set of wooden spikes with skulls affixed to them. Every other ten heads is a black flag with a golden skull on the front, the fabric rippling in the wind.

Once we encounter the fifteenth flag, we crest over a tall hill, the castle visible before the rest of the city. It's a monstrously sized settlement, so large that people live and die without ever meeting half of the citizens. Tall stone walls establish the perimeter, and civilization settles outside of the overgrown place. Smoke rises into the air from the chimneys, birds flying throughout as the ocean is Skull's Row's backdrop. I can't see it from here, but I know a couple dozen ships are manning the waters, all sailing in and out of our ports adjacent to the steep, jagged cliffs.

To the right, the dirt road winds downward in a gradual decline, leading to our more easily accessible ports that are a day's ride away—just another mechanism that makes it hard to storm our city.

It's a kingdom built by men seeking glory, riches, and flesh of all kinds.

I glance back at Jane, whose chest swiftly rises and falls as a hundred things afflict her aura.

She's awake now.

Jane better listen to me once inside. I don't want to have to kill a Zenith that she pisses off or fight through an army of them if it means keeping her daddy happy.

If that bastard gets me to Serena, I'll keep his daughter safe.

RETURNING HOME

JANE

Well... after over a decade... I—Jane Ritter—am home.

Seeing the giant, black castle they call the Spiraling Stone, my entire body stiffens with determination.

The entirety of Skull's Row is built into uneven, mountainous cliffs that line the ocean, growing like invasive barnacles to a ship. The Spiraling Stone reconnects with land about halfway up before the rest of the castle climbs into the sky.

I grew up in the area that connects back to land. I used to stare at this very ocean nearly every morning and night,

Mother often very close by and watching over me, ensuring I didn't wander too far on my own.

Soren leaves me in silence as we get closer to *the* gates. There are many entrances, but these before us are the largest, the bridge always lowered for anyone who dares to enter. Giant flags the size of ship sails billow heavily, the golden skulls haunting me from above.

The settlers outside watch Soren with excitement—a Zenith bringing in a bounty always means a fresh kill is imminent, and these people thrive on violence.

We enter a place that's created out of copious amounts of stone, brick, and wood. The labyrinth of buildings is uneven, winding streets, and alleys moving through like exposed veins. Reclaimed ships are used as entrances to taverns, sails flying high over some. Glass lanterns hang in the oddest of places, and the *sounds* scratch at my brain like a forgotten memory: people fucking, someone yelling, a brawl nearby, the clinking of a blacksmith, and children yelling as they place a bet on who can catch a rat first.

I grip the reigns tighter, not caring that my horse trots closer to Phantom, closer to *Soren*. Especially as we pass Carver's Street, home to butchers and smelling like the waste of dead animals. Men walk the streets covered in blood, red rivers spilling into the sewers from the slaughterhouses.

Underground are pig pens that are frequently stocked with bodies, to be forgotten or remain not found by paid killers.

Mom *and* Dad never let me go near there.

I spot a few wearing yellow sashes crisscrossed over their chests, walking along Carver's, amazed they're finally patrolling in those forgotten streets. Yellow denotes those who are to be completely protected, sanctioned by the Council to enforce measures of legality, calling these men or women Paragons.

The death or disappearance of a Paragon is not acceptable and if either occurs, not only will a Zenith get involved, but it will also result in a tremendous amount of bloodshed to locate who committed this act.

The streets wind upward, the giant castle of the Spiraling Stone always looming over us. We pass by a rather ominous alley, lanterns hanging in even placement, juxtaposed to the irregular world surrounding it. The lanterns are made of red glass—these are the tunnels to The Undercroft. It's an underground world that thieves congregate in, people traveling from all over to hire from their depths.

I suspect, after this, everyone will recognize the small woman with auburn hair that was guided by Soren. Fret sends my heart into an unhealthy rhythm, my gaze latched upon the castle now. The dread of worrying if Soren keeps his word is so heavy that I can't actually process it.

I jump when we pass by a crowded street, a woman's screeching echoing against the brick. It's carnal, as if magic carries the sharp edges of it, a reminder that people with powers of all kinds live here.

We finally reach a set of internal gates, one that guards a bridge with a hundred-foot drop, connecting us to the Spiraling Stone. Thick pieces of chain *clink* as the drawbridge is already being lowered, the wood hitting the cobblestone with a deep *thud*. It's as if the entirety of this place moves to allow Soren to travel without needing to stop.

The salty breeze pulls at us as we cross, everything worn and ravaged from the many storms that batter against this stone.

The bells toll.

A Zenith has returned.

I breathe deeply, my jaw almost trembling as we're guided

to a stable within. Soren helps me down, placing a firm hand on the back of my neck to guide me.

He continues to remain silent, which I don't know how to interpret. I feel more like I'm his bound captive when it's like this. Perhaps he played me *perfectly,* and that's the *true* reason they sent him.

There's a giant atrium that we walk through, passing by a wall of purple, velvet curtains. The smell of perfume permeates the air, a casket of wine being rolled in behind—an extension of Rosmertta's petals, no doubt; her color is that distinct violet. Mother had to tend to the petals on occasion when a particular client left too much damage in their wake.

A woman pushes the curtains aside to allow for easier passage for the wine, her skin glittering, and her eyes heavy with makeup. Soren ignores her wanton stares, to which she slinks back off behind the curtains like a wave of pleasure lapping at whoever passes by.

I keep my gaze ahead, as if I'm in a nightmare and perhaps I'll wake up in Coalfell, the place still untouched by scorching flames.

Soren's heavy armor clinks next to me with his movements, unable to comprehend that this man's tongue has been all over my body, his gaze boring into me as he fucked me deep and hard, all the while his belt and rope held me in place.

We approach the gilded double doors that lead us to Storm's Gathering—the great round table room for the Council of the Zenith. I've actually never even been here, only being told about it countless times. I can't miss the giant doors with golden skulls inlaid on each.

Soren leans down into my ear, his warm, rasping voice finally saying *something*. "You are very numb. I can't tell how you feel."

"Probably because I can't either," I whisper, my heart pounding with a fury.

The grip on my neck gently tightens as he pulls back. A part of me is screaming that he is about to betray me; that he will laugh and tell them all about how he had fucked me and now they can all have their turn.

The doors Dad described more than once to me begin to open, cold fear washing over my skin like the ocean in winter.

Soren guides me forward.

THE COUNCIL
JANE

Giant windows brighten the room, giving a view of the ocean. The floor is made of black stone and an enormous, half-circle table sits neatly in front of the rounded wall, potted plants contrasting the rigid nature of the room. I stare into the eyes of a wooden sculpture of a skull that's affixed to the center of the table's inlet, the whole piece of wood stained black. A candle chandelier hangs in the center like a death trap waiting to be dropped. Hooks are even cemented into the stone floor. *Where they chain people.*

All the men seated around the table carry an air of power,

one that's supported by the hundreds within their own legions that would do anything for their Zenith.

The one woman—Tempest—I had seen on occasion as a child is missing.

A Zenith seated in the center looks to be my father's age, and I recognize him right away as Antoni Blackwell. Gray stubble ages his face, permanent, puffy bags under his inky eyes, and his neck appears to be losing elasticity. A deep, visible, scar runs across his face.

Behind him is a sallow man dressed in a bright red cloak, three red lines running from his hairline to his eyebrow. A fire mage.

They're as rare as a shooting star, but the Council *always* had one on hand. *I'm still not convinced it wasn't them that burned the village.*

"You're two days late since someone rode in to tell us you found her," Antoni says, his voice icy and smooth.

"But here we are," Soren resolutely replies, his voice like warm butter compared to this dick of a leader.

All of the attending Zenith's eyes bore into me, the collective of their lived experiences a testament of how I'm probably not outsmarting the entire group of them. I stare ahead into the dark eye sockets of the table's skull, adrenaline searing my veins. Even with how awake I feel, I'm also utterly exhausted. Beaten. *Afraid.*

"Did she give you any trouble?" asks the one who has braided red hair and beard to match. "And did you find out who the fire mage was that attacked them?"

"We didn't find anyone that fits any typical description of a fire mage. And Jane was as troublesome as expected for someone being taken to present to the Council," Soren smoothly answers, letting go of my neck.

The independence from his grip is both liberating and terrifying. My muscles twitch with nerves; I'm alone in this.

I tried. I sought out the only person I thought could help, and all Cypress did was give me earrings. It's up to the fates, now.

One speaks who has dark skin, the only hair he has being a black beard with three different braids, and a single golden earring in his right ear, indicating piracy. "So no evidence of a mage, even if the spiraling fires indicate as such?"

"There are more of my kind across the black seas." A few move their gaze to eye the fire mage, whose baritone voice crawls through the room like slow lava. "As I stated to all of you earlier, it's not impossible for this to be related to a cult over there. Fire worshippers don't tend to bow to the laws of man."

The same pirate faces Soren and me. "Let's not waste time, then—show us the tattoo we heard about. Blackwell told all of us what his scouts had seen. Let's address that before the rest."

Another chimes in, "Still ruddy mad that he held that from us. We had a right to know."

Blackwell replies, "You can cry about it to your mother later. If anyone learns there is a *woman* with our mark that's *not* Tempest, it undermines the strict codes we're known for. Keeping that under control, until she was here, was worth it. I only mentioned it yesterday because I didn't expect Soren to be this late."

So, my mercenary captor was right—their *pride* is why I am about to suffer.

Fuck these cunts.

I count them all in a deliberate silence—seventeen in total. One of the seats at the head of the crescent is empty, along with one on the far right: one is Soren's, no doubt, and the other belongs to Tempest, if she's even still around. Half of the men take periodic drinks from their shiny, ornate chalices.

They're so silent it makes me more uncomfortable than if they were yelling at me.

Antoni nods and says, "Do it. Remove the shirt."

Soren walks around to stand in front of me. I'm so tired that I can't hide the way his sudden intrusion into my vision makes my bones melt, like I can actually breathe in this illusion of privacy. This also makes no sense, given who he is, but it's a reaction he can no doubt feel.

Rather than cutting the rope on my wrists, he has more and ties my bound hands to the hook in front of me—it's just enough slack so I can stand. I meet his emotionless gaze before he cuts at the front of my shirt, ripping it open before moving behind me. They're all paying attention now, a few leaning closer to gain a better look as my breasts are on full display. The room is silent, save for the random sniff, or creaking of a moving chair.

My tattoo seems to have their tongues tied.

Soren stands very close behind me as my skin raises with gooseflesh, my nipples hardening.

I hear one say, "So she fucking has one."

Finally, Antoni's voice dons the cold, mirthless edge that I'm sure he has honed after years of violence. He speaks slowly, nodding toward me, pointing at me using a hand decorated with golden rings. "How the fuck did you get that?"

I look down at the stone, not in fear, but to hopefully show an ounce of begrudging respect that might aid me. "I don't know."

A Zenith, around Soren's age, begins to laugh and I glare at the man. He is the only other handsome one of the bunch—then again, maybe that's just because the rest are working against age. He has grayish-white hair that's tightly pulled back—despite his age—and a strong jawline. Many piercings lining his face, his neck completely tattooed. I don't recognize him.

Soren steps in, his deep rasp sending more gooseflesh over my skin. "She's not lying."

My heart races, my nostrils flaring. *Keep it cool. Don't let them know you're shocked he's helping you.*

"What?" the one who had just been laughing asks. "That makes no sense. Hold a flame up to her chest. Let's see the gold change."

I hear swift movements from_someone rushing to bring over a torch, then the calculated heavy steps of Soren as he walks in front of me once more, a torch now in his hands as he glares at the younger counterpart. "I'm the fucking one who reads their truths from lies. She's not lying, *Matthias*."

Soren holds the flames against my skin and faces only me, watching me carefully as I stare up at him. A Zenith says, "She's got great tits, at least." A flash of possessiveness washes through Soren's gaze that he fails to hide. The heat is like agonizing pleasure, reminding me how cold I am. I glance down, and sure enough, the gold part of the tattoo disappears and reappears when my flesh is cool again as he pulls away.

Soren steps aside, leaving me standing there, my tunic still ripped down the front.

Antoni leans back in his chair, opening his mouth like he's about to speak harshly, but Soren must have given him a special kind of glare as the pseudo leader of this Council flicks his gaze over my shoulder, then huffs, settling on, "So this cunt seriously doesn't remember getting that? Just woke up with it? Is that what we're supposed to believe?"

Soren, standing close behind once more, says, "Go ahead. Tell them your story."

I've been rehearsing it since he told me he'd lie for me. I'm a little shocked that he's actually going to help, but I give it a try, nonetheless. "All I remember is that I grew up here, in Skull's Row, and my mom was a common whore," I say, hating to lie about how great of a healer she was. "I lived with her. She always said my daddy was special, but would never tell me who he was. Then, when I was eleven or so, I drank something that made me pass out. When I woke up, I had this tattoo on my chest. My mom said it would protect me, but refused to tell me more."

"That's a dumb fucking story," the redhead says.

The one named Matthias adds, "I don't know. Maybe she's *your* daughter and you protected her. The hair matches."

Danger flashes in the other's eyes. "If I had a daughter worth branding, I wouldn't bring her to the fucking Council like she's to be slaughtered."

Another chimes in, "It was a Zenith. The tattoo is *real*. The gold under her skin—that's *our* gold. Ferrin only gets the naprese gold when authorized. So, a Zenith decided to have her marked. He wouldn't work with anyone that wasn't us."

Ferrin... their blacksmith. I heard he died recently, and my relief is instant to know it's my word against a man's grave.

Antoni leans back over and I meet his gaze. "Bastards are common for us, but we don't mark those we don't consider our lineage. So, whoever your acclaimed father was saw you as such, and yet somehow, we have no record of a woman *ever* being listed, except for Tempest." He wets his thin lips with his tongue. "We also simply never mark our daughters with inherited tattoos."

My foot fidgets. "I know. It's why I ran away so early," I reply, spinning my lies, hidden by partial truths. "I didn't know why I had this mark." I recall the very clear memories of my father's motives that contradict those words. "I was never fond of Skull's Row, anyway."

Silence.

I wish I could see Soren's face as these men contemplate what I said. Their eyes roam over me like they want to dissect every piece of my flesh, my naked chest like a stance of confidence while also being so degrading.

They're all too calm. Does my existence make them that nervous? The one named Matthias quickly moves the conversation along and adds, "Jane has the healer's insignia. That might be easy to track, since it's from the mother's line. A healing whore would be useful and known."

I keep my head low.

Antoni chimes in, "That's a start. The fact that Ferrin never wrote it down means he was loyal to the Zenith that requested it—" he articulates very carefully as he adds "—Loyal to the degree of breaking our codes." He looks over my head at Soren. "How truthful is her timeline of the tattoo?"

"I buy it."

Antoni looks to his left. "When did Ritter die?"

"Ritter?" the dark-skinned one responds. "She looks nothing like him."

Thank the gods I don't.

Mathias says, "But Ferrin *was* loyal to Ritter, so that *would* check out. When did he die?"

"Thirteen years ago," another says. "At least that's when he fell off of Dead Man's Falls. We never found him."

Antoni asks, "How old is *she*?"

Soren replies for me. "Told me she's Twenty-one."

Please be after Dad left...

One of the Zenith at the far left of the table looks down as he flips through a book in front of him. "Then she got the tattoo ten years ago, if her words are to be true. Ritter was long gone before then, so Ferrin wouldn't have done it. Ferrin would only mark her if Ritter was present." He leans back in his seat, sighing. "It's a fucking shame that asshole is dead. Does the new naprese goldsmith know anything?"

Antoni is quick to shake his head. "No, we asked him if he did... although it might still be worth asking a second time." Antoni looks back at Soren. "Well? How truthful is this? She's not lying at all?"

"I don't have her fucking papers, but I don't feel any lies."

Blackwell sighs and raises a hand like he's out of options. "Then bring out the villager."

My blood runs cold, fear enveloping me like tendrils from the ocean's depths. I look around the room with abject horror. *Kathleen.* My mouth dries as vengeance blinds me, ready to tear the eyes out of Bones *and* Soren. They used us. They had to–

The doors open behind me and it takes everything I have to face what's behind me. If I see that familiar face surrounded by blonde hair... I'll tell them *everything.*

And yet, as I see who they bring in, I'm overtaken by the distinct sensation of being lost. The woman whom I healed back in Coalfell, whose leg still looks raw, red, and scaly, is brought through the doors. Maryanne's eyes are bloodshot, her hair covered in the same soot as back from the village, her arms bound as thick rope gags her mouth. I want to look at Soren, but looking at him for any bit of understanding would ruin whatever facade we have.

Maryanne stares at me, a high-pitched whimper muffled by the rope as she slowly shakes her head.

One of the Zenith shout, "Aye, maybe we fuck her bloody? Make Jane the lying whore *watch*. I still don't trust her. Maybe she's using magic to fuck with Soren's powers. Could be a witch or some shit."

Soren is swift in his reply, "You can call her whatever you want but don't fucking challenge *me*. Healers can't be witches, idiot. The magic source is wrong."

Maryanne's head continues to shake as the guard that guides her pushes her to her knees, tying her to the iron loop in the ground. Her sobs remind me of back to when I sobbed for Mother...

It clicks—*I'm* the reason she suffers.

I recognize Blackwell's voice, but don't raise my gaze to meet his. "So, Miss Jane... a few of Soren's men rode ahead, bringing a few villagers for questioning. I think they believed they had some sense of protection, but they also didn't realize who you were. Remove the gag."

Watching every second, I can't turn my head away as they roughly remove the rope, Maryanne's mouth burned by it, too. "Jane..." she manages out, her voice hoarse, listless eyes trying to focus on me.

Tunnel vision consumes me. We stare at each other, tears blurring my vision as I feel so utterly helpless. *This is my fault.* My lips part as I want to tell her it will be all right, but I know that it won't be. What do I do? *Kathleen... shit, she could be next.*

Blackwell's voice makes me shudder as he instructs, "Soren, what does this one here fear most when it comes to death?" He sounds almost amused.

Soren comes into view, roughly grabbing Maryanne's hair, the woman crying out in pain. He stares into her face as she sobs, quietly pleading for his humanity. Soren cants his head to the side, speaking as if the words are written on her face. "She doesn't like fire." He narrows his eyes. "Burns, more specifically." He drops her hair and even prods her infected leg with his boot. She wails in agony. "Doesn't take much to figure out why."

Maryanne cowers over, sobbing so hard that snot begins to hang from her nose.

My body is numb while my soul is on fire. What would

happen if I tell them the truth? They'll just kill her, anyway, right? *What if they start bringing more out here? Children, even?*

Soren means nothing to me now, this is all a stark reminder that while the wolf may have enjoyed playing with me, he's not above devouring my flesh if he so desires.

"Well, then. Let's bring the fire to her!" Blackwell exclaims, some of the others laughing. The fire mage smiles in the background.

"Please, I have a family!" Maryanne manages out.

Another says, "We'll have to send a note that Mother will be nice and crispy for dinner."

Maryanne fights her bindings, slicing her gaze at me as if the last will to live rears itself. "Jane, *help*," she pleads, the men beginning to strip her by cutting her clothes off. It's as if something changes in her eyes, rancor thrown my way. "This is *your* fault," she bites at the air. "They're asking us all about you. Tell them whatever the fuck you're hiding! Let me go back to my children!"

I choke on a cry as my lips tremble, watching as she snarls at me while they lather her naked body in grease. The words are right in my mouth, and all I have to do is whisper them, *'My father is Charles Ritter. Let them all go, and I'll tell you everything.'* But I can't. And yet I must, right? What's the point of surviving if this is what happens? I'm already in Skull's Row, so I've broken that promise to Melona, no matter what the debt was...

A sob escapes me, letting it all out when I know it only makes me look pathetic to these men. When Maryanne's dirty hair is lathered, I'm about to confess *everything*–

Rope is forcefully wrapped around my neck, pulling me sideways as I struggle to breathe, my arms taught as my body is stretched. Glancing up, I see it's Soren and flinch as if he's a stranger.

"Do you feel a confession coming?" he asks, speaking loud enough for the others to hear. When I want to declare yes, he pulls harder on the rope so I gasp for air.

He leans further in. "*Do* you?"

His sharp tone is laced with warning, my lungs starving for oxygen. When I internally drop the desire to say what the Council wants, Soren releases his noose, and I gasp and choke. I get the message—he doesn't want me to speak.

"No, please, I don't know anything. *Please* stop this," I plead. The words disappoint me, and I'm not even sure why I complied with Soren.

My gaze is lowered when someone cries out to burn Maryanne.

When Soren leaves me alone, I cry harder as I lift my head to see Soren grab one of the torches, everyone backing away from Maryanne, who stares at me. "You cunt! This is all your fault! I hope my children find you and gut you! *COWARD!*"

Soren stands in front of her with the fire, watching almost as if he's bored. Her voice grows frantic as she stares at it. "I don't want to burn!" She pleads. "*DON'T!* My children! *Please!*"

Soren takes the torch and pushes hard against her chest, right at her heart as flames consume her. My eyes widen as screams blur, taken back to the night when the village was burned, the bright, hot flames not matching the room.

Her screams morph into something deep and unrecognizable, the groans almost that of an animal as she stares up at the ceiling. At some point, the sounds die away as she dramatically slumps forward onto the floor. As her body continues to burn, Blackwell says, "Let the fire burn itself out. Leave her there to frighten the next villager."

The fire mage makes his way over, slowly watching as the fire cracks and licks high into the air. He holds out a hand with long, thin fingers, almost caressing the flames while Maryanne's body burns at his feet.

My body is shaking uncontrollably now, little painful moans escaping me as I can't believe I let this happen to her.

Another says, "Didn't we hear a blonde woman was traveling with them? Might be a villager, too."

I'm shaken back to reality almost instantly, about to blurt out every truth before Soren can even come near me before the behemoth snorts somewhere behind me. "Go ahead and try and take *that* one. Bones is currently having his fun with her. But once he's done? Sure. Fucking have at it."

A few mumble as if they'd prefer to wait rather than bother Bones.

Another says, "So you're telling me this woman seriously has no idea how she got that tattoo? There's *nothing* in there? Not even after that one burns?"

"I didn't say we free her," Soren counters. I can't stop hearing Maryanne's screams echo in my mind as she lifelessly lies there, my mind listless with regret. The smell of burning flesh is awful. "There's an answer inside of her, somewhere. I have a feeling she can't remember for a reason, probably tampered with by magic. Digging into that takes time. We need to look around before murdering and torturing her, because nothing has changed inside of Jane.

"I've dealt with this more than once. You cross a line of brutality that you can't undo and the truth will mix annoyingly with her desperation to tell you whatever she thinks you want to hear. What I *need* is more than a fucking hour and I'll get that done."

Antoni says, "Fine. I want this damn answer, one way or another. Depending on how well she cooperates, we can negotiate her freedom as someone's ship wench. If she doesn't help, then we continue to burn more bodies." There's a pause before he adds, "Anyone contest to this? No? Rorge, put the fire out then."

With a slow movement of his fingers, the fire mage lowers his head as he watches the fire unnaturally dwindle, the bright reflection against his eyes fading.

A deep voice, one I haven't heard yet, says, "Where will she be kept?"

Soren replies, "With me."

"As a prisoner or your pet?" Antoni asks.

"Both," Soren replies, almost as if amused.

Antoni rubs his chin before narrowing his eyes. "No. This is exactly why we abstain from this. You fuck her enough times, you might want to keep her around, seeing value in her lineage. Then your ego will dominate common sense, and you'll think you're a king."

"I'm no king, you cunt, but I do like her hair. If I want to fuck her, then I will. If I want to burn another villager in her face, then I will. She's not had a good start, so far. She's been bound in her own waste, and if you saw the scar on her stomach, it's because we stabbed her for trying to run. I'd fucking appreciate it if you let me do what I do best."

Someone violently smacks their chalice on the table, speaking over the mumbling men that surround him. "I say he has her. Makes no sense to remove her from him when he's the one that gets information. You're acting paranoid, Blackwell. She's not a threat—if anything, she's our *property*, given the tattoo, and that no one is here to claim who gave it to her. Soren will get the truth from her. He always does. However he wants to do that, let him. Even if it means she affixes herself to him in desperation and becomes his fuck toy. I don't give a shit how he does it. He's our manipulator for a reason. In the meantime, we search around for a common whore who could heal... where did you live, Jane?"

My lips don't quite work as I barely manage out, "All over."

No one will know of Jane with a mother who was a healing whore. Dad never called me Jane in public—instead, he used Ember. It's from when I was a toddler and had much paler hair that the sun's rays would penetrate and make the loose strands glow red. Over time, it darkened to the auburn color that it is now.

Which means this will all fall apart as they learn of my lies, one way or another, and Kathleen will suffer. Hells, *anyone* else suffering for this...

Soren replies, "You all look around while I work on her."

Staring at Maryanne's charred remains that continue to lightly burn, I don't know what to do.

I just don't know what to do.

STUCK IN SKULL'S ROW

JANE

Without warning, Soren grabs my neck from behind, swiftly turning me around to guides me toward the double doors that two guards open, removing me as quickly as possible from their presence. Anya and Bones wait in the distance, along with the others that I know very little of but am starting to recognize.

As soon as we leave, chatter begins in our wake. I'm trying to remain alert but can't focus.

COWARD.

I didn't say anything. I could have stopped them. *Right?*

Would they have stopped if I said something? I don't know that for certain.

And why am I hiding anymore? Truly? I hid because of the promises I once clung to, but now that they're broken or absolved... A chill grips my heart that destroys me almost as much as it did to watch Maryanne burn—I *am* a coward.

My gods... the agonizing truth that a mother died because of me is a guilt I'd never thought I'd feel. Her young children, Benny, Otto, and Eliza... I actually watched their mother burn for my selfish secrets.

Many make way for us to give Soren a wide birth to walk. The only reason my legs remember how to move is because of Soren pushing me, otherwise, I might collapse with guilt and self-hate.

Soren leans into my ear. "The more I sense you want to tell them the truth, the tighter the leash I'll give you. You'll never escape here on your own. Even you have to know that you need help for that. And telling them anything will help literally no one but *them*."

I'm right back to feeling like he's my captor, not the man that I had some semblance of... well, whatever-the-fuck I felt for him.

"It would have helped *her*. They burned her alive—*you* burned her alive," I mutter through thin lips. Melona enters my mind, her pale blonde, silky hair like an image of hope, remembering how the moonlight nearly made it glow. I trusted her words more than anything, and now I'm no better than an executioner who harms the innocents. "They can't kill more for me, Soren. I don't care about hiding anymore if *that's* what it costs."

"I know," he says, like he's not used to the act of making someone else feel better. "There's no other choice."

"You nearly choked me out when I tried to help. *That* was a choice."

"Because *I* want your secrets hidden," he hissed.

My heart beats in ways that betray survival, my eyes moving all over, not truly taking any details in. I stiffen, nearly spinning around to hit him with my bound fists. I don't care if others are watching or if I should be 'grateful' that I have any semblance of freedom.

He steadies me forward with the same force as when he had that rope around my neck. "Can you just wait until we aren't walking in the damn halls of this place before having a real conversation?"

I don't say a word after that. Nothing can absolve the near embarrassment at realizing I'm the reason for all of this, and my excuses for secrecy have vanished. I only listened to Melona *because* she said staying away was to avoid senseless deaths like these. My anger and confusion viciously intertwine. We pass by someone with a yellow tunic and black skull pinned on their pectoral—a generic servant of this place. He cautiously looks at me, carrying a tray of tea with red porcelain cups.

I lunge at him like I'm going to bite him just for staring. He nearly drops the plate he's carrying, moving quicker past us.

Soren laughs so hard it echoes on the stone walls. He looks at the servant, "Yeah, careful mate, she *does* bite."

"Shut up," I grumble. *None* of this is a joke.

"You need a damn nap," Soren rasps.

I stick my leg out before my intentions can be read by him, and it nearly trips the behemoth, but he's too skilled to take any real tumble; it merely just interrupts his smooth stride. I spin my fists around, hoping it hits something of him, but it does nothing more than lamely collide with his chest before he hoists me over his shoulders.

My emotions cascade, angry at *everything*. For how my life went. For my father abandoning me. For the fact that the only person I can remotely place any hope in is Soren, and now the Council thinks I am their property, and I'm stuck deep within the Spiraling Stone.

Angry that what I want is my own *mother*.

Enraged for the fact that I *am*, apparently, a coward.

What would I even tell Maryanne's children? I watched their mother burn because I had to keep it secret that my father is a Zenith because... *why*? There's *no* reason without Melona.

But like before, I don't fight once on his shoulder, as it's not worth it. I survey what I can, watching the castle change from this skewed point of view. We enter a platform that's a metal box affixed to thick chains, and Soren turns around so he's facing the door, and me facing the stone wall. Men who have the strength of an ox churn giant gears that raise and lower this vessel.

It's just the two of us that enter, the remainder of his men veering off to take the stairs. The door shuts and the cage lurches as it begins to move, the wall now moving downward as we go up. The lighting changes as we pass each exit.

"You can fucking put me down now," I grind out, staring at the stone that's behind the iron bars.

"Not yet. It's good you're fighting. Makes it look more like you're truly unnerved by me. Would be out of character, otherwise."

"Someone *died* because of me," I say. "When she didn't *have* to."

"I am aware," he says with a tired sigh, like my mood swings are interrupting his day. I send as much anger through my heart so he may drown in it.

He responds with, "What? Do you want me to whisper sweet things into your ear to make you feel better? It wouldn't do any good. You wouldn't believe me anyway... and I don't waste such attention of mine on deaf ears."

I snort. "Like you even know how to whisper sweet things."

With more sincerity than I expect, he says, "I'm a man, Jane. Not a demon."

"You burned her for no reason. That's what demons do."

"Oh, I *have* a reason. Just because I haven't shared it with you yet doesn't mean it doesn't exist."

My mouth opens in protest, but only empty air escapes. I hadn't considered that. I replay his words, the idea of him truly being able to say soothing things tempts me, but that's also the last thing I need when my situation requires vigilance.

Do I even deserve that?

The metal cage lurches to a stop as I stare at the now stationary wall. I can hear metal sliding, a man grunting, and the cage gives a final shake before it feels sturdy. The gate creaks open and Soren walks forward. We exit onto a platform that the sunlight beams through, although all I can really see is the grout between the stones. I grab his hips so I can lift myself, the pressure on my stomach making my recent wound ache.

Within seconds, we're adjusting, Soren leaning forward as I slide off. I wonder if he could tell I was in pain, or if it's just a coincidence since we've arrived at our destination.

I don't give him the benefit of the doubt. He's still a mercenary, and I'm still illegally branded without a Zenith to claim who left the mark, all the while my breasts are still on display.

I survey the scene as blood from my head spreads back into my body, raising my hands to cover my chest and tattoo. Especially since we're at the top, and I have no idea how to navigate this place. I never got to come up here as there are eyes everywhere in this sector... if I'm correct, one can't even enter without being escorted by a Zenith or wearing a golden skull brooch.

Dad never risked it.

Soren prods my back to keep walking. The layers of this place are completely uneven as bridges and stairs wind throughout, every doorway seemingly on its own level. The sun beams in from somewhere at the top through a glass ceiling, guiding our way to one stone bridge in particular that crosses a giant opening. I glance below, as there's about a four-story drop with more zigzagging bridges underneath to reveal a bustling sea of people, and the scent of smoked foods and spices emanates from there. "Where are we?" I blandly ask.

"In the Zenith's Rotunda. Our rooms are here on all these levels. Below is the Court of the Zenith—" booming laughter and inaudible declarations echo upward "—Lots of vagabonds and improper bastards down there, and that's where Bones and Anya stay. The rest of my men will remain at the lower level, switching out as my guards."

Across the bridge is a thick, wooden door that's manned by two people who have a serpent on their vest. They both bow deeply and open the doors. "Why'd you choose a snake, anyway?" I ask with annoyance, the detail intriguing even if my heart rages.

"Adopted it when they wouldn't stop calling me 'the viper hidden in plain sight'," he states.

Soren steps through the threshold, and I notice he doesn't have one on his own vest when I look back. Then again, he's also not wearing the same red armor.

The double doors lead to a small foyer with windows that give view to the rotunda, another set of doors waiting for Soren to unlock them. The others shut behind us, locking us in this tiny room. When he unlocks the one in front of us and pushes it open, I step through, not paying attention to how he watches me. My lips part in seeing something so glorious. The windows are tall with many panes and in different shapes, working with the grooves of the natural stone. A giant balcony tempts me to breathe in the fresh air, one unmarred by the stench of the city. The ceilings are almost two stories tall at their highest with heavy candle chandeliers hanging down. It's all dark, from the wood to the stone, save for the deep velvet red that the furniture and drapes are made of. A massive painting of a ship manning a stormy sea sits over the fireplace.

I now wonder more about my captor. Does he have naval prowess? Or is he a land warlord who simply loves the sea? Perhaps both? When did he join the gang of men that gave him the tattoos on his back, and how did he become a Zenith?

And what exactly did Cypress say to him?

That glimmer of curiosity now has me seeing him as the man he claims to be, rather than just someone who spawned out of these walls. There's an entire history that he waded through to get to where he is now.

I *must* tap into that, into the man he claims he is.

As soon as he shuts the doors—and locks it—I get straight to the point as I turn around. "They're going to know. They'll do their search and realize no one can back up my story. Especially if anyone recognizes me from when I was a child who always wore her hair under a hat and followed one of the Zenith around." I lick my dry lips, speaking anxiously. "And until then, they'll just burn more people? What's the point? I made a promise to a siren to never return, to *prevent* more deaths. Well, now I'm here. I broke my promise. And people are dying for me."

He walks through the room as I speak, sitting down on one of the oversized couches that are crowded by tables, a stack of old books sitting on one of them. He spreads his arms on each side, looking up at the ceiling, twirling one hand as he speaks, "So, first... do you want to strategize, or just do whatever the fuck Jane feels like doing? Like speaking *right* when they wanted you to, forcing me to choke you?"

I near him, that innocent curiosity about him fading as a familiar aggression returns. "Giving me the choice now?"

With one blink, his gaze is on me, looking between my breasts. "It will work best if we are on the same page, yes."

I go up to him, lean over—while he watches me with curious eyes for nearing him so closely—and I poke his chest while my hands are still bound. "Why? Why bother? *Why* did you help me? And also, why stop me? Why not just give me to the Council when it would have been easiest? I was ready to tell them *everything*."

His pale gaze slowly looks me over, a large hand running over his head to smooth back any loose strands that escaped his low bun. With a sigh, he reaches out to untie the ropes, eyeing my breasts with no shame. "There are things I can't tell you. I *did* speak to your wretched witch, as I said, and she gave me good reason to help you. That's all you *need* to know. And that means you have to keep your pretty lips shut so I can get what I want."

Once my hands are free, I jerk them back and grab the tattered edges of my tunic to cover myself in protest. Through thin lips, I reply, "I helped that woman give birth to her youngest and had to heal her when she ripped. And now? I just watched her burn for secrets I don't even know are worth keeping."

He continues to stare at my chest for a moment longer than I liked even if it's covered. "Jane, they would have burned her anyway, just for the sake of it. It didn't matter if it was by me or the damn fire mage himself, and I saw no point in delaying her torture. Aye, she got caught up in *your* wake, but it could have been anyone." He pauses as his gaze rises to meet mine. "Even *Kathleen.*"

"I would have done anything to stop that."

"Which is why we need a *strategy.*"

I look him over, the man sitting so casually while dressed in armor that has no doubt seen horrific battle and been stained with the blood of many. The scars on his face are a testament to his violent history. *Channel that. He clearly managed to survive and come out on top.* "Then give me a strategy."

"Get us a drink, first. That was a long ride and a stressful meeting," he quips, nodding to a table by a window with various bottles on its shelves.

I scoff, crossing my arms. "I'm not your damn servant."

He huffs, rocking forward and standing, the giant man looking down at me with a raised brow and actually going to do the task himself. My hands fidget, as I'm not sure what to make of Soren. I'm pretty sure he's the kind of man to tell me 'I won't repeat myself', just like when he stabbed that mayor's cousin. But not now. He even let me poke him, now that I think about it...

I watch him grab two glasses, and he looks back at me. "You drink any of this stuff?"

"It's not wine, but I'll take anything right now."

"Wine is quite the luxury." He pours two—double for himself—and turns around to hand me one, almost with attitude, as if to show that's how it's done. "Too sweet for me, so all we have is this."

Soren sits back down as I pace the room, smelling inside

the glass as one arm continues to cover my chest. It's got a smokey edge, much bolder than the stuff that Ern sells.

He takes a drink before saying, "I can arrange to have you out of here in two weeks, and the best, honest advice, would be for you to behave like my little pet until then, who's also frightened of me. And stop fighting me, as my patience for being treated like the villain will wane very thin. You abide by that, and no one else will burn for you."

I take a big gulp, my throat burning but I act like I feel nothing. My hoarse voice says otherwise. "What does 'little pet' entail, exactly?"

With the glass to his lips, he smiles deviously, the glass almost too small for his large hands. After another sip, he lowers his hand and licks his bottom lip. "Well, if I were to be in character, that means when I have meetings with other *gentlemen* such as myself, you're going to be sitting on my lap, quiet like a good girl—" he pauses when I'm about to protest "—it's just temporary, before you lose your mind. I promise they're not going to let you go so easily. They're hoping for answers, and they're hoping I break you. I've done this more than once, and they all know it." He nods toward me. "But clearly when you get pushed, you bare your fangs like an alley cat. So, it's your choice—you can either be my pet, stay locked in here, or run your pretty mouth and gamble away your freedom and risk others getting hurt." His legs spread open as he gets more comfortable. "My duty right now is to tell them that burning more people will only fuck with your memory. Most will buy it and give you to me. Honestly, it helps you *were* stabbed by Anya."

I think about that, a metaphor entering my mind that places me in the middle of the ocean. On the horizon in a nasty storm—that's the Council. I could always anchor the ship and wait for the storm to pass, but I still risk that it comes my way, especially with the way the winds are blowing. Then there's a large island that's very close by, one where Soren sits as king, and I'd be beholden to him if I sought refuge there.

I need to ask questions before getting onboard that island.

"Well, first, what's the end goal? If they want me worn down for answers, that means at some point, they expect me to talk again."

"We're going to have to play that one by ear," he suggests, watching me as I pace. His thoughts are withdrawn behind a neutral expression, but he observes even the smallest of my movements, such as when I tuck my hair behind my ear.

"Wait... so you don't have a plan?"

"Like I said, a small one. It's best to go with the tide of the ocean than to command it. I will have to amend the plan more than once, I imagine, if you actually are willing to play along."

Okay... that's not bad. That makes sense. I motion the drink toward him. "You could piss them off, though."

"And what, they'll threaten to kill me? I've been ready to die for a long time. I'm a mercenary. At this rate, it's about making my death interesting. I can't claim what Cypress offers if I don't take care of you."

Do I do it? Do I jump in feet first? I stare back at the painting over the fireplace. I can buy that Soren wants to aid me if it's for some sense of loyalty to something Cypress offered him. "All this hard work to climb their ranks and risk throwing it away on me, though? I've literally stolen your money and ran for it."

He silkily replies, "To which I chased you down and fucked that beautiful cunt of yours and then carried you here."

I cough when I choke on my drink, my cheeks reddening. His words stoke the fires that burned so hotly between us the previous night... and thinking that he wants to keep me safe—

out of a sense of self-preservation—breaks my walls down when I least expect them to fall.

He hardly smiles, but his eyes tell me that he got the reaction he wanted. "I'm a man that fights for myself, Jane. The Zenith just help ensure my power is far-reaching, but I don't need them. Work with me, and I'll get you somewhere safe, which means I fulfill what Cypress wants and you don't have to see any more villagers burn." He gets a devious look in his eyes, like he can't help himself. "If you're really desperate, though, you can let your belly swell with my seed."

My eyes widen as I glower at him, ready to pour this drink on his face.

He laughs, shaking his head. "You're too easy."

"Well, why the fuck say that?" I ask, downing more of the burning drink rather than tossing it. My veins warm as it hits my system. "You know what, never mind. I'm being serious right now. It's hard to trust you, all right? As in, it's hard for me to trust people in general, let alone this very specific scenario." My throat constricts, exposing a true layer of vulnerability. "I can't watch someone else burn like that. Not someone I know."

A semblance of his true humanity breaches that stolid gaze. The expression alone unwinds me in ways I don't have the energy to deal with, so I move over to the shelves of liquor, my mind torn in every direction. Popping the cork back into the bottle, I sit down in a chair opposite of him, hovering the glass to my lips as I feel the first serving spin my mind.

"Anyway," he says, pointing around with the hand that holds his drink, my eyes flicking in his direction. "You've got free reign of the place. No trying to kill me in my sleep or I'll just tie you to the bedpost, and as we've already discovered, it's a rather useful tactic. No leaving, because they've got eyes watching, and it won't look right if you do. You can have whatever drink, food, or luxuries you want while we play this one by ear." He eyes me greedily. "If you go against my rules, I *will* punish you. Because they have to see that, and it *won't* be the kind you enjoy."

I roll my eyes, my heart fluttering, staring at the empty hearth. I drink more at those words, rubbing my eyes.

"You need to sleep, Jane."

My eyes close at the softness of his voice, like he's someone worth sharing my vulnerability with. *Gods* how I wish he were. "Why aren't *you* tired?"

He downs his drink and puts his glass on the table in front of us, standing. His voice is gruff from the alcohol. "An explanation for another time."

Whatever. I'll dig into that later. I look around for somewhere to sleep—hoping for more than a couch—and see an open door to a bedroom. "I'm sleeping in the bed."

"Good for you." He walks past me, leaning down. "So am I."

"I want a bath," I blurt out, staring at his back as he walks away.

"As you wish, princess."

I throw my gaze back at the liquor, my mind swimming freer than usual. I drink more of it as I feel my body unwind with its intoxication. Soren seems to be examining the place, as if taking mental notes of its state, like someone searching for tampering.

"I'll play the role of your pet," I say, staring at the wooden table.

"Really?" He asks, almost shocked.

"I understand that they won't take well to me looking too free. If it keeps them convinced, then I'll play. I don't know what Cypress told you, but if it keeps others alive, that's all I care about." I look out the window across the room, desperate to go into the waters out there once again. With a distinct sense of capitulation and reckless behavior, I mumble, "And like you said, I'll probably enjoy myself... so why bother fighting what feels good? I've done that for far too long..."

I hear his footsteps, but I still tense when he leans down—the liquor nearly sloshing out of my glass—having not expected him to be so close, blood rushing between my thighs.

His husky voice is in my ear. "And you wonder why I like you."

SOREN

Memories of my life beg to be considered, like a reminder of what it took to get here. Of the sacrifices I made, of those I lost... I consider the effort it will take to secure Jane's freedom.

At the bare minimum, I know the Ritter father isn't dead. His nickname, the Scorpion, was for how isolated the man was and how swiftly hostile he became if anyone got too close. He'd survive just fine, all alone, for over a decade.

He's watching over her. Somewhere. Even if she feels he abandoned her. She knows him as a father from a childhood ruined by something tormented and deeply guarded within her heart. *I* know him as the Zenith that I revered from a distance.

An instinct, one that has kept me alive through many miraculous tales, tells me that if Jane dies, Ritter will ensure we *all* do. I don't even need Cypress to tell me that.

Which means wherever he is, he's close.

When do I tell her? The poor thing is getting soft on me, wanting to protect the other villagers that were so quick to tell the Council everything about Jane. We somehow got lucky that they truly didn't know much of her. I was told, right before we got here from a reconnaissance messenger, that Maryanne even offered to be a spy for the Council. Warm Jane up to her.

It's their fucking loss they chose to burn her rather than listen, as if I've learned *anything* from Jane, it's that she's weak for those she cares for. Burning Maryanne was easy for me, even if the heartbreak for her children bled into me more than I cared for.

Serena matters more to me than the orphans of a mother who chose to trust the wrong people.

All of this chaos is sending me down to the rotunda where the entrance to Blackwell's chamber is, knowing I need to meet with him without Jane present. I walk through a dimly lit hall with many heavy, ornate doors. Having just left Kendra's—the woman that oversees the brothels and caretakers of the Spiraling Stone, an underling of Rosmertta. Before seeing Blackwell, I wanted to ensure servants are sent up to my room to take care of Jane.

One woman named Lilith follows me out of the purple door. I look back at her as she stands next to the lantern with violet glass as it casts a unique glow on her silky clothes that barely cover anything, which is admittedly a favorite of mine. Tersely, I ask, "What?"

The pale blonde looks as if she wants to say many things,

longing and nervousness mixing in her green eyes. "Should I have your usual room ready, in here?"

Her question, while innocent enough, carries a weight of gossip. "No." I huff when she clearly has more to add. "Get out whatever is binding your tongue."

"Is there a woman in your room?" she blurts out, like this is a troubling rumor. There might even be a little betrayal in her eyes.

"Is that your business?"

Her full lips thin as she looks down, lowering her head in submission. I turn around and say nothing else when I so easily could, but I don't have time to give gentler words when it would only send the wrong message. She may have been a woman I once frequented, but the exchange was always clear. I paid her well to do the things I liked, even if she'd probably do it for free.

The hallway spills out into an area that's a hub of debauchery and musty with incense. The only windowed section is near the bar where men smoke tobacco, if one isn't counting the glass ceiling far above that the many bridges dull the light of. A full table boasts the ass of a hog that's already partially carved away at, surrounded by legumes and oranges. Men gather in a round sitting corner, black smudge hollowing all of their bloodshot eyes, a siren tattooed on all of their forearms in thick, red ink—men of Nicholas the Merciless. Their pirating captain isn't much of an inspiration, but he knows the fucking ocean like I know how to read hearts. I doubt there's a cavern he hasn't explored.

Pirates are one of the few men that look me in the eye for longer than I like, but I've learned to stomach it. They worship the ocean and don't care about the laws that govern these lands. It's one of the things I don't care for here in Skull's Row.

It's difficult to move through the crowd without wanting

to disappear back into the quiet halls. This fucking place always has me on edge with the chaos of clashing desires, emotions, or fears.

Standing against the cold stone offers *some* reprieve; at least there's nothing to feel behind me while I wait to be taken to see Blackwell. I carefully eye the few that sit in corners and are draped in thick cloaks before scanning the room further—weathered ropes, barrels, and nautical decor fills in empty spaces as old maps adorn the walls. A few skulls painted black are perched on stakes adjacent to lanterns. Behind the bar, a few men fill tankards of ale or glasses with rum as many sit on mismatched stools or couches.

They're all waiting to speak to one of the Zenith, donning a golden skull brooch for approval. I've already sent a request to see Blackwell myself, one of my men having greeted me outside of my room to approve the meeting. I'll push aside any one of these men who go to see him before me.

Time is of the essence to establish that no one bothers Jane.

I feel the familiar lawless aura of Bones before spotting him, the man sipping on a tankard as he nears me. His slightly curled hair is slicked back, his mismatched eyes keenly scan the room. About a dozen of my men mingle about the vast area, all wearing red tunics under their armor.

Drinking deeply, Bones exhales slowly as he quietly asks, "Waiting on Blackwell?"

"Apparently someone will come get me," I breathe out. "Bastard says he doesn't want us to act like kings and yet behaves as such himself.

"He's going to get himself killed doing that. Chatted with some others who say their Zenith are growing tired of him." Bones scratches the stubble on his face. "And what the hells is Blackwell even doing acting like that? He knows better."

Ensuring it's only the two of us that I sense against this

wall, I quietly say, "I'm not sure. It was hard to read him earlier with that dramatic show he put on. It's why I want to see him man to man."

Bones shifts his focus toward me. "And what are *we* doing? Now that we're here and harboring a woman the entire Council wants to dissect?"

I lean in, motioning for him to get closer. He bows his head so his ear is right next to me, and I'm so close I can smell the ale on him. "The Scorpion isn't dead." I wet my lips before adding, "He's Jane's father."

Bones's brows raise as his eyes flit back and forth in comprehension before he wickedly laughs. "Well *that* fucking makes sense. Knew life was getting a little boring." He drinks more, speaking just above a whisper. "Is Jane in on it? Is this a mass conspiracy?"

"She doesn't know that her father is still alive. And it will remain that way until *I* tell her." I inhale deeply before adding, "And tell Anya for me. You'll see her next. Kathleen can know, as well."

I wonder if he knows of Kathleen's ties to Ritter, yet. She's already aware of more than Jane, and now Bones and Anya will be, too.

She's definitely going to try to stab me at least *once*.

"Won't even question how you know. You've got my word, sir... So why are we fighting for *one* Zenith instead of the rest? Other than half of them are cunts that I don't like?"

"I saw the rubied witch... I can explain more when the time is right. But not now. All I'm conveying is that Jane doesn't die on our watch. And we need to tell Anya soon. This whole place doesn't feel right, and I don't trust anyone."

With a single, curt nod, Bones says, "Understood."

My powers are used to the familiar twists and turns of what lies inside of Bones, and I can tell he'll fiercely defend

Jane now, even if they can't seem to get along. He and I have saved each other more than once, our trust something we need in this world where no explanations are often required.

Bones downs his tankard and meanders over to a platter of food nearby, and I warn him, "That's paid for, and not by us."

"It's getting cold," he retorts, grabbing the thick leg of a turkey, and ripping at the meat with his teeth.

Someone from the Merciless's corner stands. "'Ey! Fucker! That's ours."

Bones moves his head from side to side as if looking for a piece of parchment that would have their name on it. "It was just sitting here, mate. You want me to give it back? I can shit in this cup a little later if it means that much to you."

I pinch the bridge of my nose. Bones doesn't have a magic that's clear like some of us, but the bastard is *lucky*. If he didn't have such an unnatural ability to survive everything that *should* kill him, I'd be more pissed about this.

I know he's been itching for a fight lately. He's like a farm dog that needs ran, except his escape is *violence*.

"You buy us a new one, then," the pirate counters, taking a few strides near us as his fellows stand. "I don't know if you know of us, but the Merciless men have a reputation for stabbing someone just for *looking* at us wrong. I'll give you the benefit of the doubt... I say you buy us *two* new turkeys, now, for being so gracious."

"This is already cold, like I said," Bones says, continuing to eat it. "You're *wasteful*."

"It doesn't matter why it's sitting there, does it?" The pirate looks at me as if seeking resolution, and I do nothing other than return the glare. Bones *does* have a point—no one *was* eating it. "Fine." The pirate pulls out a blade, my body instinctively reacting as I unsheathe my own in a swift movement. Bones engages with a wicked gleam in his eyes as he pulls out a dagger—turkey leg still in his other hand—and lunges forward. The pirate dodges one swipe but is unable to miss the blade when Bones flips its orientation, sliding the steel right into his opponent's gut. Bones loudly yells to the man, "Did you know *I* have a reputation of taking on twenty men at once and only suffering a single scratch?" He twists the blade inside of the man's gut. "I can take on your whole lot and eat their food afterward, too. Maybe we should place bets on whose reputation will save them, eh?"

Bones slides the blade out as the remaining pirates are on their feet, swords glinting in a wave of weapons drawn, stools dramatically kicked over in their haste. My company approaches Bones and I, along with a few others donning the black wolf label on their vests—Corvus.

I quickly look around.

Another Zenith?

I don't spot Corvus in the crowd, but if his mercenaries are reacting, he's nearby. I say to the pirates, "If you want to attack us, I suggest not doing it in *our* rotunda. You will all die, without question, over a fucking turkey leg."

One of the Merciless men puts pressure on their comrade's wound, whose shirt is blossoming with a vermilion discoloration as he sits down on the stone floor. One of the older pirates steps forward. "Get us a healer—we'll pay for her and cause no more issues. We just came to meet with Blackwell."

My first thoughts are straight to Jane, admittedly curious about what she'd do in such a familiar environment of bar fights. *Not today, but perhaps one day soon... see what my desert rose does when back in her territory.* Eyeing the barkeep, I nod to one of them as I sheathe my blade. "Get him a healer."

One by one, blades rescind as an older woman moves quickly from a hallway and into the mayhem, swiftly finding her target as she kneels down to heal him—

A presence is at my back, one that's heavy with authority. Slowly looking over my shoulder, I'm staring at the face of Corvus—his dark skin has a fresh, deep cut on his neck that's barely healed, one I didn't notice earlier. "Who cut you?" I ask, slightly amused. "It's a badge of honor if someone can mar *your* skin."

His lips slowly form into a smile. "It was my fault. Was too drunk," he says, motioning back to the wall Bones and I were against. Our men flank us and create a barrier without a single order, to which Bones joins while continuing to eat his turkey leg. The rest of the atmosphere returns to normal, as if this is all expected.

Corvus runs a hand over the front of his leather vest. "Your man likes to cause scenes."

"And I like to believe the pirates need frequent reminders that this isn't their home."

Chuckling, Corvus chews on his bottom lip as he cants his head to the side, suggesting that's not entirely wrong. His aura bleeds with more integrity than over half of the Zenith; one of the reasons I tolerate him the most.

It's his ruthless way with a blade, and his uncanny determination to deliver his promises, that's earned him his rank. I doubt killing him would even suffice; he's the kind to haunt someone from the dead if a debt is still owed. His nearly onyx eyes slowly rise to look into mine, most of his warmth fading. "What are you doing with Jane?"

I inhale slowly, thinking these words over very carefully. "She's hiding information, but there's also something not quite right. I think her mind's been fucked with," I lie. "I need to slowly pull it apart, wait for a feeling or memory to strike her that she's forgotten."

Corvus once brought me a man who had his mind altered by a witch, and within those broken memories was knowledge of the one who once tried to assassinate this Zenith. The Council nearly broke him through torture and it took me two months to pry out the truth afterward. Corvus says, "Some of the others want her chained up. They want to skip letting you work. They don't like that she was marked without any of us knowing and they're certain they can beat and rape it out of her."

A sound escapes me that's a mixture of a grunt and a laugh, which hides the ire that burns through me. "Setting that villager aflame was an absolute waste, and so would any further torture be." I stare into Corvus's eyes. "We've already been rough with her, and every time it makes her just want to fight to the death. She doesn't know the details we want, which means—" I hesitate to keep speaking when a wave of distrust fills me. Something is different about Corvus, and I'm just now catching on; a tide that's churning. I furrow my brows. "Did something happen while I was gone?"

Corvus nods, raising a hand to run over his salt-and-pepper beard that's braided into three strands. "It's with Tempest. She was missing because Blackwell is having her leave Skull's Row to fight off a warlord in the Crimson Isles, and she's readying herself to having a bunch of men fight to be in her crew tomorrow. Many disagree with risking her for something so useless. It's dividing us." He snarls. "I fear mutiny at some point. This Jane incident has them all on edge. They're starting to wonder if it's even one of *us* that branded her. Blackwell's theory, when you left, is that someone marked her so she can be claimed as a bride, like how Belstead works in their kingdoms with wedding princesses to strengthen unions."

I churn over every word, dissecting them to feel out the veracity. Sometimes, I can feel the energy of an entire place, and I still can't quite pinpoint why the Spiraling Stone feels *off*.

It *all* does.

"I don't like the energy here," I reply.

Corvus deeply inhales through his nose as he looks around, leaning even further in. My powers devour his aura like one of Cypress's hellhounds catching a scent. "Keep an eye on Jane. Someone will try to steal her, I'm sure of it, and I want to know how the fuck she got that tattoo before that happens, so don't go slow with her."

His eyes remain stolid as he adds, "Something is going on, Soren. I don't trust it. She's an anomaly. If anyone is going to understand what that is, it's *you*. And I want to know if I need to leave this damn city before it all goes to shit. I *will* cut down any one of you that gets in my way, too. This is mostly a friendly warning."

Every crevice of his essence seems to be telling the bold truth. Corvus doesn't let me respond before nodding at me and turning to walk away.

Well, that was... *enlightening*.

Great. So, none of us trust each other and they'll all be seeking out Jane, one way or another. Like men who have gone crazy with thirst at sea and start drinking the water.

Being here swiftly feels wrong.

I focus back on the energy shift of this castle and how I didn't feel this before I left. It's the sensation of eyes on one's back even if they can't find a face to point to—

I catch an impression in the air that I can't describe; it's coming from down a corridor that has an iron gate sealing it off.

One of Blackwell's men strides along it, and I can tell he's coming to fetch me. But as I stare down the stone walls behind him, I can't remove my gaze. There's absolutely nothing there, and yet something... something *dark* is there.

What the fuck is going on?

I waste no time as I near the gate, the guard opening it for me as I'm led away from the noise of the rotunda. I barely register the walk to Blackwell's quarters, overwhelmed by something acrid—if energies even had a scent. Staring at his door reminds me of Cypress's home, as if deep and ancient magic besmirches the walls.

But when it opens and I'm led inside, the storm brewing in my chest calms; if anything, it's just cold inside.

The room nearly matches the rotunda, but all the windows in here are circular.

"Looking for something?" Blackwell asks.

I roll my eyes to the man who sits behind a large desk, sipping on a brownish liquid. He holds my gaze as I dissect what I can of him, the natural light from behind casting a murky shadow over his face. Rather than play ignorant, I remark, "Your energy has changed since I was last here."

I swear his eyes flit to a corner of the room before he downs what's left in his glass. "Yes, because I see someone has been marked without our permission."

Looking over my shoulder, I stare at a corner that seems entirely empty. My magic burns into my senses, telling me I *should* see something almost *evil* there, and yet it's just two walls converging.

When I move my gaze back at Blackwell, he *too* is staring there.

I invite myself to a seat in front of his desk, my body vibrating with an absolute desire to flee this room and whatever is going on with that corner. "You realize Jane is not a threat?" I ask. "Her being marked is annoying, sure, but it's not as if she has an entire army at her command."

Blackwell inhales, raising a tattooed hand to wipe at lips before lowering his gaze to the table between us. "Someone gave her that without our knowledge. We have to figure out *who,* at the very least. If we even catch a *scent* that she's a threat, though, half of the Council wants her dead as a precaution *and* a warning."

"That's not unreasonable, but burning her people won't help, that's for certain," I counter, still miffed that he did that without consulting me. What's the fucking point to me doing what I do if they'll fuck with the one I'm interrogating? It's not as if Jane is my *actual* target, but I don't miss the way Blackwell acts more like an official leader rather than someone the others once respected.

He laughs. "Going soft and feeling sorry for that woman?"

"I'm an efficient man, and muddling Jane's heart with extreme fear will only make my job worse."

He chews on his lip before sighing. "Allright, fine. You can have whatever time you need with her. Don't particularly want singed flesh in Storm's Gathering. I'll be sending Jamie, my personal noir, to check in from time to time."

I want to nod, but as I stare at this man, I can't—I can't read him.

A sense of foreboding grips my heart, as if I realize I shouldn't be in here. I don't know why, but I just shouldn't be. "That's all I wanted to come and discuss," I reply, a dreadful chill crawling up my spine.

Twisting my hips so I can turn around in my seat when I get the undeniable sense that someone is right behind me, I glare at that empty corner again. It's a blank fucking space, but I *know* it's not.

"You're paranoid, Soren," Blackwell comments.

Deeply breathing, I slowly face the man before me. I grip my knee as I ignore the provocative statement. "In regards to Jane, if any of you fuck this up again like last time, I'm going to stab someone. It's a complete waste of my time to have *any* of you meddling."

He raises his hand and says, "Then we'll leave her to you. Like I said," his eyes sharpen on me, "we'll be watching."

This is *all* fucking wrong. Trying to read him is like telling a blind man to decipher a written riddle. He's too passive, and I can't shake the damn feeling that we're not alone in here.

Without another word, I stand to leave, almost not wanting to look in that corner.

I don't know what Blackwell has fucked with, but I don't trust an inch of this place anymore.

Soren had not lingered, leaving me inside his baroque living quarters. It reminds me of a captain's chambers, full of effects personal to him.

As nosy as I feel, I remain in my seat and slowly survey the place while the liquor buzzes in my mind. The act of standing feels like it will warrant someone to bolt in and secure me in rope binds.

Did he really just leave me alone?

My heart races as I skim the area with more purpose, especially as Maryanne's screams threaten to chase my mental state into delirium. Risking it, I rise to my feet, listening to the dead silence as if at any point, I'll hear a jiggling of the doorknob. But as I carefully cross the room to the window... nothing happens.

I stare at the glass more than at the scene behind it. "Hello..." I say, looking around. "I'm just standing in here, all alone, with Soren's things..."

Silence.

I straighten up, my face filtering through many expressions as my heart wants to unleash itself and begin crying over what I witnessed, but logic tells me I can't break; not yet. On an end table that's near me—one that sits underneath a painting of a grassy field with a small wooden home—is a globe. I spin it, keeping my gaze on the door. Perhaps they're waiting for me to upend the place, like before.

All I hear is the wooden sphere slow in its spin.

Scratching my nose, I start to consider that maybe he really did just leave me here. I even move the globe to a different spot on the end table, as if to claim I was here, before rocking back and forth on my feet.

What in the hells do I do now?

I know better than to try for the door. I want Soren's guards to give a glowing report of my behavior when he returns. A situation like this requires leverage.

But there's *another* door...

Fidgeting with the balcony door handle once upon it, I manage to open it with a rather aggressive yank. A gust of wind sweeps through, instantly enveloping me in a cool breeze as I step outside. I squint when the sun's rays invade my vision. The scent of the ocean fills my lungs, flooding me with memories of a familiar hug—I instantly recall Dad taking me down to the piers of Skull's Row during a storm, to show me how magic kept their ships protected.

It's a city all in itself down there.

In my mind, I can hear the men shouting as they work the rigs below, listening to the deep groans of their thick ropes, and feeling the droplets of salt water on my head and shoulders as I stare at the barnacles on the underbellies. There will be a few dozen ships sitting in Skull's Bay, waiting to port. A salty, crusty type of humanity haunts those wooden terraces. A pirate once told me, *'I don't feel right on shore, not even on your fucking stone. Soil is useless—'*

"Jane?"

It's a woman's voice, one I don't recognize, and coming from inside the room. I look back, but the glass of the door only reflects the clouds, the breeze having nearly shut it. Opening it back up, I peer in to see a few young women moving about, one even wheeling in a large casket of... water? Yes, that's what's labeled on the side. Anya's pejorative glare latches to me by the open door, overseeing it all.

Oh, lovely. It all makes sense now. I was only *momentarily* left alone.

A short woman with tanned skin and straight black hair looks right at me, her high cheekbones creating a unique elegance that her longer neck enhances. "There you are," she says, delicately flipping her shiny hair over her shoulder. "We are having a bath drawn for you. The casket has warm water but will need heating to make it, well... he said to make it *steamy*," she states, those hooded, dark eyes imploring that I should correct her if she's wrong.

I stumble over my words as I focus on the woman in front of me. "Well... I do like steamy baths—wait, is it for me?"

Relief washes over the woman, who is a little too clean and well-kept to not be of some service to the Spiraling Stone. "Oh, good. All right, yes. We are also just to take care of you, overall," she says with a dainty flick of her wrist, speaking more casually. "Hair trim, nails, all of it."

I raise my brows, slowly looking back at Anya, who seems to have absorbed all of Soren's callous nature in the way she looks at me like I just confessed to burning down her family home. Refraining a snarky comment nearly hurts until I remind myself that I don't know her. Or Soren.

And I don't have the energy to deal with either of them.

Looking back at the woman, she swiftly snaps her gaze back to connect with mine, as if trying to hide that she wasn't looking me over just now. I ask, "What's your name?"

"Lora," she warmly says, gesturing to a room that's between the main bedroom and balcony door. "Come into the bathing room. Please, let us help you relax."

I feel like I need to ask Lora to clarify—just to be sure this is real—as this is much different than when I got a bath because of negotiations. As I hear the door to Soren's quarters shut, I nearly reach for a knife that's been missing for the last— however many days—only to see that it's just Anya, dramatically shutting it now that everyone is inside. My heart races with wasted adrenaline, sighing to get the energy out. Anya pulls a chair over to block my only exit as she sits there. Lora looks like she wants to interject, to reclaim my attention, but she only hesitantly watches.

Anya turns the chair to sit backward on it, nodding toward me. "I know your sunder won't work a second time—not so close in usage... and if you try to get within arm's reach of me, I'll knock you out so hard you won't wake up for an entire day."

I place a hand over my stomach, feeling incredibly sardonic. "Where's the fun in that? I enjoyed being stabbed so much."

Lora watches with concern. No doubt, she has seen over a

hundred fights break out over smaller disputes. I've even witnessed two men order the same drink at the same time, the altercation resulting in someone losing a hand.

Anya snorts, revealing a rather fetching smile, even with the giant scar on her cheek. "Go enjoy your bath, little pet."

My blood burns with a fight, my arms swinging at my side. Again, I'm too tired for this. *Don't waste the bath.* "No problem. Sounds rather nice anyway. Enjoy sitting in that chair."

I briskly walk toward where Lora has been trying to guide me, wanting to stab more pillows rather than take a bath.

But when I see a large ceramic tub in a bathing room... it tames me. Glorious, floor-to-ceiling windows brighten up the dim room. The other two that join Lora quickly heat buckets of water over the fire. I peer into the casket and notice it's already quite warm. I recognize they're all wearing simple black dresses with black corsets, and matching silver chain necklaces. It makes sense, now, to see them. All the men here call them different names—bedside wenches, carers, tenders, or more commonly, the noirs. It depends on who grew up hearing what.

No matter the title, these are the men and women that take care of the elite. One doesn't have to be a Zenith to summon them, either. Warlords and rich mercenaries hire noirs all the same.

I've learned the rest of the world calls them 'maids'. As with anything else, ours are a little rougher around the edges, even if they look prim.

Taking a step near, I see the tub has a plugged hole in the bottom. They are already pouring steamy water in, tapping droplets of scented oils with each pour.

I'm a little disappointed to realize that if Anya is here, then it means Soren won't appear in the doorway to watch me bathe. The bastard easily glides into my mind like a fog, clouding the rest of the world and my better judgment. He's safe while existing within my imagination; he can't talk or potentially make things worse—

Lora cuts through my rumination. "Soren says you are fond of wine," she says, pulling out a bottle from a bag they brought.

I blink multiple times, as if it will make the scene change; but she's still holding a dark bottle. "What the hells is going on?"

Lora tries to control a smile. "Soren implores that you get as much relaxation as possible. He came to Kendra's not long ago, and we acted right away, per his instructions."

I don't know who Kendra is, but as I watch them pour more water in, I also can't resist it. "All right, I'll bite, I guess."

Lora looks incredibly pleased, like she has been warned I might say no.

As she turns around to pour some wine, a hesitation steels me as I finally understand why I feel off, in more ways than the obvious—it's like home. Mother would have baths like this drawn for us once a month. Noirs and all. I'm not sure how my father managed it without people asking questions, but he did.

It's why I hated bathing in the damn river so much back in Coalfell. I always thought that if the killers of my home took such pride in luxurious hygiene, surely others would.

But farmers bathe in the river like a common mule. Maybe it's just all they know.

Is Soren aware of how much this touches me? How much this makes me feel like I'm home? How much this also makes me feel like I have failed to stay away? It's one thing to be forced back here, but another to drink rare wine and sit in a steaming, oily bath.

Something about wine being offered, while doing this, makes

me miss my mother in ways that haven't ached in years. Oh, how I'd kill to have her sit with me right now, to tell her of everything that's happened, to share this drink with her. She'd no doubt laugh and tell me I *am* home, whether I like it or not; remind me how she chose to live here because she was born here, too.

The attempt to prune my familial roots over the last decade was clearly done in futility. My thriving roots dig deep into the soil here, threatening that they'll lash out if I try to remove them again.

I yearn for my father to be alive so he can tell me that the shit with the Council will be all right. For him to explain what truly happened and why he chose to disappear, now that I'm older and able to understand...

I wipe my eyes and pretend they were just itchy before stripping in front of the women, knowing they have seen countless naked bodies, and get into the bath. I relax right away into the warm, salty water that has a decadent floral scent, something earthy and sweet.

"Who picked this smell?" I ask, melting into the heat. I already know the answer but want to hear it.

"Soren," Lora replies, pouring a glass of wine.

The other noirs don't look at me as they continue to fill the tub, and I know it's out of respect for Soren. Lora hands me the wine in a glass. I stare at it, and another noir begins to comb my hair. My eyes roll with pleasure at the sensation of a comb against my skull.

But somewhere in the luxury, guilt pries its way back in as I recall Maryanne not just being burned alive, but stripped and humiliated beforehand. Drinking the decadent wine, my mind completely numbs itself in confusion.

Everything spirals so quickly.

Even with the noirs watching, I allow myself to weep for

Maryanne, who will never grow old to see who her children could become.

Just as my mother couldn't.

That pain of losing a parent to such brutality, even if those children will never know why, turns my sobs into an uncontrolled release of suppressed agony, the women cleaning me as if this is normal.

STORIES

JANE

As soon as they leave, I put on a ruby red robe and unabashedly walk past Anya, as if to rub it in that I'm *not* a threat, and head into the bedroom so I can sleep. My eyes are puffy, and I feel like I just cleansed my soul of everything that's tormented me for over a decade.

But I only get so far as the doorway.

As I stand in the threshold, I know this is Soren's only dwelling away from his lands—as these men all have different places that they truly call home—but this is as private as it gets in Skull's Row, and I nearly strode in like it's a tavern's sleeping quarters. As if I'm *comfortable*.

But once I see his bed, it calls to me. A thick, maroon blanket awaits me with no creases, the stone floors frigid against my feet. There's even a fire already started—possibly by a noir, as it only took one of them to dry my hair with a towel. I shut the door to trap in the heat, dropping the robe once I'm next to the bed. There's no point in looking around or being nosy. I'm exhausted, and I need to rest. I crawl underneath the heavy materials, shivering from the cool fabric. The pillowcases are black silk, and for a while, I stare at the empty side of the grand bed.

He really sleeps in opulence, doesn't he?

Eventually, my body radiates enough heat that a cocoon of warmth makes my eyelids grow heavy. I fall asleep with such ease that the next time I open my eyes, I'm in the same position and the sun is nearly down.

My heavy lids close again.

I don't know how long I was asleep after that, but when I wake up next, it's completely black outside and there's someone in the room. The bedroom door is shut, the hearth roaring with a new blaze.

Barely moving, I try to spot the intruder. On the off-chance it's *not* Soren and I need to play pretend. But my heart rushes with everything forbidden when I spot Soren's bare back, the mercenary legend returned.

My nudity feels extra risky underneath these sheets, watching him untie his hair at the nape of his neck, his chestnut waves coming loose.

His voice blends in with the warmth of the fire, his back still to me as he sits on a bench and removes his boots. "You feel extremely relaxed."

I stretch, spreading my legs and grazing against the cold side of the bed. "Well, wine and a bath will do that for you." I clear my throat. "And, um... thank you, for that." I don't want that foreign sentiment hanging in the air, as if it makes my throat itchy, so I quickly add, "When did you get that tattoo?"

He looks around for a moment, as if wondering what I refer to, then asks, "The one on my spine?"

I observe the long black lines, and how they taper unevenly near his hips. "Yes."

He leans forward again to untie his laces, the tattooed spine pronounced as the back muscles flex. "When I was sixteen."

I frown, looking up at the ceiling that mimics the wooden design of a ship. Father always said that to wear the black stripe of Death's Wing was a brutal membership, requiring terrible acts of aggression, just like the Zenith tattoo. "That's young for a tattoo like that."

Humor laces his rough voice. "Concerned for my life?"

"No," I say, almost too fast. He stands, running a hand through his hair as the fire light casts harsh shadows in juxta-position to the brightly illuminated strips of him. He places his blades on the bedside table, right next to his Black Skull mask. I glance at the skull tattoo over his heart.

I dare to meet his gaze—he's surveying the curves of my body through the blanket with a patient desire; like he's going to take his time tonight.

"Do you always sleep with pants on?" I ask, risking the sexual response in return, realizing he's not taking them off.

"If someone barricades in, I'd rather have them on. Unless you want them off, love. I assume you might, wearing nothing under there yourself."

I don't move. I don't know what I'm doing. This moment feels so... ordinary. My heart wants to leap in like this is a break from reality—my heated cheeks grow so warm that I must look as red as the comforter. I angrily flip over and give him my back, although I let a smile spread once I know he can't see me. I suppose that's a wasted effort if he can feel it.

How I would love for him to stand before me completely bare, so I may stare at the masculine parts of him, to touch him in ways that make him groan just for me.

I hear something that sounds like an amused huff. The cooler air touches my skin as the covers lift even more so he may enter. The bed takes his weight, and his rough hand instantly makes contact with my lower back, my body stiffening. It slides up to my shoulder blade, and he leans closer.

The cold side of the bed is now filled with a behemoth of a killer, and I'm nothing but willing.

He's close to the back of my head, his hand gently sliding into my slightly damp hair. "Fights are happening in the Savage Sands tomorrow. Tempest was down here when you came to the spiraling stone. There's a warlord that has taken over the Crimson Isles. They're rallying to teach him who owns those lands, and Tempest is having some men fight for her here. I'm attending to watch because it feels important that I go. You're coming with me."

"As your pet?" I ask, staring at the wall. The fire is already losing its light.

The sexual charge is electric, my heart racing so furiously with desire that I'm nearly panting. A desperate part of me wants those massive arms to pull me right into his heat, to lay over me, for his breath to mix with mine in this secluded darkness, where he reigns.

"Do you want to see how the world has changed, or not?"

"Yes," I mutter.

His hand gently grips my hair, my cheek moving against the silk pillow as he pulls my head back. I can hear him sigh, a growl laced within. He releases and glides his hand from my back to my hip, pausing with a firm grip, his breathing deepening, as if his imagination suggests many things he wishes to do. I already know that I will let him touch wherever—the silence makes sense now. He's feeling me out. He finally says, "Yes, as my pet." He adds the next words like an observation. "You still don't completely trust me."

No... why is he ruining this? Why can't he just be domineering like before? Force me into wanting him? I don't want to think about how I'm smarter than this, and how only a horny idiot would let her walls down so easily. It's not *my* fault that Soren is so tempting that it nearly hurts.

He's got the tattoos of two powerful, legendary coalitions on his body, and he's earned them. Men like him use women like me. Both my parents warned me of being coerced, and the Council even called Soren their manipulator.

I gently speak the truth, his body resting behind me in a way that makes me feel full of *want*. "It would all be too convenient, Soren, if we really are just two people who miraculously met and got along so well. It's hard for me not to think that."

He leans into my hair, breathing in what must smell like heaven to him—he's the one that picked the damn scent.

My skin is even as soft as velvet, just for him.

The next words from his mouth shock me. "What if I tell you a story from my childhood?"

I stiffen, my eyes widening. "What?" I ask with intrigue.

With one tug of my hip, my ass slides closer to him, a slight gasp escapes me. The rise and fall of his breathing grazes my back, his hand slowly running up my stomach. For a moment, it almost feels like he's holding me, enveloped in a light embrace. I don't move. I'm so turned on I'd probably do whatever he told me to do. And I just know he's taking his time because of that.

Soren fists my breast and I whimper—he chuckles in my ear—and his calloused grip moves to around my neck, holding me to him as his mighty arm wraps around me. "You want the selfish answer? I'm eager to feel you with your walls down. I will break them if I have to—and don't ask why. I don't know. But it's what I want."

"You want my affection?" I ask, smiling with triumph, staring at a dresser. The metal handles faintly glint with firelight in the dim room.

He gently chokes me, his voice roughening, my body pressing harder into his. "Just as you want mine."

"I don't even know you," I whisper. My body doesn't seem to give a damn about that. He's not wrong. I crave a side of him that only my imagination has seen.

"I'm aware... so let me tell you of myself."

What the hells? He can't do this to me. He can't make me feel these *things*. "You're trying to gain something. I just know it."

His voice is terse. "I'm done repeating myself. You interest me, and it's not more complicated than that." He moves quickly as his iron grip releases, only for one of his fingers to slide through my parted lips and into my mouth, pulling on my cheek so if anyone could see me, I'd look rather ridiculous. The rest of his fingers grip my jaw to hold it still, hooking me with his index.

"Whaf fa hells..." I mutter, trying to bite him.

His tone is assertive. "Yes, I know you can *bite*." He moves closer to my ear, his other arm perching him up so he can lean over from behind, creating an effect of dominance that makes me wet between my thighs. It's the least alluring act a man has done to me, and yet it turns me on. "Now, you can either listen to what I have to say and lay here rather peacefully with me, or I can tie you up again. Your choice."

I continue to stare across the way, not wanting to look at him. If I do, I might start kissing him. This makes me feel like I need a substantial amount of soul-searching so I can under-stand why a move like this makes me bend so easily for him. Before he can say anything else, I nod.

He pulls his finger out of my mouth, and without wasting a moment, I request, "Tell me of the time you knew you had powers."

Soren takes the same hand and runs it through the back of my hair again, and I get the sense that he's looking at me like a curious animal he caught. My eyes close at his touch, and for a moment, I just give in and pretend this moment is actually real versus layered with many hidden motives.

"They've always been there. The powers to feel others," he breathes, speaking once I'm calmed. "They've grown over the years, to the point I swear I can hear thoughts when keened in on someone, and even sense the energy of a room... but I was first aware of them when a man was thinking rather dangerous thoughts about my mother." I tense, opening my eyes. He continues to slip his fingers through my hair. "And I didn't understand at first. I saw him and knew what he intended. But still, I wasn't certain. I was only nine, and while I didn't grow up in Skull's Row, I grew up near the men who eventually gifted me the tattoo on my spine. I was used to atrocious behavior, but so far, it had yet to hurt my mother. She took care of me in that world. It's her last name that I carry."

His touch doesn't roughen, but his voice thins of its favor-able nature, donning an echo of the terror that this man is capable of. "But then he cornered her, and she cried for me." I blink rapidly as I look down at the silk pillow, where my head lay. "I could feel how he wanted to leave her raped and blood-ied, so I grabbed a blade I had stolen a few months prior and stabbed him right between the legs, tearing away that piece of him. I then looked at my mother and *felt* her fear. Fear of *me*—" for the first time, I hear the closest thing to anguish in his voice

"—then nothing but love and gratitude. And I've made it a habit to castrate those that go near something of mine ever since." His grip loosens and his tone lightens. "I've changed how I've used my ability over the years. Whores hate me for it. I can always see through the ones that are just there to make money. I'm not a very good tipper because of it. Unless she does her job well."

Something bitter festers in my heart at the image of him with another woman.

I can hear the smile and approval in his voice. "Is that jealousy I feel, Jane?"

My heart's torn between wanting him to fuck me so hard that I need another bath, while also being twisted into feeling sorry for him for all he had to overcome. My voice cracks a little as I ask, "Where is your mother now?"

"She lives a comfortable life, back in my lands."

"Really?" I ask, slightly moving so my face is closer to his, my gaze still locked ahead. "And, well... I'm sorry to hear you had to do such a thing, so early. I know what that does to someone."

"It made me the man that I am. Mother wants for nothing, now." My ass is still against the ridge in his pants that has not changed since he's laid down, my torso twisted so my shoulder is against his chest. He pulls his head back enough to look down at me while I avoid eye contact. "What happened to your family, Jane?"

Soren is good, I'll give him that. I'm so enveloped in him that my story nearly leaves my lips without thought, but the truth lodges in my throat with how deep those secrets run.

Silence binds us for a very long time as I recall the details. Soren's hand that was in my hair remains still, his arm crossed over his chest. I can feel his heartbeat through the bareness of our skin.

The intimacy nearly hooks and sinks me, but a relic of my survival reels and forces me to consider all the other women that he has told this exact story to, perhaps even while in this bed—

He leans over my face, my blood warming like Soren is the perfect liquor on a bitter, stormy night out at sea. I practically hold my breath, staring firmly at the ceiling. "Other women haven't slept in this bed, Jane. Nor have they heard that story. So don't even try."

I nearly flick my gaze at him. "What?"

Now it's his turn to ignore me. "You don't have to speak of your family, but tell me, vaguely if you must, *why* the siren gave you her song. They so rarely do it. What was offered, other than a promise?"

As I feel his powerful chest rise and fall, I lean my head into him. I don't like the memories that return. How recalling my encounter with Melona means I have to remember my mother being killed, and also how it felt to kill my first man, only a year older than Soren was when he killed his; my heart feels exposed in this setting.

I move my head so I can stare at Soren's darkened face. The words are in my throat, where they burn with a pain I've never shared with a living soul. It makes me want to cry—the recollections flood me, and I hate that Soren really is a stranger. I hate that trusting him could backfire.

A single tear falls down my face and into my ear, and that's all that I let out as I quietly say, "We didn't even get to bury my mom, or take anything of hers. Dad was there not too long after, and I held her. I couldn't tell whose blood was whose, and Dad had to pry me away. He tucked my face into his neck and carried me as I cried. He just kept telling me that I had to be strong. That—that he had to leave. They'd hunt me if they thought he was alive, as I guess *he* was being hunted, too..." My breathing grows deeper. "He gave Melona, the siren, his Zenith's mask. I didn't know it could be given away like that, but he did it. I don't know what she's done with it, either. I just know that's what the offer was. In turn, she took me. She taught me the sunder and drowned me as a means to bind her protection to me, and so I'd keep my promise of never returning to Skull's Row. She safely guided me through the waters and beached us inside of a pirate's cave that had the basics for survival—you know of all the ones stashed around these lands—and she taught me the song. I remained there for a week while she checked on me. And then she got me to shore, I made my way to Coalfell, and I never saw anyone from my life again." My nostrils flare as I frown, and I refuse to look away from him.

Softly, he asks, "Why does it feel like you've never told anyone that?"

My voice shakes as I admit, "Because I haven't."

Something flashes in his eyes, and it even reminds me a little of how Bones looks at Kathleen. Soren asks, "What of your friend? You never told her?"

"Not even her."

Yes... saying that has done something to him. This is personal, and I don't know why. He comments, "I'm surprised you didn't fight me more just now."

I don't know. I don't have a good answer, other than a piti-ful, "I'm tired of keeping secrets only I know." I've already said so much, so I might as well add, "It's lonely."

He finally moves his free hand and slides under the covers to grab my wrist. Pulling my arm from beneath the warmth, Soren takes in the circular healer's symbol.

After a brief moment, he turns my hand over to kiss the top of it, his warm lips on my skin. My eyes focus on him with sincerity. I've been flirty with many, sure, but I look at him like his lips have brushed against a needy part of my soul.

His lips part from my hand. "Sleep, Jane."

The desire to bury my face into the chest of a man as powerful as Soren makes me stutter out, "You're not going to make me scream your name?"

A grin spreads almost instantly as the fading fire silhouettes him. "Of course, but not tonight. You need to sleep more than anything else, I think..."

"You're really just letting me sleep in your bed? I'm not even relegated to the couch?"

"Does it matter?" he adjusts himself as he lays down on his back; disappointment consumes me to know that I won't be touching him more. "I'm not tying you up. So, whether you're here or on the couch doesn't make a difference."

I sigh, looking at the hand he kissed, then at the mercenary legend that moves his pillow so it's more comfortable. If I knew him more, I may have asked for him to hold me.

But I don't.

I wake up in the early morning lying on my side, facing Jane who rolls over, nearly planting her pretty face into mine.

I raise a brow, staring at her in the soft lighting of the rising sun.

She had wanted me to hold her last night, I'm sure of it. She's even after such affection in her sleep. The action seemed like a rather intriguing idea, I admit, but I need to be cautious. And I also don't want to rush Jane. There are so many layers that require delicacy in pulling back, and I know letting her truly rest will help her trust me.

Something nags so powerfully in my gut that she's in danger, beyond a reasoning that I can understand. It's as if a darkness looms closer to her, threatening to steal her light—is it related to Blackwell, somehow?

The energy of this castle is off. After meeting with Blackwell, he's more paranoid than usual, and it felt like something was haunting the fucking corner that he kept peering toward; a deep danger emitted there, even if it looked no different from the rest of his room.

Jane frowns, her lips mumbling. My desert flower is having a bad dream.

I stare at her. Her heart broke last night, a deep layer of loss revealing itself that felt as if it had never seen the sun. There's an instinct in me to gentle that pain; I learned long ago that I thrive off of someone needing me. Someone looking to me for help.

The way I feel important when everything works—no treasure can buy that. No war won can steal that. A part of me glimpsed that potential the night I stormed after her, when she badly didn't want to return. She fucking can't get enough of how I'm *Skull's Row* personified, and she eats it up like a starving woman with an endless supply of lemon cakes.

And oh, how I wanted to lick every inch of her last night... kiss more than her hand. Which is why all I do is look at her now.

This is risky of me, and I know it. I'm exerting extra layers of caution because of her father, who I swear is nearby even when I can't see him. But taking the time to tend to her brokenness? That's all voluntary.

Maybe I'm getting older.

Maybe this life is growing boring, oddly enough.

Jane is special. She is Ritter's daughter, sharing the same tattoo as me. A siren not only saved her but gave her the sunder. She has a beauty that captivates me, and she's resilient. Ruthless.

I simply do not come across women like her. Ever. She's a perfect blend of everything I desire, and the way she melted when I kissed her hand... men have gone to wars to secure and protect something as simple as that.

Some auburn hair falls on her face when she shifts. I reach over, hovering my hand in front of her, as if reconsidering. But she's my little pet today. I can't fucking help it—I will pry her open, if I must. I'm a determined fucker, and I will remove every last, little thorn she has, and stab any man that tries to do the same. Making her belong solely to me is so tempting that I don't know what to do with myself.

My hand hovers there, feeling the heat of her body. She's so delectable and inviting next to me. So soft. I want to fuck her for more reasons than a release. I want to be so deep in her, while breathing in the flowery scent of her thick hair.

I move the few strands out of her closed eyes, so as not to wake her. The gesture fills me with something that hardens my face out of self-protection, and I quietly get out of bed. These gentle moments are magnetic, and I'm not familiar with such affections. I've felt them within others, but never has it come from my own heart.

I leave the room to give her space. To give *me* space. Entering the living quarters, wearing only leather pants, I run my hand over my stubble-lined cheeks. *'You look good with stubble.'*

I'm even remembering her fucking words like they're supposed to be important to me, considering keeping my face this way. At the same time, logic tells me I had my fun and now it's time to nip this in the bud and send her on her way. Keep her at a distance while I protect her for Charles Ritter's sake— but an aggressive part of my being rejects the very notion. If I send her on her way, I'll just follow her. Watch her. Kill all the men that flirt with her. Then appear before her in the dead of night when she least expects me, relishing how I unravel Jane in ways that are completely intoxicating to me.

Whether we both like it or not, I'll haunt her shadows as if they're my own.

Which means I need to understand why this castle feels *off*, and what our next steps are.

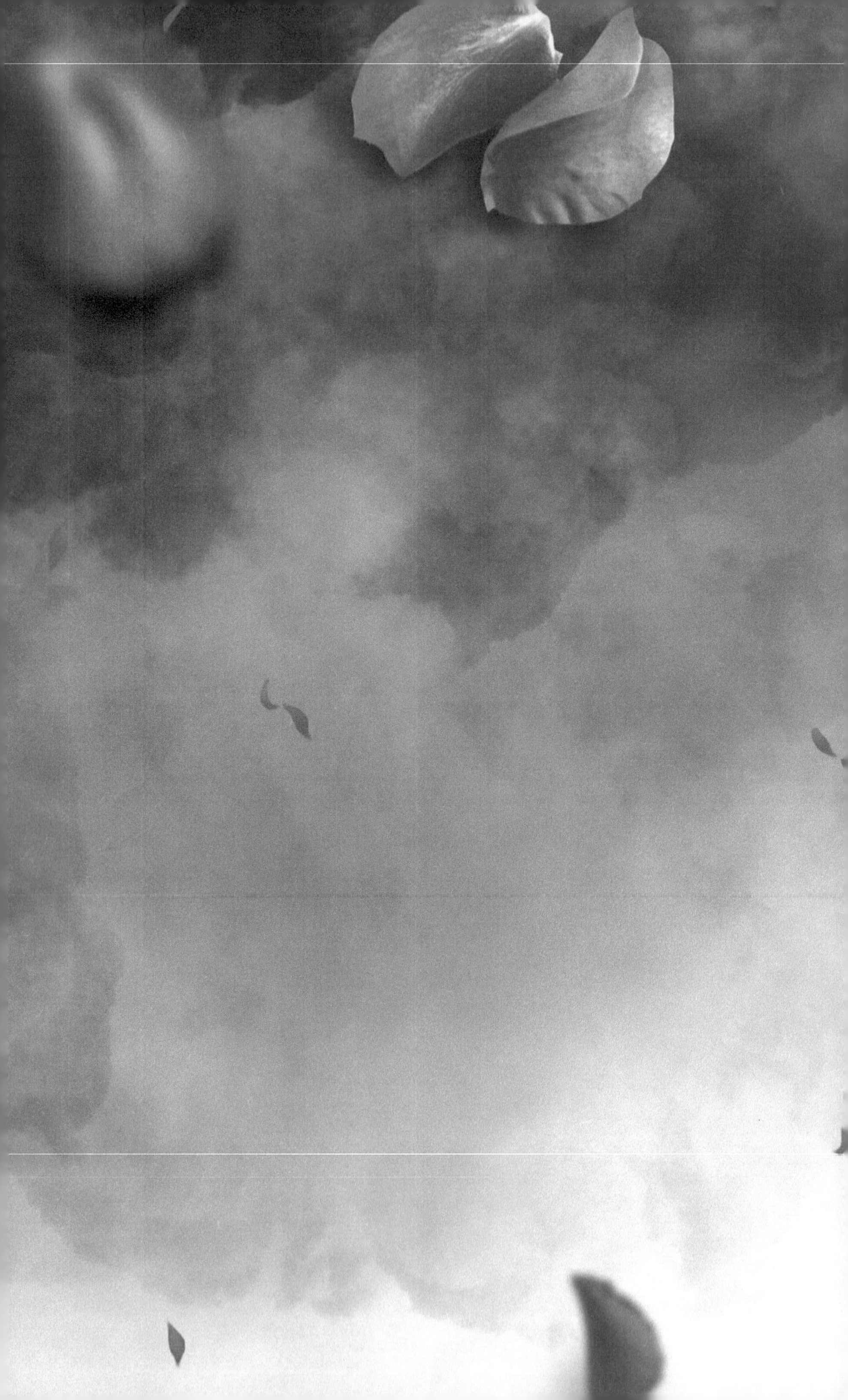

ANYA'S THEORIES

JANE

I wake to an empty bed, saddened by the lack of his presence. I reach out to touch where he once was, rubbing my hand on the cold fabric. The way my heart sinks when I confirm it's completely void of him shocks me. A whimsical, naïve part of me is eager for Soren. For a man like him. Maybe I should have pushed for more last night, after he kissed my hand like he's some kind of knight.

He's not supposed to carry such allure, or have any possibility of being gentle. And yet he's displayed that he possesses those capabilities behind whatever barrier I'm trying to penetrate, even against my better judgment.

I roll over when I feel my heart begging to wander in the forbidden land of hope. Tossing the comforter off of me, I brave the cold room as I pick up the silk robe from the floor, hugging myself once it's tied around me. Finding the water basin, I quench my growing thirst.

Placing down the cup with a soft thud, licking my wet lips as I glance around the room, I finally take it in: the sun is bright enough to indicate that morning might even be passed, and I see that his armor is still here. I stride over the frigid floor, eyeing his effects that cast elongated shadows in the dim lighting. They look so elegant and deadly, so *professional*. I don't touch anything, as he strikes me as the kind of man who remembers *exactly* how he lays his things. I do lean over, though, tucking my hair behind my ear to get a closer look.

His thick chest piece is marred by many abrasions. A handful of the marks gouge deep enough that I'm sure he'll need to repair it soon. Chainmail glints next to his leather, folded up in the same liquidy manner of silk. I continue eyeing his many blades, all with a sharpened edge, neatly laid out next to each other.

A few of his blades are out, and I nearly touch one of them —a dagger with the hilt of a snake. One end has the open, hissing head of the reptile while the other is the body wrapping around to form the handle.

I look over my shoulder at the nightstand—his mask is still there. If the bedside was cold, then it means I've been in here a while with his things.

Then again, what am I going to do—steal his armor? Wear his mask? I scoff at the thought, having absolutely no desire to touch the Zenith's face covering. Father's felt like a performer's mask in my hands, morphing into a texture of leather when he wore it. It even burned my face once when I kept trying to walk off with it.

Mother had to heal me, then.

I'm not sure why her absence seems heavier than normal. It's not as if we're in the home I knew.

Plus, that isn't even my father's mask. The golden decorations on Soren's are more rounded and elegant, whereas Father's had many straight, geometrical patterns.

It's also not going to do me any good to stand around and stare at his things like they're important. If anything, finding out where he went is the priority.

I push on the heavy wooden door of the bedroom, squinting at how bright it is in the sitting area—I realize then that the windows in his room are still partially curtained, whereas the red velvet drapes of the main sitting area are completely drawn aside.

My heart begs for me to wonder if he left them slightly shut for me.

Still, I don't see Soren. Instead, I spot Lora sitting on a couch as a few other noirs use the giant hearth to cook food.

Lora seems to sense my presence and looks over her shoulder to smile at me. "Ah, there you are."

The bedroom door shuts behind me with a deep groan, the doorknob loudly clicking. The warmth of the fire beckons me, and I near them without hesitation. "Where's Soren?"

"Training. Staying in shape," Anya answers with her smooth, slow voice that brings me no comfort. It doesn't take long to realize she's still by the front door, sitting there like a hawk who has been given strict orders not to move.

I continue to near the fire, the stone is warmer underneath my feet once close enough. "Good to see you here, Anya," I say with heavy sarcasm.

"Of course," she says, returning the acrimony.

I glance at Lora before sitting down in a chair that's closest to the hearth. The others cook eggs in cast iron, along with pork meat and, surprisingly, muffins.

That's definitely a luxury I won't complain about anytime soon.

"Do you do this often?" I ask, my grumbling stomach almost as loud as the popping fat from the meat they begin to cook.

"Do what? Tend to the Zenith?" Lora asks.

I face her, noting she looks exactly as she did yesterday. A small sliver of ink is visible behind her ear in the shape of a sparrow. "No. Tend to Soren's *pets*," I explain, motioning to myself with raised brows.

Lora nearly laughs. "Oh, no. He only deals with his pets in *their* establishments. This is my first time tending to someone here. I didn't even know he had a bath."

I frown, although my heart beats with victory, demanding I let that sink in. "Who comes in here, then?"

"No one," Anya says, as if the fact annoys her. "When he fucks, it's in another room. He's very particular about who he allows in his personal space."

Oh, that's dangerous for me to hear. The recognition that I'm actually making him go against his code strokes my ego as if it's a wild beast. I cross my arms, deliberately ignoring Anya so I don't lose myself to whimsy.

Lora leans in, both her hands flat on either thigh. "Did you sleep in his bed?"

My jaded heart prompts me to narrow my eyes, finding the question rather silly. "He set you up to this, didn't he?" I tersely ask, although the words sound funny when I recite them in my head.

Her brows knit in confusion. "What?"

I avert my gaze, watching the food being made as I press my lips together. "I—Nevermind. It's nothing."

They separate the food onto plates, one of them carrying a rather large portion near a hallway I had yet to explore. There are three whole muffins being carried by her, an entire plate consisting of scrambled eggs.

Anya yells, "You test the food before he eats."

The redhead from before silently nods and continues onwards, disappearing into the hallway. I can hear the sound of some kind of movement, and then it's silent once more. A silencing door, perhaps? Skull's Row has many of those. It's how the Zenith all live in such a compact area, but also maintain privacy that's either used for luxury or torture.

Lora, without question, takes a bite of everything on my plate. I don't trust people in Skull's Row, for rather obvious reasons, and do nothing to stop her. I would never blame Lora for doing something another Zenith told her to do. Or for hurting me in any way that she deems necessary. She has to do what is required to survive.

Once she doesn't keel over, I dig in, leaning back into the chair with little class as I slowly nod at how good everything tastes. The other noir returns like she went to feed a dangerous creature deep within its natural habitat. They even present me with a tea that I can smell from here.

None of us talk about it—I know what it is. If consumed daily, it tends to prevent unwanted pregnancies. There's a very particular pungent smell of dirt to the earthy drink, the color a deep blue from one of the roots that it's made of.

The women clean up as I eat and drink my tea, even taking my plate when I'm finished, holding the last piece of bacon in my hand. I continue to choose silence, for my benefit.

Lora stands. "I will go fetch some clothes for you, and then return to dress you."

I raise my brow as my only acknowledgment.

With that, the noirs wheel away their items and I'm left

staring through the elaborate windows as I sit here, listening very carefully for any movement from Anya.

I swear I hear her feet on stone, but she's so damn quiet. And rather than jump to my own defense, I hardly move as if to assert that she doesn't intimidate me. What's she going to do? Kill me? When Soren, at the bare minimum, wants me for information on my father? Or because Cypress is offering him something?

Anya appears like smoke, sitting quietly on the couch where Lora is. Her rank and loyalty to someone like Soren explains her otherwise unnerving silence. It makes me wonder if Bones has any traits to make him uniquely dangerous.

She slowly takes me in, every moment laced with judgment. "All right. What have you done to Soren?"

"Excuse me?" I ask, nearly choking on the last bit of bacon.

She leans her elbows on her knees. "You knocked him out, stole his coin, and yet you came back, completely unharmed." She narrows her black eyes. "And now you're in his room and smell like a king's whore, after sleeping in *his* bed, and eating *his* morning food."

"Oh, am I fit for royalty, now?"

"I don't trust you."

I suck on my fingers, staring at her. "I got that message when you stuck that blade in me."

"You're using him," she swiftly accuses, something sharp flashing in her eyes. A threat, maybe?

"Listen, lady, I wish I knew how to use Soren. It would make my life so much easier."

"You have *their* tattoo. You can't convince me that you're not manipulating him. You have the entire Council confused, which means you can do the same to Soren."

Is she serious? Sitting up, I look at her with a fire that's been kindling since the Council took me. "Excuse me, but what the fuck do I need to manipulate him for? I want to be as far from this place as possible."

I don't know If I can win a fight with someone like her. She's trained. I stopped my training once I got to Coalfell. But I can play scrappy, if needed. Let her hurt me so I can get up close. Either way, I'm ready to fight if I have to. I'm not going to let her treat me like this.

She looks around, the muscles in her face twitching as she bounces a knee. "The truth? I've just learned of your lineage this morning—" my eyes widen, my lips parting "—so you're of good stock, which means I have to watch you very carefully. Don't exactly know what you want with Soren, honestly. I just know the Zenith have immense strengths in their union, but one common weakness—they're *all* looking out for them-selves, and *you're* one of them by blood." She slowly slides her gaze back to me. "Soren is a threat to *many*. His lands grow by the year, and people serve in his ranks from all over, especially given that Death's Wing is so fond of him." She pivots so she's facing me fully. "You could use that. Maybe the one that gave you that tattoo is trying to weasel their way into Soren's private walls. Maybe not. The fact remains that I don't trust you, Jane. I'd be an idiot to do so, and you know it."

An elongated silence of us staring at the other is only punc-tured by my laugh. "*I'm* the one that doesn't trust the bastard! You have it *so* backward." I wipe my eyes, catching my breath. "For all I know, this is all a ploy to get *me* to trust *him* more. Make me so *touched*—" I place a feigned hand on my chest "—That he's giving me special treatment so my walls melt, and then he'll use me however he wants. Maybe you're the third act that's supposed to sell his kindness to me as something genuine."

She snorts, as if the idea is offensive and completely asinine. "And what could he possibly use you for? Even if your father was a Zenith, he's gone. It's not like Soren can use you for bargaining. If he wanted to breed you for your lineage, he wouldn't go through all these unnecessary measures."

My lips do a weird motion at the mention of him breeding me, an embarrassingly weird part of me turned on at the thought. "Bree—*what*," I utter with a high-pitched voice. "*No!* You know what, don't worry about it. We're clearly in a stalemate. Except *you* at least aren't a prisoner. And I don't give a shit about the tattoo anymore. I barely remember it since they gave me something to make me woozy," I confess, lowering my voice. "My, you know who, wasn't even around when I got it done. I was just told to go with some people, chew on a certain bark, and the next thing I know I'm getting marked on my chest. I'm *useless* to you, and currently held against my will."

She throws her hands up, motioning around her. "Yes, you're so miserable when you're screaming Soren's name, eating his food, and sharing his bed, in this *shabby* castle."

My brows slowly fold downward. I nearly whisper when I say, "Are you jealous?"

Her black eyes widen. "What? Hells no. I like my men *softer*," she replies, eyeing me as if I'm mad. "But he *is* my leader, and has saved me more than once. And he relies on his powers too much, thinking he knows people because of them. I don't blame him. I would too. But that's also why *I* am here, to keep that in check."

I'm stunned for a moment, absolutely desperate for the powers that Soren has. "Why would he treat me like this, then, if not to use me?"

"I don't fucking know," she grinds out, raising a brow as her face seems to age at those words. "Unless he genuinely finds you interesting. Wouldn't be shocked. His bloodthirst has matured over the years, and he's pickier about the missions he takes. There's only so many times you can nearly die and come back before it loses its luster." She continues to talk like she hasn't shared this theory yet, shaking her head as she eyes the floor. "You're feisty enough for him, and he likes women with your hair. And you're of *our* world. I can see the temptation." Those onyx eyes flash my way. "But even then, I don't trust you, Jane. Trust here is built by bleeding for another. It could be as simple as you just want an out and are using him for that."

I look down. I *did* consider that.

She backs off, as if she had her answer. My gaze finds the hallway that Soren must be down. I hear a heavy door open behind me, and Anya looks over to say, "You can dress her, now. No speaking. I'll be listening."

Lora gestures to the bathing room when I glance over my shoulder. I sniff from the coldness of the room and sigh, standing to follow her. I'm too lost in thought for any retort to Anya.

Inside the room, Lora places a canvas bag on a large table, taking out the many pieces of whatever I'm to wear. It's all black, save for the sheer fabric that's a deep red. The rest of it is black silk, and I reach out to run my fingers along it. One side of me wants to immediately burn this for the insinuation that will give the Council any thoughts of superiority over me, but the other reminds me that there's no strategy in openly defying anyone this early.

My pride can be quiet if it means getting to live long enough to search for the perfect time to strike.

Wouldn't it be fun to tempt Soren, too?

Anya is right, though—trust here is built on more than words. And I haven't known him long enough for his actions to win me over. All I know is he has his own personal reasons to keep me alive.

Lora dresses me in silence, down to the perfumed oils that

she dabs at my neck and wrists. The outfit is quite interesting, honestly. The bottoms are undergarments made of fine silk, with strings tied around my waist. The ruby red sheer fabric is a long skirt that covers my very visible legs. The top is black silk that reveals my cleavage in a way that both boosts my confidence and makes me blush, tying around my neck, delicately bound together like a corset in the back.

It's a very revealing outfit, with my arms, shoulders, and upper mid-drift still completely exposed.

Lora pulls out a black cloak to lie it on the table and as quietly as possible, says, "Soren requested a cloak for the cold, but said he wants to see you in this outfit, first."

My heart races at his request. I give her a nod, trying to conceal what I feel. "Thank you."

She looks like she wants to ask a thousand questions but refrains with a bow of her head and departs.

For a moment, I awkwardly stand there.

What do I do now that I'm alone? Wait for him? Sit prettily by the window? Or sit in the biggest seat I can find and tell him I'm only dressed like this because I don't want to be cooped up in here?

I deeply inhale and near a mirror, looking at my wavy hair that Lora said I'm to leave alone—Soren wants it undone.

My dignity demands I rip it all to shreds as I did in those dungeons, and yet, some kind of delicious desire thrives at knowing that he made sure I'm exactly as he wants me.

I'm not sure how long I'm alone when I hear his heavy footsteps; I was in the middle of examining my face, noticing how it has aged since I was last in Skull's Row. My heart skips a beat when the heavy steps cease, and I glance over my shoulder to see Soren in the doorway.

MIRRORS

JANE

S oren's chest is bare, his thick and muscled stomach
breathing heavily, sweat on his face. Whatever training
he was doing clearly exhausted him, even if I couldn't
hear it.

He slowly takes me in with tired eyes burning with vigor,
approval laced in his gaze. "That is almost *too* appealing."

"Why does that matter, if I'm on *your* lap?" I ask, raising a
brow.

His pale gaze slices to meet mine, the door shutting behind
him as he nears me to touch my hair softly before lacing his
fingers to pull and hold my head still. My heart races with a

need for Soren, especially as he looks at me with possession, like he's threatening the mere thought of someone trying to take me. I can almost hear the many words he wants to speak, and yet he refrains.

In a fluid motion, the mercenary leans down and crashes his lips onto mine, kissing me with a depth of his power. He smells of sweat, but it only makes me eager for him. I grab his shoulders and kiss him back, touching him without hesitation. He reaches underneath the sheer skirt and unties the bottoms. I say into the kiss, "Don't you dare ruin my top. Took a while to get it on."

Those perfect lips hover over mine, his calloused hands sliding on my smoothly oiled body. "I only need these removed, love," he gruffly says.

I don't fight him in the least. My bottoms are removed as if he's done this more than once, his touch moving to my inner thigh before sliding through the part of me that wettens so easily for him. A finger pushes inside my pussy as he reclaims my lips, his tongue sliding through my lips as I moan into his mouth.

"I love how fresh you smell, just so I can ruin you," he growls. He rubs my clit with his thumb while he's fully inside of me, that powerful hand holding me still, his other one still fisting my hair. I whimper into our kissing, running my hand through *his* hair.

Without much transition, he pulls away and grabs me by the hips, lifting me so I'm bent over the large table which my clothes had initially been laid upon. He adjusts me so I'm looking right into the mirror of this washing room, staring at myself as I'm bent over. He gets behind me after untying his pants as I greedily stare at his hard, veiny cock, lifting my sheer skirt and holding me still with one hand. I watch as Soren aligns himself before his cock disappears from view and I feel him fill me in one thrust. The way he just moves me around like this, and watching him do so... I was never born to be with gentle, or proper, men.

I hardly blink as we make eye contact in the mirror, his expression breaking its stolid glare as he lightly rolls his eyes when he finds a perfect rhythm.

He leans over to wrap an arm around my navel—not caring if he ruins the rest of my outfit—the other hand bracing himself on the table. I can see his hand move between my legs, stimulating me, his hand working with precision as his cock hits everything perfectly. My moans grow needy as I watch him undulate, the table shaking.

Soren is so large compared to me, and leans down to crowd my body, breathing raggedly into my ear, still staring at my reflection. "I plan to fuck you every time before we leave this room, Jane. And even in front of the others, if I have to assert who the fuck you belong to when we're out there."

My eyes roll as his words push me to an edge that he seems to effortlessly control. I can't get over how deeply he fills me, how that pleasure builds in my navel. How his statement fucking turns me on, how I almost *want* him to have to assert himself.

"Say you want that," he groans, the table moving with our bodies. His tone is needy, like he has to hear me confess what he senses.

I don't even try to hide it. I want to hear him unravel, and I swear it's the heat of the moment talking for me. Staring with intention, I'm completely unabashed as I say, "I want you to fuck me every time I leave this room. I want your cock deep in me, Soren, and for some fucking reason—" I moan when he rubs me faster"—I *really* want them to know I belong to you."

The sound he makes sends me right over the edge, a guttural groan of pleasure emitting from him. The way he looks at me through that mirror, like he's willing to kill many men to keep me as his pet... it happens so fast; waves of pleasure wash over me in a powerful explosion as my body shudders.

He gets rougher, holding me still with both hands, my breasts jostling wildly, his body so massive behind mine now that he's standing. I've just finished, but I'm already feeling an excitement return by how basal this position is; how he probably means it when he says he'll fuck me every time before we leave.

His body stiffness not shortly after that, pushing as deep as he'll go, his eyes slightly rolling, his tempo slowing. There's nothing left untouched inside of me, now coated in his cum. I don't know what we're doing or how long his spell will hold me. Anya's behavior makes me wonder if I really am—

"You go so quickly to feeling negative after being fucked," he chides, disappointment written all over his face.

Once he pulls out, Soren examines me like he wants to make this scene a painting. *Gods* he better not demand something like that. I stand, feeling the aftermath between my thighs. I lean against the table, finding my balance. He quickly begins to wipe his face and chest down with a towel in the room. The sound of water trickling off of the damp fabric after he dunks it in the water basin before he hands me one for myself.

"Like I said—for some reason I really like the *idea* of you—" I say, waving an arm at him. "Of the whole fucking picture. But you could seriously get *any* woman," I pant, glaring at him.

He sighs, as if he's about to ban the topic in the future. "Yes, because random women are so interesting to me."

"What do you *want?*" I blurt out, giving him some of my insecurity as I slap the soppy towel on the table. I hope it bleeds through so he can feel it. "Seriously. Give me *something.*"

Thankfully, he seems to consider this. His voice is muffled in a towel as he wipes it clean from sweat. "What I *want* is the Zenith's daughter that rips rooms apart when she's angry. It's not more complicated than that, and I'm tired of having this conversation."

My heart flips, and I swear when the towel comes off his face, I see a satisfied smile. He even looks at me, coming back over to grab my jaw with that veined hand that held my hips still, his mouth hovering in front of mine once more, the scent of sweat lessened. "Did you know you rolled over to lay against me when you were sleeping? And I felt how removed your walls were, and how eager you were to be close to me?"

My eyes widen. "You're lying."

He doesn't answer right away, and doesn't move, either. He just stares into my eyes. "What's there to lose, Jane?"

I quietly say, "I grew up here, Soren. There's a *lot* to lose, and I promised myself I'd never let someone make me believe they'd take care of me, when instead they *left* me. That's... I don't want to do that again."

Those beautiful eyes of his roam my face. Rather than give me more words, before pulling away, he simply caresses my cheek in a ruminating way. My gaze falls to his lips, eager for him to kiss me, but when he drops his hand and gives me his back, I let my disappointment ooze out of me.

"Shall we go over the expectations?" he asks, walking out of the room. I grab the bottoms he undid and follow him.

"Yes... fine. Expectations," I begrudgingly say, tying the bottoms back on. "I also have some of my own, you know."

"Such as?" He sounds entirely amused, like he really wants to know what I'd expect from him.

"Well, two major ones, honestly. I'll do *anything* as long as you promise to keep Kathleen safe, and no one else touches me."

He pauses, slowly looking around, almost back at me, but seems to hesitate to make eye contact. I can see that maybe he even narrows his eyes. He stares at the floor, considering something.

I lick dry lips and add, "If you're going to hesitate—"

He returns his attention to his armor. "No, I will not hesitate to chop off hands or gouge out eyes, even to defend your friend. I was contemplating something else."

"Like what?"

"Private things," he states with finality, lacing his vest. "Anyway, to what *I* expect, it's pretty simple, today. Won't look right if you're completely meek," he looks at me. "But I know you're smart enough to figure out that you should probably listen if I give you instructions. Or else it's a whole fucking mess we have to clean up. You also do not interfere with *anything*, no snarky comments. And you'll wear a chained collar around your neck so it pleases any suspicious hearts. I also don't want you fighting the collar *once*, or pushing back against *any* orders. I'd dare to say that obedience reigns here, but that might just set you off to phrase it that way."

A collar... of course. Nonetheless, I nod. "If no one touches me, then fine. We have a deal and I'll wear whatever you want without complaint." My heart races, realizing I'm really about to do this.

He grabs something from the table and turns near me, some of his armor still not put on. He sighs, as if deciding whatever rests on his tongue is worth uttering. "I also need to say that if you run on me, when we're out there," he says, nodding to his bedroom door. "I *will* come for you. Council or not. So don't even try it."

"As fun as that would be," I say, not lying; the idea excites me a little. "I won't run... today."

Soren undoes the goat skin in his hands and shows me the earrings. "Wear these, too."

"Really?" I ask, happily taking them. They're not the same as having *Mother's* earrings, but they're something. As I look at them in my hand, Soren leans in to gently kiss me... just like I wanted earlier. I completely melt, emotions ripping open that make all the danger feel less intimidating.

A dying part of me wants to keep these desires guarded, but the other—the one that makes reckless choices—just wants to see whatever the hells this is between us.

He inhales, as if breathing in the scent he opted to cover me in. His lips graze on mine as he says, "Go out there and wait for me. And let no one tell you where to go unless it's me."

JANE

Life has a way of really making someone question everything, doesn't it?

Sitting next to Anya while waiting for Soren is such a fascinating development in my life. Here I am, freshly pleasured by him, smelling as he wants me, dressed like I'm his trophy, and the woman next to me recently stabbed me; a cacophony of my new reality.

Silence doesn't linger for long when the handle to his bedroom door jiggles, and my entire body focuses on that threshold, my heart absolutely infatuated with the notion of his undivided attention.

Soren emerges from his room, partially dressed in his armor, wearing a rather intricate black leather tunic instead of his armored chest piece. The opulent, onyx attire is just as hypnotic as his red armor, his hair tied back into a low bun. Scabbards and their blades line his body, all the way down to his ankles.

I can't help but accept the amorous thoughts of finding him almost *beautiful*, even if that seems ridiculous. His outfit is so dark while his gaze is so light, his strong jaw flexing perfectly when he clearly clenches it.

"Grab her cloak, Anya," he instructs, nodding to the couch that it drapes over.

My nostrils flare as I try to calm myself down. I've decided to go with the route of trusting him today. My father trusted Cypress, and even though my burned heart wants to think he abandoned me... what if he didn't? What if something happened to him? If that's true, then I trust his judgment with the ruby witch, which means if she didn't warn me of Soren, then maybe he's *not* my enemy. Plus, she clearly told him something so profound that he lied to the Council about me. That counts for something, right?

I found myself choosing between the jaded part of me that is afraid to have her heart broken again, or to lean into fate a little and see where *that* gets me.

The last time I trusted fate I was a girl hopelessly waiting for her father to find her.

It's different now. Everything is different.

Standing, I face the entrance while Soren's gaze dissects me. His invasion of my privacy is fascinating, alluring, and yet disturbing. There's not even a crevice for my heart to hide within.

Soren nears a table with a metal collar and a long chain on it. The metal clinks together as he picks it up, motioning for me to come forward, and opening it up. Before he says anything, I lift my head to expose my neck. "Get it over with," I grunt.

The corner of his lips rises upward as he places the cold, heavy metal around my neck and locks it, putting the key in his pocket. He grabs the chain and pulls slightly so I have to take a step toward him. He leans down into my ear. "You begin to act out, at all, in ways I don't approve of, and I'll have you gagged and bound."

"I know the bargain," I confidently reply.

He hands the chains to a smirking Anya as she eyes the power that she has over me, my cloak draped over her shoulder.

At least my hands are free. I guess that's an upside.

Despite the wreckage of my heart and what I've just survived, I focus on how I'm actually quite curious to see the Savage Sands today.

Where many fight in the main arena of Skull's Row for pure entertainment, those fighting *here* strive to be noticed for their brutality, in hopes that it gives them a leg up on becoming a Zenith.

I was only ever able to sneak into the main arena, attending as a curious child processing her violent world, watching from her father's fierce shadow. *I almost wish Dad was here now so he could be the one to take me.*

Walking across the walkway, the vibrant halls contrast Soren's quiet wing. As we enter the rather unsteady lift, and not chucked over his shoulder this time, I can see how dangerous this lift is. It's a steel cage that is held by a hook as large as my torso. It's only Soren, Anya, and I that enter, while the others descend the stone stairs.

"You know, I really should have a dagger or something on me," I whisper, standing straighter, speaking like we're teammates discussing a strategy once the platform begins its jerky descent.

"Honorable attempt," Soren grumbles. "But I'll be doing the stabbing and torturing for now."

Anya dutifully remains silent, guiding me forward once the lift stops at our destination. The crowd thickens on these lower levels as we near an interlocking of staircases. Soren strides with purpose, the crowd naturally parting wherever he moves. There are so many onlookers here, many dressed in the Skull's Row version of aristocracy; leather, weapons, expensive tunics or dresses, and *lots* of jewelry. Especially gold. One woman even has tattoos all over her neck and face.

The men and women here move like a pack of hyenas, always willing to bite the other if they see fit.

My heart rate triples when I spot a familiar face, the wind stolen right from my lungs. It's an older noir from the Silver District, someone I doubt would recognize me. At the same time, panic sets in when I envision her staring me down like she might somehow remember me from all those years ago, and I start to feel rather exposed, made worse by what I'm wearing, or lack thereof. I've physically matured since people only saw me as a scraggly girl, my hair was paler then, too. And shorter.

It doesn't help that *everyone* steals a glance or two at me, no doubt intrigued by who Soren has at the end of his leash. I swallow thickly as if afraid that I have it written on my face that I'm Charles Ritter's daughter.

Maryanne's screams echo in my mind of her calling me a coward. Is that what I'm being now? My cheeks maintain a solid blush as we descend, dark, thick wood layering on the walls and ceilings as oil lanterns hang for light. My shoes clack on the stone, but it's drowned out by the rest—there's even someone singing a hearty song of manning a ship and wanting to return to his lover.

Bones is among a group of Soren's men at the bottom, a rowdy duo shouting over something in the distance as more people join in on the singing. Some even begin to tap their wooden mugs on tables to offer a steady rhythm that many voices sing to.

Reaching the final step, the smell of cooked food wafts through the air as a trolley wheels past—it's some kind of meat I used to eat as a kid. I don't have time to spot what exactly they're eating as Soren guides us, Anya yanking on my chain to regain my attention.

I glance at Bones, who is as dark and dangerous as ever, a wild gleam in his eyes. A new necklace of knuckles hangs below his older one, the second row as bright as whitecaps compared to the worn ones.

Kathleen better be all right, and those knuckles acquired from protecting her, wherever toad-face put her. He better be worshiping her and killing any man that gets too close.

Bones places his hands on his hips and addresses Soren. "I see we've chosen chains."

Soren replies, "Makes it easier to lock her in place if I need to leave her for a time."

I stare at the stone wall ahead, eyeing the intricacy of an archway so as not to meet anyone's gaze.

Once, I would have laughed and reveled in Soren aiding me in this giant lie to keep me safe. But now? I still see Maryanne's glowering eyes burning into me before her flesh blackened and her soul left this world.

Now, I just want out of this damn city.

Down below is another, more private way to access Skull's Row from the Spiraling Stone. They check every inch of whatever is being transported, and it's not easy to make one's way down there in the first place. It's a secondary bridge that connects two archways carved out of the cliffs, tunnels linking it all together like rope.

Hearing the ocean crash below us is both liberating and isolating, the raw nature like the edge of an escape plan.

Would Melona pull me under if I tried to find a ship out of here? Or is Cypress telling the truth that I've paid my debts to her?

Crossing into more tunnels is not quick or easy, with guards and Paragons investigating everything. One even gives a hard yank on my chains, as if to prove I'm actually bound. Soren doesn't watch or look my way as they do so.

I can smell the salt water before we're upon it, the tunnel opening to a moderate, pseudo fjord. I've seen these from far above, knowing in reality that these are just calm waters that are fed by a waterfall from Skull's Row. They eventually end up in their own massive waterfall that takes one over the rocky cliffs. But here? I can't stop looking around at the breathtaking scene. The once-natural stone and water have been tamed by ingenious hands, worn wood covering the gentle body of water beneath us. Plants and vines wrap up and around, ropes hanging all over. Carved-out windows punctuate the stone where wooden homes affix themselves.

"I've never been here," I quietly say to no one in particular, wondering where the Savage Sands fighting pits are. So far, this reminds me more of a pier town. Anya remains silent next to me as Soren finally looks down.

"Really?" he asks, guiding us to an oversized bridge that will take us to what appears to be the more bustling side.

"*He* wouldn't let me go near the piers. Of any kind. I was only allowed to go near the fighting pits in the main city, not here," I reply, trying to be vague, knowing Anya can hear me. I still don't like that she knows about my dad, but I don't have a voice in the matter.

"Wise of him. Pirates don't owe loyalty to anyone but their ship. They don't even care to follow the Zenith's rules."

"Then, why do you trust them?" I ask, eyeing a building that's a combined pleasure house, tavern, and inn. *Of course. People stay here and then watch the fights, I bet.*

"Tempest keeps control over them."

"*All* the pirates?"

"Maybe one day you'll see her command the ocean. She's sailed through countless storms and hurricanes, and never once lost a ship." he replies. A cart full of bananas ricochets its weight through the wooden platform before I see it, nearly running into us as they apologize profusely. Soren ignores them and keeps walking. "Some think her ship, The Sea Wolf, is special. But I've seen her command a fucking canoe through impossible waters. Her man o' war can, and *will*, hunt anyone down."

My dad spoke highly of Tempest, although never embellished too much. I honestly didn't know she was so inundated in the pirating world, only knowing she frequented the areas I was forbidden to roam. I crane my neck to look up at the scene above me when I hear flags flapping heavily in the wind against a sky of overcast clouds—more Zenith flags.

The more I think about it, the more I remember dad telling me to stay away from men and women of the sea. I always thought it was just because he was worried that I'd find them interesting and want to join.

Maybe he didn't trust them, either.

I keep taking in the various structures, wondering who in the hells lives down here full-time. Do all these people support the Savage Sands? Does this place even have a name?

Once we cross the bridge that looks like the reclaimed hull of a ship, a group of men—all wearing a single gold earring on their left side—slowly crowds us as if they might pass, but instead they stand still, all staring. Anya pulls gently on the chains controlling me, as if to halt me like I'm a damn horse.

As I take these men in, it's like the child inside of me from over a decade ago revs with curiosity. These are *real* pirates, and I've rarely seen so many that look so *weathered*, dried out from the salty waters they worship. More than one has only one eye, and my brows raise when I spot a man with his arm missing from his elbow down, a blade replacing his forearm. A man approaches Soren who has the cleanest and most trimmed black beard, large puffy bags under his eyes. His clothes are finer than the rest, his captain's coat a deep emerald. My gaze fastens to Soren until I steal a double take around the behemoth when I see Bones pull out an apple with a small blade to start peeling at it.

Well, at least *he's* confident.

The one in the front bows his head, and I snap my attention back to him. "The name is Nicholas the Merciless. Your man, the one with the apple, stabbed one of our crew, Lord Zenith." He speaks politely, although his forced smile not only reveals dirty teeth, but also an undertone that he's using that title mockingly.

"And I'm supposed to care?" Soren quips.

Nicholas furrows his bushy brows, raising a hand that's so cruddy I can see the thick black lines of dirt under his nail beds. "Wouldn't need a healer if it wasn't *your* problem. Over a turkey leg, I hear." Nicholas points at Bones. "And we're not leaving until *that* one has paid a debt. Healers aren't free, you know."

Soren rests his hand on the pommel of his main sword. "One of your men said you'd pay for that healer without issue. Going back on your word?"

"I prefer to confront a Zenith's broadside. And I also never did say *I* play fair." He wickedly smiles, a few of his men chuckling. "That man was Cook, and he's known for being our *mediator*. I decided after the fact that I wholly disagreed with him."

My brows raise as I feel like a spectator in a pre-show to the Sands. Is this really happening? Is this man *really* going to challenge Soren like this?

Soren takes a step forward, the weight of him creaking the wood even in that one motion. I watch with bated breath, the weight of the collar extra heavy as I feel a need to be armed. Soren slowly pulls out his sword from his scabbard, holding it to the side while not removing his gaze from the pirate captain. "Anya, you have Jane."

Swords are unsheathed like a wave of talons, Anya pulling out her own dagger. No way... they're going to fight! What the hells do *I* do?

Nicholas is last to pull out his cutlass, his eyes alive with a fight. "We have quite the reputation for being men that don't get attacked without the rest of us fighting back. Zenith included. All we want is your man, or we'll give no quarter."

As if those words were a signal, I look over my shoulder to see more crowding us from behind to lock us on this bridge; it's a dozen of Soren's men against three dozen pirates.

Bones speaks after biting into his apple. "You can't handle me, love." He takes one last bite before adding, "Your man's fine, and you've got plenty enough gold. It's what you're known for. At this point, you're just *bitching*. But if you insist—we do need to stretch our legs a bit." Bones throws the core of his apple over the bridge, the blade he used to carve it pivoting in his hand as without warning, he throws his full body weight with the small blade that flies from his grip, striking one of the pirates dead in the eye as he slowly topples over.

All mayhem breaks loose.

Two of Nicholas's men charge before him to attack Soren, who perries with little effort, pulling a smaller blade from one of his scabbards and stabbing one man in the throat, slicing it open before kicking him away and slashing down with his larger sword and chopping a hand off of the other attacker. Fear flashes in the pirate's eyes before Soren grabs his head and stabs him through the face, yanking downward to free his blade as the body falls.

Everyone around us moves, men yelling and screaming, metal clashing on metal. One pirate climbs on the side of the bridge to evade the fighting, hopping over facing Anya. I'm completely useless as she drops the chains, to which I quickly gather so no one can drag me or hang me.

Time simultaneously moves with urgency and stillness. Bones dances among a handful of pirates, slicing brutally at them as blood smears the wood, his hits landing without mercy as the flesh is viscerally torn open and bodies land limply on the ground.

While Anya squares up with *another* pirate that's on her, I watch as a Merciless man climbs over in the same manner, gripping the exterior wooden fencing as he makes his way toward me, climbing over the rails once he's close enough to me. I scream in shock at first, but when he smiles with a dirty set of teeth, I wrap my chains around his neck while he clamors over the rails. I tug so hard in an effort to choke him like it's a rope. His eyes nearly bulge from his sockets, and he's about to stab behind him to stop me, but not before I see a hand grab the man's clothes and lift him like he's a small dog.

I release when I see its Soren, the pirate gasping for air once free of my chains, but not before the Zenith's long blade plunges through his enemy's heart. Behind him, Anya guts one of her assailants, looking back at us before continuing her assault.

Soren raises the body on his sword with *one* hand as the pirate chokes out blood, the Zenith moving away to toss the fallen man at the feet of Nicholas, who has yet to join the fray. The body slams down on the bridge, and Soren's voice rasps, "Use that sword, *Merciless*—"

From somewhere above us, a woman cries out, "Put your damned swords away!"

It takes a moment for everyone to look up, not wanting to distract themselves and create vulnerability. When Soren cranes his head up, I do too—

My lips part as I drop my chains that rattle to the floor.

Tempest.

"He," Nicholas says, motioning to Bones. "Stabbed my man. Right in the gut. Was expensive to heal it, and he refuses to pay."

"As if you can't afford it," she silkily replies.

Bones moves his blade in his hand like he's twirling a stick, blood smeared all over as he seems completely uninjured. Five bodies are at his feet.

Walking down a flight of stairs, the energy shifts as Tempest nears us, the rest of the piers watching on like *we're* the entertainment. She's aged since I last glimpsed her; Tempest's dark brown skin is creased around her lips, rings clinging to her slender fingers. Her long black hair is dreaded, gold decorations lining her strands as a black bandana keeps them out of her face. She wears fitted pants, her leather armor contouring her feminine frame. Many glinting weapons are hoisted all over her body.

Tempest still carries herself like she's the ocean incarnate, moving fluidly like water.

Her reputation precedes her with tales of being as dangerous as a calm day on the ocean with a hurricane lurking in the distance. Very few men have ever breached the eye of her storm, protected from her fury.

Her smoky voice curls at the end of each sentence with a slight rasp. "Easy, Soren," she hums, narrowing her deep brown eyes that black smudge hollows. She nears Nicholas, those around lowering their head in respect to her. She gets in his face, looking up; she's shorter than I remembered her to be. "*I* rule these piers, not you. So, if you want to bloody these decks, fight him *yourself*."

He stares at her before looking around, and then nodding as he sheaths his sword. "Aye, sea temptress."

"Now move, because if I'm late, I'll tie you to the bottom of my ship on my next sail and keelhaul you, *just* high enough so you don't drown right away. Then, I'll take your crew and make them *mine*." She looks around. "What's left of them, anyway."

Nicholas takes a step back, and his men mirror him as they shuffle out of the way, some panting. The one with a blade for an arm doesn't have any blood on him either, just like his captain. A few rush forward to examine the injured, someone yelling for a healer as he puts pressure on a wound.

I'm *definitely* not helping.

Bones sneers at them all, pulling his little blade out of the eye socket of the first one that fell.

Tempest addresses Soren, a wind picking up as it blows a few strands of hair into my eyes. "Let's walk together."

"You ended the fun," Soren grunts, looking around on the bridge to find a dead man's shirt to clean his blade with.

"You don't have room to complain. Looks like none of your men are dead."

Everyone begins to wipe their steel before sheathing, blood smeared or spattered on all of our faces. Anya grabs the chains once more, although quietly to me, "Well, at least you're not useless."

"Good of you to notice," I say with pride. "The *Merciless* sure is, though."

She snickers. "He's known to let others fight for him. There's no way he'd fight Soren unless it was a dirty blow. Nicholas has value in simply existing, and his men are only on his crew for the money. As long as he pays, he doesn't have to fight."

The reasoning behind one's loyalty to their leader makes me realize I don't even know why Soren's men follow him. "And what of Soren? Why do you all risk it for him?"

For once, she doesn't look at me with acrimony. "Many join because of the promise of valor, always eager for a reason to fight. The rest stay because of how he treats us, and of the security he offers. He takes care of us."

I ruminate on that as we step over or around the blood, which drips down through the cracks of the wood. Tempest orders Nicholas to clean up the mess, her brown eyes haunting me when our gazes connect, like she can see the ghosts of my past.

Soren watches Tempest with great caution, and I'd pay a lot of gold coins to know what he feels about her at this moment. Is she going to barrage me with similar questions like with the Council? Subject me to all of her pirates?

Get it together. It will be what it is. Just like that, we carry on as if we didn't stop to stab and kill some men. Once we're moving toward an opening in the stone and enter another corridor, flanked by both Soren's men *and* hers, Tempest looks back as torch light casts shadows on her face. There's a lot of chatter from the group behind, echoing against the walls as she quietly says to me, "Now, let's all have a chat once we get there. You've really grown up, little Jane."

CHANGING TIDES

SOREN

ell, that's fucking bold.

Many things transpire in my mind as Tempest insinuates something so fucking dangerous—does she actually know? The need to pin her against a wall and stare into her eyes until I can only sense the truth nearly overtakes common sense.

Not in these tunnels, though.

Jane stares at Tempest like she's a ghost of her past, honeyed eyes wide while Anya watches very carefully. Blood spatters the Zenith princess's face, danger emitting from her aura.

Tempest's mahogany eyes glide to look into mine as we continue to walk.

My mind races with a cascade of decisions that will need to be made in a very short span of time. If Tempest knows, that could change *everything*. How far will I have to take this? As much as I'd hate killing Tempest, I will, if I have to. If keeping Jane alive truly is my way to Serena, I'll burn this whole city down to ensure it.

Plus, keeping Jane around for the mere sake of it feels important, too. Jane's scraps of affection have set me on a path that I won't stop haunting until I get what I want; a desire I'm still navigating. I'm not sure what that means for my hunt for Serena, but perhaps I'll merely take Jane with me as my healer.

Not if this shit disrupts our plans.

Tempest merely smiles and faces ahead. "We can speak in a moment," she croons. "I'll let you try and read me until then. I'm on your side, you know."

I snort, still moving as if her words don't bother me. Underneath that is my heart screaming that I fucking hate dealing with politics, and that's all this damn place is.

I probably wouldn't bother being with the Council if my instincts didn't do most of the work.

Admittedly... Tempest feels the opposite of Blackwell. Seeing Jane brings her warm memories—and yet Jane stares at her like a stranger.

The sound of a crowd grows louder on the other end, pulling at my attention. The Savage Sands presents itself before us as even the overcast sun makes me squint after the bleakness of the tunnel. Banners fly over the stadium that's carved into the stone. We pass by noirs, to which I tell one to bring towels and water to clean our faces with.

We all make our way up a few flights of stairs to enter the Zenith's wing—a raised wooden seating area that we all congregate within, stretching around the crescent shaped fighting pits to give each one a sense of communal privacy.

"In the corner," I say to Tempest, finding the furthest chair away from anyone, spotting that not even Blackwell is here. It's just a handful of us, although the redhead named Alistair is present, who eyes Jane like he might be willing to swipe her from my hands.

He's a newer Zenith, still learning that we all have our roles and that I've done something like this more than once to gain reliable information.

If Alistair tries to take her, I'll gut him in the very sands below us.

I arrange the ornate, wooden chair so my back is slightly to him. I'll feel him before he can reach me, and I don't need him trying to read my expression. Jane's chains are handed to me by Anya, I pull on them so she kneels. To my surprise, she doesn't fight me. Anya takes a few steps back, and I look over my shoulder. "You and Bones keep the others away."

Facing Tempest, I nod.

She squats down, resting her elbow on her knees and stares at Jane like she's a fascinating oddity. It's almost hard to hear her through the crowd as she speaks quietly. "Ritter trusted me, you know."

Everything becomes loud in my mind, the energy around like clashing riptides as my magic nearly explodes from an adrenaline rush; hyperaware, ready to move and act in any direction. It's one thing to hint at this, and another to confirm it so bluntly.

My hand tightens on the chains, trying to grasp onto Tempest's aura, but all it can latch to is Jane's desperation to be hidden; withdrawn, even from *me*.

That just pisses me off more.

Does Tempest not understand how much effort it took for

me to unwind Jane? My unnatural gift latches so tightly to her that I don't even know how to get it off.

I swear I feel amnesty in Tempest's aura when I *can* focus, but again... she's as wicked as a hundred-foot wave, even if she can be as calm as a flat day at sea.

"What do you want, Tempest?" I grind out.

Is *this* why my instincts yelled at me to come here today? To meet her and learn this about her?

"I owe the Scorpion," she flatly replies. Trickles of deep, clashing emotions flood her calm. In my experience that only happens when someone is recalling the truth, especially a heavy one.

Lies taste too pretty, too organized, before it becomes utter chaos. Truths follow a line, even if it's jagged or smeared with complexity.

Tempest grins when silence is her only response, revealing three golden teeth. "Cheeky of you to take his daughter as a pet. Especially in chains."

"Why are you saying all of this?" Jane asks, her expression nearly terrified. At least it sells the show to anyone watching.

Tempest chuckles, and I glare so hard at her that the smile doesn't linger. She maintains her gaze on Jane. Familiarity. Protection. Intrigue. Tempest is stern about those feelings. "You get it from your mother." Jane's heart skips a beat, everything in her uncertain. "And you get that glare from your father. If *he's* truly hurting you," she nods to me, "I know how to hurt him in return."

"Now that your cryptic entrance is done, why are you telling us this?" I ask.

"Again, I owe him. Especially now that the Council knows of her tattoo. Although, it's working as intended. It's meant to send out red flags, signaling they found her."

My body stiffens, the surrounding sounds drowned out by shock. "What do you mean?"

"I remember when it was done. The tattoo." Jane's fingers tap fiercely on her thighs, the chaos inside of her like a needy, angry storm. Tempest adds, "How else do you think they snuck you in to get it? It was on *my* command after Ritter arranged it with me. It's why no one can remember who exactly did it. That took quite a bit of social puppeteering," she explains, twiddling her fingers as if strings are attached.

"And now?" I ask, trying to maintain patience.

Tempest languidly looks at me. "I'm just checking in on her. And letting *you* know that I'm watching."

Tempest stands, and I can't feel anything other than the truth, which for some reason makes me trust it less. "We will speak later."

"Good," she says, flashing Jane a smile before walking away, carrying with her an aura so thick that I wonder if she even knows her reality from the lies.

I look ahead, rubbing my chin, my blood so fucking hot it matches the temperature of Jane's scalding baths.

"What if the others learn?" she quietly asks. "That she's involved?"

"I need to think."

I stare at the back of her pretty head, her auburn hair as soft as the silk she wears. Tempest takes her place, the crowd cheering for her as I consider a hundred decisions at once. The sandy pits below are empty until two men enter, shouting their allegiance to Tempest as cheers roar in the air.

I don't care at all for the fights anymore. All I *do* know is that when I consider returning to the Spiraling Stone, indignation claws at my chest like a warning of betrayal, as if the castle has raised bloody flags. I glance down, wondering what the fuck is going on in this world. First, it's Jane being Ritter's daughter. Then, Cypress and Tempest enter like they have the right to alter this world. And now, returning to the castle feels like swimming into the jaws of a shark.

Logic is juxtaposed with the force within that has guided me my entire life, *hating* when I don't trust my magic. As I watch the two men fight and stain the sand with their blood, the answer finally comes to me.

"You told them your mother was a whore. It looks realistic to visit a whorehouse for a few days, perhaps a week or more. It's what I would do if I were trying to regain your memory," I say, breathing deeply, catching her unique scent with the floral perfume as the wind blows. "To answer your question, we're not going to worry about the others learning. Instead, we'll go to Rosmertta's for now and get away from the Spiraling Stone. That's all we can control."

She looks to the side in interest, her gaze still on the floor. "Which of Rosmertta's establishments?"

"To her primary residence in The River sector. Your friend is there."

Her eyes brightened, Jane's wave of trust washing over me, making my fists clench tighter. I fucking need the unmarred part of her heart that's utterly wrapped in thorns, and I no longer bother to decipher why. I just do. I lean over, pulling on her chain so she has to listen to me.

"I have a proposition," I offer, figuring this might be our best way forward. For the both of us. For my curiosity. For her to relax for a damn hour.

"It's not as if I can say no."

I smirk, unable to restrain myself. She's such an unique figure in Skull's Row when so many don't understand just who she is, and *I* want to be the first to claim her. I want to fuck her so hard she's haunted by me while her heart is wide open. I want to feel the rawness of her soul, in ways only I can. "Give me your unguarded self, for a single day."

She narrows her eyes, but I can feel the curiosity. "What does that have to do with anything?"

"Tempest reads true, for better or for worse. Which means we lie low until I speak with her again... until then, we both could use a little enjoyment."

"That's it," she states, not believing me.

"This is purely for my desires, love. I like to *live* when danger is so close by. It's the best time to do so."

She wants to. I can feel so many things swirl inside of her, secrets locked deep. Hurt. Anger. This woman, if Ritter had maintained power, would have been the most desired daughter in all of Skull's Row. What would this place do with the Scorpion's daughter who is undeniably beautiful and as fierce as a mercenary?

I can feel her plucking away at the neglected part of me—one that I ignore because it's useless—and how it's become fascinated by her. Craves her. The way she rolled over this morning to seek my affection, with absolutely no reservation, stirred something within me that won't shut the fuck up now.

If this is all going to shit, then I'm not going to hesitate.

"Do it, Jane," I softly command. "We both know there's no point in fighting it. Might as well enjoy ourselves. You've said this yourself."

She exhales, raising an impatient brow. "When does that day start?"

"From when we get to Rosmertta's until tomorrow night."

Both brows raise. "That's *more* than a day. It's only late morning right now."

"Not if a portion is spent with your friend. I'm a greedy man, so I'll make sure not a moment's wasted."

I sense the forced protest, the one stemming from a necessary obligation to protect herself. The most bizarre aspect of this is that she doesn't *have* to protect herself from me. I don't fucking know why, but I'd let her stab me, many times, before I'd ever stab her in return. Even if I did, I'd never hit anything vital.

She can have her tantrums as long as she learns she'll submit her ferocity to me in the end. I'm not a poet, or a philosopher, but I *am* a man. If this is how some form of infatuation works for me, then she's going to have to be patient, and understand she's not shaking me.

Not as long as I feel how much she wants me.

Being this close lets me feel her more, and I can even decipher that despite the words soothing her anxiety, she wants gentler professions. A foreign part of me *wants* to give them to her, and yet I'm also reserved, because I don't know what I'll do if she rejects me. *Truly* rejects me.

That might be dangerous for her.

She breathes heavily, her heart tired. So damn tired. I even reach to her face and she partially yanks back, but I clear the hair in her eyes, then drop my hand.

"What do you need from me to trust me?" I quietly ask. "You didn't agree to my proposition."

There's no hesitation. "If Kathleen wants to leave Bones... You. Let. Her. Leave."

Fucking mutiny will erupt if I take the kitten away from Bones, but I also know what that oppressing love can do to a woman if she doesn't want it. I've seen it in my mother.

My mother's pain is the only reason I have any morals in this world.

"I'll promise to do what I can."

She's unconvinced, but curious, and even relieved to give in. Jane breathes out, "Okay."

"Okay, what?"

She heaves a sigh. "You get my undivided attention for the next day, once we're at Rosmertta's."

The crowd roars as she says that, one of the fighters losing his head as the other stumbles, screaming over his victory.

I want to tell her more of what I know about her father, and yet it doesn't feel right. Even admitting that felt too close to the edge, like Cypress is telling me it's too soon—I eye the ruby earrings Jane wears, caution stilling my tongue. No doubt *that* would help earn her trust.

I lean back into my seat, allowing my mind to wander with the possibilities of everything now that I've temporarily soothed the rage inside of Jane.

Who fucking knows where all of this chaos will take us.

Thank the gods I thrive in this environment.

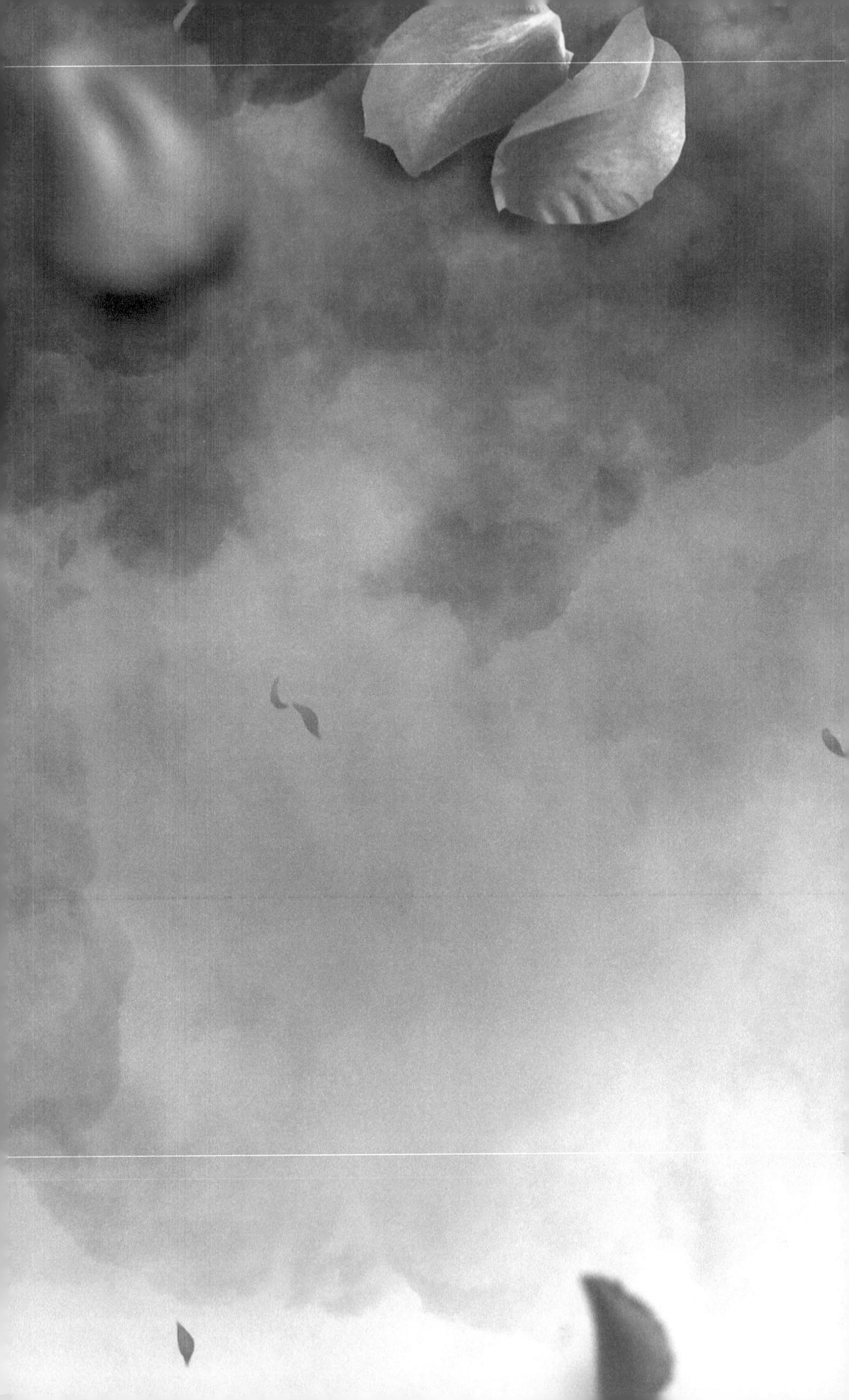

SEEING GHOSTS

JANE

The crowd cheers, drums sounding off to a steady rhythm. The third round has just finished, and I watch with a bated breath as someone is carried away with a nasty wound to the thigh, blood discoloring the sands in a blotchy mess.

I've already cleaned my face after a noir brought some towels, wiping the dried blood away.

Anya startles me when she nears Soren, although the Zenith hardly seems surprised. She leans down to his ear and I can barely hear her say, "We secured Rosmertta's in The River sector."

He looks down at me, his leather crinkling with the movement. I crane my neck to look between the two. Anya had come to us not shortly after Tempest left, Soren requesting that she secure rooms for his men. In the meantime, we've sat here while other Zenith have looked our way. If one came near, violence brimmed in Soren's glares, and that's apparently all that was required.

As I stare at him, he deeply inhales, his unblinking gaze connecting with mine. I'm not sure what silent conversation we're having, but he finally stands, my legs aching with the sudden rush of blood when I mimic him. Anya takes the chains once more, and rather than fight the heaviness around my neck, I simply look away and walk closely to her.

We retrace our footsteps around the cliffs, entering through another tunnel lit by large torches. Anya says, "I sent Rasmus and a few others to secure Phantom. Figured we could ride to Rosmertta's rather than walk."

Bones sighs out, "Always so on top of things, Anya."

"Better than starting fights for no reason," she quips.

He scoffs. "I don't tolerate horseshit, and you know it. Fucker acting like he was put out. Plus, Soren can read me like a book. If he wanted to stop me, he would have."

We approach heavily manned iron gates that open instantly once Soren is identified. Over a dozen horses are waiting, and as always Phantom stands out among the rest in his size and fur color. Soren runs his hand over the horse's face, looking at his followers. "A handful of you ride ahead."

Almost instantly, five of them swiftly mount their steeds and take off, hooves clacking on cobblestone. I'm standing next to a nickering horse when Soren says to Anya, "Give her the cloak. She gets covered up in the streets."

Anya hands me the cloak she brought, and I quickly pull the wool fabric around my shoulders. I won't complain about avoiding any extra eyes while out here. Once I've mounted my ride, Soren takes the chains. The clouds overhead thicken and turn gray as we make our way. I'm not sure which sector we're currently in, all I know is it's *not* where I grew up.

It smells like horseshit, baked goods, and filthy humans. All these sectors have their "safe" zones where commerce is highest. They also harbor unkempt streets full of secrets, lies, and lurid humans. Nearly everywhere feels overcrowded as many live in squalor, while affluent homes are erected among the poor.

The atmosphere shifts like walking through a veil once we're in this lower portion: people keep to themselves, many walk with their weapons visible or in hand, and the sunlight is blocked out by tall, lopsided buildings that intensify the shadows.

My eyes widen when we pass by a building with many eyeless, onyx statues and gargoyles—more worshippers of Solerin. A collection of men and women sit outside with lips painted black, chanting the same words as they watch us pass by, one of them skinning a rabbit.

They all wear ruby earrings.

I touch mine before averting my attention, suddenly creeped out by wearing them.

I never meddled with the affairs of gods in this world, only aware that legends claim our magic stems from them. Some healers even worship a goddess of light, but Mother said the goddess would either be with us, or she wouldn't, and we never really talked about her after that.

Either way, it's a good reminder that people out here *do* participate in rituals and offerings, as it can make the most devout extremely dangerous—*if* they're granted powers. Or hells, they're made dangerous just by their fanaticism.

It's not long until we're away from the devout. The city is

so vast, something I admittedly *did* miss. Town squares are markers for where one's at. All I can remember is that there's one that's centralized around a very old oak tree, and another of a statue of sirens pulling a pirate underneath the water.

Eventually, after traversing many narrow lanes that are flanked by gas lanterns, Soren halts his horse and dismounts at a stable large enough to house four families. *This* town square consists of a willow tree that has a row of gallows built into it, so people hang from the branches.

One person is chained to a stone pillar, and children throw rocks at the man as he pleads for food.

I dismount my horse, and to my surprise, Soren drops the chains and begins to unlock the collar. I stare at his chest as he does so, not about to question him.

"Don't care if anyone sees you down here without these on. You wander far from me, and you'll be pulled into the shadows before I feel you're missing. Don't take this as a sign to wander, or you'll regret it."

He drops the chains by a stable post, and I rub my neck. I'm so happy to have them off that I even choose to flirt with him. "I owe you my day, anyway, and I don't go against my word."

"I was holding you to it whether you wanted to or not."

I throw my hood up as I hold back a smile and closely follow Soren, glancing around at my environment. It's so damp in these streets, townhomes stacked and mismatched. The red lanterns indicating The Undercroft stand out as we pass them by—

My heart nearly stops.

In the shrouding darkness stands a man who inspects his blade, swiping it on his forearm before sheathing. In the same motion, he leans against the wall with a leg up, crossing his arms with a slight slouch. I can even hear Mom tell him to fix his posture.

Soren turns on his heel before anyone even notices I've stopped, he must have sensed me. His hand is on his pommel, the other one touching his mask. "What is it?" His voice is laced with danger.

"I... thought..." I shake my head, closing my eyes. When I open them again, he's gone.

"Jane."

Words collide in my throat, preventing any cohesive sentence from forming. My gaze trails over every minor detail of that alley, tunnel vision blinding me to the rest of the world.

Did I really just see him?

Dad?

No—his blonde hair wasn't the right color, which is supposed to be jet black. That face was also rounder than what I'd expect, the nose too wide. And yet the man acted like him. Stood like him.

My eyes burn in my refusal to blink, like it will permanently erase any possibility of it truly being him. His minute existence—even if in my head—fuels a validation I didn't know was starved. I've spent years in bitter resentment, but the idea that he's actually alive makes it feel like hardly any time has passed.

The moment is exceptionally brief, and yet I haven't felt as if Dad was truly alive since I first arrived in Coalfell.

The concept drastically shakes my foundation.

Soren is patient, until he's not. The behemoth nearly stands in my line of sight, but I sidestep him—what if Dad comes back? Or, not *dad,* but someone *like* him...

"We need to go, Jane," Soren commands, uncertainty laced in his voice, eyeing the alleyway all the same, his hand still on his hilt.

My lips barely move, unspoken words resting on my tongue. I still can't get over the way it struck me to even *think* I saw him. So far, my father began to feel like a made-up figure of my mind, like perhaps my entire identity was irrationally not real.

But seeing a man that at least *acted* like him? No, that childhood *was* real.

I'm not just Jane, I'm Jane Ritter.

Repressed memories burn with new life. My childhood creeps in—my youthful dreams, memories of walking in my father's shadow...

Once that overwhelms me, my mind empties. I stare, unblinking, my heart racing so fast I'm almost dizzy. Soren's rough voice cuts through my haze, the Zenith leaning in. "*Jane.*"

I lift my head to eye the brutally handsome man. "Right," I mumble, and look back down.

His voice is controlled, despite his words of warning. "No matter what you saw, we need to act normal when out in the open. Come."

"All right," I pitifully reply.

My mouth is like cotton; I can't focus on anything. My gaze latches to a random barrel—it's as if my identity finally seeps into my skin, like I'm soil thirsty for moisture after a bitter winter, my roots awakening, digging deeper. I *am* Ritter's daughter. Charles Ritter, the Scorpion. He was *real*.

I'm real.

My hand reaches for a blade that's not at my hip, as if I'll stab the first Council member I come across, finally awakened—

Soren's hand reaches out. My attention snaps to his chest, my veins burning with revenge and death. His grip on the back of my head is almost gentle, like he's attempting to be soothing. The Zenith rumbles, "I won't hold you back from that revenge, either, before you worry. But we need to move. I don't know what you saw, but we can discuss it later."

The gentleness of his voice shreds through every emotional wall—I don't know why, but his words mean something to me. I hotly sigh, trying to calm down. My lips fail to speak, until I finally say again, "All right. Let's go."

Without much transition, I numb it all. Ignore it. Assert to myself that it's not real, or even if it is, something is massively wrong with the situation.

Clear your mind.

Closing my eyes as I exhale, I center myself. It wasn't Dad, that's for sure. Besides, this entire situation is too dangerous to let my emotions run wild. I have to concentrate on what's before me. The fact that for some reason my village was burned down and that my only friend is currently residing at a whorehouse for safety. Let alone the shit with the Council, or how Tempest is reappearing like a rescue ship when I'm stranded at sea. I almost wish she'd come back so I could ask her a hundred more questions.

Opening my eyes, I give a nod to Soren, one he doesn't seem to believe until he finally drops his hand and walks forward. I follow so close I nearly step on his heels, staring only at the intricacy of Soren's armor. Of the thick leather straps, the vambraces, and the thick belt at his waist that everything hangs from.

I only look away when I smell what must be Rosmertta's before I see it, relief lifting my worries when I spot guards outside an elaborate building on a cleaner street.

The perfume's quite pleasant, even if pungent.

Kathleen's close.

The sound of people fucking is clear as day, along with laughter and loud talking—such clashing energies compared to the rest of the streets. The building is four stories tall with evenly placed round-arch windows, steep gable roofs with large dormers, and a flag that hangs which depicts a purple rose on a black background.

I'm aware of how easy I have it when accompanying Soren. Packs are required to survive in Skull's Row, reputation is almost as solid as steel armor, and he's akin to wrapping myself within a steel ship.

A woman rushes out onto a balcony that overlooks the streets, purple curtains billowing behind her before she disappears back into the fabric, no doubt announcing the arrival of a Zenith. Guards are already on their feet, a few of Soren's men standing by the entrance in matching displays of a snake on their chest.

We enter the building without question. Candlelight creates a warm, golden atmosphere against the umber walls, a large staircase in front of us that winds up to all four stories. Thick velvet drapes cover windows, and lewd paintings hang within gold-painted frames—there's even one of a giant orgy over a hearth in the drawing room. It draws my eyes to the statue of two people fucking right in front of it, as if it were merely a nice sculpture of a bird.

I'm *not* in my comfort zone. Mother had to heal many broken men and women from these establishments. Then again, she also never let me go near one of Rosmertta's buildings due to the high-profile clientele; someone might recognize me from the Silver District.

A shirtless man with smudge painted around his eyes bows his head as he rings a bell. Almost immediately a woman with oiled skin descends the stairs to greet us, her body decorated in golden jewels. Her mahogany hair is pulled back as loose curls drape around her aged face. Deep red lips smile at us.

"Soren. It has been a while since we've seen you," she

welcomes, her voice deep and raspy. "I kept the entrance rather empty when I heard you were coming."

This must be Rosmertta.

"What all were you told?" he asks.

"I don't question those who pay, and your men handed me a very heavy bag of gold. You have the entire top floor, while your guards are scattered throughout in their own rooms. It has all been arranged."

He nods. "We'd also like to start our visit with the one named Kathleen."

"Ah, yes, Bones is quite fond of instructing us how to handle her." She looks over my head at Bones before connecting her gaze with mine. I immediately think of an expensive wine that's aged well—worldly, yet clean. Rosmertta observes me like she's about to place a bid. "And who is *this*? She's not a petal of mine."

Soren shifts so I'm no longer in her view. "Her name is Jane, and she is with me. *Only* me."

"Of course," she swiftly replies, her tone immediately obedient. "I'll take you to Kathleen."

CLAIMING HIS DAY

JANE

Soren pivots on his heel, looking over my head at his men. "We're here for business right now. You can come back and fuck whichever one you want later once I'm in my room. I need all of you on guard for now."

Soren's pale gaze falls down to mine, penetrating me in a momentary dissection before he turns around as we follow Rosmertta. I'm almost used to the exploratory nature of his powers, like it's something I have to accept if I'm to be near him. Peeking around the massive man, I see Rosmertta guiding us through a long hall that's away from the entrance and up a separate flight of stairs.

Dragging out a sigh, I do my best to ignore the many sounds of sex coming from rooms that we pass. I even hear the crack of a whip as a woman tells someone they've misbehaved, moans breaching the wooden door of their room.

We near a large archway with open doors—the only room with drawn-back curtains. I nearly squint at the natural light, the room as large as a grand dining hall with many moving bodies.

One-and-a-half-story windows overlook a man-made stream, water flowing through carved-out stone, and buildings packed together that use it for commerce and travel. It's so crowded that I'm shocked people can even traverse the waterway.

We are taken to rather spacious quarters in the very back that are filled with food and many casually talking. I spot a blonde woman by a slightly curved window, sitting among a collection of empty couches and chairs. She stands out among the darkness of the room.

I move to bolt right past Soren, who steps aside for me without hindrance.

Kathleen stands when she spots me, revealing her thin yet elegant white dress. We embrace, and she smells just like wisteria. I let the unique scent stain my lungs like it's a fresh day of spring after a long winter. We're friends that never quite did anything more than indulge in the other's presence, and yet here we are, in Skull's Row and trying to survive.

She shouldn't be here, though, and I need to find a way to get her out.

Her heavy-lidded, green eyes examine my outfit. "Miss Jane, what are you wearing under this cloak?"

"Oh, it's a story that will require some ale," I reply with a smile, taking in every detail. Her skin is smooth and clean, her beautiful blonde hair soft and washed. I take one of her hands in mine. Even her nailbeds are pristine. "You're okay," I state with relief. "At least, you look okay."

She smiles, then waves at another. "Ale for my friend and I."

I barely process our environment as she moves me to a chair that places my back toward the entry. I glance over and both Bones and Soren are watching from across the room in their own enclave, more of Soren's men standing by the entry. I face Kathleen who sits very close to me.

The room quiets at the presence of a Zenith, only for Rosmertta to clap her hands. "Act as normal. Patrons, if you feel more comfortable, there are more rooms downstairs."

An awkward air hangs as I know half the room wants to move but doesn't want to be offensive. A gang of men in a corner raise their glasses in Soren's direction, a few holding onto petals of all shapes and sizes.

Immediately, I don't like those men. Something dances in their eyes that reeks of violence with no boundary. Especially as one grabs a woman with so much force she winces. My blood runs hot as I sneer, but I still face Kathleen, refocusing on her. "Okay, but Bones. What is going on there? Are you sure you're all right? You look great, but are you bound here? Forced to do anything?"

Dark eyebrows rise as if I've asked her the most personal question. "I'm going to need about three mugs of ale to talk about *Bones*," she laughs, one of the only times it's ever shaken with uncertainty.

"I worry about you," I implore, spotting a necklace that looks like *his* around her neck—a bunch of bones on a leather string. I lean in, having seen too much of the world to take her clean appearance at face value. "Are they making you do anything you don't want? Is *he*?"

"No," she immediately replies, adamant. "It's quite nice here. Rosmertta runs one of the few houses that lets the workers choose their clientele. She has her limits on what is allowed. People go to darker districts for *other* things," she scowls, her eyes flashing with disgust. "Of course, it's Skull's Row, so pain is always just around the corner, but I mostly just help where I can. Do their hair and make-up. Cook."

"You've become their *maid*."

"Not much else to do, honestly. It's been good." She takes ale from a man who lowers a serving tray for us, and I do the same. "They all know everyone, and everything. It's the best way to learn Skull's Row. No one touches me, either." She grabs the bones around her neck, surprising me that she touches them with ease. Speaking with a contemplation, she says, "Bones made this for me."

"What *is* that?" I carefully ask, although I'm pretty sure I know.

"The knuckles of a man who tried to force himself on me when I got here," Kathleen says those words like Bones gave her a necklace made of gold, and then her eyes widen as if realizing the tone she used in admitting that.

I take three large gulps of my ale. I mean, I'm happy to hear he's kept others away, but does she even want to be here? "So, when you get that?"

"About two days ago." Kathleen downs some ale herself before hesitating like she's finally committed to a confession. "You're going to think me crazy, Jane."

"Look at what I'm wearing." I laugh as I gesture to the corset I wear, down to the nearly see-through fabric. "I won't judge you, Kathleen. You can tell me. Are you doing okay? Like, truly?"

She speaks like it's a secret she's eager to share. "He is one of the most intense men I have ever met." She leans in. "But I think I want to keep him. I mean it's not like I have a choice, probably. I think my tits have made him see new colors. He's not going anywhere." Shaking her head and looking out the window, a ghost of a smile on her elegant face, she adds, "I've become a mad woman, Jane."

My laugh doesn't quite leave me like how I intended, and I end up staring at Kathleen like she's the only familiar thing I trust. My gaze drops down to the ale inside the wooden mug, the drink still frothing. How do I explain to her that men like Bones are more familiar to me than the ones in Coalfell? And that her desire for him is something that makes *me* feel normal?

"Jane, what is it?" Kathleen asks, drinking more. "You better perk up. Your Zenith is now eyeing you funny."

Soren. "Oh yes... I can't hide a single feeling from him," I mumble, still staring at the foam.

Kathleen gently says, "Bones told me that's why he was sent in the first place... because of your *tattoo*."

My body stiffens; of course, that's already spread. "Yeah," I mutter, looking out the window, watching a crow fly by.

"Your father was a Zenith, but the Council doesn't know which one?" Kathleen leads, like trying to coax it out of me.

I snap my gaze back on her. "He told you that?"

"Soren told him to. To see what reaction I had, and also mentioned something about you needing someone to confide in." She licks her lips, and it's impossible to miss how she's trying to be gentle. "It's fine, Jane. I'm your friend. This all makes a fuck ton of sense."

It's as if her words take the very weight of my heart and carry it away. Having someone say it—and not in a panic—makes me feel like a normal person. I don't know how to feel about Soren sharing this information as if he knows what's best for me, but that reaction feels so useless, too. Because damn him, but it *did* help. With a cracking voice, I mutter, "That's the gist of it."

I glance her way when I notice her posture change, Kathleen's tone clipped, her eyes scolding. "Look, I understand you being quiet before, but it's making me feel less like a true friend that you won't talk to me."

That shocks me out of my stupor. "You're right. I'm so sorry Kathleen," I reply, motioning my ale toward her. "It's just so much to process," I begin, spilling my heart out once I begin. "My life. Where I was sure it was heading... and then Coalfell and now I'm back, like the ocean has finally pulled my ship to its depths..."

"What's happening, Jane? Why do they want you?"

"I don't know." I glance around before holding her gaze. "I mean that. I don't know." I eye the knuckles around her neck. "I think Soren is handling some of it. But I don't know what that means. As far as I know, I really think it's just because they're confused and pissed that I've been marked. Wondering if it's one of *them* that did it." I don't mention Tempest, as I'm still honestly processing it myself. "Daughters never get marked. Ever. I broke their code, and they're not a forgiving bunch."

With a single nod, Kathleen heaves a heavy sigh. "So why trust Soren in all of this, then?"

Looking at her face through my lashes, I counter, "Why do *you* trust Bones?"

She rolls her head to look away, going to touch the necklace, and then refrains as if realizing what she's doing. "He's got obsessive issues, ones that confusingly intrigue me. I think he's sparing me just for the novelty of me, at the bare minimum. I trust *that*... is that the same for you?"

Some nagging voice yells at me to declare he has said as much more than once, and that my skull is too thick to hear him. "I'm lost, Kathleen. I'm *so* lost," I confess, dropping my gaze to the floor. "I don't know who to trust. I don't know what to do. I'm scared, worried, anxious, enamored—" I stop when the shocking need to bawl my eyes out nearly does me in, embarrassed that I even said that.

She touches my knee. "It's all right, Jane... is Soren treating you all right, at least?"

I sardonically laugh, blinking rapidly to remove the tears in my eyes. "He's a great brute that I enjoy fucking. Even had me in chains earlier, and yet I wasn't scared of him once. That's insanity, right?"

Her smile genuinely spreads across her face, the image immensely comforting, reminding me of times before all of this. "There you go. Always knew you needed the right man," she says, drinking more of her ale before she dons a serious expression. "So now what? What's the plan with him? You need to have one. He's watching you right now like he's picking your soul apart."

"I'm an idiot if I blindly trust him," I reply, but curl the end of the sentence almost as if it's a question.

"Bones says you're special to Soren. New, yes, but he's smitten, even if a bargain has been struck," she says with a smile. "I don't think you're an idiot, Jane. Maybe a bit daft if you want to have his babies tomorrow, but I think he likes you. That's how some of those men are. Even the women here are like that. They see something rare, and they snag it."

My head spins in a way my heart has been eager to, but my mind refuses to allow. With a partial smile, I mutter, "Did he pay you to say that?"

The muscles in her face twitch as if the question catches her off guard, but she laughs it away. "Hells no... I wouldn't do that even if he offered me a castle. I'm not like that." After a deep drink, she leans forward again, the scent of ale mixing with her floral perfume. "My honest advice? Emotions removed? Ride that cock right on out of here, then escape if that's what you want—"

Kathleen's eyes peer over my shoulder, the warmth of them hardening. Turning in my seat, I watch as a man sits on the couch next to me. He's someone I saw earlier in the pits, recognizable only for all the red tattoos on his pale chest and arms. He's minorly cleaned up, but still rugged.

"Can we help you?" Kathleen asks.

He looks between us. "Was just wondering what you two are talking about."

"Does that often work for you?" I ask, raising a judgmental brow.

He smiles before connecting his gaze with mine. "The name is Shade."

My heart gently flutters at the eye contact, staring with confusion at another dangerous man in this world. At the same time, I know, deep down—or perhaps finally accept—*why* they have this effect on me.

Dad, for as much as I am bitter, killed many men to free me of this place, and those from Skull's Row would do the same. Their brutality is what I crave, because I was raised to accept nothing else.

With a cracking voice, I choose to be snarky. "Did your mother name you that?"

This side of me is why Dad often kept me at a distance in public. I was prone to saying things that frequently got me into trouble, which could blow our cover—although he *always* paid someone to trail me. I even had a large kid sit on me once when I was seven, crushing me because I couldn't hold my tongue until someone smacked him upside the head with a cane...

I eye the fighter's bandaged leg. Blood cakes the hair through his gashed pants. It's as if he wants to show off the carnage he endured. He's not even wearing a shirt, displaying his ink and scars.

Leaning back into his seat, he's hardly phased. "I don't know what my mother dearest would have called me if she stuck around. But this nickname has stuck." His muscled, dirty stomach moves in tempting ways as he breathes, and faces Kathleen. "Anyway, *you've* been requested." He motions to our side.

"Oh, *what?*" she mumbles.

"Rosmertta sent me to fetch you," he explains slowly.

Kathleen looks behind me before facing me. "She does seem to want me. I'll see you soon. I hear you're staying?"

"Of course," I assert.

I watch Kathleen walk away, Bones immediately following her, the tall yet lean man—for what it's worth—looking at her with gentler eyes than I would have imagined he'd ever have.

I glance Soren's way, who raises his brow, watching me, but not moving. He slowly sips his drink, eyes on me and *only* me. I turn around, noticing that Shade isn't leaving.

Shade takes immediate advantage of the isolation. "So... I hear you're Soren's pet. A new one," he observes, leaning forward. "You're too pretty to be ruined by him, you know that? Although, he does enjoy his things pretty so he can break them. Always digs right into their chest and knows how to manipulate."

I snort, only for a heat to threaten its bloom through my cheeks. Screw it. I need information, and this man is the first person outside of Soren's ranks who might have answers for me. "So, he has a penchant for the pretty ones?"

He scoffs. "Fucker has had many men of power trying to get him to marry their daughters. But he's a hard bastard to catch. No one has been long-term that I'm aware of." He stares me dead in the eye as he says, "That's why *you're* very curious to me right now. He doesn't usually keep his pets leashed so close."

I narrow my eyes. "First, I'm not leashed. Right now, anyway... And second, why does this matter to you?"

He grins, the smile rather pleasant. "As I said, came to tell Kathleen that she's wanted and figured I'd ask. Although I don't like the way he's looking at me now, so it's probably best I leave. I'm rather fond of living."

Just like that, he stands to leave me alone. I watch him walk away, and once he's out of arm's reach, Soren finally motions to Rosmertta.

In quick succession, everyone rises when Rosmertta taps a very small gong, the patrons leaving made more dramatic as they fade with the sound that ordered them.

As I stand, she motions for me to remain, and it's evident that Soren has just cleared the room for us.

THE MERCENARY'S TOUCH

JANE

I'm not quite sure why she's doing this. Moving my gaze back to my Zenith, the stark lighting of the window makes him look almost regal. Like he's a warped king watching over his subjects.

When the door to the vast space shuts, and it's just the two of us in sudden silence, Soren stands, his heavy footsteps the only sound in the room. I don't need powers to read that he did not like Shade coming near me. It's ruffled his pretty little feathers, and I'm honestly curious now.

He cants his head to the side as he nears me, a controlled

frustration laced in his brutal, rough voice. "You so easily give him your attention..."

"What? I give it to you," I counter, standing.

"I mean your *undivided* attention..." With each step forward, I take one back until I'm against a cold wall that he flattens a hand against, towering over me. Deciphering his mood seems almost pointless. "Your nerves even calmed when he talked to you, in ways that he's lucky I don't feel like staining Rosmertta's rugs in blood for. Is that what you want? A gladiator?" He leans in, hovering his face in mine. "Perhaps have them fight over you in the pit?"

His intensity, after such a gentle moment in his room the previous night, confuses me... especially since it actually makes me trust him more. I'll trust a man's anger over his niceties any day, even if I'm not entirely sure where it stems from. Is it territorial? Jealousy? Both?

I still can't hold my tongue. I'm a damn daughter of this world, not a cowering peasant. "I did, actually," I reply, as if he casually asked me the question. His body stiffens, his breathing deepening. "I fantasized about that very thing when I was younger and in Coalfell, especially when I still allowed myself to miss this world—" I want to make him squirm, especially after learning he has a penchant for 'the pretty ones'. I lean into his cheek, so ours are touching as I speak into his ear with the confidence of a Zenith's daughter. "If I had been known, and my father still relevant, many would have fought for me. I'll never forget that, no matter how much you dress me up as yours."

He reels ever so slightly, growling in my ear, "How right you are."

Soren fists the back of my hair, watching me as he holds my gaze. I pant, the pain from pulling on my scalp just enough to steal my breath out of surprise, my eyes flitting back and forth between his. I can't get enough of *his* undivided attention; of hearing that others really don't sleep in his bed. Of Kathleen's theory that he might just genuinely be captivated by me.

As I am, admittedly, to him.

His lips are so close to mine that I could lick them. He rasps, "You're so misguided when it comes to judging me, Jane."

Confusion overwhelms my needy heart, believing his sincerity with more ease than before. I want him to kiss me. To touch me. The more I'm in Skull's Row, the more I crave the life I should have had, as if living this out will fill the void that loneliness and misery have carved out.

In some way, I think I am mourning a person who *should* have been, and having Soren fuck it out of me is as sweet as punching men at taverns. I bleed the desire out of me, hoping he picks up on what I want. When a flash of intrigue appears in his eyes, before he covers it, I ask, "You're not going to kiss me?"

"No," he muses, then thinks on the answer. "No... I think *you* should." He runs his nose alongside my cheek, inhaling deeply, no doubt catching lingering traces of whatever floral scent he covered me in. "You promised to give *me* your undivided attention. So, kiss me like you want to keep that word."

I'm so fucking confused. Some part of me completely believes him, and the other screams that he wants something from me. But if he does, what's the worst that will happen? He breaks my heart, and I spend the rest of my days figuring out how to kill him? What's the best? I get to engage in... whatever, this is? "I don't think you even know my middle name," I tease.

"What is it, then?"

With zero pushback, I reply, "Marella."

His icy eyes flash with intrigue. Even then, I don't move. It's the weirdest feeling to want him so badly and yet be utterly afraid of that desire. He sighs, knowing I need more. I love that

I don't have to say anything as he adds, "Do you know how hard it is to find a woman with as much danger as you, who is also as gorgeous as you?"

My lips wordlessly part as my body relaxes. He seems intrigued, raising a brow as he adds, "I call you my desert rose because they don't grow in the desert... so to see one would be special enough to kill others for it." He brushes his lips on mine, the grip on my hair tightening so I can't lean into the motion. "And I revel in the way it feels when your heart unwinds for me—that's from selfish reasons, Jane, that have nothing to do with the Council, Skull's Row, or Cypress."

Those words slither deep within, entwining with every fiber of my being... I'm reminded why I hesitate so much.

His affection *means* something to me.

It's been over a decade since I opened my heart like this, even if just by an inch.

Give in. Even if it hurts you. So, you can live and hurt the rest. Including him if he deserves it.

It's as if the thought is the permission I've been desperately grasping for, effortlessly pressing my lips against his, despite the grip on my hair. His hand on the walls drops to touch me like I'm something he's yearned to find. He's ruining my outfit with his rough grip, but I don't care. Not when his tongue parts my lips, or when he wraps his arm behind my back, readjusting us so greatly that I wrap a thigh around him for support. He even lifts me, pinning me on the wall, both legs wrapped around him. His armor hurts my inner thighs, but it means nothing to me.

If anything, it just reminds me who holds me.

Soren doesn't understand how much he hooks me at this moment. When I was a teenager, missing home and trying to enjoy the boring life around me, I often thought of here. Of tending to a young gladiator.

Of finding romance that way.

Maybe, I could sneak back into Skull's Row as a healer.

This kiss is very different from the others. Fear is replaced with desire, giving this questionable man a true bit of my trust—it's senselessly divine.

I've never kissed a man while feeling *any* emotion.

Everything about him morphs in my mind, imagining the potential I have with him. My body freezes when the concept overwhelms me. I'm still in danger. Still alone. Our lips part as his gaze bores into mine.

"Don't pull away from me, beautiful. That's not a part of the deal. I want all of you."

His expression bleeds with so much desire that I can nearly read *him*; I touch his cheek with affection, his icy eyes are vulnerable, like the beast has a heart so closed that he, too, doesn't know what to do when it's open.

Whatever emotion sprouted is drowned away, his reluctance mirroring mine like his own heart might actually be threatened, too.

We are both in need of rapture, afraid to touch the light.

So, instead, the Zenith fucks me inside of the whorehouse with carnality rather than sentiment, and I'm grateful for the familiar intimacy, or lack thereof. The sounds we make nearly echo in the giant, empty room. He rips at my clothes, gripping my neck so tightly it might bruise as he fucks me like I'm his pleasure to own.

I cling to him like I've never grabbed a man before, eager to touch someone lovingly while they're at a violent distance; practicing what it would be like, amorous, without the fear, and uncertainty of rejection. I even come twice in the brutal exchange, and he ensures he's as deep as my body will fit him when he spills into me.

When we're both spent, he grabs a towel and even cleans

me up with his cock still out, silently observing. Once I'm standing and his pants re-buckled, Soren attempts to repair the damage to my elaborate outfit as he ties it in the back. I stare out a window, watching the many boats as they congest the river. He's helping dress me after bruising my thighs from how hard he fucked me against a table. He quietly asks, "Did you really see your father in the alley?"

Old habits initially protect my words before exhaustion unleashes them. There's no wall guarding my heart as I say, "It makes no sense... but I swear I did."

He tightens my binds one more time before tying them. In our solitude, the safety he provides is magnetic. There's no reminder of who he really is, and he can just be the man I'm enjoying passing the time with.

"What do you mean you swear you did? Was he hard to see?"

"You'll think I'm crazy."

"We're beyond that, love."

Smiling, I decide to give him everything as I say, "It didn't look like him—physically—but he moved like my dad. When our gazes connected, I *felt* him. It was... healing, almost. Even if it's not him. I've spent so many nights crying, wishing for the impossible. At some point, it was almost like my life was made up. Even when you came for me, my dad felt like a figment of my mind." I breathe heavier, speaking without restraint, "I don't know. It's like having a dog that died and seeing one that looks exactly like them. It reinvigorated me. Made me realize I can accept who I am, rather than tame myself for the sake of the villagers in Coalfell."

The dead air behind me fills with his body as he closes all space between us, the man tenderly wrapping a hand around my throat, his breath is on my ear. "Let that part of you open, Jane. I can feel it, and you need to heal. Which you can do here, as we're staying for an undetermined amount of time. They'll think I'm trying to open you up, but if your daddy's showing himself, things are about to get very colorful, and whorehouses have a way of keeping secrets. Especially if you pay them well. You'll be sleeping with me, and no man is to touch you."

I lean into Soren, his touch nothing but gentle even if it might look aggressive from the outside. His other hand runs through the back of my hair—I'm learning he likes to play with it. "What of your duties to the Council? Surely, they'll know."

"Those bastards have a lot of fat that needs trimming." His nose burrows into my hair as he adds, "I have a feeling those that burned down your village are still out there. Something is going on, and it's more than just them wanting to know who marked you without permission. Blackwell and his ilk are too distracted by their magnitude to remember we're *all* fragile when the ocean's storm barrels into us. I'm planning to ride into the eye."

I believe him. For better or for worse, I trust that he's playing chess rather than being entirely selfish or senseless. Perhaps it's all simply too much and I'm forced to believe him for my own preservation.

But if intuition is a real guide, then mine tells me that Soren smells blood in the water and is letting the Council bleed out before claiming what's left. Maybe my appearance makes them all realize they're more fragile than they'd like to pretend.

He shocks me when warm lips press against my neck in a kiss before he says, "We will worry about that later. You still owe me a day, and I have every intention to drain even the last minute out of you."

There's no point to my usual words of protest, ones that are like dirt in my mouth now.

I want to live.

"Then, I'd like another warm bath, some wine, maybe a foot massage, and the freedom to ask you ten questions."

For the first time since meeting him, his laugh sounds like it comes from a normal man rather than a callous mercenary as he says, "Deal."

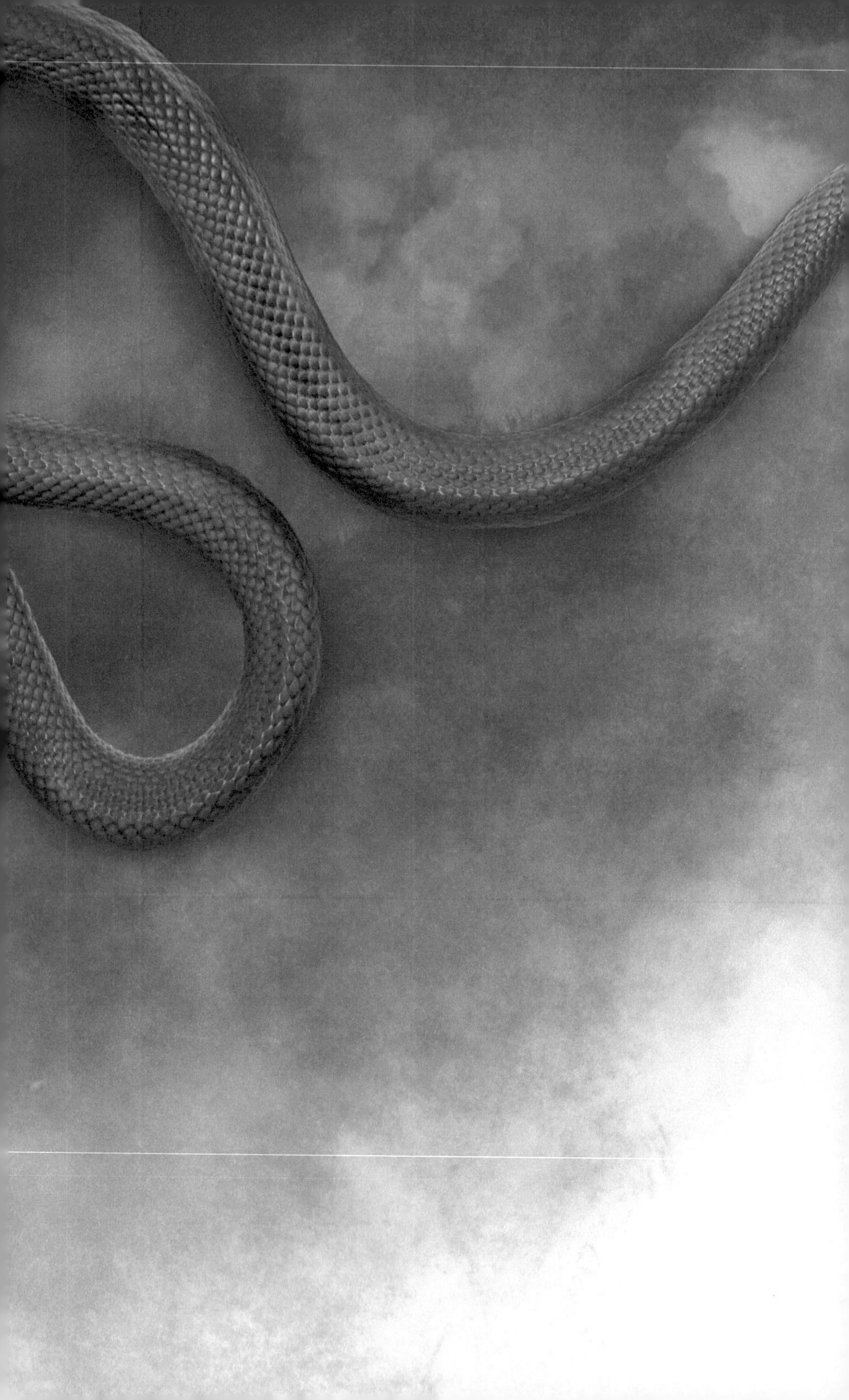

SOREN

Skull's Row is full of escapists who are starving to appease all carnal desires of man. Many establishments do well to offer the finer things in life, like a carrot at the end of a fucking golden stick.

In the basement of Rosmertta's is a private bathing room for that very purpose, the water from a nearby stream trickling into a basin reserved for the finer customers.

And being me, I get whatever I want.

But we're not here for my *own* desires. I don't need these luxuries, as I already have it all—the carrot and the stick, all doused in liquid gold.

No, I'm here to dangle this carrot in the face of someone that I can't force to take it. My innate abilities mean that I can always tell when an emotion is forced, so illusions are nothing more than bitter attempts to assuage what can't be manipulated.

Miss Jane is going to get the luxurious bath she so desires, and she *better* let me in.

It's the strangest turn of who I am as a man, as if I met her two years ago, then she wouldn't tempt me like she does now. I simply didn't crave this type of temptation.

That change didn't occur until I smelled death so close in my shadows, swearing I felt his putrid breath on the back of my neck, and I awoke to feeling older... wiser. My wine didn't taste as delicate, and fucking women hungry for my affection was nothing but empty.

Nearly bleeding out and waking up a week later changed me. It wasn't the first time it's happened, but it was different than the times before.

It even made me miss *home*. The kind that only lives in memories.

Something is missing in my life that no swipe of a blade can claim, and I crave it more than I ever did before. Even if my sister is still out there, I want my *own* family.

I want what inspires the Scorpion to risk everything and break all the rules.

Jane relaxes in her steaming bath as her beautiful, wet hair dangles behind her. My feelings are multifaceted and also incredibly basic—I want her. I'd swing many blades to claim her, but her heart is still something she has to *give*.

It's addictively maddening.

Her being the daughter of a Zenith fills in every gap that's ever existed when bedding other beautiful creatures. Violence is as natural to Jane as breathing, yet she's soft. Feminine.

She'd kill a man for me if she harbored enough loyalty. I know she would. And she makes me earn her favor.

I wonder if she knows how much I enjoy her, how she's an escape that's so different from everything else. I'd even dare to say I enjoy unwinding Jane more than gutting a man.

Gods how it would be different if she trusted me without question. Opened up to me like how she does to Kathleen. I thrive on being someone's stability, on having her need me. Of being the darkness that keeps her safe.

It's what I was born to do.

In that, I understand that having someone like her loving me for the truth of who I am is what's lacking in my soul.

Death felt hauntingly empty when it recently tried to ensnare me.

Rounding the bathtub, her eyes lock onto me, trailing down and taking me in. I wear only my tunic and pants for both of our comfort.

She could see many sides of me if she so chooses.

Blood pounds harder in my veins when I notice her warm eyes are different. Less reserved.

Such a good violent little creature.

I place a stool right next to the tub, the sound of wood on stone the only noise against these brick walls. Warm candle-light flickers all around, and a more sensitive man would even find this romantic.

It's when I see the matching tattoo on her chest that I feel the romance—a woman who doesn't just walk in the same darkness as me.

Jane Ritter was born in it.

"Foot out," I gently command.

Her wet, lithe body creates ripples as she moves, the water cloudy from soap. She requested to wash first. I don't think she believed I'd actually follow through.

"You're really going to rub my feet?"

"As long as you keep that heart open to me," I reply, staring her down. Maybe it's selfish of me, but I know once she lets me in, I'm not going anywhere. She's addicted to understanding me just as I am with her, but refuses to break because she knows once she does, she won't be able to back away.

So, I'll be the first one to do it. "I also want to ask you one question before you ask yours," I say.

Where she might have been a pain in my ass before, she relinquishes and lifts her leg out of the water, resting her ankle on the edge as her skin shines in the golden light, little water droplets hitting the floor. "Deal."

I can't stop the smile that forms, her cheeks reddening, and not from the steam. I run a hand against her warm leg, rubbing her calves first.

She does her best to pretend like a hundred streaks of lightning didn't just blaze right through her. We both know how much of a waste that is with me.

I touch her like she's mine, gently and with care. It's just as important for me as it is for her, as I know this is what her damaged heart needs. "When did you start assaulting people at taverns?"

Her chest rises, slowly exhaling as she looks away. Those lost eyes flash with many decisions. I feed on every flexion of her emotions, staring at her face. When she speaks, I hear the truth. "My mother used to heal injured whores. It's why I don't like these places very much... This one time, there was a man who came barreling in while my mother healed someone, and he threatened the poor woman. He was a cunt—" her voice thickens with disgust. "My mom stabbed quite a few men and women that have crossed lines, and so I took it upon myself to stab *him* in the balls—" I poorly stifle a chuckle, gripping her calf tighter as my other hand thumbs the heel of her foot. The tension in her heart loosens significantly. "Mom nearly killed him for me when the prick realized what I had done. She healed him right after, you know, so he wouldn't die, but I don't think his cock quite worked after that." Her face scrunches, a maelstrom of emotions confusing what I feel. She quietly adds, "I think Dad killed him later. Just as a precaution, so he didn't hurt me. I'm starting to realize Mom used to let him finish those tasks. I think he was just better at disposing of them. So, I don't know... going to the bars to search out the assholes almost reminds me of home."

Gods how I fucking love her history as a daughter of a legendary Zenith. Someone like her would never question my behavior if I felt the need to murder anyone in cold blood if he touched my family.

Fleeting thoughts cycle through Jane, uncertainty like a whirlpool she can't escape. It's wearing her down, too.

She sees me as a life raft, but is convinced I'll take her away and throw her back into the unforgiving riptides. I need to give her more. Convince her I won't throw her aside. Gliding my hand down to work her foot more, I offer, "My mother is a healer."

That snags her attention. Her leg tenses as she connects her gaze with mine. "What?"

Her skin is so soft in my hands, something I could get used to touching. Speaking to Jane is effortless, as if I know she won't tell others of this side of my life. "She often healed women in childbirth." I stare her down. "I grew up in a sea of vagabonds. Injuries everywhere. She was quite busy because of it. Lots of bastards, too... including myself. She was a caretaker to many."

Immediate affection blooms in those warm eyes before mistrust distorts them. I grip her ankle so she can't pull away, her lips parting before pinning shut.

"Jane."

She raises a hand and rolls her eyes to look at the ceiling. "Oh come on, that's a great lie to tell."

She tries to yank her foot away, my hands tightening in a reminder that as long as I have a hand on her, she's not escaping me. "Every word everyone has ever spoken could be a lie. You have trust issues, love. We just have to mend that."

She clears her throat, leaning back into the tub and relaxes her ankle with a sigh, watching as I resume working on her foot. Those words stroked something immensely tormented inside of her. "Okay," she concedes, something between us bonding. She takes her time to think before she slyly asks, "What's your favorite color? Let's start there."

I grin as I stand, moving to the other side. "Red," I reply, sitting back down. She sticks her leg out expectantly, watching me as if she hopes she'll suddenly learn how to read me like I read her. I stare her in the eyes as I say, "Your hair is a very nice, dark shade of it."

There it is—the flicker of affection that bled out of her from earlier. I begin gently rubbing the other foot as I felt nothing of her heart.

I narrow my eyes on her when I detect something I don't like, nor understand. I swear every time a thorn is removed, another one fucking grows back. "Why do you think of daddy dearest when your heart opens to me?"

She seems to nearly choke on air at the way I read her like a book, tilting her head back, looking up at the ceiling in annoyance. Silence sits between us for a while, and I don't push her. Maybe I need to peel back the raw layers, force her to stare at her own imperfection that prevents her from giving herself to me.

Her eyes flick back and forth like she's searching for a

secret message above her that will give her all the answers. She's so desperate to love. To trust. So lonely.

I patiently reply, "I'm a man before I'm a killer, love. I've already told you this." I continue to run a hand up her calf, massaging it. "You're the first woman in a long time, Jane, that has made me desire affection." Her breathing stills. Gently, I add, "That's all I want right now. Your affection... if you want to guard your heart, you can. But I'll seek you out. I'll give you patience, but I'm a mad fucker that is known to hunt what he wants, and as long as some part of you wants me, I'll hunt you."

Her body relaxes as if she wants to be pulled under. She's almost forlorn as she quietly says, "It scares me that you excite me so easily." I stop my movements. She looks me in the eye and continues, "I've seen elaborate schemes to get to someone... my father always said that the only ones who can betray us are the ones we trust. I'd never forgive myself if I fell for a scheme now."

That's fair, but she *will* give in to me.

"So then, ask me your questions, " I say, looking down at her foot. "You don't have to believe the answers. But I'll tell my truths to you, regardless. Just know that no one gets my time like this. That's a truth anyone can answer."

Her eyes close, and I gently massage the pads of her feet. So far, I've counted seven scars, one even on the bottom of her right foot. I have the strangest desire to learn about each one...

"What do you think of the sirens?" Jane asks, opening her eyes.

"They are a part of the magic of the ocean. To disrespect them is like angering a god."

Her body relaxes, my hand trailing almost to her knee. She connects her gaze with mine as she asks, "What do you fear the most?"

Superficial fears cover the ones that truly haunt me. "That is very personal."

Picking up the stool, her heart is almost disappointed that I'm moving away, and I grin. "Such a greedy desert rose," I rasp, moving behind her with the stool. "Worrying that her pampering is done."

I hardly blink as I devour her sentiment. She doesn't reply. How can she when she wants to pretend like we're not in the very situation we're in?

Something about me comforts her like nothing else, and it makes me ravenous.

Sitting down behind her, I grab a brush from my pocket and begin to comb it through her wet hair. She laughs, pure joy radiating out of her for the first time—well, it's a first for *us*. She feels that same relief when with Kathleen. "What are you doing?" she asks.

"Brushing your hair, then I'll braid it," I reply, watching the rich auburn strands congeal through the wooden teeth as it straightens.

"How do you know how to braid hair?"

If only she could feel how personal this is. How much I am giving. How my next words are delivering a true piece of my identity that only Bones and Anya know of.

But I'm a risk taker, and these details could yield extreme rewards. "I have a sister," I reply, touching her hair more intimately for my desire. "When we were little, my mother was very busy. Serena liked her hair braided and I hated to see her cry. So, I learned to braid it for her." I lean down, almost as if I can smell her emotions, my voice stiffening. "What I fear most is what happened to her."

Jane breathes heavily, her genuine sympathy touching me through the stiff air between us. I quickly pull back when the foreign sensation brushes against me, even if there *is* something pleasant about it. I'm not used to being soothed in such a manner.

With sincerity, she quietly says, "I'm sorry to hear that, Soren."

"We were both adolescents when men came to pillage. I've searched everywhere, stalked every trail. She's across the Black Sea somewhere, and traveling to those lands is the second time in my life I've nearly died. I've never found her. Failure of that measure is something I've never experienced. All I know is that Cypress told me she's alive... so what I fear most, Jane, is that her entire life has been wasted and stolen. That I will *never* find her." I don't consider Serena's death, as that thought hollows me out in ways I have no comprehension of processing. "I agreed to become a Zenith because they have more resources and function as a collective. I assume it will be easier to find her that way. That's my *true* motive among them. None of them know that, but they can sense I'm here for selfish means. It's why they told me very little about you, I'm guessing. They know whoever marked you has power they weren't aware of. Which means they'll lose their minds when they realize it's Tempest *and* your father. It's what Cypress told me back when you escaped, and why I agreed to help."

I pull back, running my hand through her hair as I begin to section it, clenching my jaw as I concentrate on reading her. *Don't disappoint me with your response, love...*

Her sympathy turns to burden, and I nearly grip her hair in painful ways when all I sense is a stormy sea inside of her. Jane's voice is laced with apology. "I'm sorry, okay? Maybe I *am* too broken. I can't shut off the voice that says you're just trying to make me fall in love with you like the idiot women in all the songs, so you can just use my dad for a favor..." Her hazel eyes almost look pleading. "I don't know if I know how to open up."

I lean over. I am far from being in love with this woman,

and yet I can feel everything needed to build such a connection. I dip my chin so I can peer into her eyes. The possessive, avaricious, and reclusive side of me can't stop from speaking, "Any man who inspires you to speak of love that isn't me, Jane, won't live to see the rising sun. *That's* the kind of song you're stuck in."

Her eyes widen as those pupils eat at the warm color, and I don't waste a second of her affection as I claim those lovely lips, Jane's hand rising to run through my hair. It's gentle enough at first as I dip my tongue further into her mouth, a moan vibrating into mine. So breathy, so light. I don't understand the hunger it spurs; the kind that wants to devour her flesh and soul and harvest every bit of her, just for me.

What's the point in dissecting what I want when it won't change how I feel?

I just let it be.

Dropping the wooden comb on the floor, my hand dips into the warm water, sliding over her soft body until I reach down below her navel, the ends of my rolled-up sleeve soaked. In a swift movement, I grip her hair and slide my middle finger knuckle deep inside of her. I scour her body for a response.

All I feel in return is a needy heart that doesn't want to think about the world.

That doesn't please me as much as I want it to. I want her to give herself to me because she wants to, *not* as an escape.

Sliding another finger in, her warm hands touch my arm, holding onto me. I love feeling like an anchor, especially with the way she looks at me when our lips part.

She seems to give herself to me this way.

It's a place to start.

Using just my hand, I have a point to make her come this way. "Stop fighting, Jane. I only have to use my hand and you're already writhing."

"It's safe to want you like this."

Do I blame her? No. But *I* need more. "It can be safe in other ways, if you let it."

I plunge a third finger in when I feel her hesitation, my thumb rubbing her clit. She melts just as fast. "*Soren...*"

It's almost a plea to make her believe. I don't know how to convince her. Not when she doesn't know my ways or can't understand how many of my own rules I've already broken with her.

"You'll come for me, Jane. Without question." Her body tenses, that lovely cunt clenching my fingers. "Your body bends for me because it knows the truth. You know, deep down, I am your reckoning. You need a man that will kill many just to ensure not a single hair on your head moves." I brush my lips against hers. "And I'll do that without question."

She pants before kissing me again, touching me with hardly any reservation. I allow that sensation to build until I can feel her body tensing.

"Come for me. *Now.*"

Her grip tightens around my neck as the orgasm rolls out of her, bath water lapping at the edges of the tub. I bare my teeth in a wave of suppressed desire, the thought of ripping her out of the water consuming me, but my instincts are screaming at me not to.

When she's relaxed, I do something I greatly don't want to —I stand to leave, gently pulling on her unbraided hair, leaving it like that. Maybe it will make her ask for me to finish it later.

"Where are you going?" she asks, panic elevating her soft voice.

"You'll finish your bath alone. I'll be outside," I grind out, adjusting my cock as I near the only door to the room, my right arm soaking and smelling like floral oils.

"Well, what was that?" She asks. I grin with my back to her, realizing why this is so important—she's expecting me to use her for my own pleasure, so when I get too close to her heart, she can spin lies about how it's only for me. "Soren, what about every minute of this day?" she coaxes.

"You need some time alone. I'll be outside when you're done," I answer, turning to face her as I shut the door.

I smile at her when she's twisted around to look at me, disappointment hitting her pretty little heart harder than she was ready for.

My intuition is *never* wrong.

That's how I will conquer her. She will have to stare the truth in the face, one way or another—I won't betray her like she thinks I will.

If anything, I'd care for her in ways she's nearly dying to feel.

Time for her to stew on that.

The hall outside is dim and empty, sensing only my guards at the end of the tunnels, my mask sitting on a lone chair next to Jane's door. Placing it at my side, it adheres to my belt loops like it's a pet that hates to be put down.

If a man comes in here, he can sure as hell try to fight me while I wear this thing. It's almost as if time slows for the one who dons it, able to maneuver a fight like none other.

And I swear blades don't cut as deep when I'm wearing it.

One of my guards strides over, a man named Michael. He bows his scarred head in my presence, the young bastard born with a penchant for violence that will no doubt get him killed within the next decade.

Some merely prefer to die young and in the heat of a fight rather than let old age rust their bones. It's not my place to question them.

"My liege. Rumors spread of a man with hell hounds in The Undercroft. But still no mention of the Scorpion."

Strange.

I eye the lines of the stone wall in front of me.

"Blackwell has given me a month to work on Jane's heart," I say. "That's how long we have. Gather more information on this man with the hounds—actually, find Anya and tell *her* to look into it for me, and tell Bones to secure Rosmertta's for the night and be on duty. We question everyone who comes in and pay her extra for any business missed. Only those within our legion may man the doors." I connect my eyes with his nearly black ones. "And no one goes near Jane unless it's for her protection, to which you'll have to explain to me later."

Michael deeply nods before parting, his armor clinking against the silence of the tunnel.

Meanwhile, I sit and stare at the stone for however long Jane decides to take in there. I even try to separate myself from my fascination with her, focusing on all the moving pieces around us.

I'm almost in a trance by the time I hear the water rippling and moving, the sound of her dripping onto the floor making me lower my gaze.

Blood rushes south when I think of her body all wet and glistening against the candlelight, my cock still wondering why the fuck I didn't spread her legs and leave her dripping with *me*. Rubbing my chin, I chuckle to myself, listening to all her movements.

For once, she doesn't seem to be searching for a way to kill me.

The door opens and Jane exits, wearing a black dress and robe, her sandals clacking on the floor.

She peers around as I stand. "It's so empty."

"Until I understand whatever is wrong with this place

more, you'll only interact with me, Bones, Anya, or your friend."

Her attention snaps to me, hope blooming in her chest. "Kathleen? Really? Does that mean you trust her?"

Great. I nearly forgot about the deal Kathleen struck with the Scorpion and how Jane doesn't know. Even then, it's not quite time. "I've got a feeling she's a blade you think is dull but could skin the hairs on your arm if she so wanted." My gaze rakes over her without reservation. "It's why Bones likes her."

"He likes her for the tits," she chides.

"She's not the first woman with tits that large. He'd have fucked her, left, and talked about her until he found the next one." I stare her in the eyes just in case it helps her hear me better. I've felt a part of Kathleen I don't think my desert rose knows about, a side that's utterly ensnared Bones. I speak to her with more than one meaning. "He likes her for who she is."

THE SCORPION'S RETURN

JANE

Two weeks have somehow passed, the days and nights rather uneventful. If anything, the stagnation of drama concerns me, anxiety flourishing in this limbo, waiting for danger to strike. Every shadow looks a bit darker, and I question the motives of *everyone*.

The only bright side is that despite all of that, it's also been the hardest that I've slept in years.

There's a familiarity in Soren now, having either been on my knees between his thighs or lying in any and all manners for him.

The most foreign thing occurred on the second night when

I slept in his arms. We shared stories in the dark of the most bizarre thieveries we've ever witnessed, and with his strength wrapped around me, I genuinely forgot about the danger just outside our door.

We don't say many amorous things, as I have a suspicion that he's enjoying just feeling me.

Perhaps that's how this man loves.

I've never really fallen in love before, so these emotions are entirely new. Maybe that's why I push them away with such veracity—although it seems pointless now. Especially after what recently happened when I had been crying when thinking of my father, so confused and needy for a parent. At first, the man in the alley had been liberating for me in my imagination, but now I can't stop thinking about how I *wish* it was him. Why did Mom choose a man who would abandon me for over a decade when I needed him most?

Her judgment is something I've trusted my whole life, and I loathe how I question it now.

The sobbing began when I let myself miss my mother like I used to when I was a teenager. Crying in front of others makes my skin crawl, so I tried to get it all out before Soren saw me next.

I half wonder if he can feel my distress even when we're not close, the Zenith having entered our shared room within minutes. I refused to meet his gaze, embarrassed and also too fucking tired to pretend like I was all right.

Soren didn't say a word as he quietly fetched someone to bring me food and wine. Some of the workers left a tray at the door, per the rules Soren's established, and he brought them in himself.

No one is allowed inside our room. Ever.

Only the two of us.

He broke my resolve when he gently touched the ends of

my hair before leaving me alone with everything I needed. It was almost loving.

This is much better than in

Soren conquered a part of me that day and I've slept like no man or beast could touch me ever since.

When the Zenith isn't tending to me, Bones is stationed to keep a very close eye on me, which came with the welcomed surprise of Kathleen's presence. I'll put up with mister-bones-around-his-neck as long as he takes care of her. I'll even admit it shocked me to see that he stares at Kathleen like she's hung the stars herself. That's not even when he's looking at her tits —it's just when he looks at her in general.

Watching that develop only confuses what courses through me for Soren. Am I really developing affection for him? Would I miss him if something separated us because I want *him*, and not just his protection?

When my Zenith isn't here, he's either speaking for long hours with others like him or spends the remainder of his time training like he's about to enter a tournament in the Savage Sands.

Sipping on my ale at the same bar where I initially met with Kathleen, I'm alone for the moment. Soren's legion is banned from interacting with me, save for Anya or Bones.

There's a possessive edge in that demand, but I also know he's establishing a barrier that keeps suspicions to a minimum. It also means I remain looking like I'm his pet in case any spying eyes are in here. If the Council is asking about where I am, no one has told me. There's been hardly any mention of Tempest since, too.

Kathleen is recovering from some kind of cold, or else she and I would be chatting up a storm. If we can somehow survive this, we will be friends for a very long time. Perhaps even tied to the hip of deadly mercenaries.

I snort at the idea of us all having violent little families, one day.

All because I wound up in Coalfell, just where father placed me.

My head tilts back while I drain the remainder of whatever they serve here, glancing to the side when Anya barrels through the door.

Sighing as I slam my mug down, I frown and cock my head to the side when she makes her way right toward me.

I swear if she stabs me again...

"Been a while, Anya," I say, observing her, the men and women of the tavern eyeing her with interest. She's been gone most of the time, only having returned to us two days ago.

She nears me, but I don't move. Once close enough, I can smell Skull's Row on her, mixing with the smell of rain. She leans into my ear, my body stiff. "Jane. Soren is injured. He said to move fast and without suspicion."

"What?" I leave my stool, alcohol burning through me as I nearly stumble. I don't even think about it as I speak, "Take me to him."

She seems to have expected this reaction, already heading to the door, and grabbing me a cloak. I'm still adjusting the fabric as we leave, trying to keep away the light rain by throwing my hood up, moving with purpose as I dirty my boots. Yellow sashes of Paragons crowd Rosmertta's now that Soren's established his presence, a few even following when Anya motions to them with her hand before resting it on her pommel as if daring any man or woman to challenge her.

I breathe steadily, my heart racing with fear when I realize how serious she is. What if he's gravely injured? I failed my mother by being young and afraid and not thinking my actions through.

The idea of Soren no longer existing...

Numb. I'm completely numb, focusing only on keeping up with a worried Anya. A clear mind could be the difference between life and death.

We near the area where fighters tend to beat each other into submission around here—a large dirt-covered field surrounded by buildings—before diverting off into a bakery. The gray skies above are so bleak and heavy that it feels like a premonition as the rain begins to heavily drizzle.

"Why's he here?" I ask, my voice determined, licking my wet lips, moving hair out of my face that slightly sticks to my skin.

"The baker offered. Put some sugar on his laceration," Anya explains, barging into the building that smells like fresh bread. There's hardly any illumination inside, like the place is closed. "He doesn't want to be outside while you treat him."

I scan everything with my eyes, spotting a knife I could grab if I need it—caution is my friend with these frayed emotions. I almost consider the possibility of this being a trap, but it's not worth wasting these precious seconds. Anya guides me to a room in the back that has stacks of flour and two butter churns. Sitting next to a bag of sugar is a giant man covered in blood, his hand pressing on his neck, sitting next to a window that casts stark shadows. I've heard about sugar being helpful for fresh wounds–it's nothing I really use because of my abilities.

My cloak flies off when I see Soren's very much alive but losing large amounts of blood, immediately swatting at his hand that covers a sticky wound. I apply pressure as he watches and pants, pouring every ounce of controlled power that I have into his neck, looking over his shirtless chest for more injuries.

Nothing. It's just this one nasty gash.

"You trying to lop your head off?" I ask, my voice cracking

as I close my eyes, focusing on exploring the way my magic feels within him. I always sense where the bleeding is heaviest and try to heal that first.

The blood slows from his neck, the sensation vibrating in my hands when torn muscle heals as I pour my life's energy into him. I open my eyes to observe him—he's quiet and pale, panting as he stares at my face, but even then, his glacial eyes are amused. "You worried for me, love?"

"You die on me and I'll find a way to bring you back just so I can stab you again," I mumble. When he seems rudimentary healed, I search for a pitcher of water and a rag, to clean the blood. He doesn't speak as I clean him. Dropping the heavy, bloody fabric, I touch his neck again, blue light emanating through the cracks of my fingers.

My heart steadies when I feel confident he'll be all right, even if the dirt floor is covered with his blood.

He winces when something sews back together, his large body tensing. Parting his lips and connecting his gaze with mine, all emotion drops as he begins to speak, "I saw your father."

The blue light glows so intensely that it reflects off his eyes, the beast of a man snarling from the pain I cause. Too much too fast and it burns like a hot cast iron.

Somewhere in the recesses of my mind, I register that he doesn't touch or scold me in response to the pain I've caused.

I gently pull back. "I'm so sorry," I say, almost touching his face in apology. Then, I stare into those pale eyes that tell me to replay what he just said. I blink rapidly before looking down, the rain pattering against the glass now. "Wait, what did you say?"

"Spotting him caught me off guard. He was standing in the crowd. It's why this strike hit, even though I knew it was coming."

Oh, shit.

My eyes widen and my heart furiously pounds, matching the rhythm of the rain on glass. "Maybe... maybe someone looks like him," I dumbly state, denial returning like an old friend. "I swore I saw someone that reminded me of him, too."

Soren doesn't blink or remove his gaze, forcing me to hear the truth. "He doesn't look like himself. Don't know how. But I *felt* him, especially when our eyes connected—he wanted me to know." He readjusts, sitting with a grimace until he's only a foot from me. His face hardens when he looks over my shoulder, Soren putting an arm in front of me as if he doesn't feel encumbered by blood loss at all.

A crack of thunder shakes the unlit lanterns, Anya standing in the threshold of this room. She pants, staring at Soren with a concern I've never seen in her.

"There's a man at the front... he says he's the Scorpion."

TO BE CONTINUED...

I hope you had a lovely journey with Soren and Jane in this book!

The sequel, and final installment of their story, is to be releasing Fall 2024

This book has been living in my head for quite some time, and I absolutely fell in love with the idea of a woman who has an identity to reclaim, which is why Book 2 will have the subtitle of "Reborn".

And let's not forget Soren... we've just cracked the surface of his tough shell.

If you enjoyed this book, I'd greatly appreciate a review! They go a really long way for supporting a novel and getting them seen.

PERSONAL THANK YOU'S

I have my lovely beta readers to thank for their exceptional input. Tori, Ashley, Samantha, and Amna <3

I also want to thank my PA, **Baddie**, who has been immensely helpful with brainstorming, editing, and being there through all my antics. She's been an incredible friend and supporter!

Fleur DeVillainy is the author of *Sky of Thorns* and is another wonderful person I'd love to thank. She is my dear author friend who has been a wonderful supporter, idea bouncer, and listened to all my concerns. Her story is about a unicorn shifter who finds herself entangled in a good versus evil plot. The prince sent to capture her hates shifters, but of course, she annoyingly is an exception and makes him question where his loyalties lie. It's a lighter read that punches with suspense, so it's worth checking out!

www.ingramcontent.com/pod-product-compliance
Lightning Source LLC
Chambersburg PA
CBHW020052310726
48970CB00007B/2520